Johanna returns to Earth from her exploration mission with a heavy burden — the survival of two peoples is at stake, menaced by an all-devouring creature. Now she must convince mankind that helping the foreigners is rewarding — and at the same time, she must defeat the human opponents who threaten to destroy everything she ever built. Time is running out — will she be able to return, and if so, will she still find someone to save?

Expedition
Copyright © 2021 Valerie J. Long
ISBN: 978-1-4874-3327-7
Cover art by Martine Jardin

Published by eXtasy Books Inc

Look for us online at:
www.eXtasybooks.com

EXPEDITION
ZOE LIONHEART BOOK 24
LIONESS TRACKS IV

BY

VALERIE J. LONG

DEDICATION

For Lin

PART ONE—SECRETLY

CHAPTER ONE

At an easy ten percent light speed, our Barracuda sailed toward Earth, wrapped in its protective nestle field.

"Should we eventually report back?" Francine asked cheerfully. "They could put the champagne into the fridge."

"Nanette always has champagne in the fridge," I disagreed. "Congratulations, by the way."

"What for?"

"The *Besson compensator* is working fine. I never had such a pleasant wormhole transit. It's sleek."

Francine made a face upon the mention of her name, but grinned on my last remark. "Sleek?"

"Like lubed. Oh yes — if you don't like the name *Besson compensator*, should we instead call it *Francine's lubricant?*"

"No!" She sat up straight.

"All right." I grinned back. "Just a joke. On your question — no, I don't want to report back. Right now nobody needs to know we're back already. Our mission went quite differently than planned, first of all shorter, and I don't want to explain the reasons across such a distance. Most importantly though, I must consider how I can tell our people that I must return there as soon as possible."

"Why? That's as plain as day. There are Dragons who need our help." Her face showed nothing but serious worry.

"Thank you, Francine, that it looks so plain to you."

"But isn't it?"

"No. For you and me and many of our people on Earth, it's a matter of course to help anyone we see in need for help. But not everyone thinks that way. They will ask—why should some Dragons in a distant star system concern us? What will it cost to help them, and what would we gain? Those are questions I must find compelling answers for before going public—or it might even be better to present them with a fait accompli."

"No, I think that would not be better. Not with such an important decision. Whatever you'll do, you'll commit all of us, not just yourself alone. So you'll have to give people a chance." She spread her arms. "People must at least be able to tell themselves they had a say in it. Only that way will they pull their weight—well, at least most of them. And, who knows, perhaps there will be enough people ready to help selflessly."

"Why should they?"

"Because they're not all such selfish assholes? Because you've been a role model for caring about others long enough?" Francine leaned forward. "Perhaps you just have to kindly ask for it."

"Ask the UN boneheads? Not in a hundred years!" Flaring up didn't help, I advised myself. "I'll have to talk with Rashid. We need a communication strategy. Then I'll have to write down a concept together with Reginald about what our help could look like and how we can adapt the construction program—somehow we'll need more freighters, even at the expense of defense."

I asked myself if I could sell this idea.

"On no account should you trigger the impression you were no longer committed to protect Earth," Francine argued. "That would cost you a lot of sympathy. You have to clarify that our defense stands and we're only changing the method of danger prevention in the *Worries* system—because we can find allies there."

This made me pause. It was too easy to only see the *Mamba* in her, the intransigent killer, or the focused, imperturbable space pilot. Behind her pretty face she hid a keen mind.

"You're right there," I agreed. "Okay—doubtlessly there'll be some people who oppose it anyway. But the prospect of more Dragons that'll be ready to help us will surely benefit us."

"Exactly. And in case we'll have to get them here quickly we'll need interstellar transport capacity." Surprising me once again obviously made her happy. "Hey, Jo—you really don't have to do it all alone. We can help, if you let us."

I leaned back with a sigh. "Yes. It's just—I can't ignore the responsibility. If anything goes wrong and the Jellies catch us unprepared, or if this brown pest comes for us . . ."

"Nobody expects you to take all that burden."

"That's not true, Francine, and you know it. I announced I'm Dragon, and I've already performed a few miracles and feats. That's now the benchmark people compare me with—nothing less than the next miracle, and then another, and so on."

She sighed, too. "Yes, you're probably right there. So we have no choice but working the next miracle all together, have we?"

That made me grin. "For now, a cup of hot chocolate would be marvelous."

"That's feasible. I'll get you one." She rose. "Anything else?"

"No, thanks. We must be patient until we're home."

"And until then?"

"I'll check why we still have three percent emitter failures. The *Besson compensator* fine tuning probably isn't programmed properly."

Francine mimed a toss, and I raised one arm in defense. We both laughed.

CHAPTER TWO

Francine was focusing on the virtual screen that *Mischief's* computer was projecting before her as if she could hypnotize any threat away.

Nothing among what was flying around in Earth's orbit outside could seriously endanger us—not the countless small pieces of scrap metal, not the larger still-complete satellites the Jelly EMP had silenced, not even the remainders of the last space station—our nestle field would protect us against it just as against interstellar particles, while we were approaching these pieces at significantly lower speed.

Our goal nevertheless was to avoid collisions—only that way could we remain mostly invisible. Any larger flash could give us away, and we didn't want our return to become known. For the same reason, we shouldn't send out radar signals.

So Francine kept her focus on the enlarged image of our surroundings. If indeed a chunk came against us at about 28.000 kilometers per hour, she had only fractions of a second to dodge it.

As long as she did nothing, *Mischief* slowly descended toward the south pole. We expected the least air traffic and the fewest direct observers there who could notice us obscuring the view on an occasional star.

That's what the return home of the first two humans having visited a different star system looked like—not the heroes' triumphant entrance, but the clandestine sneaking up of thieves.

5

I asked myself — could I deny Francine the former? Hadn't she earned this public recognition with her eternal patience and dedication — where there had been no guarantee of a return?

No, I couldn't, and yes, she had earned the right to become known not just as Knight Francine Besson of the Order of the Dying Lioness, but also as the first interstellar pilot of a spaceship entirely built on Earth. However, that didn't require everyone tracking our approach.

A buzz told us we were leaving the critical area and descending into the denser layers of atmosphere where we no longer had to expect debris. Francine took a deep breath and stretched her limbs.

Thereafter she rearranged her virtual dashboard and took *Mischief* under manual control. She almost lovingly stroked the few real parts with her data glove before activating it.

"I know the computer could do it better," she commented with a slight shrug of her left shoulder. "But . . ."

I remained silent.

"They'll take her away from us."

"I won't let that happen," I promised.

"Yes, you will. Our baby needs a general overhaul after these hardships anyway. Before that comes the search, though — what's broken that our deep diagnosis didn't catch? What's the emitters' condition, and what conclusions can be drawn from it? Well — and our data comes on top, and then your changes to the code. I'm sure they won't let us fly again before everything's processed and reworked."

"We don't have that much time — no, I want to say, the *Worries* Dragons might not have that much time left."

"You'll need at least one Phoenix anyway."

"Several. But what should they bring along? No. I must return as soon as possible, and the first Phoenix must be ready by then. I can tell Achrotzyber what we'll need, and the first shipment can follow."

"In that case, we'll have to change to one of the other Barracudas. Hopefully it won't take that long to integrate the compensator."

"That's what I have to talk with Rashid about."

"Fine. Where?"

"New York."

CHAPTER THREE

The risk of being detected on our approach to New York despite camouflage and darkness was too high, so we traveled underwater, and the Mischief remained parked underwater in the East River—her airlock didn't care whether there was water or empty space outside.

Francine did care, as her following comment told me. "For having to dive in this stinky brew you owe me one."

"Yes, sure. Now take a deep breath and shut your mouth."

We wouldn't need a breather for the short swim to the shore, and the pressure difference didn't make me worry—as we wouldn't stay underwater long enough to let our bodies adapt to the higher pressure anyway.

The water quickly rose in the lock, and it didn't smell appetizing indeed. I didn't want to know what the people were putting in it—New York wasn't done cleaning up yet. I didn't even know whether the Bronx was already conquered back from the Slicers.

The outer hatch moved away, and I grabbed Francine and pulled her with me. Soon we reached the shore.

My pilot gasped for breath and made a face. "Ugh. That stinks." She gazed at me. "We won't remain undetected with that smell."

"No. Don't move." My outer skin's nanos quickly removed the repugnant ooze. I had to send out a nano column to help Francine. Due to her conveniently short hair, that didn't take long.

"So. It's better now."

"Thanks." She stepped away from the river and took a sniff at her arm again. "Yes, that's okay. Which way?"

"Straight into the city. We'll arrive at Central Park's southern end." A brief mental command created a black suit matching Francine's skintight combat and space suit. "Let's go."

A few rats scurried away from us, but otherwise no one noticed us. To keep it that way, we watched our surroundings, stuck to the shadows, and avoided unnecessary noise.

Francine couldn't become invisible — her suit wasn't made for it — and didn't need to. Where it was about roaming a strange town inconspicuously, the *Mamba* was even better than me.

Only once did we have to evade a group of four young men who were patrolling up Park Avenue, collecting paper shreds and checking out doors and passages. Each wore a blue armband with a large eye symbol.

We arrived at the hotel delivery entrance unmolested. At this late hour, the door was locked, but that was no obstacle for me. Francine nodded approval when I locked the door behind us again and reactivated the alarm.

Now we only had to reach the top guest floor unspotted, but even this only required a little patience to pass the more frequented corridors near the kitchen. An emergency staircase took us up.

CHAPTER FOUR

The door to the large top floor suite opened upon our approach. Francine flinched, but immediately relaxed when we saw Achrotzyber standing in the door. Of course, my Companion had sensed my arrival.

There he was, in polo shirt and long white slacks—and I was reminded that I'd almost never seen him again. If some more emitters had failed on our way out . . . if Francine hadn't come up with the compensator idea . . . if the compensator hadn't worked as planned—my arms almost automatically wrapped around his neck, pulled me up, my legs hooked around his waist, and I pressed my face into his chest. Briefly hesitating, he put his arms around me and held me tight—that was good, as I couldn't and wouldn't hold back the trembling anymore.

Next, he held out one arm, and Francine snuggled up to us. Sure—she'd risked her life, too.

Being embarrassed about my selfishness didn't help me overcome my distress. My *Analogy* could've helped me, but that subject was settled—it wasn't advisable to suppress emotional stress relief. So I let my tears run and enjoyed my Companion's warmth. The world had to wait.

My Companion wouldn't wait.

I don't understand, Companion. What happened?

I'm feeling safe in your arms. Now I may show the fear I had suppressed during our journey. I believe Francine feels the same.

You felt fear?

Big fear. So much could have gone wrong.
You shouldn't have gone, then.

Of course not. But how would discussing that with my Dragon have helped me? *We've gained valuable insights.*

More valuable than you?

I couldn't answer that. *Someone had to go. It was logical to assign the most qualified person with the highest odds for survival. The course of events confirmed this decision.*

Achrotzyber had no chance to prove me wrong, as I hadn't reported the events yet. That's what I had come for, and before this fruitless discussion could go on, I should start doing it.

Footsteps approached.

"Can I get you anything?" Zoé asked. "Oh—I'm sorry."

"You're welcome." I detached myself from the hug. "Two cold beers for Francine and me, and then we'll tell our story."

CHAPTER FIVE

It was already dawn when I put down my sixth bottle of beer on the small table at my side. The sand-colored leather chair groaned. "The next moment, we went into transit."

"And what does that mean?" Rashid asked.

"That we can find potential allies there." That was my most important argument, and this argument had to strike home before we would discuss any details. So I gave him a moment to digest it.

Finally, the UN Secretary for Interstellar Defense nodded. "I understand. If only for their mission, all Dragons in this galaxy are our allies. Should we manage to evacuate them without catching this brown pest, and should they agree to become our guests, we could hope for their support against a second wave."

"A little more than that. I expect them to accept my authority as a Golden One." I glanced at my Companion. "Achrotzyber?"

"That's logical. There is no other option." He cocked his head. *Rashid need not be informed about the indoctrination, right?*
Right.

"Well, then . . ." Rashid placed his palms together and rested his chin on the fingertips.

"It's also logical that they accept our hospitality if we can't decontaminate their planet," I added. "That leaves one big *If*—if we manage to evacuate them in time. I have no clue how much time we've got, but it will surely be counted by months rather than by decades."

"What are you up to?"

"To a change of our priorities. If we want to profit from these powerful allies, we need interstellar transport capacity soonest. We don't just need a single expedition ship, but an airlift in space—a spacelift."

The secretary started to answer, paused, and then spread his arms. "You know what you're asking for."

"Yes. It's about the preparation of a defense against an interstellar invasion—against two invasions, to be precise. We have to arm Earth so that we can defeat the Jellies, and we have to arm Earth so that we can repel the brown pest, if—or better, once—this lifeform gets hold of another interstellar spaceship. I have to assume this will happen sometime in the not-so-distant future."

These considerations weren't new for Francine, and Achrotzyber accepted them with Dragonish serenity.

Zoé wasn't as untouched. "How soon?"

"Hard to say. Twenty years, perhaps a hundred?" I didn't take my gaze away from Rashid. "We can't afford to be un-prepared. We need space fighters, torpedoes, bases elsewhere in the Solar System, supply vessels for these bases. We need Phoenix-class carrier ships, and we need freighters of the same size. We can't afford to forego external support if we can get it. But we can afford to prioritize our construction pro-grams so that we can collect that support."

"That's easy to say—we can afford that. Sadly, I have to tell you we can't afford it all by far."

"So."

"It's not easy to get the necessary funding. The economy suffered heavily from the Cartel's shadow economy during the last decades, and there are still many places where we can't get anything done without certain—well, procedures."

"Corruption?"

"As well, yes."

"Okay. Tell me names, and I'll talk with those people."

"Johanna—"

"No, Rashid. If someone sidelines our funds, that's a war crime, and it's dealt with accordingly. We only have to make that clear. Very clear."

He considered that. "I haven't seen it that way yet. Okay, but we can play this card without you, too."

"Tell me if there's trouble. And now back to the funds— how did it work during the Second World War? There were supply convoys from America to Great Britain, and in parallel, you could build thousands of planes and hundreds of ships, not to mention tanks. It worked some way, and that was only about a bunch of megalomaniac dictators with their followers and not about the survival of all mankind."

"Maybe it's just that, Jo," Francine chimed in. "It's easier to fight *for* something than *against* something. Leave out Jellies and the brown pest for now, and let the people fight for the spacelift and at the same time for the conquest of space. Give them a reason to strive for flying to the stars."

"What are you thinking about?" I asked.

"About research stations around the Solar System, about valuable resources in the asteroid belt, about the chance to see the rings of Saturn from one of its moons. Explain to them we have the technology for it and are ready to give it to them. If someone comes with the money to fund such a station, we'll rent the transport to him at reasonable, cost-covering terms— and along with it, we'll be erecting a depot, a maintenance station, and perhaps a defense base. The UN will provide military police, just in case. This way, the funds for a few lifters will come easy. And then—whoever's living out there will pay some taxes in exchange for access to our defense bases' healing nano tanks. First class medical care, protection against long-term radiation damage and so on. We just shouldn't leave the raw materials mining to those slave drivers who

14

regard their workers as expendable resources."

Rashid had placed one hand on his knee. The other covered his smile.

"Knight Francine, I'm ravished. Is there a chance to win you over as my assistant?"

"When I'm too old for this pilot job one day, sure. Until then, you must wait in line." She smiled, too. "Well, and re-garding *Trouble*—who knows what rare treasures can be found there, once the planet is secured? Offer war bonds. Only bond keepers will gain the right to participate in inter-stellar trade—at least for the first fiftyish years."

"Some will do the cherry-picking," I objected. "And then we'll have a new *Cartel*—whatever it's called then."

"Limit the influence on this trade cartel to, let's say, sixteen shares per beneficiary, natural persons only, and allow the forming of cooperatives. The more cooperative employees own their own shares, the larger the cake slice will be, only you can't boot out the employees without losing the shares."

"How do you come up with all this?"

"I had a lot of time for thinking on our trip."

CHAPTER SIX

We had a sumptuous breakfast. Rashid had ordered everything the hotel kitchen could offer, and in quantities. A Dragon man's healthy appetite had to explain the reason, as of course the staff shouldn't learn about Francine's and my own presence. Accordingly, the chambermaid had to stay out this time — no, the conference was still going on, and interruptions were unwelcome.

"It won't be easy," Rashid said. "It won't be easy, but your suggestions might work. Just give me some preparation time."

"That's what we're here for," I answered. "To give you time for preparations before we return with the *Mischief* — before Terra's first interstellar spaceflight will end and the crew members will be welcomed as bright heroes to then report what they've found. Because two things are clear — firstly, not just science but most of all the press will bombard us with questions, and secondly, we can't keep back such an important information as the presence of Dragons in the *Worries* system."

"Why not?" my Companion asked.

"What do you mean, why not?"

"Why do you have to unveil information nobody knows you could have? Just the opposite — I do not consider it wise to divulge this knowledge."

"Explain."

"How did you learn about the presence of Dragons? They did not radio you. Your ability to sense Dragons across distance is not publicly known."

"It is. I've publicly announced it during a press conference in Gladstone before."

"On this planet, yes. But not across millions of kilometers in a foreign space system. Furthermore, it was not a permanent signal. What would have happened if the foreign Dragon had woken up a few seconds later?"

"I wouldn't have noticed."

"Then it need not have happened."

"If we know nothing about Dragons there, there's no reason to force our transporter construction program," Francine argued. "We'd have to stick to our current priorities until we've discovered their presence officially during a second expedition. That way we'd lack a substantial motivation for accelerating our efforts."

"That is logical, Francine," Achrotzyber confirmed. "But as you already provided us with a better reasoning for building transporters, we do not depend on this motivation."

"That's logical, too, Companion," I agreed. "Only this reasoning has less emotional value. Whether we're settling on the first Saturn moon this year or next year doesn't matter. Saving the *Trouble* Dragons' lives is a goal with much more urgency. You've come up with an important issue, however — I really shouldn't mention that I can sense Dragons across such a large distance. Nobody needs to know that I can do that."

"On the second point, I agree with your Companion," Rashid said, "and I have to concede the first point to Francine and you — we need the Dragons as motivation. In fact, in a double role — as victims we must aid quickly, and as allies, as reward for quick action."

"Achrotzyber, what do you think?" I asked.

"I am but a hatchling. I accept your greater experience with human motivation." He managed to disarm his remark with a smile. "In which way will you have gained knowledge of their existence, Companion? Do the *Mischief's* mission protocols include respective clues?"

He had me there, or didn't he? I smiled around. "Of course not. Or, put differently, the respective communication means aren't available to *Mischief's* computer. Dragon confidential."

Rashid winked at me. "Well, if the Imperatrix doesn't want to disclose this information, she can hardly be forced to, and I don't think it will matter."

He didn't voice it, but I could read it from his posture — we'd have trouble enough to carry our point.

"Are there any other topics to discuss before our official arrival?" I asked. "Otherwise we should get to the details now. It's our show, so it should be our script."

CHAPTER SEVEN

Not for the first time I admired the tranquility with which Francine guided our spaceship out of Earth's gravity sink. This imperturbability was probably owed to her *Mamba* training—girls that had easily become nervous hadn't survived the drug treatment.

I was really proud that they all had opted to follow me—that they were gladly following me, and themselves felt pride and joy about it.

Now and then I should tell them. But Francine beat me to it.

"I've got the best job in the world." She pointed at the image of Earth on one of the screens, where the southern Pacific was slowly passing below us. "My home is paradise on Earth. My job encompasses the entire universe—plenty of responsibility, but also an incredible lot of freedom. My boss is Dragon—and she loves me. What more could one ask for?"

"A cock once in a while?" I said to cover up my embarrassment.

"Their importance is overrated."

We both had to laugh.

"Moreover, I can get as many cocks as I want," she added. "As often as I want, if I want." She waved around. "Only not always when I want. But what does that matter if I can have the universe?" She touched one of the controls, checked the system's acknowledgement, and nodded contentedly.

"Doesn't the thought of what could be waiting for us out there make you fear?"

"It should, shouldn't it?" She shrugged. "I believe you still don't really understand what makes us *Mambas* tick. We've learned not to fear death. It will come one day anyway, and until then, every day is a gift. At first, during training, every mistake may be your last, and to think about it too frequently only distracts. After a while, you learn to accept the possibility of your death. After a while, you also recognize what you're trained for — to be a tool. An expensive tool, but still expendable. You learn that each mission includes the option of your death, and after a while it becomes a matter of course." She waved my attempt to speak up aside. "No, don't say anything. I know you've got a different self-conception, that we're not just tools for you. But to me, just like to Tess and the others, it was always clear that we'd take the hottest jobs — including the option of death, and not because you'd consider us expendable, but because it would be even more dangerous for anyone else — because we're the best. Isn't it so?"

I could only nod.

"So — death can't frighten me. Someday he'll come and get me, and until then I want to have fun. Until then I'm the pilot of the hottest ride in this galaxy." She winked at me. "There was a saying — the good girls go to heaven, the bad girls go everywhere. I'm a bad girl. I go everywhere, and the sky is mine!"

CHAPTER EIGHT

"You know, Jo, we should really be worried," Francine said.

"About what?"

"That a spaceship can sneak so deep into the Solar System and can even land on Earth without being noticed. What if our enemies could do the same?"

"We'd be fucked up." I found that thought discomforting, but there was an even more discomforting corollary. "If we can't notice it, how can we be sure it hasn't happened yet?"

"Oh, that's easy. We're not fucked up yet. I'd know."

"Francine, your logic is irresistible."

"I have another argument. We can almost certainly rule out that there is a second Johanna Meier in this galaxy. So our enemies don't know about the Meier effect, and thus neither of the derivations like the nestle field or the *Meier gravtunnel.*"

"Or the *Besson compensator.*"

"Whatever." She grinned like the Cheshire cat. "Yes, that a second Johanna would meet a second Francine is much more unlikely, isn't it? And even if—how likely would it be to happen almost simultaneously, that is, giving a thousand years more or less?"

"And if it happened more than thousand years ago?"

"The Jellies would long be fucked. There wouldn't have been an invasion."

"Damn, yes." I stared at her. "Yes, that'll be the next step, won't it?"

"What?"

"Fighting the invasion of this galaxy. As soon as we've cleaned our doorstep."

Francine watched me for a while. Then she nodded. "Yes, of course. You couldn't just sit still if you know you could help, right?"

"Angry April couldn't, either. *As long as there's a spark of life in me, I will not rest until that race is erased from the face of our galaxy,* she swore."

"You're well on the way to walk in her steps."

"Me? Angry April?"

"At least you've got the right height."

If looks could kill, I'd have had to control myself. So she just shrugged off my scowl with a loud laughter.

But I couldn't get her remark out of my mind. We had the means to detect wormholes. If we could manage to find the Lionheart transits, if we could pick up their tracks . . .

PART TWO—PUBLICLY

CHAPTER NINE

Francine nodded at me and showed a thumbs-up. I pointed at her and nodded back.

Me? her expression asked.

I nodded again.

She shrugged, and then she activated her microphone and the camera. "*Mischief* calling Earth. *Mischief* calling Earth. This is Francine Besson speaking. Folks, we're back. Just put me through."

Was that her entire speech already? One small step for us, a giant leap for mankind? No, she was just warming up. The first signal was just an advance warning for the senders around the planet.

"*Mischief* calling Earth. Get ready for a broadcast in five minutes."

Five minutes—okay. I left my seat and moved to the kitchen. That meant time for a coffee.

Francine remained comfortably seated and watched the computer counting down the seconds. At minus two I brought her the coffee and took my own seat.

She sipped once, then she placed the thermal mug down

and made sure it didn't show on camera. Minus one. My pilot winked at me and pretended to arrange her hairdo.

During the last ten seconds, she allowed the computer to show her image, reclining in her seat.

Then the time was up.

"People on Earth—This is Knight Francine Besson speaking from aboard the first interstellar explorer *Mischief*, experimental vessel of the United Nations and the Dragon University. We returned from our journey to the one-hundred-and-forty light years distant *Worries* planetary system! We're bringing proof that mankind can even conquer the barriers of light speed if collaborating, as my friends at the University did, and as the countless helpers and provider employees did. Always remember, whether it's the steel of our spaceship's body or the coffee in our onboard kitchen—people all around the Earth contributed to our mission's success. Every human is entitled to be proud of this mission and to say *we* did it, all of us."

Nicely put. I held up a thumb.

"It will take a few days until we reach you. While the flight from star to star is unbelievably fast, we have to go slowly inside a planetary system. Even my words need many hours to reach you. That's why there can't be queries, and that means I must guess what journalists and moderators would ask me, as if this were an interview. I will make every effort not to be boring anyway."

She leaned forward. "For those of you asking themselves why we did this journey with completely untested technology at all, and why we did it right now, I'll sum it up."

Francine took one hand down. "It wasn't long ago that Earth was the target of an interstellar invasion for the second time. My sisters-in-arms Sylvie and Zoé helped the Imperatrix Aurea and her Companion to repel this invasion, and for that we were appointed Knights of the Order of the Dying

Lioness." She raised her hand again and attached the order brooch to her chest.

I hadn't even known she had brought it along!

"We wanted to check if there's still a threat originating from that distant system — to be able to fight it before it could reach our own Solar System. Although our primary goal was exploration, we were prepared to fight the enemy there — even for the price of never returning. That was an important mission goal, and I openly admit — we didn't achieve it."

She folded her hands into her lap. "We didn't get to fighting, and the main reason is that our explorer was severely damaged during its first flight. We weren't battle-ready, and our return was on a knife's edge until we had found the cause of the damage and fixed it. The second reason is that there's currently no other interstellar spaceship in the *Worries* system that could mean a threat to us. So everything's okay? No. The enemy is still there, and as soon as he's built another spaceship, we're in trouble again." *Unless we beat him to it.* But she didn't voice that.

"Okay — you're asking yourself how I can know that the enemy is still there. As I promised you not to bore you, I'll leave all the data we collected aside, and get straight to the point. We know the enemy's still there because he hasn't won there yet. And herewith I hand over to the Imperatrix Aurea. Johanna, your cue."

Francine let the camera picture pan to me. I flashed a brief smile — friendly and authentic, as my past clients had appreciated it — and became serious again.

"Yes, right. There's still resistance in the *Worries* system, and this resistance was able to send me a call for help. I'll relay this call to the people on Earth. I need your support. Keep in mind that your help will contribute to keep our enemy away from our home. I ask you to help me, like the Dragons once came to Earth to help us. Let us repay a bit of that, let us support the *Worries* system. I beg you! Let's help the Dragons there."

Francine cut the line and indicated the end of the transmission to me.

I took a deep breath and gazed at her. "That wasn't my strongest speech, I think."

"But authentic. Let Rashid and his marketing professionals wrap your message up nicely."

"Yes. He'll have a few days then."

In a few hours, when our broadcast reached Earth, he'd start to pull the strings. Until then . . .

Mighty?

There was a brief pause. *Companion.*

We've sent our message. It's starting. Are you on the island?

Yes.

Good. We'll start the data transfer now. If there are questions about the Besson compensator, *call me.*

This term is new to me, Companion. Besson is the name of Francine's line?

It was her idea. I'll send the formula package, the controls implementation, and the measures first. Perhaps the team might want to have a look at that. In any case, we should upgrade the other Barracudas and develop a solution for the Phoenix class.

Of course, Companion. I will pin the respective cards to the board and tell Reginald.

Thank you.

"All okay?"

Francine's question startled me. "What?"

"All okay?"

I briefly listened inside. "Yes. I must have been lost in thoughts."

"No new problems?"

"Not that I know of. In any case, Achrotzyber didn't mention any."

"Well, we'll get them soon enough." My pilot waved a hand. "There's always something."

"I'm good at getting problems," I agreed. "Problems and I, we always find each other. And I'm talking of the really big, difficult problems, not the little hiccups."

"So then, all is fine."

"Yes, exactly."

Chapter Ten

I placed one hot chocolate next to Francine and carried the other to my own seat. She swept a course display away and called up the communication board with a snap.

"The first reply to our hail could arrive within the next seconds — if they didn't wait until I finished."

Shortly after, the first light flashed. Francine tapped it.

"Mischief, *this is Gladstone. Welcome back, fearnoughts!*" After a brief pause, the voice went on. "*Five minutes? You're keeping us in suspense. Okay, I've passed it on. Probably the phone will soon be running wild. Well, I shall tell you from the boys around here that we're darn glad to hear from you again. Take your time to come down in one piece. We'll have to put the beer in the fridge first, you know?*"

Francine nodded at me. "When we're back, I should visit the blokes. They're really okay."

"That was Ed, wasn't it?" Ed was the leader of Gladstone Control. According to his own statement, he didn't sleep well, so he worked the second night shift. He'd reach retirement age soon.

"Exactly."

Francine didn't comment further on her short reply, and I didn't dig deeper. Instead, I had to think of Uncle Bob, even if that was an unfair comparison with Ed. With a little empathy we could have a lot of fun together.

"Mischief, *this is Gladstone. I know when you're hearing this, it's all long been over, but the big stations confirmed — you're live.*"

I nodded at her and then raised my chocolate cup to inhale

28

the wonderful smell. The five minutes were almost over. How long had her speech taken, and how long my brief addition?

"I'm getting good signals from several stations," Francine said, and lined up several virtual screens before us, all with her in medium shot. Tickers or fixed subtitles in different languages marked the image as live transmission. Aside from that, all images remained uncommented and uncut.

Next she began to sort the image streams according to their delay compared to the earliest signals. There were differences of more than five seconds.

"Like an echo," she commented. "Funny how big the difference is."

"It depends on how often the signal runs around Earth, and how slow the digital repeaters are. That's a simple, visible example for the kind of problems I'm fighting with in the compensator fine calibration. Just imagine that the wormhole transit will only work once all streams are synchronous again."

"Oh. Okay." She frowned. "That's surely much too simplified, but nicely clear. You know, I'm glad you're here and taking care of everything, but I think we can't afford this specialization. Before I'm flying interstellar with such a small thing again, I must learn how all the technical stuff works in detail, how I can adjust it, and, if necessary, how I can find a programming bug and fix it."

"Isn't that a bit much?"

"Yes. I get my brain tied up in a knot just by thinking of it. But there's no other way. Aboard a Phoenix, you can carry a team of specialists along, but everyone traveling on a Barracuda must be his own engineer." She watched my gaze. "Don't make such a sour face. Of course I'll fly with you again before I've finished learning. You can't wait five years until I've finished my studies. Only, in principle I must start *now*. Well, and here are the first calls."

CHAPTER ELEVEN

Francine waited until I had gotten rid of the next caller and terminated the line before she placed my coffee down before me. Our computer still reported twenty-seven incoming signals.

"One should think they got it by now," she said and stepped behind her own seat. "Do you have to talk straight with them?"

"Perhaps I should. But why should I be unfriendly to them? Okay, they're importunate, annoying, and don't know the word *no*, but that's their job."

"You're very lenient toward them."

"Sure. After all, they don't want to shoot me, and I've been lenient toward a killer before."

Francine frowned at me.

"No, I'm not talking about you Mambas, but about the killer in Denver—he also was just doing his job."

"What happened with him? Did you kindly ask him to leave you alone?"

"Well—I broke his shooting finger and wrecked his knee. Thereafter he had to abort his mission."

She laughed. "Oh boy—yes, then the press people can count themselves lucky. But they're still bothersome."

"Naturally. Neither of them would skip the chance to write our story down. The one who manages to get an exclusive interview with you or me—"

"With me?"

"Yes, sure, with you. You're one of two women in this Solar

System who's traveled to another star. Moreover, you're the only witness who can tell what I did and said there. The one worming such information out of you has got it made. That must be worth some millions of dollars."

"Some millions?" Francine pretended having to consider it. "Perhaps I should auction the right for the first interview. A nice girl can live long on those returns — and a not-so-nice girl even longer."

"I know some juicy details about you, too," I warned her.

"No, it's okay. I'll need all that money to bribe you into not giving the seat in your cockpit to someone else."

"I'd rather not do that. On the other hand, if the price is right . . ."

Francine's expression became clouded.

"Seriously," I began. "I don't want to miss you. When we're flying next time to deploy the rover, I want you at my side, no doubt. But if it's about who I can trust an accompanying ship to, there's not much choice."

"What do you mean?"

"I think you should get a captain's qualification in addition to the engineering studies, not just the astrogation stuff, but also leadership and all. Just wait for it—the query for our qualification will come earlier than you'd expect, and I don't want to pass the command of this mission."

Francine sank into her seat, took her cup with both hands, and stared into the black liquid. "Do you think people will play along? Once you open that door, there'll be enough people putting spokes in your wheel."

"You're right. That's why I shouldn't advertise it publicly. We'll find someone from the order to teach us everything we need. Regarding space flight—you're the standard pilot. Nobody but you and me can set the limits for a Barracuda. We'll be writing the rules against which all spaceship pilots and commanders will be tested, and thereafter we'll give each other the exam—after all, nobody else can do that. All other subjects will be administered by an order member or even a commission. I'm sure these people will treat us fairly. Once we've worked that through, the rules are nailed down for further candidates, and then we'll present these rules to the United Nations."

"You've planned far ahead."

"Aw no, I haven't. I've only picked up your idea and spun it out. Later on, I'll pass that on to Achrotzyber, and he can warn Walter, so that we can tackle that topic right after arrival."

"Right after arrival?" Francine pointed at the screen. Meanwhile it showed seventy-three contact requests. "Aren't you forgetting a tiny detail there?"

CHAPTER TWELVE

Not just the press was among the importunate callers. Diplomatic channels were filling up as well. Should we touch down in New York, close to the UN, or better in Nevada to have more space available? On top came invitations from Abu Dhabi, Moscow, Peking, Paris and half a hundred more metropoles around the globe. Every city, every nation wanted to adorn itself with the return of the first interstellar mission.

Thus, each of these offers was a diplomatic landmine. No matter how I decided, it would be called favoritism, and any number of political explosives would be interpreted into this decision.

The chaos created by such a short-term decision, by the chosen host having to organize the welcome party, the big reception, the world leaders' summit, and the press conference within a week, and by having to bear the rush of visitors from all around the world, would be blamed on us — on me — as well.

I decided to tackle the topic head on and string all mistakes together.

I arranged the agenda on the screen. After brief consideration, I rearranged them once again.

06/04/2069, Tuesday — Gladstone — Arrival, party, press announcement

06/05/2069, Wednesday — Canberra — Reception, report back

06/06/2069, Thursday — Manhattan — UN, summit, press conference

06/07/2069, Friday — Abu Dhabi, academy — military

06/08/2069, Saturday — Tokyo — Science conference

06/09/2069, Sunday — Velvet Island — Coming home, consulta-tions

06/10/2069, Monday — Gladstone — Colloquium technical col-lege

I showed the list to Francine. "What do you think?"

She returned an indignant glance. "Now don't ask me to assess the political consequences."

"I'd like to hear your thoughts. Just with regard to con-tent."

"Well then." She quietly read the list and then placed her fingertips together. "Once around the world, right?"

I nodded. "I rearranged it to have less back and forth."

"Some participants will be grateful. But we'll travel east, with very short days."

"Yes. Sorry, there'll be little time for sleep. But you can phase out now and then."

"Nah — I've got a better idea. Ask Sylvie whether she'd like to fly us. So we can sleep on the way."

"Good idea!"

"Okay, well, the ordering makes sense. Why do we start in Gladstone?"

"That's *Mischief's* port of origin. Here we departed, here we return."

"That town will soon be better known and more important than Sydney."

"Maybe. A small return for the hospitality."

"Ah — that's why Canberra comes next?"

"Exactly."

"And all the *important* people have to wait until Thursday. I guess you'll have to explain that."

I shrugged. "They're welcome to join the party. We won't be running out of beer soon."

Francine laughed. "And you'll disappoint them if they're raising political topics."

"Exactly."

"Well, fine. Security will make Tess and Kenneth burn some midnight oil, but that's nothing new. What are your plans with the military? You surely don't want to just say hello to Fatima."

"No. It's not just about the infantry. I'm the boss, and it's time for me to address the full spectrum. Of course, the United Nations council will be invited, and I want to have Jenny, Zoé and Walter in. I don't know yet how to fit the entire agenda into one day — it will boil down to me throwing everything at their feet and letting them deal with it."

"As always."

"Yes." Yes, as always. As always, the slave master Jo would drop in, toss new problems at the overworked people's feet, and disappear again.

"Jo?"

"Mmm?"

"It's okay. You can't do it differently if you don't want to do it all on your own. Just consider what the people get from you in return. Not just a pile of new problems, but rescue from the Cartel, from interstellar invaders — who'd come without you anyway, let's not fool ourselves — liberation from Earth's gravity prison, from the limits of light speed, and just along you're also helping this planet's poorest, who are forgotten all too often."

She was right, and anyway — even by me, this planet's poorest were forgotten all too often.

Mighty, you'll have to do something for me. Papua New Guinea, Owen Stanley Rangers, the Kokoda Trail. There's a small village. I want all village people to join the party, new clothes, food and drinks and all included. You'll need two Tigersharks, there aren't many people left. Tell them the Golden One sent you.

What party are you talking about?

Welcome party in Gladstone. I'll send out the schedule at once, and then I'm curious about the reactions.

CHAPTER THIRTEEN

There were no objections. The diplomats had expressed their wishes, and the Dragon empress in her infinite wisdom had condescended to present a pragmatic proposal. Of course, it didn't meet the hosts' preferences, and of course, some people felt unhappy about it—but at least the proposal was feasible.

I had only added a short postscript to the message with the schedule and the respective agendas— *You can discuss it or use the quite short time for preparations. Without me, neither event will take place anyway.*

Thirteen days were tight but sufficient for the basic logistics—that is, providing appropriate amounts of beer. In addition, the short timeframe limited the number of participants who could arrive.

The people of Gladstone had catered for a party before. They just had to rely on the old plans and make everything a bit bigger. Did I have special requests? Cold beer, tender steaks, happy people, the rest was up to the hosts was what I had established—and no talk of the topics of the following week.

"Gladstone Control, this is *Mischief.* In a few minutes we'll enter the outer atmospheric layers."

"Francine, dear, we can't wait. Airspace is cleared on all levels. So don't let your steak be burned and your beer get warm."

"As you like, Ed. We'll hurry up." She entered a few parameters and let the computer calculate a new approach. "I'll be with you in thirty-seven seconds. *Mischief* out."

"Thirty-seven seconds?" I was just asking, but Francine had already released the new course, and our Barracuda dashed toward the surface under protection of its nestle field.

Like a feather, our spaceship came down to a rest on the pavement of Gladstone's airport — of course, perfectly aligned to the marking.

The space around our landing spot was generously cordoned off. No, I had to correct myself. There was only a white line on the pavement, around our landing spot, and the people remained behind it respectfully. There were a few high steel scaffolds for the cameras, and large screens ensured that everyone could see what happened. Three huge stages had been erected at the far end of the runway, and I asked myself for how many days flight traffic had been canceled to allow that.

One by one, Francine deactivated the screens, then her data glove, and finally, the computer announced the successful integrity check completion. Thus our journey had truly ended.

Upon her questioning glance, I pointed at the airlock. She sighed, nodded, and rose. I followed her to the exit. The airlock was large enough for two.

After the racy approach, the airlock cycle appeared infinitely slow to me. Until the inner hatch had closed and the outer hatch had completely opened, it felt like hours to me.

Perhaps that was good, because we needed a moment to get used to the incoming Australian heat.

"Now I know what I missed the last four and a half months," she said.

"You missed this heat?"

"Yes. Thirst makes me enjoy the beer."

The outer hatch was open now, and we looked down on the bare pavement. Francine stepped to the edge and gave me another questioning glance.

I showed her a thumbs-up, and she jumped out. Outside, she quickly scanned the surroundings before making way for me. She had insisted on that—she wasn't just a pilot, but also a Mamba and as such member of a unit that had set the goal to protect me.

Such protection shouldn't be necessary. But who could predict which crazy ideas a group of fanatic Dragon haters might come up with? And if there were no Dragon haters, maybe isolationists, luddites, or committed activists who had decided that gravtunnels would irreparably damage the structure of the universe.

Perhaps the latter would be right there—but if so, wormholes were more detrimental by orders of magnitude, and if we aspired to stop this kind of environmental destruction, we had to travel where we could find the culprit. So we had to continue making small holes to prevent the large holes.

Such considerations wouldn't get me anywhere. I stepped over the edge and dropped down to the landing field, slightly bending my knees to cushion the impact. Now, how did our *Mischief* look from the outside?

The spindle shape had remained, but only a loose mesh was left of our once tight nano hull, unable to hide the scars beneath. It was remarkable that the steel shell had survived.

"There's the welcome committee coming," Francine said, thus pulling me out of my moody thoughts.

In three places, one person had emerged from the crowd. All three were ambling toward us leisurely. I recognized Jenny, Sylvie, and Zoé, and all three were wearing the same black, skintight suit as we, each with a silver brooch over her left breast.

"If we don't want to cause anyone to run, we'll have to wait here," I commented drily. "Just let's make a few steps forward, so that we're visible next to the *Mischief*."

The three indeed reached us almost at the same time—in the end, Jenny held back a bit. She was wearing the headband with camera and microphone.

Sylvie approached Francine and hugged her. "Welcome back, sister!"

Zoé wrapped her arms around me. "Welcome back, Jo!"

Thereafter we swapped, and then we each hugged Jenny. And now?

Jenny hugged me again, pushed me away at arm's length, and held me tight. "I'm sure many millions, no, billions of people around the world would like to hug you now and thank you for the risk you took for us—and for safely return-ing home. Just feel hugged by me in place of all of them."

"Thank you, Jenny," I replied. "I'm speaking for Francine and myself now—we're glad we could safely come back, too. In the beginning, it didn't look like that. But today, we don't want to talk about the hardships, also not about any future topics. Today we just want to party with you and be happy that everything worked out in the end. After four and a half months in this tin can that nicely carried us to the stars and back, we're both glad to be back among people. I think after such a long time we may grant ourselves one day and evening to remember who we made this journey for—for all of us, for mankind."

"Thank you, Jo." She turned around. "Francine, would you like to add something?"

"Sure I'd like to." Francine smiled into Jenny's camera. "I've got the best job on Earth. I'm flying with the best boss and the most brilliant *inventress* on Earth. The galaxy is mine—but if I want to have a fresh, cold draft beer, I have to return to Earth, here, to Gladstone. Mothers, cover your chil-dren's or husband's ears for a moment—men, for a cold beer you can have anything from me tonight. So, let's get the party started!"

CHAPTER FOURTEEN

Sylvie's voice sounded far away — while she was just sitting in the cockpit and I was sleeping in the rest area, only few meters away from her. "We've arrived in Canberra."

I tried to get my bearings. Where was up, where was down?

Hasn't the alcohol been metabolized yet?

— Metabolizing of toxicants has explicitly been revoked until recall. —

Uh. And I was no longer used to the good stuff.

Recall.

Next to me, in the neighboring berth, an indignant growl sounded.

"Francine?"

"I'm not there."

"As you like. One beer too many yesterday?"

She turned on her back and stretched. Her rosy nipples were nicely pointing to the ceiling.

I sat up, looked around — yes, her suit was under the berth.

"Alcohol doesn't affect me."

The effect on me faded quickly now, too, owing to my nanos.

"So, were many admirers taking you at your word?"

"I couldn't down the beer as fast as they arrived with new glasses."

"Sounds like you had a fulfilling evening. Do you still know how many?"

"I stopped counting at forty or fifty." She rolled on her side and grinned at me. "Not what you're thinking of. Nice fathers asking for a photo together with me, or with their little daughter and me, or the occasional bold one asking for a kiss."

"What, no sex?"

"Well—three, no, four quickies once the children were gone, and toward morning two somewhat longer encounters."

"Disappointing."

"Yeah—once the blokes had acquired the Dutch courage to ask me for sex, they were too flat out to get it up." She sat up, too. "Okay, you did it. I'm awake. So, let's get it over with, shall we?"

I nodded. "There's still time for a shower. Isn't there, Sylvie?"

"The car to pick you up for your breakfast with the prime shall arrive in eight minutes," her answer came from the cockpit.

I nodded at Francine. "You go first." After all, she was already undressed.

She rose and stepped into the plumbing unit. "You didn't say yet how your evening went. How many lobbyists did you have to turn away?"

"Countless." I tried to remember.

— *Retrieve recording?* —

No, thanks. Just don't.

"After the first few importunate guys who just didn't want to learn that they'd picked the wrong time, I simply merged with the crowd of ordinary citizens and started kissing random strangers. Even the most tenacious reporter had to recognize that he wouldn't get an answer while my lips are busy. Well, and once the blokes understood that I wanted kisses, they formed a line."

Refreshed and dried, Francine returned, placed a kiss on my lips in passing, and bent down for her suit. "Only the blokes?"

We could have set our Barracuda down in front of the estate, but that might have been inappropriate. The shiny black Martian blended in better with the ensemble of Olde English cottage, tall trees, green lawn, and white gravel, and for a moment I reflected on where I had left Phoebe behind — ah, yes, in Paris.

The security guard at the entrance briefly frowned when we climbed the stairs to the Australian prime minister's residence, but then his gaze fell on Sylvie's order brooch, and he let us pass without a word.

Only when were a few steps away did I hear him report, "the Imperatrix with *two* companions."

I made an effort to approach the young man at the next open door slowly, because I heard sounds of hastily rearranged furniture from behind it.

When we entered, two young ladies were busy adding another place setting of silver and rose-white china on the white tablecloth. The prime minister approached me with outstretched hand.

"Johanna! I'm so glad to see you!"

"Percy, the joy is on my part."

He shook my hand, then he turned to my company. "Knight Francine. Welcome back! And Knight Sylvie. Welcome!" He smiled and pointed at the table behind himself. "May I offer coffee or tea? Harry will arrive soon. Johanna, here please, and Knight Francine opposite, and Knight Sylvie, please there."

Francine stood next to the chair to his left. Before she sat down, she nodded at Sylvie. "Please leave out the knight, Percy. We don't need that, do we?"

"No, of course not — Francine. Sit down, please."

He waited until we had taken our seats, and just as he had adjusted his own chair, his minister for foreign affairs arrived, and we rose to another round of greetings.

Finally we were all sitting around his breakfast table, and everyone had a full cup of coffee.

"Pardon me if I don't stick to the agenda," the prime minister began. "I'm curious. Would you like to tell me a few impressions of your journey, without too many technical details?"

"That would be Francine's part, then," I replied. "I've spent the major part of our journey with technical details and hardly found time to gather other impressions."

"Our computer often was more communicative," the Mamba agreed. "Well, okay. Until the first transit initiation it was a routine flight. Then we left Einstein space . . ."

Percy and Harry kept their silence long after Francine had finished speaking. Their coffee had become cold. Quiet sobs filled the background—the two young ladies who should have served us breakfast could no longer hide their distress.

"So your return teetered on a knife's edge," the prime minister finally stated.

"Several times," Francine affirmed. "The end of the first transit alone could have shattered us—and if Jo hadn't managed to reconfigure the remaining emitters fast enough, we'd literally been grinded. Thereafter, we were safe—but it would never have sufficed for our return."

"If Francine hadn't come up with the compensator idea," I added. "That was the decisive factor."

"And that you could code it with the remaining emitters."

"That was craftsmanship."

Percy pointed at his cup and waved. "If it's so risky, we basically can't responsibly send anyone out again."

"Oh no," I quickly disagreed. "It's *been* so risky. The compensator works."

"Nevertheless," the prime minister insisted. "It's

43

venturesome."

"Yes, it must be," Francine agreed. "It's like the early time of seafaring, when men like James Cook or Abel Tasman went out to sea in small, fragile wooden ships, entirely submitting themselves to the vagaries of weather—and yet, reliably found their way back home. The technology back then was controllable and fault-tolerant, and still you had to deal with storms and be cautious about reefs in foreign waters. We survived our Cape Tribulation."

"Our learning curve is steep, and our technological progress is, too—because we're able to implement innovations quickly." One of the two girls served me a fresh cup of coffee. I looked up at her—tears had smeared her eyeshadow. "Thank you for your sympathy."

Now there was another drop in the corner of her eye. I reached out, placed one hand on her cheek and wiped her tear away with my thumb. Along with that, my nanos repaired her eyeshadow. Thereafter, I kept my hand at her cheek until I felt her calm down and relax.

"What's your name?"

"Evangelina."

"That's a very nice name."

"Y-yes. Thank you. Would you like eggs and bacon?"

"Gladly, both. Fried eggs, sunny, please."

"You're doing it again," Francine said, once Evangelina and her colleague had disappeared to the kitchen with our orders.

"What?"

"Enchanting people." She winked at the prime minister.

He nodded. "Yes, I feel it, too. I just want to trust you. How do you manage to convey this feeling of your unconditional honesty to other people?"

"Because that's what she is," Sylvie burst out. "She can't help it."

Percy smiled at his minister for foreign affairs. "Harry, what should I do? Leave her my job?"

"No!" Harry and I exclaimed like one.

For a moment we looked at each other, then Harry nodded and reclined.

"No, I don't want your job," I said. "I've got enough on my plate."

"Well, ye-es." Percy wrapped his hands around his cup. "You're scheduling my appointments, commanding my party budget, controlling our economic and foreign affairs, providing new immigrants at your own discretion—what's left for me?"

For a few moments he almost managed to make a serious face and deceive me. But his eyes flashed, and when I let my head hang down and quietly said, "Sorry," he could no longer hold his laughter.

Harry pointed at the door where Evangelina just had appeared with three plates. "Let's eat breakfast now and talk about the serious stuff later."

"That was delicious," Francine praised after she had swallowed the last bite.

"Your first breakfast after your return—the food on the journey is more samey, isn't it?" Harry asked.

"No and no," Francine said. "No, not if Jo takes care of the meals. That makes every award-winning chief pale with envy. And no, it wasn't the first breakfast. Regarding our return, we've cheated a bit."

"Cheated?"

"We've been back for four weeks," I said. "I had to discuss our findings with Achrotzyber and Rashid. It's inevitable that we start a second expedition as soon as possible—but it will be a humanitarian expedition."

"One moment." Percy rose. He walked to the door and

waved at one of his people. "We don't want to be disturbed. Nothing but a Jelly invasion is important enough, okay?"

He closed the door and returned to the table. "So. Now tell us. It's about the last sentence of your message, right? Help for the Dragons in the *Worries* system."

"Exactly. We need to change our whole fleet construction program as well as the parameters for the Solar System's defense — and then, Francine had another good idea."

"I'm curious," Percy said.

All gazes turned to my pilot.

"The thing is, we have to motivate the people to actively participate in our plans. If we make them pester us, if we find promoters, we'll get what we need, too. We don't want mere understanding and tolerance for our plans but excitement — the right kind of excitement that's fueled by investment power. It's about the commercial development of the Solar System."

"And that means?" Harry dug deeper.

"Raw materials mining in space. Space stations and moon bases. Regular commuter traffic between Earth and Saturn. Factories in the asteroid belt."

Percy and Harry glanced at each other.

"That's an entirely new perspective," the prime minister noted. "But what does that mean for Australia in particular? I expect the United Nations to govern the whole thing, right?"

"It can't work otherwise," I agreed. "We don't want Cartel-like organizations in space with miner slaves and — well — peculiar views on legislation or drastic methods for maintaining monopolies. Every investor shall be allowed to make decent money, but not at the expense of fundamental values. Australian companies may participate like all others. In the medium term there will be additional institutions in need of a location, which they might find here." If he wasn't already buying into this vision, I had more. "There's also a short-term part. I'm expecting us to educate a lot more people in Dragon technology very soon—at least the applied part—and I'd rather not leave that entirely to others. Therefore, I'd like to expand the University in Gladstone. The same applies to the production of certain key technologies. There, we already envisaged a factory outside of Earth, but the control remains with us. We need a true spaceport—perhaps farther inland and connected to Gladstone by express rail."

"If we want to run the rescue mission through it, we need a high-performing distribution center—with harbor and airport," Francine added.

Sylvie raised her hand. "Gladstone's airport is too small already, and I've heard that new companies which would like to settle close to the University can't find affordable sites anymore."

"I see," Percy said. "However, if we allocate the new University part not in Gladstone, but for example in Rockhampton, and connect the express rail from Rockhampton via Gladstone to the new airport and spaceport in the hinterland, we can allocate commercial premises in Rockhampton or near the airport. Beyond that, there's a prospect of extending the express rail to Brisbane or Sydney. What do you think, Harry?"

"That's plenty of explosives—environmental protection, regional politics and all—but for our economy, it would be a blessing. We have to check that with the respective department ministers."

"And if I told you the spaceport must be up and running within one year—including the express rail connection?" I asked.

"Impossible." Percy shook his head. "Planning procedures, administrative decisions, formal objections, tenders, and then the construction itself—that cannot work."

"Talk with your ministers about how it *can* work," Francine recommended. "For this topic, *No* is no answer for Jo.

Right, Jo?"

"Right."

The two Australians glanced at each other again—but the idea had already caught in their heads. If Australia could put the first commercial spaceport worldwide into service, what would it mean for this country?

CHAPTER FIFTEEN

Sylvie's disapproving glare held me back. "You don't want to go out like *this*, do you?"

I glanced down at myself. My black combat dress was impeccable, and the same applied to the matching boots — of course, all made of my nano material and thus perfectly fitting my body.

"Why?"

"Why, she asks!" Sylvie nudged Francine with indignation. "Jo, you might not be naked technically, but that's still no getup for such an event!"

"So." Yes, perhaps she was right. I had become so used to wearing this suit or nothing at all that I no longer thought about the subject of clothing. In turn, the people used to me didn't comment on it either.

"Jo, for the Gladstone party it was okay — and authentic. And Percy and Harry have known you long enough. But meanwhile you've had two days, and that's more than sufficient to dress up for shore leave. Show these people you consider them worth this effort."

"Okay." That was another way to see it. "Thanks for the tip."

Both were watching me and waiting.

"If you want to go shopping, you should get going," Sylvie advised me.

"Oh no." That was the true issue! "You want to go shopping? Do that — pick something pretty."

"And you?"

I focused my mind.

Ghost. I need pants, tight only around my butt, flaring out to my ankles, with a transparent, loose, long-sleeve blouse. Over that, a vest, straight cut with deep V cleavage and band collar. All in black, and matching shiny boots.

The red brooch goes on the left breast and a small silver star with nine points on the right. And one golden laurel leaf each on the right and left collar patch.

Clear?

— Clear. —

Execute.

It took just one moment, and I was newly dressed. The two women stared at me — they'd seen a lot from me already, but not this trick.

"Well?"

"Great, Jo!" Sylvie said.

Francine nodded. "The laurel leaf is clear, that's for the Imperatrix Aurea. What does the star mean?"

"My own command over a long-distance-flight capable spaceship. Ah, one moment."

A vertical silver wedge below, please, pointing down.

"There's a silver wedge for every kill of another spaceship. I'll transfer the code into the computer at once, so that you can have your suits programmed accordingly."

"What rank will we be then?"

"Aw, shucks!" I hadn't thought of that!

What did my Mambas need ranks for? To command other people? Yes, perhaps. For not being ordered around — surely.

My own rank was set, and of course I could give my own people ranks as I liked. But I also had to consider how this would fit into a larger organization later, where they'd have to collaborate with others. It wouldn't be good if an identical rank didn't encompass a similar qualification.

As ordinary Mambas and agents they actually didn't need any rank at all — but as fleet members, they would. Or perhaps especially these two wouldn't need one, as they were already knights, but I still had to install a regulation.

"I didn't want to cause you trouble," Francine said. "The ranks can wait until later."

"No, it can't," I disagreed. "When you go to town as special officers of my forces — that is, in uniform — you need the insignia, and you must be able to tell what they mean. You are the ones who'll carry my ideas into space, so that's what you'll call yourself — my *wings*. And that's your collar symbol — a Dragon wing in gold. This symbol can be carried in addition to a regular rank insignia, but it always comes first — that is, innermost on the collar patch or outermost on the shoulder."

"Nifty," Francine said. "Isn't it, Sylvie?"

The great hall was occupied to the last seat, and I didn't want to know how many *last seats* had been added to the otherwise usual seating. Was it called General Assembly because *everyone* attended?

This wasn't my first visit to the United Nations, but my first General Assembly. On my previous visits, I had only met with *my* Interstellar Defence Council.

This time, it wasn't just a council, and not even just the member nations' usual UN ambassadors, but in most cases additionally at least the foreign affairs minister, if not the respective head of government.

Zoe had stood before this assembly previously. I remembered every single word, and even if I was not a good speaker, I could rely on that.

"About ten thousand years ago our neighbor galaxy was run over by an invasion," I began. "Without chance for organized resistance, the individual peoples of hundreds of thousands of star systems fell prey to a voracious and parasitic train that knows no restraint. Very few found the courage to stand up against them at all."

51

Did they recognize the words?

"Two peoples developed a plan to impair the parasitic advance. One of them commanded the technology of faster-than-light travel as well as genetic engineering, the other people's members were fierce and determined warriors. They joined forces and gave up their homes and their unity as people, ultimately. They retreated to another line of defense to surprise and defeat the invaders there, to give the peoples of another galaxy a chance. You."

Some listeners gave each other questioning or knowing glances. From here on, I had to modify Zoe's words, though.

"You know the warrior people — the Dragons. A small tribe of Dragons settled on this planet, made it their new home, determined to defend it against the invasion once it reached us. Ten thousand years the Dragons remained silently waiting. Finally there was an agreement between Dragons and mankind, a contract on the distribution of duties regarding the defense of this planet. This distribution of duties arranged for the Dragons to take the lead in case of an interstellar conflict, with the Imperatrix Aurea as the highest rank. The invasion began, and the Dragons kept their side of the contract — they fought."

There was bitterness in Zoe's memories.

"After the invasion's first wave, the contract was unilaterally suspended by mankind, and the Dragons — all Dragons living on Earth back then — left the planet. Well, you know that's not the whole truth. The Imperatrix knew that mankind wasn't ready yet to continue the joint path, and she left assistance and her knowledge behind for you."

I placed my right hand below the order brooch on my left breast. "Me. In the beginning, I wasn't ready to accept that legacy. I had seen way too much egoism — starting with the financial crisis more than forty years ago, the root causes of which, namely greed and exorbitance, you still didn't remedy, up to the Cartel's worst excesses, for the emergence of which you're responsible yourself, too — and I had made safeguarding my own survival my most important goal. There I excelled. Yes, I learned my lessons, I learned to put myself first and follow my own goals. That I dealt out blow after blow to the Cartel, that I repeatedly freed victims from the Cartel's claws, was just a side effect."

Many listeners tapped their earpieces. Had they got their simultaneous translation right?

"Yes, you heard me right. The Cartel was my adversary only because they didn't want to leave me alone. But they chose the wrong opponent, and paid the highest price for it — their eradication. That's a warning to the world outside — while I take many an affront as good sports, it's not advisable to set a killer on my tracks or to try to blackmail me with a threat against my people."

I smiled. "My people, that's all of you, humans and Dragons of this planet. Because in the time of my fight against the Cartel I've met many wonderful people who're not just looking after themselves. People who are helpful and trustworthy — people who are worth fighting for. That's the reason why I finally accepted my legacy, that I accepted to walk in the way-too-large footsteps of a Zoe Lionheart and follow her tracks. And that's the reason why I took the threat of another interstellar attack — after the raid two and a half years ago — as reason to turn the tables. For you, I ventured on a test flight in a spaceship with untried technology, without guarantee for a return, to spy out the attacker in his home system, and to prepare for an attack on him in a follow-up mission. This new aggressor made a big mistake — he challenged me."

My smile made some listeners shiver visibly.

"But that wasn't his only mistake. He made a second big mistake — he expanded his fight before he had cleaned up his own doorstep, and perhaps he did that because he had to —

because the fight in that other system, in the *Worries* system, isn't won yet. As I already told you in my first announcement, there are still Dragons, and if we ally with these Dragons, I'm convinced that our joint enemy has no chance."

There I arrived at the difficult part. "The sooner we're able to support and strengthen these potential allies, the fewer of our own forces we have to deploy to gain victory in that other system, before the enemy can advance on us again. That's the military aspect. Well, a moment ago I talked of side effects caused by angering me. One of the side effects of this enemy angering me is the development of a demonstrably operational interstellar drive, after we already had shaken off the chains of Earth gravity. Many of you might not have internalized it yet, but a flight to Mars isn't much more expensive for us than a trip from New York to Sydney, and may take perhaps a week on an economic route. That's so cheap that you could launch a two-week commuter traffic service. Only, to our astonishment, so far no one called us and asked whether we could provide transport means to Mars. While we could— even though there'd only be a few seats today."

I paused to give the translators time to catch up and took a sip of water.

"The concepts, the construction plans, a few body shells are already there. To lay a few transporter keels is just a question of funds—there's enough yard capacity. And anyone who can send a spaceship to a far star system can build a Mars station, or a mining station in the asteroid belt."

Here I had to pause again. This issue had to sink in—my audience should develop their own associations, at least for a brief moment.

"The opportunities are nearly endless, and by the way we're thus creating the means for a supply bridge to the *Worries* Dragons. Once the Jellies' second wave arrives, a not all too far day away, the same transport ships can take Dragon fighters back from *Worries* to us, to support us and return some of our aid. You know Dragons do such things."

This argument was weak. It was logically comprehensible, but it didn't reach the heart. There I had to catch them. Like in the saying — *don't teach people how to build spaceships, but rather teach them to dream of the stars.*

I placed my hand on my left breast again and gave my nanos another order.

Transform.

"The people who I learned to know, who caused me to accept my role as new Golden Dragon, will help me, of that I'm sure. You all, you're part of that. Help me. And do the next step together with me — fly with me to the stars."

Except for the blood-red brooch and the small star on my chest, everything of me was golden — my nano suit, my hand, face, hair — and even my eyes.

"I thank you."

Before the door to the small boardroom I briefly paused and took a deep breath. Next came the most difficult task.

For my goal, people of the General Assembly beginning to consider my proposals sufficed. For the press conference, me not blundering would suffice to not endanger Rashid's campaign. But I had to win the seven people waiting behind this door together with Rashid over to my side — after I had just passed them over again.

Oh yes.

Restore.

I took another deep breath, gazed down at myself, at the familiar black in an unfamiliar cut, then I knocked at the door and pulled it open. The boardroom behind was paneled with pale wood and indirectly lit and furnished with one table and nine chairs only.

Eight interested pairs of gazes followed me to my place at the shiny polished table. I nodded around at each of them before I took my seat.

"Good morning, ladies and gentlemen. Thank you for making this meeting possible on short notice. I'm aware that I've messed up the appointment calendars of many important people for this week with my unilateral proposals, and I'm regretting that especially in your case, because it's very important to me that you can do your job in the best way possible and without interruptions. But at the time of my departure my return wasn't predictable yet—as you've heard, not even granted—and setting up a meeting across several light hours is tedious at best. As we're at war—even though there's no current fighting due to the long distances—it was important to me to have the first information meeting as soon as at all possible. Again—I expressly apologize for pushing like this—but my head is about to explode from all the stuff I yet have to do, or that's been neglected for almost half a year. So, and here I've talked enough for now."

My gaze directed straight across the table, I waited for the storm to hit me. The council members had every right to vent their anger and reproach me for my overbearing attitude.

But the seven men and one woman remained silent.

Finally, Sheikh Hassan cleared his throat. I had expected him to do the talking—if there was one member of this circle who'd have a problem with a woman in leading position, consciously or subconsciously, it was Hassan. "There are two points we urgently need to understand better. The first one concerns your return. In what way was it endangered?"

I looked up. He focused on me, stern and attentive.

"Okay. Let me say a few words about the basics. I already illustrated in our first meeting how faster-than-light spaceflight works, only that was before Benjamin joined us." I nodded at Benjamin Goodman, the representative for North and South America, and tore a sheet of paper off the pad before me. I folded it once and pierced it with one claw. He flinched, and I quickly retracted the claw. "We're drilling a shortcut through the spacetime continuum, thus saving a large part of the flight distance. The Jellies are creating a large hole for this purpose — the astronomers call it wormhole — which then remains open for days. The flight across has side effects, though — for higher lifeforms like us, the transit is unconditionally lethal. Why that doesn't apply to Jellies nor to this brown substance is something I don't know yet."

I placed the sheet down, looked around and focused on Hassan. "Our new method is more economical, more elegant, and healthier. We create a bubble around the spaceship with which we slip through between the paper fibers. That requires so little power that we could build the necessary aggregates into a Barracuda. Because the required power partially depends on the entry speed, we accelerated to twenty percent lightspeed and then went into transit. This procedure is no longer lethal, as I said, but our sensual reception during the transit became, well, let's say upside down. While the ship was in transit, we had to rely on the computer that terminated the transit as planned in the destination system, one-hundred-and-forty lightyears from here. All this worked exactly as calculated."

Hassan leaned forward.

I held his gaze while I went on, "There was one factor we hadn't factored in, as we didn't know about it — a difference in the gravity potential. I don't want to delve into complicated formulas, so let me compare it with a flight from the Himalaya summit to Abu Dhabi. The air pressure is much higher, and the temperature, too. Once you open the transit bubble, you get hot, thick air thrown back in your face. It was similar for us — at the moment of change, our little spaceship got to feel the gravity differences quite abruptly, and we — Francine and I — couldn't do anything. We didn't know about the problem. Okay — within its programming, the computer did what it should. It maintained the transit bubble until we returned to normal space. With the effect of eighty percent of our control quark emitters burning through." *Too technical, Jo.* "These are the devices that create the transit bubble—and that are responsible for wrapping the spaceship into a protective shield. This shield was missing now while we were passing at twenty percent lightspeed through the fine interplanetary dust— that's the stuff that makes comets glow, okay?"

Hassan slowly nodded.

"At this moment, we could have failed two ways. With a bit more gravity potential difference, the emitters could have failed before the end of the transit. I don't want to know what that would do to a spaceship. In exchange, I know too clearly what would happen to a spaceship crossing a planetary system for some time at that speed—the hull will be burned off, and once the hull is gone, its content burns, too."

"You were aware of that?" Hassan asked.

"After the transit? Yes. I needed a few seconds to read this situation from the controls, and thereafter I had a few moments to reprogram our remaining emitters before they'd worn off by the attempt to protect us."

Benjamin chimed in. "I don't understand yet how you could return after you lost eighty percent of your aggregates. Did you bring so many spare parts—and wasn't the return flight as abrading?"

I didn't take my gaze off Hassan. "No, we didn't have enough spare parts to replace all emitters. First it didn't look like we could return."

"Yes, but," Lasse Jorgenson, the European council member began. "What did you do then?"

"We had a task." I didn't look at him. "We made that journey to gather data about the *Worries* system, and even if we were no longer able to return home, we were still able to complete this task. So we fixed the *Mischief* as far as getting her maneuverable, and then started our exploration of that system."

"Without a prospect of return?" Hassan asked. "How could that have helped you?"

"Little—aside from a chance to land and spend the rest of our lives fighting the brown pest. But it could have helped you. If we hadn't found a way to fly home, I'd have been able to send you the data in a different way."

"And which way to return did you find?" Hassan continued.

"We didn't find a spare parts store, sadly. We removed the *Mischief's* linear gun emitters. With them, we replaced some of the burned hull emitters."

"Which hull?"

"Our spaceship's hull. I had to work outside, in a protective cocoon that we improvised."

"Did that suffice to replace the eighty percent?"

"Not by far. The key to success was my pilot's idea—the *Besson compensator*. Francine proposed to do the gravity potential compensation gradually. Sticking to my example—if you adjust air pressure and temperature during the flight, you can open the cabin door in Abu Dhabi and nothing happens. And here we are."

"You had just one idea and didn't know whether it would work?"

"Oh, I had calculated everything several times. After all, we had recorded data from the almost failed transit, so that I could verify my formulas. Moreover, we first did a few very short transits within the *Worries* system to test the compensator before we ventured on the long leg."

"Your faith must be very strong if you took such a risk."

I spread my arms. "I trust in the skills I acquired, and I recognize the necessity to take this risk. Someone has to do it, and nobody else is qualified." He still focused on me, and I focused on him. "I wouldn't burden anyone else with a risk I'm not willing to take myself."

Thus we were sitting there, face to face, like two duelists waiting for who made the first move. No one else interfered.

Finally he lowered his gaze.

I had won an important victory — but ultimately, we all had won.

In the end it was Hassan breaking the silence. "You stressed we are at war. Formally, that's correct, as that's the reason for this council to exist. But I had the impression that you meant a different aspect, and we should better understand that aspect."

My reply didn't come quickly.

Jack Turner, the Kiwi, chimed in. "Is it because you assess the situation from the Dragon point of view?"

"No. No, my point of view is entirely human, although it well and truly takes some patience to live with the results of my musings. We've been attacked — twice already. First came the Jellies, then this brown pest. Between them were more than twenty-four years. That's a strange war if there's just one short but intense battle every few decades, and between them it's seemingly peaceful. This peace is treacherous — it only means that the enemy hasn't finished his preparations for the next attack yet, or, in our case, neither of the enemies we already know of."

"How do you mean that?" Lasse interrupted.

"Hold on, Lasse. The critical element in this war is that a single defeat, in a single battle, can mean total annihilation for us. It's not about occupation with following resistance — that's not an option for us. Or at least not for me. The idea that millions of people are agonizingly tortured while a handful of warriors are executing minor attacks from the underground, and in the unlikely case of a late victory will dare a new start with a few thousand survivors on the rubble of our civilization is unbearable for me. And therefore, I cannot stand to watch us slacking in our preparations, doing less than would be possible."

Only now did I release Hassan from my gaze and glance around. "In a hot war, like for example in the Second World War, the question of whether the factories are working for war doesn't arise — the only question is what kind of weapons are built. Our war is more like a cold war, like at the time of the old ironsides, when news on the situation on the far frontline needed years to reach home."

Sergej Markoff, our Russian, smiled and briefly glanced at Benjamin. Nellie Okonambe, the African representative, nodded, and Wei Ching signaled me to continue.

"Back to Lasse's question. We know from the Lionheart's farewell address that the Jellies migrate from galaxy to galaxy with a large fleet and harvest inhabited stellar systems like a locust swarm. Sooner or later, their second wave will reach us. That's enemy number one, the enemy I wanted to prepare us for — until enemy number two, the brown pest, got into our way as a surprise." I fetched a glass and a bottle of water and poured. "Interstellar travel is costly, as we had discussed in the beginning. To build a spaceship the size of a Jelly mothership you need enormous resources. Who can afford that? Who's got the technology for it? How likely is two peoples completing such progress nearly at the same time and then showing up at our door? That's statistically so insignificant that it's not worth computing that number. That's not my worry, though. What makes me pause is that the brown pest arrived here in a Jelly spaceship. That's already the second case we know of that another people appropriated Jelly technology."

"The second?" Benjamin asked. "What was the first then?"

I grinned at him. "Why, us."

After a moment of silence, Sheikh Hassan chimed in again. "We should now get to your *desires* toward this council."

His face didn't allow us to discern how his statement was meant, but his voice seemed to carry a hint of irony.

"Yes. I know we have to discuss numerous topics I couldn't tend to during the last months — I need to know which decisions you made and which questions are still open. But I proposed this meeting in the first place to raise the urgent topics that accrued lately. Before I meet with the press and say something that could be understood as precedent, I want to discuss and agree with you."

All but Rashid showed surprise.

"I've already stirred up enough of a storm with my proposal to advance the commercial and scientific development of our Solar System," I explained further. "Not entirely selfless, sure, as the primary purpose is to unburden our budget by partially refunding the strategically necessary production of transport capacity as well as the maintenance of desirable supply bases around the Solar System. I won't delude myself — the topic would have come up sooner or later anyway, so I prefer to sit in the front seat and be able to intervene. Surely we don't want to have any kind of Cartel in space, with slave work and other atrocities. Thus I have some proposals what to do about it. Proposals, Sheikh Hassan, and I'm expressly open for alternatives."

He nodded and signaled me to continue.

"Thank you. I'd rather not see the space flight technology we're using in private hands. In the long run I wouldn't have an issue with ordinary, grav field driven commercial transport ships, and fusion reactors are freely available anyway nowadays. But our nestle field, and most of all the means for interstellar flight, should remain under control of the United Nations. That means freight space or passage are only leased away, and in case of a military conflict we've got the entire space traffic—with its telltale emissions—under control. That way no piracy can develop. Likewise, the United Nations should exercise police powers for all installations outside Earth. Or reversed—anyone with the desire to erect a base, for any private purposes whatsoever, has to maintain a supply station, a hospital, and a police station. We provide advanced nano science and all. As I said, that's just a proposal."

The idea didn't meet immediate protest, so I went on.

"Every spaceship officer bears enormous responsibility—outside Earth he represents law and order, and in case of an interstellar expedition also our foreign affairs. People we're trusting with such responsibility have to be diligently chosen. I thought whether it would be good to provide them with a United Nations commission—but that's something only this panel can discuss and decide."

Sergej smiled, glanced at Hassan, then at the Chinese, and picked up the thread. "We've been discussing this topic area during the last three months. Although you've only just proposed a different fleet construction program prioritization, we were aware we'd soon need experienced officers to command the first spaceships, and that a simple retraining of wet Navy officers wouldn't suffice. In all sincerity I'm glad you're not presenting us a fait accompli here. I agree with the basics of your assessment—it will be better if we set the principles for space colonization and don't have to catch up on developments."

"I'd have a small request there." I glanced from Sergej to Hassan.

Hassan again gave Sergej a didn't-I-tell-you glance. "What would that be?"

"A transitional solution for those of my people already playing that role—primarily Zoé, Sylvie, and Francine."

"The knights?" Hassan seemed to be surprised again. "I wouldn't have thought you'd ask this question."

"We agreed that these three — and you yourself, Johanna — are the persons best qualified to train new officers and decide upon the first commissions," Nellie said.

"At least with regard to the handling of the new technologies," Lasse added.

"And with regard to Dragon leadership style." Jack grinned. "We agreed that our officers might, well, have to catch up there."

"Nobody in this council will question the proven qualification of a knight," Hassan said. "May I openly concede that I'm admiring your staff members' dedication?"

I stared at him for a moment. He held my gaze with a question on his face.

"You took me by surprise. May I openly concede that I've assessed your attitude toward female leading personnel differently until now?"

"You may." Now he was smiling again. "Your assessment was well reasoned. But even the Prophet himself couldn't ignore what you achieved."

Jack winked at Hassan, then at Rashid, and finally at me. "Not to mention the feats a certain infantry commandant achieves one military exercise after the other."

Rashid seemed to grow in his seat, but didn't say anything.

Nellie smiled, too. "We should try to discuss a few more details before Johanna has to depart for her press conference."

CHAPTER SIXTEEN

I wouldn't have been surprised—and many journalists would surely have been happy—if the press conference had been scheduled in the Madison Square Garden. The way it was, the admitted press representatives had to make do with a hotel's large conference hall, and a significantly higher number of journalists remained out. They were lining the streets along our way, kept at bay by fences and mounted police.

But it wasn't just members of the press—including radio and TV—who were lining the streets with their cameras. It looked like all New York had gathered to wave golden flags and cheer at our convoy.

"So many!" I marveled.

"The New Yorkers didn't forget you, Johanna," our driver said, a bull-necked giant with a deep scar at his upper arm, and steered the Martian around another corner. "We know what we owe you."

"You, too?" I leaned forward and pointed at his scar. Somehow I sensed that he had a story to tell.

"I was in Central Park on that day, *Protectress*. You know why?"

"No. Did you belong to the Bones?"

"I've got a daughter. She's grown up now. Her name's Rebecca. She's working for a New York Police special unit, cleaning up in the Bronx. I objected when she told me about it—the Slicers are still dangerous, at least at night. But I couldn't talk her out of it. She said she did something foolish and let someone else pay for it. It would only be fair to pay off a small share of her due. You know what I'm talking about?"

I nodded.

"I remember her," I told Francine and Sylvie at my side. "She and four other girls . . . I never asked how it happened, but the Slicers — a loosely organized gang of violent criminals in the Bronx — kept those five captive. For their *entertainment*."

Francine's and Sylvie's faces showed dismay.

"You can't imagine what the Slicers did with their victims back then," the driver said.

"Yes we can," Francine said. "We've both witnessed and experienced ourselves what men do with little girls. In the ZONE."

Our driver remained silent for a long while. Finally he began, "Well, then — "

He paused and firmly stepped on the brakes. I glanced forward. A little dog was jumping back and forth on the street between cars and horses and barking.

"Wait," I ordered and opened the door.

"Don't," Francine started and swore when I still disembarked. She followed on my heels.

The cheer rose outside when people spotted me — which only stirred up the dog more. I made a few steps toward him and *quickly* picked him up before he could understand what happened.

He calmed down in my arms — or simply held still because he didn't know what to do.

I watched and listened around, reached out with all my senses. People were waving their hands all along the curb — and I didn't spot rifle muzzles on the roofs around. To the right, a girl was waving a leash, her eyes red and wet, perhaps just six years old.

A mounted policeman carefully bridled his horse between her and me. He looked down at me. "You should get back in the car, *Protectress.*"

"There's no reason to worry, officer." I nodded right and left at my Mambas flanking me. "We're safe here. After all, we're in New York."

"If you see it that way . . ." He made his horse step back, clearing my way to the fence.

Many hands reached for me to at least manage a brief touch. I ignored them and walked up to the girl who was watching me with big eyes. Her dog seemed to recognize her, as he was trying to get to her.

I gave her the dog across the fence. "Here. What's your name?"

She took the dog, who immediately began to lick her salty cheek. "Johanna, *Protectress.*"

"In the future, take good care of your dog, Johanna. You are his protectress. Don't fail his confidence."

"N-n-no."

"Goodbye, Johanna." I nodded at the people around and returned to the car.

"That was risky," Francine said once we were sitting in our Martian and the convoy proceeded.

"I know," I admitted. "Not everyone in the crowd is necessarily a New Yorker, and I have enemies. But I also have to show that I can't be intimidated, that I won't hide away."

"Nobody could easily produce a gun among these people," our driver said.

"I thought instead about a fragmentation bomb," Francine said. "Or a disruptor field."

"I checked that. It didn't smell like explosives, and I didn't sense telltale stray emissions."

She stared at me, then she grinned and punched my upper arm.

CHAPTER SEVENTEEN

The conference hall was too small, I had heard. Nevertheless, several thousand people were waiting behind the door for our appearance. My *Analogy* could have sorted their whispering and murmuring, but I wasn't interested in it.

"One minute!" someone called. "Where's Ike?"

The conference would be broadcast live around the world, and we didn't want to make the TV people nervous, so we were patiently waiting for our cue.

Francine was calmness incarnate, or at least didn't let on she was anxious. Doing so had to be easy after having learned to suppress even drug-induced nervousness.

I had learned from Dandy how to hold still even when someone applied the knife. That didn't reduce the tension, though. It's not like your appearance in Central Park, I told myself.

My grim face was mirrored in the startling of the young assistant just looking up from her watch.

"Sorry," I said. "Old memories."

"Oh. Yes. Protectress — Knight Francine — ten more."

A gong sounded in the hall, and the whispers faded.

"Ike — now."

A man in dark-gray suit hurried past us through the stage door. Applause sounded and faded.

"Welcome, ladies and gentlemen!" Ike shouted into his mike. "I'm Ike Snyder, and together with my team I'll moderate this conference."

The assistant tried to get my attention. She pointed at the

door.

"Ladies and gentlemen—here they are, Earth's first inter-stellar spacefarers, Knight Francine Besson of the Order of the Dying Lioness"—Francine strode out and was welcomed by deafening applause that hesitantly faded when she took her seat at the table—"and the Imperatrix Aurea, Dragon Protectress, New York liberator, Paladin Johanna Meieeer!"

My cue, and the assistant frantically waved toward the door. I winked at her before I stepped through. Despite his announcer-style introduction, I wasn't entering a boxing ring, I reminded myself.

The applause seemed to be trying to blow me back out of the hall anyway. *It's just noise, Jo.*

With an amused smile I waved at the assembly, shook Ike's hand and sat down to Francine's left.

Several hands already shot up. Ike waved. "Just one moment, folks. Protectress Johanna, are there any restrictions?"

"None, Ike," I said, as agreed before. "With regard to military secrets I reserve the right not to answer. Everything else is okay."

"Fine." He pointed at a screen behind himself. "For our spectators—a randomizer decides the order for simultaneous requests. The inquirer's microphone will then be opened, which you can recognize by a light, and name and media will be shown here. Number one."

Number one was a German reporter. "Protectress, what gives you the authorization to draw us into a war in a distant star system which we've got nothing to do with?"

Francine at my side briefly bent her fingers, but didn't make a fist.

I made a friendly smile. "I'm not drawing us into this war. As before, with the Jelly invasion, we're all pulled into a war that's not ours without our doing—as resources or even as a food source. We don't know the invaders' original motivation, but they don't come to exert power over us or to permanently incorporate us into their territory. We're nothing more than the fruit they're plucking from a tree in passing by, or the tree they take down for making a fire. We're not part of their war mission. That's what we've got in common with that distant star system — they're another resource for this incomprehensible war. And there's one more commonality — the Dragons there who are ready to fight for their protected and to sacrifice themselves. In this war, I'm your Imperatrix, and with my claim to spare you pain and horror, I seek to wage this fight as far away from Earth as I can. That's a Protectress' mission, and that's enough authorization in itself."

"One follow-up question is admitted," Ike reminded. Every participant had received the rules in advance. "Please keep it short — question and answer."

But words had failed the inquirer.

"Next inquirer, please."

The next one was Russian. "Protectress, isn't it presumptuous if you call yourself Paladin?"

I examined him thoroughly before I replied. "Do I? I primarily call myself Protectress or Imperatrix, or simply Jo. The Lionheart was the one who set the rules for awarding this title, and other people were the ones deeming this title appropriate. I accepted this title from you, from all people, because it relays a sense of acceptance of responsibility to you and thus having repaid a debt — a responsibility for having let it come that far."

Again there was no follow-up.

The third inquirer spoke with French accent and represented a large French news magazine. "Protectress, is it true that a large part of your spaceship is of French make, and what's the reason for that?"

I read his name from the small screen set into the table before me. "Renard, that's partially true. The hull was made in

Austria and the raw nanos on Velvet Island itself, and we've acquired a large share of the control emitters and the auxiliary aggregates from French companies. At the time I triggered the orders, I was still on the run from the Cartel and couldn't afford a public tender. Back then, when I met a French industrialist, I grabbed the opportunity, and he utilized his French connections to run the procurement in a way that the French Cartel wouldn't learn about. I may add that I'm entirely happy with quality and reliability. One further inquiry?"

"Protectress, is it true that you also procured sex toys for your spaceship?"

"No. The connection to that company lies in the involved persons alone, and even that was by chance. For me, only the qualification as the buyer and intermediary counts, not the previous occupation."

Next one. "Protectress, what qualifies your pilot for such a mission?"

"Oh, there's so much I'm not sure whether I might miss something now." I glanced at Francine. "I believe in the first place it's her enormous stress tolerance. She manages to stay calm in situations where other people have long despaired — she's the antithesis of panic." Francine grinned at me, surprised. "Hand in hand with this imperturbability goes her diligence. Loyalty, reliability, discretion, competency and eagerness to learn go along, fast reflexes, and of course a smart brain we're owing the *Besson compensator* to. At the same time she's got humor, is kind and a good buddy — what else could one ask for on such a long mission?"

"And — sex?"

Ike reached out for his microphone, but I was faster. "Ike, the question is permissible. The answer is yes, and if anyone thinks this is the place for further details, I will unveil them without censorship."

The next question gave me a break.

"Knight Francine, what's your stance on your commandant's idea?"

She glanced at Ike and leaned forward. "Please state your question more precisely—which idea, and which commandant? I have different superiors in different roles. Ike, that doesn't count as further inquiry yet."

"Pardon, Knight Francine. What's your stance on the Protectress' idea of sending out fighting units before we're able to protect our own system?"

"I don't know any such idea." She raised a hand before the inquirer could protest. "During the first invasion, Earth commanded one company of armor suits and one Taipan wing for its defense. For the second invasion we had two space fighters and one Taipan and didn't need the armor suits. Currently we command a regiment of armor suits on the way to a division, we are training a Taipan wing, and in addition to the three active space fighters there will soon be four more, once their pilots are ready. From my point of view, we're better armed than ever before—as long as the enemy doesn't concentrate his forces. If we want to prevent that, we have to convince him we're no worthwhile target. From my point of view, we can't afford to pass up allies. But that's my personal opinion. Strategic questions are jointly decided by the Imperatrix and the United Nations Council for Interstellar Defence."

"You've got no say in that?"

"I'm part of a military unit with a clear chain of command, and at the same time of a Dragon unit where logical arguments count and are heard. I provide advice and regard it as my duty to point out things that might have been missed from my point of view, but once a decision has been made, it's my duty to implement it. Yes, I've got something to say, but I don't have the final say."

The light jumped on. "Protectress, why should the enemy in the *Worries* system still be a threat to us? Didn't you destroy the Jelly spaceship he captured and arrived in?"

"That's correct, and we didn't find another Jelly spaceship in the *Worries* system. But we found more than one habitable planet there, and evidence for interplanetary space travel — residue of chemical fuel in space."

The inquirer frowned.

"I wasn't finished yet," I said. "I want to follow this train of thought. The technology to build a spaceship exists in the *Worries* system. We cannot rule out that an enemy who managed to capture a Jelly spaceship and conquer its artificial intelligence commands the knowledge to build another interstellar spaceship on this foundation — even if he has to rebuild some of the tools for that. So we have to mitigate that risk — with low to medium occurrence probability, but extremely high damage potential — within our means. And we have the means."

"How do you arrive at this assessment?"

"Mmm — that's hard to answer briefly. The probability is high if we have clear evidence, medium for first signs, and low for assumptions, okay? I regard the damage potential as extremely high if our existence is at stake. The council agrees with this assessment. Next question, please."

Why did I suddenly feel so impatient? Something was wrong here.

Analysis. Give me a hint.

Meanwhile, it was the next inquirer's turn.

"Knight Francine. From your point of view, what's the most important skill for a space pilot, and what's the greatest weakness?"

"That's actually two questions," Francine replied. "Whatever. There's not the one skill, but there are two very important qualities. The first is patience — even though we're flying very fast, the distances are still so large that often simply nothing happens for days or weeks. You must be able to bear that. The second is attention — once finally something happens, there's not much time to react. Believe me, it's damn hard to remain attentive for weeks. Yes, and there's not the one weakness, but again it's a pair—claustrophobia, if you're locked into a tight, windowless tin can for weeks and months and there's no escape, and agoraphobia if you realize how much nothing there is outside the thin steel walls."

"And how do you see yourself?"

"I have the strengths, and I've learned to live with my weaknesses and not let them influence me a long time ago."

"Thank you, Knight Francine," Ike chimed in. "I'll let that go as Francine decided so, but I ask for discipline. No more double questions."

"Protectress. What is your main concern?"

"Oh. That's a broad question. I'll try to give you a decent reply anyway. Since I accepted my role as Imperatrix, my main concern is to look after mankind and first of all protect it from dangers from outside of Earth. I don't have the stomach for human politics, that's not my area of expertise, and nevertheless—the protection of the weakest, of those who have no voice, is important to me. Woe betide the one using his powers to abuse young girls if I learn about it. But in the current situation I don't want to help the people on Earth exclusively. I want to help the people in the Worries system, too, because I'm firmly convinced that these two goals correlate."

"Thank you—and what exactly do you expect from us?"

"From you . . . no more than a little selfless helpfulness—after all that's what humanity is about, isn't it? I'm expecting no more than that you consider what you'd expect from others in a similar situation—that someone reaches out a hand and helps you to get up."

— Result available. Three suspicious subjects identified. —

The next question was for Francine. I took the opportunity to look into the analysis result. Three of the admitted persons seemed to be less eagerly waiting for a chance to raise their questions. Instead all three had gazed at their watches and to the exit at different times, but multiple times.

Okay, perhaps they just weren't heart-and-soul journalists, perhaps one had a pregnant girlfriend about to give birth, but two of them also seemed concerned about their large bags. Why? I sent out three nano threads.

"Protectress Johanna, what are your next steps?"

Oh — my question. "Tomorrow I'll have a first discussion of the military aspects with my people. What options we have, what we lack, how we could proceed. You can't just pull such strategies out of a hat. On Saturday in Tokyo, science has its turn — okay, I'll be asking for help there again, but I also have a lot to offer, and I want to make clear that I'll support science for science's sake, too. And thereafter I'll return home, to the University. I couldn't plan beyond that yet — and I fear I won't find rest for the next half year."

"Are you able to cope?"

This question had come spontaneously, and I immediately saw the inquirer berating himself. For this closed question, a yes sufficed, and I'd be out.

"In this regard, I'm just another human. I can cope with stress better than others, and I can rely on my Dragon part when things get tight — but in the long run, I need my time for recovery. When else should I contemplate new developments? So, if I can't grant all your interview wishes in the next half year, please bear with me."

"Knight Francine . . ."

I faded out again. What had my nano threads found?

The two large bags held no immediately dangerous substances — taken separately. But the slight outgassing around one bag was suspicious, and what purpose should the thin layer of tough substance between outer leather and inner lining of the other bag serve? What would happen if the contents of both bags came in contact with each other?

Prepare to isolate the solid matter.

I knew that Sylvie was watching through the stage door, and gave her a brief hand signal. Francine noticed it, too — and remained calm as usual. Her answer didn't stumble.

I had no paper and no pen and no mobile phone at hand, but I had my nanos. I let them form a shuriken, made the information appear on the surface, and flipped it across the table toward Sylvie. It pierced the doorframe next to her, out of the audience's sight, and the sharp tips instantly disappeared. She hardly flinched, pulled it out with caution, and read. With a brief nod she then turned away.

"Protectress, grant me an out-of-line question," a scrawny woman with silver streaks in her stubbly hair chimed in. "Who created this plain-elegant pantsuit you're wearing?"

"I gladly allow it, Lynn. This question has a tradition, doesn't it? Well, this suit is my own creation, from design to manufacturing, and that also has tradition. The functional cut offers much ease of movement for the arms, plenty of space for rank and other insignia, and protects the bearer in all kinds of weather."

In her eyes I read a question she didn't ask. Instead she went on, "And your other accessories?"

"Everything I'm wearing is my own creation," I said. "As you see, I'm not wearing jewelry or a watch, and as my breasts don't need support, I don't wear any. Pardon, Ike, just a moment. Lynn, you didn't ask, but I *remember* your interview with Zoe, on the evening of the ninth of December, 2018. You're looking good, Lynn. If you want to visit us on Velvet Island to see what became of Zoe's legacy, you're welcome anytime."

For a moment, she stared at me as if I had slapped her. Then, a tear formed in the corner of her right eye, and she sat down. "Thank you. I'll gladly come."

Sylvie reappeared in the door frame and showed two fingers. Without looking at her, I lifted one finger to confirm.

"Protectress Johanna, what does it look like in the *Worries* system? You surely had a chance to have a look at the planets, didn't you?"

"We had a chance, yes. But I was busy programming our tunnel field while Francine had a look around. May I pass the question on? Francine?"

My pilot smiled kindly. "Gladly. Well, the *Worries* system has got three planets, two of which are in the habitable zone. That is, they're not as hot as our Mercury and not cold enough that any matter is permanently frozen. Where the innermost planet, *Trouble*, is significantly warmer than Earth."

While she continued her illustration, I took care of the potential threat in the hall again. The two suspects were visibly nervous now. Even at the beginning of my career as a little shoplifter I hadn't acted so obviously.

Should we notice the two?

Where was the true threat, then?

The hall had no windows, with several large, two-winged doors at one side and at the far end each, and smaller doors on both sides of the stage at the front face where we were sitting. The air conditioning provided an acceptable temperature and sufficient oxygen. The hotel staff provided sufficient mineral water for the participants, and for this purpose, the side doors remained open.

Zoe's *memory* of a nuke in the basement, a long time ago in Ramstein, wasn't helpful. A run-off fusion reactor or a disruptor field would have a similar effect.

Companion?

Mighty, we have a problem. I summarized my findings. *If there's a second strike, I have no trace of it yet.*

Which target would such a strike have? I will come to you.

Which target . . . *Stay where you are. Silent alert for the island.* Oh.

Yes, oh. But we weren't safe here yet.

If it was about gas, the most effective way to distribute it would be via the air conditioning. I sent another nano thread.

If there should be a second strike, I'd execute it once the confusion from the first had maxed. So I let the text *NO IN-TERVENTION* appear on my palm and held it in Sylvie's direction.

Her eyes widened in surprise, but she nodded and took a radio from the guy next to her.

"No intervention," I read from her lips. "Yes, by the Imperatrix herself." A moment later she showed her okay.

Would she come to the same conclusions? It could take some time before my nano thread found something.

"Protectress Johanna. Do you have hobbies or are you collecting anything?"

The young man asking this question would quite well match my collection of erotic adventures—but this reply would be rather inappropriate now.

"No and no," I began. "Or at least that was the first reply I was thinking of. But it's not entirely true. The last few years, I had no time for any hobby. But I might as well say that my efforts to establish the University and for Earth's protection are my hobbies."

"But you surely get some kind of pay?" the young man asked. Ike checked the follow-up.

"My pay is my employees' happiness. I don't get money. I own a few savings that allow me to afford a coffee or a meal once in a while, but all money the University earns go into research and development. I didn't answer your question about collections yet," I quickly added before Ike could call the next inquirer. "I don't collect anything tangible. I have no room and no need for it—basically I own nothing but what I'm wearing. No dresses, no shoes, no jewelry—I have no personal communicator, no music collections, no books. I left all that behind many years ago, just as my hobbies of the past—

martial arts, bicycling, marathon. Now and then I get an opportunity for swimming, but rarely. When I need time to think."

And it was the next inquirer's turn.

"Protectress, where do you find the confidence that you can permanently protect us from interstellar threats?"

"Oh, that's an interesting question. Am I indeed confident, or rather driven by my concern that our preparations are going too slowly? In fact, it's a bit of both. I'm confident that we *can* have the means to permanently protect us. I'm taking that confidence from my teammates, from our recent research successes, and from the unbroken will to resist that I'm sensing in the people. Look at the applicants for our fighter division, for our future space forces, or for the armored infantry. They all know they're applying for fighting forces in times of war! And not least the citizens of New York only recently proved to me how ready they are to fight for a good cause. Yes, all that makes me feel confident—and still I'm concerned because I suspect it will be about making good use of our time. Only then can I keep my confidence, only then can I sleep in peace. Aside from that, I believe we owe our soldiers the best possible preparation. It would be deeply unfair to slack in our efforts only because we have a handful of active fighter planes, in order to send a dozen inexperienced pilots into battle against several hundred Jelly fighters. Yes, doubtlessly Knight Zoé would accept the challenge, and her students would follow her example. But, folks, we want surviving victors and no dead heroes!"

Turning toward Ike, I shrugged. "Sorry, that went a bit beyond the original topic."

The inquirer seemed to be content, though.

"Protectress, couldn't you spend your time better than in such an interview session?"

Yes, for example by searching for the assassins. I didn't voice that, though. "The list of unfinished issues in my brain is long—I've got enough to do for the next hundred years. But events like this are far up on my list, because I'm not doing all this for me, but for you, and thus it's important that I take you along with me, that I explain to you what I'm doing and why I'm doing it, and what kind of help I need. I need help from all people, and I need help from professionals when it's about talking with people—professionals like you."

"So we shall be your mouthpiece?"

"Yes. And at the same time you shall be the people's voice, collect their questions, worries and troubles and confront me with them, so that I can take care of them. I need your critical voices as well, because I'm not immune to making mistakes or missing things. That's what critical journalism is for, after all."

What I couldn't miss was the tandem arrangement of a small, pressurized gas bottle and an even smaller metal cylinder, connected by a valve with a radio receiver, that my nano thread had just spotted in an air conditioning duct. It *reminded* me of another evil installation which Zoe and April had been confronted with a long time ago.

Zoe had learned much later to disarm such installations by the laying-on of hands, and she had been very successful. So I didn't have to reinvent that procedure from scratch—and I didn't have to lay my hand on the casing. For that I had my thread, and before anything could go wrong, I interrupted the line from receiver to valve.

That way I had helped myself to another problem—how could I plausibly explain this mechanism's detection without unveiling my abilities?

And then, a new, evil thought crept in—if there were two cascaded assassination attempts, could there be a third?

I would be sensible to follow up on the inside assassination attempt, which required an evacuation to the street, with a sniper outside.

Toxic gas in air duct verified, neutralized. Check assassin or sniper outside was the next message I sent Sylvie by shuriken. Had she already noticed that the first one's nanos had returned to me?

Again, she showed a little surprise, but then nodded and hurried away.

"Protectress?"

Had I been inattentive? *Repeat.*

— *"Protectress, which faith do you belong to?"* —

"Excuse me. That's a bit more difficult to answer than you'd think. I've never been accepted into any religious community. I believe in my own strength and responsibility, and I believe that nobody has the right to escape responsibility for his own actions with reference to his belief. Anything beyond that isn't mine to judge, that's each one's private business."

"Do you believe in the existence of a divine being?"

"I'm accepting the possibility that one or more such beings could exist. I've got no respective evidence if I don't accept the existence of life itself as such. Or put differently — No, I don't believe in a specific manifestation as already described in any religion, but at the same time, I do believe in the possibility, and thus I'm no atheist by definition. In any case, I believe — no, I know that Dragons exist."

The next question gave me time to consider our precarious situation again.

"Knight Francine, how strong is your bond to home?"

"If you mean Velvet Island, very strong. There's no other place I'd call home."

She further explained her affinity. Turning a deaf ear made it easier for me to not blush. At the same time I realized how vulnerable we were.

Mighty, I might be imagining things, but I'm worried.
What kind of things?

Oh. It's a saying. I wanted to express that my risk assessment yields a negative result, and I'm unable to come up with a logical reason.

So it is an intuitive assessment. I have difficulties to comprehend this process, but I have learned that the human way of thinking is different. There are subconscious thought processes that yield conscious results, correct?

Correct.

If your treasure trove of experience yields such results, they are worth being observed.

That was an important point. *Okay. My subconscious signals a significant threat for Velvet Island. There could be an assassination attempt. We discussed that before. Now I'm regarding this as more likely, and if it comes to that, it could be a multilayered plan that aims at driving you away from the island and hitting you at potential retreat positions if the original damage doesn't suffice.*

I understand. I have to brief Tess. She is standing next to me.

This conference more and more tested my patience. I should be outside, with Sylvie, utilizing my skills to search for terrorists. Anyone could sit at a conference table.

No.

Remaining seated at a conference table with the knowledge of several imminent assassination attempts and calmly answering questions was something not everyone could do.

"Protectress, how can it be that we're talking about the construction of weapons for a war on distant worlds while children here on Earth have to starve?"

Where did that come from? The inquirer shrank back as if my glare had impaled him.

"It's not true that children here on Earth *have to* starve. There's enough food available—you only have to distribute it. Meanwhile I'll make sure that nobody can destroy the world that's feeding these children—and that nobody will come to feed on these children."

"Wouldn't it be appropriate to make sure first that these

children survive long enough to live through their rescue? Like the Naomi Jan Heer Foundation does, for example? Wouldn't that be a worthier task?"

"Yes, it would be." I gave the dedicated young man a very friendly smile. "This foundation makes a very valuable contribution to the situation of countless children in the poorest parts of the world, and I'd really wish that this initiative would get a lot more support."

"Why not by you?" the young man called.

Ike raised his hand.

"It's okay, Ike," I stopped him. "That's not a follow-up question, that's just a different wording. Let it stand. The foundation is very dear to me. I founded it."

The young journalist gaped at me, but like many others in the hall, he hadn't made the connection yet.

"Naomi Jan Heer is an anagram for Johanna Meier."

It took a while before the press people had digested my disclosure and were ready to return to the questions-and-answers game. Luckily the suspects hadn't used this pause for their assassination attempt, so Sylvie had gained some more time to have a look around outside, and Achrotzyber might have some time left to take care of the University.

"Knight Francine, which privileges actually come with knighthood?"

"Privileges?" Francine shook her head. "Knighthood alone — the honor coming with it — is a privilege in itself. Benefits aren't part of it, at best additional respect. As a knight, I don't strive for benefits. At the most — maybe some countries bury their knights in a war cemetery. That's surely a privilege, but once I'm dead it means nothing to me."

"But you take advantages from it — you participate in exclusive meetings and get invited to expensive events?"

"The first is no advantage and it's got nothing to do with

knighthood, but is part of my duties on the Imperatrix' staff, and regarding invitations I'm not sure who profits from whom. But as I have no personal income, I have no qualms accepting free offers."

Several participants listened up. The next inquirer cast a glance on his tablet, shrugged, and placed his question spontaneously. "Knight Francine, what do you mean by saying you have no personal income? Shouldn't you get some compensation for your efforts?"

"I meant it as I said it—I have no income. Jo—or the University, respectively—offers me shelter, the clothing I need, food and drink, and if I have another wish I can get what I want. But I have scarcely any time to develop wishes. In space I can't go shopping anyway. I have little use for material goods. Instead, I'm allowed to fly the fiercest gadget ever built on Earth. So what I'm getting in exchange can't be expressed in monetary terms."

"Don't you have any of your own stuff? Dresses, shoes, anything like that?"

"Hm—the stuff we've been wearing for dinner in Brisbane should still be somewhere. Otherwise—no, actually not. I don't miss it. In the ZONE, I had way less than now—there, I didn't even own my own body."

The follow-up question was already used up, but the last and the next inquirer reached an agreement with glances and a nod.

"Knight Francine, please tell us more about why and how you arrived in the ZONE and what you experienced there."

"You know you're opening a whole new can of worms there, don't you? If I were to tell everything, the rest of the day wouldn't suffice, and, to be honest, I don't like to remember it." She shrugged. "Well, why did I arrive in the ZONE? I didn't choose that. I'm a child of the invasion, so to speak, the result of a random encounter of two stray people—I never met my father, and I don't remember my mother. She must have been unable to cope with the situation — at least that's what I made out later — homeless, jobless, clueless, and with an unwanted child. As far as I can remember I've always been in a group home. At first, it was an ordinary orphanage, and I don't remember the name of the village, but it probably was outside the ZONE. Only that the ZONE slowly grew — not just the radioactivity, the occasional fallouts against which we got medication. No, much faster than radioactivity, lawlessness spread out. I guess I was seven or eight years old when the men came. They wanted their *fun*, they said."

Not just the inquirer made a face. Several female journalists in the audience sat as if frozen, and the usual background noise — whispers, rustling, clinking — had fallen silent entirely.

"They had their *fun* with some of the older girls, but only after they had killed our nurses. Watch what happens to you if you're not nice and obedient, they said — and I don't want to remember what came next."

Francine paused, lowered her gaze, took several deep breaths, and then looked at the inquirer again.

"I had a few girlfriends in the orphanage. We'd been playing together — sometimes the Flight Of Nine, sometimes the Steadfast Five."

I placed one hand on hers and squeezed gently. *I'm with you.* At the same time, I felt guilt — I had never asked my girls about this.

Francine briefly smiled at me, then she focused on a spot at the ceiling and went on, "Late at night, when most men were dead drunk and asleep, and a few others had their fun with the girls solo or in pairs, we worked together. Our strongest held the arms, two of us each. Two pressed the pillow on the face. One of us wielded the knife."

You could have heard a pin drop in the hall.

85

"It was a large, sharp butcher's knife from the kitchen. Each time a clean cut across the throat, as quick as possible so they couldn't cry out. We took turns — once the pillow, once the knife. The sleepers had no chance. But there were the others."

Her voice was trembling now, and her hand under mine became wet. This no longer was my imperturbable Francine. Should I intervene? This emotional striptease was so hard for her.

"There were the others, five strong men. We agreed we had to take them all at the same time. But we were only seven girls, and what chance stands an eight-year-old girl against a strong man? We broke up. The three little ones together, the four older, stronger ones each on their own. Then we took our clothes off. Completely."

Again she took a deep breath.

"It worked — almost. I went into the parlor where he just —" She stared at the table before her. "Where he just had his *fun*. He didn't notice me until I had almost reached him. Naked, and with my hands on my back, and I was smiling. He should think that I —" Her hand twitched. "He looked at me, so lecherously. I couldn't hide anything — I shouldn't turn away, and I shouldn't cover myself. That would have spoiled the plan. Yes, and then he showed me his tool, and I showed him what I had in my hands. I tossed that handful of pepper at his face and stabbed my knife into his eye."

She stretched, sat up straight, and looked into the eyes of the people before her.

"I had to stab two or three times until I had hit his throat right, and of course he lashed about. It hurt, but I knew that it would hurt more if I failed. And then there were my friends. They weren't all successful."

Many attendants in the front rows couldn't withstand Francine's gaze. They were looking down, embarrassed.

"I had to help them to kill two more men. One with my

knife, and the other—well, that's no longer important. Only the outcome counts. They were all dead, and only one of us. Two were injured, but what does a broken arm count? We all had scratches and bruises."

After a while, one of the female journalists in the first row asked, "Couldn't you have called the police?"

Francine gave her a friendly smile, and the journalist returned the smile, then frowned when my teammate didn't reply right away.

"They were seventeen men, and the worst of it was that we knew them. It was the entire team of the local police district." She pulled her hand out from under mine and spread her arms. "Why? I don't know. In any case, other men followed after them, men with guns. They looked at the carnage, and one said, oh look, they did our work for us. They instantly understood what had happened—after all, we were all covered in blood. Look, these girls have true fighting spirit. Such is what we need. Then they took us with them."

She placed her hands on top of each other before her. "That's the story of how I arrived in the ZONE. I think that's enough for tonight."

Nobody seemed to be in the mood to object. There was a pause while everyone digested Francine's account. Ike had to address the next inquirer twice before he recognized it was his turn.

"Yes, ah, Protectress—one moment."

With a friendly smile I granted him his moment.

Companion?

Yes, Mighty?

Tess says you cannot help us, so you can focus on your surroundings. I agree with her assessment.

Well—crap. Sadly he was right.

"Protectress, your plans appear very unilateral to me. To explore our Solar System, you need factories for your spaceships, spaceports, bases on other planets—what's your position with regard to environmental protection?"

"Let me first fix an unfortunate choice of words—these are not my plans, but our plans. I don't need factories, *we* need factories. These are not my spaceships and spaceports, but ours—primarily yours. We need all that for environmental protection—envisaged on a large scale, to protect our environment from a Jelly invasion. Have a look at the environmental devastation from the last invasion and make up your mind whether it's better to intercept the Jellies long before they can reach Earth, whether it's worth making minor sacrifices here. Once you've answered that question for yourself, we get to environmental protection in the narrower sense. Our University, Velvet Island, is located in an area of special protection, the Great Barrier Reef. From day one, environmental health was on top of our agenda. You surely heard we're usually nude on the island? That saves on detergent. Our trash and our bodily waste are a hundred percent nanotechnically recycled—even the birds leave more dirt than we do."

The audience laughed.

"Our research results don't just serve defense. Our recycling facilities are continuously improved. Our modern transport means are emission free." Even Freddie's yacht was running on fusion power. "The only greenhouse gas we're emitting is our breath. Our facilities radiate less heat than a human body. Yes, I'm sure we're doing more for environmental health than ever before."

"And what's your position on endangered species?"

"I'm favoring genetical diversity and natural selection. Overspecialized species that—put exaggeratedly—can only survive within a single square kilometer on Earth, are an evolutionary dead end, a failed experiment. We must allow this failure to happen. At the same time I'm confident that the total of our efforts offers much better conditions for nature than during the last two thousand years, and that's no exaggeration—I *remember* how people treated their waste at the time of the Delian League."

The inquirer nodded, deep in thoughts.

Francine grinned at me, but then frowned. Had I made such a grim face?

No.

My nano-optical receptors showed me dark shapes behind the stage door, sharp blades in hands, and a security guard just going down.

Assassins!

Maybe they were thinking I couldn't see them as long as I didn't turn my head. Maybe they hadn't noticed Francine's frown yet. Maybe this assassination attempt was just another puzzle piece in a greater plan.

Such *maybes* didn't get me anywhere.

In any case I couldn't allow them to blithely kill more guards behind the stage door.

The two suspects in the hall flinched hardly noticeably, and almost at the same time, my nano thread in the air duct registered a signal.

Neutralize agents in bags.

One of my fingers aimed at the shapes in the next room. In quick sequence I distributed three tiny anesthetic needles. I sent the two potential assassins in the hall to sleep as well—I wasn't interested in learning what else they might have planned. Only then did I rise.

Ike gave me a startled glance.

"Just a moment, please." I nodded at the audience. "I guess someone's not feeling well outside."

In the anteroom, I met three drugged assassins and two dead guards. Ike's assistant was leaning on a wall, trembling and with closed eyes—but alive.

I became invisible and accelerated. Where else in this building were more assassins roaming? But I didn't find further suspects on my way — only two more dead guards.

Then I heard the muffled but characteristic bellowing of several rifle shots from the street.

Where was Sylvie?

When I reached the exit and the street, everything was over outside.

Mounted policemen tried to calm down the excited crowd. Their colleagues on foot, staring up at the roofs, rifles in their hands, weren't really helpful there. A team in protective vests was just storming the opposite building.

In three spots farther down the street I saw the police pulling individual people from the still assembled crowd — and obviously having to prevent their targets being beaten to death right on the spot. I wasn't needed there, though.

How did all that add up? A ragtag collection of assassination attempts, all meant to drive the press conference audience out on the street, where snipers were already waiting on roofs and in the crowd — for whom? For me? What chance of success could such an assassination yield?

Unless all that was just a distraction.

My gaze fell on a manhole cover — a cover like thousands of others in this city. Nothing about it was unusual. But from the sewer below I sensed the control quarks of a just awakening micro-fusion-reactor's nestle field.

Why there, why now? Nobody could know that the target — me — had just left the building.

On the other hand, everyone with a TV could watch my empty seat at the conference table. How likely was it for me to be taking a look at the place where shots had just rung out?

And the assassins in the hall, in the anteroom, on the roofs, among the crowd — all cannon fodder to conceal the great plan? That probably wouldn't matter after the deaths of the many thousand innocent had already been counted in.

Oh no.

A fusion reactor needed only seconds to start up and to reach full power. To run away thereafter — or create a disruptor field — required only another blink. Too fast for countermeasures?

Too fast to lift a heavy manhole cover. A generous serving of devouring nanos simply made it vanish, and I jumped into the shaft.

I no longer needed camouflage. Instead I prepared myself for sending out control quarks, just in case.

The reactor was resting at the shaft bottom. I dropped straight toward it, stopping my fall only at the last moment with hands and feet pressed toward the wall, landed next to it and reached for the emergency stop button.

No.

I'd better send a nano threat inside. Someone who could manipulate a reactor wouldn't stop at the controls.

That moment — of all times — I sensed the stray emissions of two more starting reactors from both sewer tunnel directions.

A voice sounded from somewhere. "Goodbye, Joha—"

My nano thread fanned out to the emitters of the reactor at my feet. I knew its design very well — I had envisaged the Meier effect specifically for this model, and I knew the control parameters for each single emitter as precisely as each of my body cells — or as the formula set to create a *Meier gravtunnel*.

My *Analogy* only had to rearrange the formulas and send new orders across my nano thread to the emitters.

Two strong quark showers filled the tunnel in both directions with orders. The reactors there had no choice — their envelope field failed before it was completely established, and that only left emergency shutdown — without meltdown and without disruptor field.

The reactor below me warmed up. Its control quarks had neglected their duty to maintain a stable envelope field and instead burned themselves out. This reactor went into emergency shutdown, too. The fusion process stopped, and my own control quarks maintained the envelope field just long enough to protect myself from unpleasant side effects.

" —nna." The cheap digital player escaped its fate, too. Who knew, perhaps this device could tell the FBI a decisive story?

But after this stunt, I needed a few deep breaths. The last action had cost me power.

The already dim shaft became darker again. I looked up to a head covering the manhole.

"Hello, anybody down there?"

"Yes," I replied and rose. "Johanna Meier. I'm coming up."

That was what I did —slowly, to recover. By the time I had arrived at the top, four police officers had gathered around the hole.

One policewoman addressed me. "Protectress? What's going on?"

The nametag on her chest was conveniently on eye level for me. "Officer Welch. I neutralized three manipulated fusion reactors down there. Please have them —and a digital player —examined by experts."

"Manipulated, Protectress?"

"Yes. I guess they were meant to create a very big hole in this street."

She paled.

I went on, "I'd like to know who could install them here unmolested. For the time being, the threat's been averted. Please send another team into the hotel to collect the five suspects and to salvage the four dead security guards. I'll go inside now and talk to the guests. After that, I'll be at your command."

Francine was no longer sitting behind the conference table, but on top with a wide stance, hands at her hips, and showing the audience a grim stare.

When I entered through the stage door, she relaxed.

"Any trouble?" I asked.

"Two of our guests felt unwell, just after you left. No problem, but there was another with a gun—nasty, made of plastic parts that don't show up in the scanner."

"And?"

"His neighbors *convinced* him to deliver the weapon. I didn't have to intervene. Nevertheless I thought I should get a better overview. And you?"

"Later. Sit down."

I took my seat again and looked at Ike. "I'm sorry, Ike. The questions must wait another moment." Turning toward the journalists, I went on, "If you didn't hear it from your colleagues outside—there were a few troublemakers in the street, but the police got the situation under control. I don't want to anticipate the police investigation, so I can't answer respective questions, but sadly, I must tell you that four people from the security team lost their lives tonight. I ask you for a minute's silence in their commemoration before we go on."

Strangely enough—although the entire hall was full of journalists, probably the most curious species on Earth, it remained silent for a full minute.

The pause allowed me to listen for my Companion—but as long as he didn't call or change his signature, I didn't have to worry about him.

By and by, whispering spread around the hall.

Before Ike could call the audience to order, a man in a dark suit entered and handed him a small chit.

Ike read it, frowned, nodded, and then tapped his microphone. "Ladies and gentlemen." He waited for the whispers to fade. "Ladies and gentlemen, thank you for your attention. Out of respect for the police investigations regarding the cases of death, we sadly have to terminate this event for today. Moreover, I have to ask for patience — for the same reason, not all exits are available for emptying the hall. Knight Francine, Protectress, on behalf of all participants I may thank you for the always detailed answers and at the same time express our desire for a continuation. Protectress, please."

I had to wait for the applause to fade before I could reply. "Thank you, Ike. Friends, I've told you earlier — you're important to me, because the tasks before us can only be solved together, and because that will only work if we talk with each other. So there will be surely not just one follow-up session but many, all around the world. I only have to ask for some patience, because you know — the next events are already scheduled. So, see you soon."

I rose and walked to the stage door, where the gray gentleman was already waiting for me — doubtlessly to steal some of my time.

As soon as I had answered the friendly FBI agent's questions, Sylvie approached us.

"Hadn't I said nobody may — " He paused when he spotted her brooch. "Sorry, Knight — ah."

"Sylvie Moreau," I assisted.

"Knight Sylvie, of course. Sorry, it was just . . ."

"Doesn't matter." The way Sylvie smiled at him made him involuntarily shy away. "Jo, Francine, let's go."

Francine waved me forward and then fell in line at Sylvie's side. "Is it quiet outside?"

"The atmosphere is somewhat heated up," Sylvie admitted. "But that's not directed at us, but at the assassins and their cockiness thinking they could hide in the crowd. They were darn lucky the police reacted so level-headedly—I've seen some cops clenching their fists."

That matched my observations.

Sylvie pointed at the hotel corridor's ceiling. "Then there were the snipers on this roof and the roof on the other side of the street."

"I heard shots," I added.

"That was me. I first took out the two on this roof, quickly, cleanly, and quietly, and then borrowed one of their rifles to eliminate the three on the other side before they could have caused bigger damage. Sadly lethally—but I had to make sure."

Francine placed one hand on Sylvie's shoulder. "We didn't ask these people to prepare for an assassination. Our primary task is to protect Johanna, and, if possible, innocents too. These people had no qualms about killing four guards. They were here to kill more people. You had to prevent that. You don't have to apologize for that."

"I know. Don't rack my brains. Jo, what's next?"

I stopped, turned around and smiled up at my body-guards. "An old acquaintance invited us for dinner, and perhaps a bit more. We should treat ourselves to that."

"Oh, I'm curious about that bit more," Francine said. "Who's the host?"

"An old fool. Wait and see."

CHAPTER EIGHTEEN

"Where to?" our driver asked.

"Father awaits us," I replied.

He raised his eyebrows, but then pulled out without comment. The police let him pass without another check—they probably had memorized the license number.

"Are we dressed appropriately?" Francine asked.

"It's a private event. No dress code."

"Like this?" Sylvie asked.

"Exactly. We could show up nude, and no one would be offended."

"But one would take notice."

"For sure." I had to suppress a grin when I remembered my return from the Bronx, and immediately I felt a shiver. "Almost the entire population of New York has seen me naked, back then in Central Park."

"If anything, we'd remember your blood," the driver chimed in. "I don't think I can ever forget that."

"No. Me neither," I admitted.

Thereafter we sat in silence while our car rolled into Harlem. This part of Manhattan was still characterized by people with dark complexions—it remained a mystery to me why this of all features should bring people together or apart.

Francine pointed at a group of four men in white trousers and white baseball bomber jackets. "That's the third such group. What kind of uniform is that? Current fashion?"

"Bones," I said. "They're ensuring peace in Harlem. The police can't be everywhere."

"Ah."

Francine didn't ask further. She and Sylvie patiently waited until we stopped at a small venue.

"We're there," the driver said.

"Okay." I pushed Sylvie out and followed.

Francine came around the car and stopped next to the entrance. "Here?"

"Here." I pulled the door open and entered. Except for the innkeeper behind the counter, the venue was deserted. "Hello, Ezekiel."

He looked up and smiled. "Hello, Velvet. A beer?"

"Three."

"Okay." He placed a glass under the tap and pulled the lever.

"I've been here before," I told my escorts. "Back then, I still had to convince Ezekiel to serve beer to a white woman."

"Convince?" Francine asked doubtfully.

"Her charm was irresistible," Ezekiel chimed in and held his hands up, pointing at a fine cut line. "She healed this one just by laying-on her hand. Well, and when she brought the girls home from the Bronx . . ."

"Someday you should tell us the whole story," Francine said to me.

"I'd like to hear it, too." Ezekiel fetched the second glass. "We all only know some fragments."

"Actually we've got an invitation," I tried to object.

"First we all have a beer together, and then you're telling," a voice came from behind the kitchen door. The door opened, and Father came in, as I knew him—black shirt under the white double-breasted suit, and except for the gray eyebrows, completely bald. Right behind him followed another familiar face.

"Good evening," I saluted them. "May I introduce everyone? Father, head of the Bones. Our host, the mayor of New

York. Francine, Sylvie, my knights."

"You're early," the mayor said. "Of course I understand that the press conference had to be canceled, but the kitchen isn't ready yet. In exchange, I'm eager to hear your story."

"Well then. But if I tell this story, you get Rebecca's father inside, too. Francine, please?"

"Sure." She turned to the door.

"Ezekiel, that makes another three beers, please—and one for yourself, if you like," Father said and pointed at a table. "Have a seat, please."

We sat down and waited until Francine returned with the driver and Ezekiel arrived with the beer. After the first sip, all gazes were on me.

"Okay. Back then, I had come to New York to get an idea of the situation." My audience didn't need to know about Nick's unofficial assignment. That was my private business. "I quickly learned that I couldn't leave it at that. It was too awful. The Syndicate controlling the city had been performing periodical torture shows, and the people took it lying down. Someone had to show them that it's possible to change things. I had to show them that it's possible to go to the Bronx."

Father nodded knowingly. The mayor didn't know this part yet. Our driver's eyes were glistening wet.

" . . . and in the end, Mona and Theresa took care of the girls. Thereafter, I didn't hear about them." I nodded at our driver with his wet cheeks. "Until he told us about Rebecca today."

"The story still sounds unbelievable," Father admitted. "Although our girls told us the same back then. Of course we didn't know back then that Velvet is Dragon."

"Back then I wasn't Dragon. Only equipped with some Dragon technology—the suit and the healing nanos."

"Quite like our story," Francine said to Sylvie. "Jo goes in and brings people out. The Bronx was a testing ground, so to speak, right?"

"Back then I didn't know about you yet."

Father and the mayor both watched me very closely — and seemed to be slightly on edge.

"What's the situation?" I asked.

The mayor leaned back and glanced at Father. Father smiled and pointed at his empty glass. Ezekiel nodded, rose, and walked behind the counter.

"After what happened today, it might be presumptuous to claim the situation was under control," Father said. "We will follow up on that."

"And in the Bronx? I heard there's a special unit cleaning up there?" I briefly glanced at our driver.

"Rebecca," Father agreed. "Yes. She's very committed."

"Successfully?"

"Not always. Every time the special units show up, the rats hole up, and we haven't found out where yet."

"The situation has improved," the mayor said. "Initially, our patrols were attacked regularly. They no longer dare to — our special forces are shooting back, and they're good at that. Initially they rebuilt the road blocks each night, and the next morning, we cleared them away."

"Material consuming," I added.

The mayor showed an evil smile. "We deployed snipers. After three nights, they had learned their lesson."

"The Slicers had some snipers, too," Father said. "We lost a few men."

"And then?" Francine asked.

"Two of them attacked Rebecca's patrol." Our driver blotted his cheek and smiled. "That was their mistake. Rebecca left the car, didn't waste time looking for cover, but attacked that single shooter head on — advanced on his position, emptied one magazine to keep him down, and once she was inside the building, he had no chance. She took him out. Okay, there-after she needed a new protective vest."

"And the other sniper?" Francine asked.

"Tried to shoot her and forgot her buddy. His last mis-take." He took a new glass of beer from Ezekiel. "Thanks. Well, Rebecca got a dressing-down for her aggressive behav-ior."

"And next an award," the mayor added. "Whereafter her colleagues felt motivated to follow her example."

"That couldn't work out well," Sylvie said.

"But it did. The Slicers are not an organized gang but a bunch of individualists with common interests. Getting one-self shot down isn't among those." He shrugged. "The patrols got a few more scratches. Then word got around that we're not intimidated. Only — our people can't be everywhere."

"And where they aren't, the rats come out again," I rea-soned.

The mayor only sighed.

"I know about rats. Been there, done that. You need help."

"I didn't want to —"

"Yes, you did," Father interrupted the mayor. "We wanted to ask for help. We can't do it alone. Oh, of course we could request armor suits and then smoke out the entire Bronx house after house — or flatten the entire borough."

"But that's not what we've been fighting for," I interrupted him. "That's not what I stood up for in Central Park. We want the people to get their city back themselves. For that, we must show them that it's possible. Rebecca saw that. She showed her colleagues that you don't have to put up with everything. This is principally the right way. Only when evil is rooted too deeply, this doesn't work without external help. Armor suits are one option. I'm another, and I'm ready."

"Not alone." Francine instantly decided and glanced at Syl-vie.

The ginger Mamba nodded. "Not alone. Don't you think you could have all the fun for yourself."

"It's not entirely risk-free," the mayor said.

Francine nodded. "Yes. I could break a finger nail."

Father laughed out loud. "Johanna, where did you find her? She's right!"

I only grinned and winked at Francine.

Ezekiel came back to us, cleared his throat, and thus spared us a reply.

"Oh yes." Father looked around. "The kitchen is ready. Should we have dinner?"

CHAPTER NINETEEN

The Bronx didn't look any better than I remembered it. The rattling footsteps behind me grew louder, came closer. I hurried around a corner, almost stumbled across a heap of garbage bags, panted heavily — and then I stood before a wall. Dead end!

I made a half-hearted attempt to climb the wall and failed. Then my bloodhounds were there — three men of about twenty wearing the same kind of rag pants, shirts and sneakers as I. With that they wore a mean, lecherous grin though, while I presented them with a fearful face. I could imagine what would happen next, even before the first unzipped his fly.

"Do you want it the hard way, or will you drop your pants voluntarily?" he asked.

With resignation I unbuttoned my pants. "If it must be, at least I want a hard-on," I joked and let my pants drop down.

"Shut up, slut," he barked at me and slapped me with the back of his hand.

"Ouch!" I cried out and felt my cheek. No wetness, no blood, okay. I had expected these thugs favored violence.

"At least she's not wearing undies. Bend over!"

I obeyed.

He felt my crotch. "Damn, is she wet. Well, let's see."

Next, I felt the tip of his cock at my labia, and then he had penetrated me with a firm push. "Ohh, is that tight. Whoa, how phat."

While holding my hips with both hands, he humped

eagerly. I uttered some cries of joy, assisted with tensed pelvic floor muscles, and so he came within minutes.

I came, too, and announced it with a loud cheer.

"You even enjoy that, what?"

He pulled out and slapped my butt. "Well, we'll have to resort to other means then."

"Let me first," one of his buddies asked.

Cock One stepped aside. I heard him pull his belt from the loops. Meanwhile Cock Two pressed between my messy labia.

"Ah," he wheezed. "Ah—ah—ah—ah—ah, oooh."

What, done already? Indeed—he lingered there for another moment, pumped some more of his load inside me, and then he pulled his tool out and moved away.

Slap! Cock One's old, jagged and frayed leather belt hit my back. "Ouch!"

It didn't stop at one slap. He let off steam for a while, and I delivered the appropriate soundtrack with my loud cries of pain, while their juices slowly ran down my left leg.

Wouldn't the third guy want to shoot his load, too?

Yes, he did—but not inside me. He wanked off with noisy groans while watching my beating orgy. In the end, he shot his load on me, thus messing up my sore butt and my new-old shirt, too.

This was the sign for my torturer to stop his efforts. He panted heavily, and I uttered a quiet whimpering.

"Pull up your pants, slut," he finally demanded. "You'll come with us."

"To the Duke?" Cock Two asked.

"To the Duke. That cunt can take some, he'll like that."

Yes!

Two of them dragged me out to the street, down a few blocks, then into a nondescript house. We went down two stairs, then followed a poorly lit cellar corridor to a boiler room, where

Cock Three pulled a heavy metal lid away from a hole in the floor.

"Down there, go," Cock One ordered.

The hole smelled humid and foul, and the narrow ladder didn't look trustworthy, but I obeyed. Beneath me it became even more dark.

"Wait."

What else should I do anyway? I was standing in a narrow, low, unlit tunnel, and the only obvious exit was blocked by those three blokes climbing down the ladder one by one.

"Right." Cock One shoved me forward, and I had to watch out to not fall down on the slippery floor. "Stop."

I quickly recognized the reason for the second command — there was another door in the side wall, only revealed by a little draft. Once Cock One pushed the door open, our corridor brightened up.

Behind the door was just another passage. At least it was lit, but the men still had to stoop.

While passing the secret door I held tightly to the frame. A rubber strip seemed to be meant to suppress telltale flare.

"Go on."

I quietly obeyed.

The new passage made a twist and ended in a larger tunnel, which in turn finally led to a subterranean hall, three stories high with circumferential steel balconies and wide ladders leading up. The hall's floor was elevated with knee-high platforms and runways. A smelly brew ran through a channel below. Cock Two and Cock Three took me between them, each clutching one arm. Cock One moved ahead.

I counted overall thirty-four men on platforms and balconies, some in leather clothes, some in jeans, and equipped with the most diverse weaponry. The four young ladies, each chained to a steel pillar in the middle of a platform, wore nothing at all.

"What are you bringing to us?" a voice echoed through the hall. I identified the speaker as a surely two meters and twenty centimeters tall giant who was lolling in a huge throne made of scrap metal, thereby swinging a dildo like a conductor's baton. "A new toy? A bit short, ain't she?"

"My Duke!" Cock One bowed. "She's short, but she becomes wet quickly. Most of all, she bears pain well. I believe she'll entertain you for quite a while."

At this point, I failed my role — I should have expressed my horror about what he just had indicated. Instead I remained silently standing there.

"Bring her over."

Cock One stepped aside, and the other two pushed me forward.

"Undress her."

Cock One stood behind me, reached around my hip and opened the button, then the zipper. His buddies grabbed my shirt and pulled until it ripped open.

With a little help from Cock One, my pants slid down to my ankles.

"Do you like what you see?" I called out loud, easily shook off the two men at my sides and pushed them away so that they almost fell from the platform edge. Then I stepped out of my pants and placed my hands on my hipbones.

The Duke stared at me as I stood there in a wide stance, proudly presenting my chest and my butt, as if I had nothing to fear. And still, he saw just a stark naked, short woman among all his strong and heavily armed men.

"Who are you?" he asked with a frown.

"Do you like what you see?" I repeated and slowly walked once around an imaginary pole with swaying hip. "Should I dance for you?"

He considered that. Then he sat up straight. "Why not? Show what you got to offer, and if you please us, you might be our guest for a longer while."

Before it's time for the torture. Yes, you've recognized I'm buying time. Enjoy it while you can.

Let's start.

And I began to play with my imaginary dancing partner.

My face was twisted in the sweet agony of *petite mort*, my right hand twitched a last time along my clitoris, flung a few drops of my wetness across the steel platform, my heels rose from the floor, the half-bent knees moved outward, and with an extended yell I announced my orgasm. "Yeeeeah!"

Wheezes sounded from all around, and then it rained sperm when most of the three dozen men came. Even the four chained girls had blushing cheeks, and their labia glistened wet.

The Duke's cock rose hard from his open crotch, with a white drop hanging at its tip. What had worked for Uncle Bob back then, an infinitely long time ago, worked for these young men most reliably.

He clapped his hands three times. "Very good."

I wiped a shot of sperm away from my shoulder and lustfully licked it off my finger while slowly straightening.

"I think we will keep you for a while. As reward for your performance you may choose a place where we will chain you to."

Bastard. I smiled sweetly. "As reward for watching me so patiently, I grant you to bow to me."

His eyes widened, he briefly grimaced angrily, then he laughed out loud. "You haven't lost your humor yet. That's good, you'll need it."

He rose and pointed at two of his men. "Bring the chains."

His erection hadn't really faded yet when he came to me. "Now, which pole shall we chain you to?"

I placed one hand around his shaft very gently and felt it hardening again. "This one."

He wheezed when he felt the slight pressure from my fingernails.

"Well?" I placed the index finger of my free hand under his chin. "Do you give up?"

His right hand dashed forward, toward my head. The intended slap didn't arrive at his target, though, because I let him go and jumped two meters back.

"Insolent slut!" he yelled. "I should have the irons heated up right now!"

My refined senses recognized a new, different smell. It was time to end this game.

"This iron is too hot for you, *Duke*."

I pursed my lips and aimed past him at his throne. "Pft."

He flinched and stumbled backward when the small but hot fireball flew past him. Several of his men made a step back, and at the same time, I heard surprised calls.

Those continued when the first golden shimmer covered my skin, then formed into scales. One leap brought me onto the throne's backrest, and the seat's red glow mirrored in the gold of my armor, my wings, my long claws.

"Dragon!" someone cried out in horror.

"Police! You're under arrest. Guns down, hands up!" a voice from the entrance demanded now. I heard quick steps from the other end of the hall, then a sequence of dull noises.

Then silence fell.

The hall was cleared. Members of the police special unit that had arrived together with Sylvie and Francine had waltzed the terror-paralyzed *Slicers* off and also taken the four young women away.

Except for my Mambas and me there was just a lone young police officer left, unsure what to do.

I had recognized Rebecca right away, and not just for her award. What was she waiting for? After all this, would she need a confirmation for her achievements from me?

No, of course not. What she did need, though, was the confirmation that *I* had taken notice of her deeds, that I regarded her dues as paid. She wouldn't stop doing what had to be done—but she would stop asking herself whether she met my requirements, and that might save her life one day.

So I looked into her eyes and nodded. "Thank you, Rebecca. Now you know what kinds of holes these rats are hiding in."

"I must thank you. You helped a lot. We couldn't have done this." She also nodded at Francine. "We wouldn't have found the bait."

"And that would have been lethal for the bait," Francine replied. Only the enhanced Mambas had been able to follow my concealed markings and lead the special unit to me—which had spared me from taking out all assembled criminals.

"If the old plans won't tell you, ask an expert for echo sounding," I recommended. "That way you'll surely find the other holes."

"You mean there are more?" But Rebecca didn't wait for the answer. "Yes, of course. There are more than just a couple handfuls of Slicers in the Bronx. We'll establish a new search approach and smoke these ratholes out."

"They'll adapt, too," Francine noted.

"Naturally." Rebecca nodded. "And if we manage to corner them, it gets unpleasant. We might have to cut back occasionally instead of taking the conflict to the extreme. I want to survive for another while."

"That's a very healthy attitude," Sylvie said.

"It's not about eliminating a specific group of Slicers," Rebecca went on. "It's about showing them all that their power over the Bronx will be broken—step by step. I don't expect us to finish this task within a few months."

"That doesn't exactly match the story of your heroic deed," Francine said.

The young policewoman grinned. "No, it really doesn't, right? I stand by my actions. I still believe it was the right thing to do, that we had to set an example. But I had some time thereafter to consider my actions. Protective vest or not, it hurts if you're hit. It's better that I try to avoid such in the future." She gave me a contemplative glance. "I had thought of Jo, what she did for us. I thought I couldn't do less. I recognize that's nonsense. I can't do what she's done—I'm not a Dragon."

She raised a hand before I could say something. "No, it's okay. To stand here with you now and talk with you as if we were just colleagues—just as we worked together earlier—that's recognition enough for me."

Francine reached out a hand. "I've gladly been part of your team, Rebecca."

The policewoman stared at the offered hand for a moment. Then she took it firmly. "Thank you, *Knight* Francine."

Sylvie offered her hand, too. "It was an honor, Rebecca."

Rebecca had found her countenance again. "Thank you, *Knight* Sylvie."

"I thank you, Rebecca," I said. "Good work, officer."

"Thank you, *Protectress*." She shook my hand, too, then stepped back, went to attention and saluted.

We returned the salute, and then Rebecca hurried away.

Francine watched her until she had disappeared in the dark corridor. "She's good." Then she gave me a look of reproach. "And you had all the fun for yourself again."

"Fun? Well." I briefly remembered the hits with the belt and felt my rear. To make the hits sound right and look right, I had to recall my armor.

Francine pointed at some large sperm stains. "I mean this here. I saw the end of the show. Admit it, you had your fun, too."

"Yes, okay. My orgasm wasn't faked. But after all, I had to find you some time to get in and sneak up behind their backs."

Sylvie grinned. "They were *very* distracted."

"And now? Do we report to Father?" Francine asked.

I shook my head. "No. Now we have a go at the true puppet master here."

"What do you mean?" Francine asked after a while.

"I mean the Slicers are staged to appear poorly organized, like a wild bunch of criminals only randomly connected—but there must be more to it than a few guys of the Duke's caliber. We've got an entire borough here that held off police *and Syndicate* for years, even though the Syndicate wasn't gentle at all—and even had armor suits. No, you can't maintain a restricted area with a few thugs. There's more to it, a lot more, and I want to know what's going on here."

"And you'll investigate that all alone?"

"I'm not alone. I've got two Mambas."

"So." Sylvie placed one arm on her hip and frowned. "That clarifies everything. The three of us will venture out and decapitate the Hydra so decisively that nothing regrows for the next hundred years, and thus finish something that neither Syndicate nor authorities could do in years—and of course you already know where we have to go?"

"Naturally." I smiled. "I've got some experience in decapitating crime organizations. Naples, Palermo, Marseille, Paris—okay, I took my time in Manhattan. In any case, whoever's running this show needs intel about what's going on with all these Dukes, Earls, and Whatshisnames. That means this shop is bugged."

Francine already smiled.

Sylvie looked grim. "Now, too?"

"No, not now. I've neutralized cameras and microphones. But before, when I danced, I had a few additional spectators, and quite a clear idea where the signal arrived and where the control signals for the concealed cameras came from, because I measured the latency. It won't be long, though, until they learn about the successful police raid, and not much longer until they figure out what must have happened here—it's no secret that the Dragon empress is in town. So we should hurry up now."

That made Sylvie smile, too. "And I thought you'd grant us none of the fun."

"Oh, you'll have fun."

The six-story building with the rusty fire escape told no tales about its crucial importance for the distribution of power in this borough. Trapped between a lower corner building and a wider building with only four stories that nevertheless lacked only one row of windows in height, it stretched out to the next street.

Upon the second, more critical glance, the building still didn't unveil any of its secrets. Nothing stirred behind the windows at this late hour, and except for the occasional rat dashing across the sidewalk, the street was quiet, too.

Our observation post on the parking lot's roof, at the same time the uppermost parking level, gave us a good view on Third Avenue and East 154th Street, on our target vis-à-vis and its adjacent buildings right and left. We also had a good view of the garbage heaps at the curb, on the cracks and potholes in the road surface, and on the greens forcefully reclaiming their terrain.

Francine and Sylvie were kneeling next to me behind the railing and silently observing. In their attitude I sensed their great confidence that I surely had earned, but that I also had to reinforce from time to time. There, I couldn't afford unnecessarily risky gambles.

This one was no unnecessarily risky gamble. Surely I didn't want to underestimate the unknown opponent who, after all, had managed to keep the police and Syndicate in check with an extremely undisciplined pack, who had sustained the *Slicers* as a continuous source of trouble. But I also observed the large scale — this still unknown party hadn't reached any significance outside the Bronx' limits.

Or was there some outside guidance? And if so, who was behind it? Which other power was ruthless enough to support such a gang, whose power was based on violence and abuse? And most of all — why?

Insufficient data.

Gathering more intel was the true reason for our presence. Helping the New Yorkers to clean up their backyard was a welcome side effect, but no task for a Dragon empress. As much as I despised the Slicers — I was really excited to find the true puppet masters and thus my true antagonist.

Then and there I was the one pulling the strings — or deploying them — and until my nano threads provided me with better data, my Mambas had to be patient.

After all, we didn't want to run into a trap. I couldn't and wouldn't rule it out — that the whole Bronx situation was a trap set up long ago.

Set up before anybody knew of Velvet or the Dragon empress? *Hang on, Jo. You can afford some healthy paranoia, but reasonably.*

On the other hand, it was quite possible that someone had made good use of the current chaotic situation and turned it into a trap. Who were the suspects? Remnants of Cartel or Syndicate? Or the same people that were responsible for the press conference assassination attempt, who had expected me to come to the New Yorkers' aid?

In that case, I couldn't even rule out that they had a spy somewhere among Father's people — who might already know about our mission.

So I'd better send out some more threads.

My Mambas watched me expectantly when I finally snuck away from the edge and then rose behind the cover of the staircase.

"That entire thing is a trap labeled Velvet," I whispered. "There are two options. The first — we'll quietly sneak away now to return with reinforcements later. The second — we'll spring the trap, or even better, sneak past it — and take that shop apart."

"What kind of trap do you expect?" Sylvie asked.

"The whole hog. Toxic gas, explosives, fire, and at least one run-off fusion generator, most likely several."

"Ho-hum. And the three of us will take all that apart?"

"Yes." I grinned at her cheekily. "Bit by bit, silently. If we appeared with a big team, we'd probably have to tear down half the quarter. Among the three of us, we can sneak from trap to trap and disarm the more dangerous installations."

"And what would be our part?"

"You'll have my back against possible troublemakers — primarily for their own protection."

"Makes sense. Where do we start?"

"With the puppet master."

The installed traps showed me that someone had done his homework — as with the assassination attempt before. Many of my tricks were publicly known, but not all. First of all my spies, my nano threads could go everywhere without ever springing a trap. Light barriers, step-on traps, induction barriers, magnetic sensors, motion detectors — none of them could detect a nano thread, and nothing could stop such a thread. Even bulky steel doors only provided additional raw material for my nano machines.

I could probably have got in there without extras — all these technical gimmicks could only be as smart as the one installing them, and during my time as Velvet I had gathered a lot of experience in finding gaps and bypassing security installations.

I didn't want to stress my teammates' patience that much, however. Moreover, time was short — our next appointment in Abu Dhabi should begin in the early afternoon, and the sun had long risen there. The night would be eight hours shorter for us.

So instead of wasting my time with nano curtains and mirror tricks, I simply hot-wired a critical part of their power supply and stormed forward. Before my opponent noticed that his spare reactor's starter battery had failed, we were at his doorstep.

He had deployed a dozen helpers with sturdy leather jackets and machine pistols there. But they didn't even get to grin or smile — Francine and Sylvie made short work of them while I kicked the door in, the hinges and bolts of which my nanos had simply consumed. I had to grant myself at least that much of a show effect.

Inside a U-shaped setup of desks and shelves with keyboards, computer boxes, screens and carelessly scattered wiring, one lone man was standing. The large basement room was otherwise empty.

He wore knee-length leather pants, wristbands with electronic gadgets and data glasses, but neither shirt nor shoes.

The way he was staring and gaping at me, he didn't appear to me like the highly intelligent mastermind that his setup suggested.

While I ambled across the dropped door, he began to smile again. "Velvet! Or should I say *Protectress?* I don't know how you managed to get in, but welcome anyway — to your doom."

He snapped a finger at his wristband. Nothing happened. He tried another switch — in vain. Hastily he reached behind, maltreated a button, stared at me.

I smiled. "Malfunctions? It's over, trickster."

"My men . . ."

Francine and Sylvie entered and took positions on both sides of the door, arms crossed. They clearly showed him that he shouldn't hope for his men outside.

As a sign of resignation, our opponent dropped his arms and shoulders and waited, but he couldn't deceive me.

"The dead-man switch has a malfunction, too," I advised him. "Like your poison pill. You've got an appointment with the New York Police now."

CHAPTER TWENTY

Fatima intercepted me before the door to the conference room. But instead of raising her concern, she frowned. "You look tired. Not enough sleep?"

"Almost none," I admitted. "We departed from New York only two and a half hours ago. We had to dig out a little crime ring first."

"Two and a half hours ago? But that must be more than ten thousand kilometers!"

"Eleven thousand, and then some from Manhattan, yes. We made a hop through space to avoid interfering with flight traffic. I used that time for sleep, but it wasn't much anyway. In exchange, Sylvie and Francine can have a break now. I told them I'll do this alone. By the way, it's snuggly warm here." I briefly examined her skintight, white colored armor suit—of course without backpack and linear cannons.

"The Emirates are always warm." Fatima smiled. "But this summer it's very hot. In New York, too?"

"No. Less than twenty degrees Celsius. New York was hot, but in a different way."

"I saw it on the news brief. An assassination attempt on the street in front of the hotel, which the police quickly got under control, with a little aid by some pedestrians, and a few people shooting around inside."

"Okay, so nothing slipped through despite the heavy press presence. Sylvie took out a few snipers outside, and moreover, the masterminds had planned a toxic gas attack and a few run-off fusion reactors."

"What?" Fatima seemed to be shocked.

"I'll tell you later. Sadly, we couldn't find out who's truly behind all that. Depending on the craziness of their motivation, you could be endangered as well."

"That's always so. We attract our own share of religious zealots. We're as prepared as one can be if you have to expect anything and know nothing for sure."

"Fine."

Fatima gave me a tiny microphone clip. "Here. You'll need that."

"Didn't you have something on your mind?"

"Yes. I wanted to warn you. Some of the guys are a bit disgruntled by the way you scheduled the date." She studied my face. "But that doesn't worry you, right?"

"No. Thanks anyway. But now I shouldn't let those people wait any longer."

Those people were the participants of this military conference at the United Nations academy in Abu Dhabi—all members of the United Nations Interstellar Defence Council, generals and admirals of the great power blocs, military attachés and military consultants, as well as academy lecturers, together with Fatima and her officers far more than two hundred persons.

The spacious auditorium's furnishing was plain and functional. The seats looked comfortable. Nevertheless, most participants were sitting on the edges and leaning forward when I entered.

Someone had prepared a high desk for me, even with a platform that probably should make me appear taller. I didn't need such help that day. Instead I stopped a few steps away and took a look at my audience.

To my surprise, they rose almost simultaneously and applauded—only very few hesitated, but then joined the cheer.

I memorized their faces.

The applause remained military-style short, and then the people started using their comfy seats. Still a share of their tension remained. Meanwhile, I knew that they were curious about what I had to say.

"Good afternoon, ladies and gentlemen. Many thanks for the friendly welcome, and many thanks that you all made your participation in this conference possible. I'm quite aware that I simply ordered this meeting, but at the same time may I remind you that you're here voluntarily. I'm simply offering an opportunity to hear what I have to tell. The formal meetings and consultations will follow separately." With slightly spread arms I invited them to continue listening. "Of course we didn't meet here just for a cozy chat. It's important to me to brief you as early and as comprehensively as possible about the new findings that our journey—the first interstellar journey of a terrestrial spaceship—yielded, and to highlight the military aspects there specifically. As you know—and the installation of the United Nations council confirms this—I regard us, that is Earth, mankind, and Dragons, at war."

Those spectators I gazed at nodded.

"It's a strange war, where there's no fighting. But that applied to earlier wars, too. That was owed to the long distances and the slow transportation. Only modern technology made our world shrink so much that we're seeing daily war action as normal. But for the kind of war I'm dealing with we must remember, and I believe you're much better versed there than I am. We were drawn into a war where the journey from battlefield to battlefield is measured in months and years, and where between two such journeys not years, but decades and centuries can pass."

Now Zoe's *memory* came to my aid. No, her mother's *memory!*

"Think about the campaign of Alexander the Great, about the Crusades, or even Hannibal's journey across the Alps. The military as well as logistic challenges for this kind of war are immense — but they were solved back then, and I'm sure I'm not demanding too much from you when I say — we can do the same today, too. Of course, our situation isn't comparable in many ways, but there are still analogies. We're the target of a conquest campaign, and worse, by two competing parties — the Jellies and this strange brown lichen organism. Both parties got themselves a bloody nose here, but that was just one battle each and not the entire war."

All that wasn't really new to my audience, but my point was to establish a common denominator with them. If I claimed to be a warlord, I had to show that I knew what I was talking about.

"We all know Angry April's answer to this problem — forward defense. She and her folks departed to carry the fighting to the enemy and thus wrangle some air for us to breathe. I wish her only the best, but we all know that her campaign won't spare us from assuring our own defense. There's no tangible front line in space, and the only thing protecting us is our Solar System's gravity funnel — it ensures that our enemies cannot appear right above our heads, but at the system's outskirts, so that we see them coming. Accordingly we can align our defense efforts."

If I didn't want to bore my audience, I soon had to get to the point.

"The first time, we had to allow the Jellies to deploy their landers. You know what that cost us. The second time, we could repel most of the attack in space. That only cost us a single space fighter — a painful loss, as we only had two of them back then, but nevertheless a worthwhile investment. I assume you know the reports about the one scout that got through — if not, better catch up as soon as possible — and so you can imagine what would have happened if such a lichen creature had landed in three hundred or more spots on Earth. We'd been caught with our pants down." Which I was very well versed in.

"We're working on improving our defense. Aside from better means close to Earth, like our Taipans and the Armored Infantry" — I nodded toward Fatima — "we're slowly ramping up our small fleet of space fighters. You know all that, but you haven't seen the whole picture yet — most of all, you probably don't know yet how much our most recent journey has changed this picture. So let me highlight how our Solar System could look like twenty years from now. Join Cadet Li on his first journey."

CHAPTER TWENTY-ONE

Flight 81 has been called. A half dozen people in the departure lounge of Gladstone Interplanetary Port are getting up.

Cadet Li shoulders his duffel bag and follows the other passengers to the apron, where the slender, spindle-shaped express shuttle is waiting. Its shape reminds him of a space fighter, but the interior is laid out for passenger transport. You don't need a central linear cannon for that.

Taking the express shuttle spares him a flight to one of the orbital stations and transfer to one of the huge freighters that regularly carry raw material to Earth and supplies to the outer posts. As the shuttle takes the direct route, it only needs a few days and not several weeks.

With some curiosity, Cadet Li watches the other passengers and wonders what motivates them to travel — research, business, or field service?

During the next few days he gets the opportunity to make their acquaintance — the female geologist, the physician, the United Nations inspector, a recycling aggregate technician, and two mining company foremen who earned the direct flight as a special bonus. Of course, he's way more interested in the friendly young female pilot, but that doesn't belong here.

Five days later, the shuttle arrives on station Rhea One, the Saturn moon's central base. From here, the geologist and the technician will travel on to the research station Rhea Two, and the foremen will mount a short-range shuttle to the mining station. The physician will routinely relieve his colleague in Rhea One's sick bay, who will return home with the same shuttle, and the inspector will pay a visit to the Sheriff — responsible for the safety of the Saturn region — in *the station's military section. Some simply call it Space Patrol, but in a state of defense that unit will act as part of Earth's defense with accordingly far-reaching authority.*

For rescue and patrol flights, the Sheriff commands a Barracuda space fighter – at the same time, this space fighter is part of the Advance Defense Task Force. Cadet Li is eager to complete his pilot training aboard this space fighter. After completion, he will receive his commission as United Nations Space Officer, which will make him, just like the Sheriff and the female pilot, a United Nations representative in the entire Solar System outside Earth – with all-encompassing police authority to maintain order on the outer planet, moon, and orbital bases, the research and mining complexes and of course all of the United Nations' spaceships.

The burden of this responsibility doesn't worry young Li much yet. What counts for him is the fact that only United Nations commissioned officers may pilot a spaceship with Dragon technology, no matter whether it's a space fighter, a freighter or one of the large carrier spaceships. War is something distant. War happens, if at all, only in another planetary system, about a hundred and forty lightyears away. So Li doesn't think about every United Nations officer's responsibility that Dragon technology may never fall into the enemy's hand – even if that means the own ship's self-destruction.

His superiors know of that, and they're trusting Li that he'll live up to this responsibility. Without him noticing, he passed numerous tests – if he had failed, he could still become a United Nations officer, but not as a pilot or commandant of a spaceship or one of the few space forts.

Li's thoughts are circling around his latest tactics lessons. With a space fighter he'd have covered the distance from Earth to Saturn within less than a day – despite the compulsory limitation to one tenth of lightspeed. But shuttles are flying even slower to reduce the risk of collision with small interstellar objects and to minimize the wear.

Or Li would have done an intrasystem gravtunnel passage and thus shortened the flight time to a few minutes – for acceleration and deceleration. Such a maneuver would be a hard surprise for any invader!

CHAPTER TWENTY-TWO

I found a fascinated gleam in many of my audience's eyes. *Oh yes, folks, there's something coming up!*

"So, ladies and gentlemen. Of course, this was just a sketch of what could be one day. But I guess you've already recognized where your knowledge and your organizational talent are demanded. It won't do to just commission a few more Barracudas and train a few pilots technically. We need a well-founded training program for these pilots and space officers that will encompass much more than just flying, We need a new military doctrine for the space fighters that utilizes the newest options — and that doesn't rely on a dedicated amateur like me improvising an offhand more-or-less-working solution."

My wink disarmed the last remark, and my audience accepted my self-criticisms with amusement.

"Based on this doctrine, we can develop a defense strategy for this system. Where should supply bases and space forts be placed? Where should space fighters be deployed? How many ships of what type do we need to maintain order and logistics? And so on. You can do all that so much better than me. My University provides the technological progress, and I'm providing primarily one thing — the vision. No, don't argue." I waved a hand. "Some ideas from my little story — for example the exclusive United Nations ownership of spaceships that renders excesses like piracy practically impossible, the rental of freight space for commercial purposes, the combination of military bases with research and mining facilities that will ensure police supervision as well as healthcare, and at the same time refinances our military logistics—are sourced from my pilot, Knight Francine Besson, and not from me. Just like her, I encourage you, too, to add your ideas to this vision. The message should be—it's not just a defense necessity to fly to space. It's fun, and it can pay off."

As Francine had recognized—it paid to offer people something they could dedicate their efforts to. Even seasoned generals and admirals could get excited.

I raised a hand, and the murmurs faded.

"I toss you the rough ideas, and you make them work. This will surely not be our last meeting on this subject, but I have a second one."

They needed a moment to become receptive to that. So I waited before continuing.

"I'm asking the joint expertise in this hall—if you had the choice of letting an invasion force superior in numbers and weapons technology come ashore at your own coastline, in a spot chosen by your enemy, or attacking the enemy before his invasion fleet could embark—and at the same time gaining support of an ally—which would you prefer? Please raise your hand for the first option—let the enemy come."

A few hands went up. I memorized these faces, too—they could probably add valuable ideas to the discussion.

"Thank you. Hands for the second option, please. Yes, that wasn't surprising. Naturally, the second option grants us more ways to learn about the enemy, just as the enemy will learn more about us before equipping his invasion fleet. Nevertheless—I'm Dragon Empress not just by title, and I can't just watch the enemy running my kind over. I want to help them, I want to win the Dragons in the *Worries* system as allies, and I want to take the fight to our enemies."

That caused some frowns.

"You're skeptical. You're right. A moment ago I was

talking about long distances and long travel times. This still applies to our enemies and their unwieldy ships that depend on expensive wormholes. It doesn't apply to us. Once we've build somewhat larger ships, we're able to redeploy large forces within a few weeks between our planetary systems — our air force and infantry to them or the allied Dragons to us. The only precondition is reasonable logistic planning. Ladies and gentlemen, at the moment we're fighting galleons with torpedo boats, and once we can deploy a few aircraft carriers, we're quite well able to defend more than just our own system."

The difference between boys and men was said to be the price of their toys, and that probably applied even more to soldiers. Well, this hall was full of big boys in uniform, and I just had announced to them, not as fiction but very real option, the ultimate toy — a faster-than-light carrier spaceship with countless swift fighters aboard!

After a brief glance at Fatima I added, "You've got a lot to talk about now. Let's make a longer break, and two hours from now, we're doing a questions and answers session. Grab the opportunity to talk over a cup of tea or coffee with each other, with me, and with the United Nations council members. Thank you."

As expected, I didn't get to fetch my own coffee. If Fatima hadn't deployed one of her teams to take care of me — and to protect me? — I wouldn't have got anything to drink, because I was so beleaguered and assailed with questions. My only comfort was that Rashid and the rest of the council didn't fare any better.

"You said before that we need several carrier spaceships to defend more than just our system," the British General Whittaker began. "Doesn't that mean conversely that we can't even protect ourselves without such a carrier?"

"No, that's not what it means." I smiled at him. "We've already proven the opposite empirically. Our carrier is Earth itself. We need carriers as a safe base in a distant system. With just one carrier we can certainly start an operation. Only if we think of a more permanent deployment, and thus about regular crew relief, there should be several."

"Ah. How large should the fleet be then?"

"I hope that one day you can tell me—not today, not here, but in the near future. To provide you with this food for thought is why I'm here today. I can only tell you one thing—as one of those who will stand up against the enemy, I'd rather have more firepower than last time."

His neighbor, a Russian admiral, frowned. "I had understood that one Barracuda would be enough."

"We had two, and we were successful. We killed the opponent as planned. The fact that we could bring one of our ships back, and that I can stand before you today, was pure luck, though."

"Luck."

"Envisage the situation, Admiral. Each of our two Barracudas could fire *one* shot before exposing itself to hostile fire. Each enemy hit could conversely annihilate one Barracuda. We had brought one untested torpedo and thus had three free shots against four opponents—the mothership and the three landers."

"Those are good odds—that only left one opponent against two Barracudas."

"That's a fallacy. Our Barracudas aren't able to incapacitate a target with one shot. Let me sketch a comparison—a torpedo boat can score a critical hit against a battleship and thus sink it, but before that happens, the battleship can return fire several times. For the mothership alone we needed four hits until its gun turrets could no longer endanger us—by then, the *Martyr* was already destroyed. The landers couldn't predict our dodges quick enough, so that we got several more shots away. But one chance hit would have done us in."

"And then?"

"Then you'd have had to take care of the lander or the landers. You'd have had a few weeks left."

He shook his head. "You can't wage war with such odds."

A French general stepped forward and nodded at me. I recognized General Cousteau from Marseille, who said, "It's not as if we'd have had a choice, Admiral Donskoi—as if the Imperatrix would have had a choice. The enemy wouldn't wait."

"Pardon. I didn't want to criticize. I only wanted to express my unsettledness about these odds." The Russian gave a short bow. "You already are Paladin, otherwise you should have been awarded knighthood, like your comrades-in-arms. I realize that I didn't sufficiently research the parameters of this first space battle, and I guess it's the same for many of my colleagues here. Could you tell us more in the questions session? We have to understand these new weapon systems better before we can design a military doctrine. I believe dry reports are no substitute for a first-hand story."

"Your analogies are very illustrative," General Whittaker said. "I'd like to hear more about the potential of a gravtunnel. Is it comparable with a submarine?"

I had to ponder that briefly. "No. You can detect submarines while they're approaching. The close end of a gravtunnel can only be located a few seconds before the approaching spaceship exits, when the spacetime structure at the destination is warped—and only if you know what kind of change you have to look for."

"That sounds like a quite nice surprise."

"Indeed. On the other hand, the crew's disoriented for a few seconds after the transit and thus unable to act, and the computer is busy reconfiguring the emitters. If you're spotted, you're a sitting duck for a few seconds—under laser fire, that can be too long."

"Assuming we could agree to follow your proposal for a forward defense," Admiral Abramov began cautiously. "What would we have to expect? What do we have to prepare for? In which way shall we help, and how would we have to fight? That's been rather vague until now."

General Hernandez, Admiral Decker, and General Badawi pricked up their ears, and the two armor suits from Fatima's unit stopped to listen to my explanations.

"My pilot, Francine Besson, described the target area in detail during the press conference. Did you watch the conference? If not, try to catch up on that. Let me go into the military aspects. In principle, we'll be facing a hot drop into a war zone, with an opponent the capabilities of which we can hardly assess yet. The system has three planets, two of which are habitable—one is very hot, the other so extremely cold that an unprotected human would freeze to death within minutes."

"How can it be habitable then?"

"Below the ice or with protective clothing. Dragons can adapt. I suspect this environment would be rather uncomfortable for brown lichen—but this guess would yet have to be confirmed." My listeners nodded. "The ice planet could be better suited for a first bridgehead, because we could protect ourselves better there. After all, we still know way too little about the local situation. From my point of view, our first goal must be building a robust base of operations, then gaining intel about the situation, and only then can we decide whether and in which way we want to intervene in the fighting." I glanced at Fatima, who was talking with a different group. "The local commanders need a lot of leeway for their decisions—comparable to an expedition corps from the time of old windjammers. Regarding our help, I can only guess again.

Worst case, we might have to prepare for establishing something like the Berlin Airlift—only under hostile fire—and that we'll have to orchestrate the defense against a superior enemy with insufficient means to retain something worth salvaging."

"A kind of suicide mission? Can we expect such from our people?"

I looked Abramov deep in the eye. "I won't expect anything from anyone. I'm looking for volunteers. But one thing's set—I'll be in. I won't ask anything from anyone what I'm not willing to do myself."

The time for the questions and answers session was almost up. If I wanted to spare a few minutes for Fatima and her people, we should finish on time.

The last request to speak came from Rashid, at one end of the first row. He rose and turned to the audience. "My sincere thanks, Protectress, for taking so much of your time to provide us with such rich information so early. The questions, the talks around the event, clearly made us feel the empathy you shared with us about the chances, risks, and necessities ahead of us. I think every one of us has realized that mankind's avenue to space can't be barred—we can only govern this way if we actively share it. Most of all, however, this is about the military aspect. The council arrived at the conclusion that an all-encompassing military operation in a distant planetary system is currently far beyond our means."

I swallowed a reply. That wasn't what I'd hoped for—wasn't it too early anyway to make such a decision?

"At the same time, we came to the conclusion that we cannot ignore the threat from the *Worries* system. So the council proposes to mandate the Imperatrix Aurea to a *robust* reconnaissance mission in order to gain a better foundation for future decision making. This mandate will be tracked with highest priority. The reconnaissance mission should start as soon as the *Mischief's* overhaul is completed and she's rigged with a technically mature *Besson compensator.*"

Only the *Mischief*? That wasn't what I regarded a robust command. But Rashid wasn't finished yet.

"To improve the odds for a successful mission, a Phoenix should escort the journey as auxiliary ship. Its commissioning should be given highest priority as well—not just for the mission, but also as a test vehicle for new technologies for future carriers and auxiliaries. We urgently need this knowledge."

That sounded more like my ideas—and perhaps people had to be led toward my goals in small steps.

The sheik placed his fingertips together. "We're aware that we'll temporarily deprive Earth of a major part of our defense that way, but we should take that risk. Many of today's discussions crystallized that we can't just dig ourselves in if we don't know what kind of enemy we should prepare for. To gather this intelligence is the most urgent goal for this mission." Now he focused straight on me, raised his eyebrows, spread his arms, and cocked his head. "Most of our conversation partners showed concern about a potential contamination during the reconnaissance—but didn't express their reservation toward the Protectress. We know why. If necessary, she will forbear from returning rather than risk taking the foreign organism back to Earth."

I nodded. This part wasn't new.

"Well, Protectress, do you want to address the audience a last time?"

"Naturally." I rose, even though that didn't make much of a difference. "I'm asking you all for support for this reconnaissance mission, not just by approving the council's proposal—but with your experience, so that this mission can start with the best possible preparations. In that case I'm confident that I'll be able to return such a mission's voluntary members home to Earth."

Fatima followed me outside.

"What do you think, should I address your people, too?" I asked her while we were ambling toward the side exit. Her tandem partner Moses joined us.

"Not now. Give them time to review the recording and talk about it. This *voluntary* reconnaissance mission is something hard to digest."

"I'm serious. Volunteers only. There should be no pressure."

"Johanna, we know that. But there's also something like peer pressure—and many of us feel compelled to follow your example." She glanced at her partner. "First of all women of the Arabic world. Without you, I wouldn't be where I'm now. The suits are the best of the best, and I'm their commandant. I can't help but volunteer for this mission—and that's okay for me. That's the way I chose for myself."

"Fatima wouldn't be who she is if she wouldn't go on this mission," Moses added. "And we wouldn't be a good tandem team if I wouldn't feel the same. You may count on us, Protectress."

I gave both a warm smile. "Naturally. Just as you may count on me. I will do everything to protect you."

"No!" both exclaimed almost at the same time. Moses added, "No, Protectress. Exactly that may not happen. We're replaceable, you are not. If it comes to extremes, you must be ready to leave us behind. You must accept our sacrifice."

"That's what Achrotzyber says all the time." After taking a deep breath, I placed one arm on Fatima's shoulder. "It will be our task to not let it come to extremes, to not enter unnecessary risks. Not even to save these foreign Dragons. Tell that to your people—it's a mission parameter. But I want to mention voluntariness again. I can't take all suits with me. Some must stay behind to protect Earth, to instruct more suits — and for the Space Patrol. As powerful as the suits are, a single tandem couple can guarantee safety for a space base or inspect a civil freighter. With three couples you should be able to defend a space fort against a small invasion. In short — we need you here, too."

Fatima briefly glanced at Moses. He nodded.

"Understood," she said. "We must make a selection."

"There can be reasons someone wants to remain here," I added. "Your people joined to defend their home, not for traveling to distant stars. They could expect the usual share of home leave, and that will not be the case here. The mission can take years, and even if we get the hostile organism under control, there may be a quarantine. Whoever has an old, sick father or is obligated to his family should stay here and be sure I don't think badly of it."

"I hadn't seen it that way yet," Fatima said. "But then . . ."

"There will be enough volunteers," Moses said. "We know our people. They will consider Johanna's concern, and some will decide to stay behind, but I don't think anyone will see that as an easy way out."

"No." She frowned. "I just don't want my father to see this as an argument to keep me here."

"He won't," I promised. "For that, he's way too proud of you." Again, I squeezed her shoulder. "So, and now I have to go. Science is waiting."

CHAPTER TWENTY-THREE

Sylvie briefly looked up from her dashboard when I dropped into the seat at her side. "Had a good rest? How did it go with the generals?"

"Cut short, and it went well. But you asked for me?"

"Yes. I just got a call from below."

"Below?"

"The Chinese. About half of the eight thousand kilometers between the Emirates and Tokyo run above China. Even though we're about two hundred and fifty kilometers high, air traffic control insisted that we have no permission to pass through their air space."

"That's no air space at this altitude."

"Perhaps a translation issue—his English was not that good. In any case, they're bitching every two minutes. Next should come up any moment—ah, here."

"*. . . trespassed Chinese air space. Reduce your speed and descend to flight level five hundred. Our interceptors will escort you to an airport.*"

"What crap." Sylvie got upset. "But I didn't want to just ignore it. Who knows what's in it politically?"

"You're right. I'll handle that."

A gesture conjured a virtual microphone up. "Chinese air traffic control, this is United Nations spaceship *Mischief* under command of the Imperatrix Aurea Draconis. Earth is in a state of war, and while that continues, the Imperatrix ultimately decides on flights in near-Earth space and beyond. This corresponds with the applicable Dragon contract."

"*Spaceship* Mischief, *any objections will be examined by the responsible authorities after your landing. Follow the instructions or we will have to force you down.*"

How would the Chinese do that? No, this threat didn't terrify me, but the danger of a resulting escalation did.

"Chinese air traffic control, you're neither authorized to terminate a Dragon contract nor to apply force against myself, the Imperatrix. I will ignore your instructions and continue my flight. At the same time, I will address your illegal threat of an act of terror against United Nations forces to the United Nations Interstellar Defence Council."

Along the way I checked the status of our nestle field. Sylvie forwent the shielding functions and only used it as drive — in principle that was sufficient, but I prepared a more protective configuration and pushed the trigger over to her panel. She acknowledged with a nod and one raised eyebrow.

"*Spaceship* Mischief, *our weapon systems are well able to hit you even at your current altitude. We're asking you one last time to follow our instructions.*"

Go fuck yourself, I thought, and showed Sylvie my middle finger. She grinned.

"Chinese air traffic control, I'm well able to come down, drill you a second asshole and serve you to your government on a silver platter. You're lucky I've got better things to do. So don't overreach yourself."

"*You've got no authority . . .*"

Ah — *had I finally coaxed him out of his narrow-minded shell?*

"I'm *Dragon.* I've got the authority to barbecue you, and that's not just figuratively speaking."

"*Uh.*"

A second voice chimed in.

"*Spaceship* Mischief, *Imperatrix Aurea, this is Commissar Chen speaking. Please ignore the previous communication and continue your flight. Have a safe journey!*"

I smiled at Sylvie. "Thank you, Commissar Chen. I assume

that the previous conversation didn't happen and won't ever happen in the future. *Mischief* out."

A snap of my fingers made the microphone disappear.

"And what was that now?" Sylvie asked. "Just a try?"

"I don't know for sure. Perhaps a test of how far they can go with me."

"In that case you put a nice shot across their bow."

"Yes. As soon as I threatened to apply force myself, the commissar was ready at hand to call the dogs back. Very convenient."

I was woken up by a draft behind me and recognized that I had fallen asleep in my cockpit seat.

"Good morning," Francine said, and I automatically focused on the image behind my back that my nanos provided for me. "What's up?"

"A storm above the Sea of Japan," Sylvie replied. "I flew a small detour, but we're already above Japan. In fifteen minutes we can land in Tokyo."

"Okay."

"Slept well?" I asked. "Ready for science?"

Francine shrugged. "I still don't know why I should come along for the eggheads, of all things. I guess I would have gotten along better with the soldiers — would've been more interesting."

"Maybe — but for one, you could hardly keep your eyes open, and for two, I'll need you today. I hardly took any notice of the analyses above *Trouble*. Only you can say anything about that."

"That's the price I'm paying for having diligently completed my mission tasks." But she smiled.

Francine hadn't chosen her profession as warrior, had voluntarily trained for pilot — but I knew there was more in her. The *Besson compensator* was no chance hit — she knew how to use her brains, she only lacked knowledge and experience in scientific work — and that this hadn't changed was due to my selfishness. I needed her, or at least I thought so, where she was. That wasn't fair.

"Francine, what would you think of studying Dragon technology? The real way, at our University, I mean?"

Her smile froze, and her eyes widened. She swayed a little and quickly reached for my seat's backrest. "Me?"

Sylvie briefly glanced at me and nodded, then she focused on our approach again. I swiveled my chair around and watched my teammate.

"You. I believe you can do it, and you could even have fun doing it."

"But, me . . . and my duties?"

"Francine." I didn't let her avoid my glance. "You've already done more for me than anyone could ask for. You've got every right to think about yourself just once and do what you'd like to. We'll find a solution for your duties."

"But — and the mission?"

I took her hand. "I want to have you along in any case, but perhaps not just as my pilot and bodyguard or flight engineer, but also as my student."

Her eyebrows went up, then the corners of her lips — and then she threw herself forward into my arms. "Oh, Jo!"

CHAPTER TWENTY-FOUR

Sylvie gently set the Barracuda down in the inner courtyard assigned to us at Tokyo's university. The roofs around were lined with armored Imperial Guard warriors, and our screen showed the reason in front of the university entrance — accompanied by the uniformed Shogun Nakamichi, the Tenno was waiting for us in a light-gray suit. Why?

Why should I rack my brain? I'll ask him.

"Ready?" I asked Francine.

"Naturally."

She was the cool Mamba again, self-control incarnate. Forgotten was the one moment I had penetrated her walls. And yet — her stance had changed. No bit more or less confident than before, but at the same time easier — like she was relieved from a heavy burden.

"Then let's go."

The airlock's inner hatch was already open. We stepped inside, it closed, and with the outer hatch opening, Tokyo's humid air gave us welcome.

Francine held me back when I was about to jump outside, and left first. Her gaze swept the place, then she nodded at me, and I followed.

The Shogun saluted, and the Japanese emperor bowed so deeply that I almost had a hard time copying him.

"Welcome, Protectress, on Japanese soil," the emperor said. "We're grateful for the honor of your visit."

Actually he was saying in flowery words that the soil wasn't worthy to support me, but I had learned to interpret

138

the submissive-formal way of speaking. My reply turned out as formal, but raised him to equally-ranked conversation partner.

"I'm grateful for the hospitality and the friendly welcome." Even though I kept my focus on the emperor, I didn't fail to notice the Shogun's tension. "Should we go inside?"

I allowed the host to hold the door open for me. Francine followed, then the emperor, and finally the Imperial Guard commandant.

"Welcome, Knight Francine." The emperor bowed before my escort, too. "We're feeling honored and are delighted to make your acquaintance."

Francine bowed as well and replied, "Many thanks and good morning. Pardon my insufficient Japanese."

Before our host could lose himself in elongated excuses I had to intervene, for Francine's benefit in English, too. "We're not just meeting for a welcome here and now. What else is on the agenda?"

The Japanese emperor squinted. "Ah, the Dragon way is very straightforward. It requires some familiarization to walk this way. Like your language requires familiarization. Pardon." He pointed upward. "The Imperial Guard is here for your protection, not mine. We're concerned. The New York incident rather fueled our concerns. As it seems, someone's orchestrating opposition against your activities. My experts cannot figure out the objectives this new opponent pursues."

"If it is a new opponent," Francine commented.

"We know too little. But there are signs." Our host looked at each of us in turn.

"What kind?"

"If two promising Dragon University candidates are disappearing without trace in short sequence, our criminal police will be worried. Once a micro fusion reactor maintenance expert goes missing, too, our experts are alarmed. However, we fear it's just the summit of the iceberg."

"The tip," Francine corrected automatically while staring into the ceiling.

I resisted the temptation to ponder the implications of these findings. Instead I kept my focus on the emperor. "To tell us this, the Tenno wouldn't have had to trouble himself personally."

He hesitated, then braced himself. "Back then, after you put down the rebellion against my government and me, I had sent you away. I had expected thereby to discharge the oncoming conflict. But the opposing forces in our country were too powerful—especially the Dragon cult was too powerful. Together with the Yakuza, the cult effectively controlled the whole country. Then it was beheaded. A Golden Dragon allegedly interfered." He smiled knowingly. "Thereafter, the cult fared badly all over the country. The Yakuza prevailed, not the police, but nevertheless, we're better off today, because certain typical atrocities of organized crime are no longer tolerated—in such cases, Yakuza and police are working hand in hand, if the culprits don't lose their heads right away. It's said the Dragon will interfere if this self-control doesn't work anymore. Obviously the Yakuza doesn't just respect the Dragon, they fear the Dragon—and if I hadn't sent the Dragon away back then, cult and Yakuza wouldn't have gained such power." And without flowery paraphrasing, he added, "I made a mistake."

"And I allowed it to happen," I replied. "I deemed this de-escalation strategy conclusive from a Dragonish point of view. It simply didn't work."

"Thank you for your understanding."

"Both of you didn't have enough intel," Francine said. "That's frequently the case—and that's why the next mission is so important. We must not allow the enemy in the *Worries* system to become too strong. But at the same time we must not allow our enemies here on Earth to become too strong. Someone should take care of this problem—no, not you, Jo."

"I didn't say a word."

"You didn't have to. Your Majesty, I think we're due."

CHAPTER TWENTY-FIVE

I paused at the auditorium entrance. Francine watched me with curiosity.

"You would think that I'd got used to talking to large numbers of people by now," I said with a sigh.

"Perhaps you should show up naked," Francine joked.

"You might have a point there." I winked and placed a hand on the handle. "But as you're the main actor today . . ."

"No!"

The remainder of her protest was drowned out by the noise in the auditorium as I pulled at the door. But the conversations quickly faded. Curious gazes and numerous camera lenses followed us on our way to the centrally placed microphone and the older Japanese next to it. My *Analogy* took the image apart.

– Two hundred and sixty-four participants, forty-one of them with press card. –

Okay.

"Ladies and gentlemen, welcome together with me Protectress Johanna Meier and Knight Francine Besson from the Dragon University," the Japanese spoke into the microphone in English language.

The applause gave us another moment to reach our place. We bowed before the audience, each shook the speaker's hand, and once he then raised both hands toward the audience, the room fell silent.

"On behalf of Tokyo University—welcome. I am Ishido Motosawa, this institution's president. We're excited to hear what you'll be telling us."

The microphone stand was much too high for me, but fit Francine and the Japanese well. I didn't want to fumble around with it. Instead I took the microphone from the stand.

"Good morning, ladies and gentlemen. Many thanks to our hosts for making this event possible on such short notice. Many thanks to you for the great interest—and that also applies to the many listeners before their screens—and the trouble you took to come here. We'll make sure it's worth it."

That earned me a few smiles.

"After all, we achieved several technological and scientific breakthroughs. We traveled faster than light to a planetary system a hundred and forty lightyears away—and back—in a spaceship entirely built on Earth, and brought a tremendous amount of data back with us, among it observations of two planets in the habitable zone. I admit—scientific findings weren't the primary goal alone. It was about the flight itself and reconnaissance of a system from which Earth had been invaded before. Nevertheless—we were traveling on our own scientific account, for example for the empirical confirmation of the *Meier gravtunnel* theory. Only—upon arrival in the *Worries* system, we found ourselves in trouble."

I summarized the first minutes after the transit.

"Pardon me if I don't go into further detail. The creation of a transit bubble is relatively easily described, but behind it is a hell of a lot of theory. I want to make better use of our time today than for a crash course in Dragon technology. We have more interesting topics, and the primary person responsible for both is my partner and pilot, Knight Francine Besson." I pointed to my side, and Francine made a bow.

"While I was busy analyzing the cause of our rough arrival and finding a way we still might be able to return, she proceeded with the system's survey and observation as planned. So she will give you an overview of our results and answer questions about them afterward. But we also have an entirely different astrophysical and not just gravity-mechanical topic — differences in the structure of space. These parameter differences in the gravity-mechanical potential were the cause of our transit problem, which we then could solve with the *Besson compensator,* and our findings about these parameter differences are the second topic, for which I will answer your questions in a parallel session. So you're spoilt for choice where to ask your questions. You can watch the recording of the other session afterward."

Many participants showed surprise — obviously they hadn't recognized this aspect of the invitation yet.

"You don't have to decide at once. We'll now show you a very brief summary of the data we obtained and permit a few questions that allow you to make up your mind — and you should have a chance to agree on your choice with each other."

CHAPTER TWENTY-SIX

Francine stood in the entrance of her lecture room, sur-rounded by scientists, and her gaze at me was seeking help. I pushed my way through the people, who at first re-acted indignantly, but then made room for me once they rec-ognized me.

"Folks, we have to move on. Really." I focused an older guy who seemed to be especially unwilling to let my pilot go, and read his nametag. "Professor Maraschinow. I propose that you first check the measurement data again, collect your questions, sort them into several subject areas, and then pre-pare a one-week congress, for which Francine will join you. Would you like to take care of organizing this conference? And would your university provide the rooms?"

He paused. "I must check that. The funding . . ."

I pointed at his immediate neighbors. "Professor Li-Yung, Professor Cormac, would you support a joint sponsoring of this event? Great, so we already have three heads for the con-ference committee. So, and now we really must leave."

With these words I placed one arm around Francine and pulled her with me. The researchers moved out of our way, their attention already directed on the Russian.

"Sorry, we didn't agree on that before," I whispered to Francine. "Bad?"

"One week? No, not at all. I was astonished how little their questions made me sweat — and what ideas the folks came up with! Time was up much too soon."

"Sounds as if you had your fun."

"You bet! I mean, you've seen it—they wouldn't let me go. Oooh damn, I guess I'm just beginning to realize what I missed until now."

She stopped and looked into my eyes. "Don't get me wrong. I like my role as Mamba in your service, and also the kick that comes with it. I like my job as pilot. I don't want to let go of either—but I want more of this. I want to understand what my instruments are recording, and I want to be able to draw my own conclusions."

"Okay. In that case I want a Mamba with a grip on the technology we're using, a pilot who can make sense of the recorded data and a researcher who can deal with threats and isn't just a passenger aboard my Barracuda."

Francine smiled. "Watch out what you're wishing for. Some wishes come true."

"Thanks, same to you."

We grinned at each other, and then she laughed, linked arms with me, and pulled me along.

CHAPTER TWENTY-SEVEN

I woke up from a slight touch at my right shoulder. I wanted to turn on my back and look around, but an arm around my chest, one hand on my breast, held me tight. My back felt humid — Francine, snuggled up to me in spoon position.

"Jo?" Sylvie whispered.

"Yes?"

"We'll be there soon — I have to return to the cockpit. How will we do it? The island's landing pad is occupied. Should Harry pick you up in Gladstone?"

"No. We'll just jump out and swim to the jetty."

"Okay."

Sylvie left, and I sensed a stir behind me. Francine grumbled, then she loosened her grip. "Did I just hear something about jumping?"

"Just a little refreshment before we can sleep in a real bed."

"Then I'll be awake."

"You'd be anyway if we had to change our ride in Gladstone. Perhaps Nanette has a nightcap for you."

"Well then." She rested on one arm. "Then I don't have to don the suit."

"Nah." And my nanos didn't have to shape a suit.

The pressure from Francine's body disappeared, and I felt a cool draft at my back. Now I could turn away from the wall and get up, too.

"Gals, we're almost there," Sylvie called from the bow. "You can enter the airlock."

We did, and when the outer hatch opened and we saw the Pacific Ocean's gentle sway glisten below, we jumped out.

147

I didn't have to overcome my fears for that — someone who's jumped from a skyscraper roof before doesn't fear a ten-meter drop into water. I wasn't so sure whether it didn't bother Francine, or whether she had to resort to her Mamba drill, but she jumped.

After resurfacing, we found ourselves about thirty meters away from the jetty in the salty water — a few swimming strokes took us to the ladder, and soon we were standing on the jetty in the cool night breeze.

Next to us, the air flickered, and one of our suits became visible.

"Welcome back," Orry said. "Reginald and Tess are already waiting for you."

I gave Francine an apologetic glance. It didn't look as if we were allowed to go straight to bed.

"Okay," she said. "So it's the nightcap."

Our communication center sat silently and seemingly deserted under the palm trees. That it was dark aside from the dim glow of a few strip lights meant nothing — out of consideration for the local fauna, lights were turned off in the late evening. Whoever desired to stay thereafter had to make do with the moonlight.

Tess was snuggled into Reginald's left arm and only opened her eyes when he took his hand from her breast and whispered, "Hello."

"Oh, hello, Jo, Francine," she said. "Welcome back. Sorry, I'd dozed off."

"Hello, both of you," Reginald said. "Welcome."

"Good evening," I replied. "Thanks — we didn't expect to see anyone except the guards."

"Hi. I'll get us something." Francine went for the counter.

"Yes," Tess said and sat up. "I guess there will be a big hello at breakfast, and then we won't get to it — while you were gone, a lot of things happened here you should know about. Arko told me he didn't deem bothering you necessary, but I see it differently."

"Was there an attack on the island? Or anything planned?"

"No, no, nothing like that. It's about our mission. Meanwhile, we've visited all *instruments* on your list and brought the researchers who would come. As expected, almost all wanted to. Only Robert Wilson didn't."

"How's he doing?"

"Good. He's researching nature in Vietnam."

"That he shall do. Any trouble?"

"Yes. The last few times, we met organized resistance. Several researchers had been moved together to let them design miniaturized laser weapons, and they were guarded by three strong lone warriors — warriors with booster. Arko calls them *Dragonlings,* and he said Zoe had already met such Dragon-human crossbreeds. Cologne and Cairo, he said. Does that ring a bell?"

Indeed. The emerging memories were expressly unpleasant. "Greenhorn. He was strong and fast. What about the girls?"

"All well, no worries. Nothing the tank couldn't fix. In any case, we found hints about a breeding station in Switzerland and went there for a visit."

"That was risky."

"Yes — but to us it seemed riskier not to follow the lead. We did it officially via the Swiss army and dug the base out. That wasn't easy — those guys are darn strong opponents — but thanks to Arko we had no fatalities. Instead, and that's the issue, two of them joined us. That's what you should know before you meet them."

"Oh." I tried to imagine a fight between such men and Mambas. How could they have persevered?

Francine returned and handed three beer cans around. She

kept the fourth.

"For the others we had to use plasma guns, and finally Arko applied his venom. They could barely be stopped."

"I don't understand. If there was a fight, why didn't the two of them join in?"

"Because we made them an offer — like you did for us back then."

"An offer? How?"

"Monique went to them and delivered the offer — and then the fighting started."

"Monique?" Of course I knew which Mamba Tess was talking about. A brunette, usually rather quiet and contained.

"She was very courageous."

"I'd like to hear the story in context again. Let's see when I find a chance to talk with Monique."

Tess nodded. "She surely deserves that."

Reginald chimed in. "The station had a few attendants and ordinary security — the girls left them to the Swiss. Who they brought along are the involuntary mothers. On advice of our shrink, Peter, they're not living on the island — perhaps you might want to look after them."

"Yes, sure." *Yet another task!*

I had another idea. "Was that the only breeding station?"

"The only one we know of," Tess admitted. "There are no leads to other centers and sadly no usable traces to the masterminds. But there must be someone who sent the Dragonlings to the researchers. Someone's running the big gun here — not like the Cartel, organized crime all over the place, but covert."

"And the New York attack?" Francine asked.

Tess shrugged. "Maybe — although I don't understand what they thought to gain there."

"Me," I said. "I'm an obstacle. All the rest was façade — calculated collateral damage to corner me. I only don't know what plans I'm blocking."

"The University," Reginald quickly said. "Well, unless they are ordinary criminals who fear you as global police, or some primitive vendetta—"

"Primitive is not the word for their approach," I objected.

"Okay, sophisticated vendetta. In any case, no other motivation appears plausible to me. It won't likely be the vanguard of an alien invasion."

Tess placed a hand on Reginald's leg. "I'll talk with Kenneth about it. This is nothing Jo should worry about now."

"No, okay. Sorry, Jo."

"It's okay." I sipped at my beer again. "Anything else?"

"Yes, I've got one more point. Jo, we've seen your speeches, and our people are excited about your new ideas and plans, space bases, trade fleet, and all that."

"Francine's ideas. Oh, by the way, from now on she'll dig deeper into our subject areas."

Reginald raised an eyebrow.

Tess smiled. "Congrats, Francine. Did you finally find your true calling?"

"That's yet to turn out," my teammate replied. "But I will always be a Mamba. Sorry, Reginald."

"It's okay. I appreciate that, Francine. Come to me if you're stuck. So, where was I? Oh yes, the new ideas. Our people are excited, and we've got a lot of new cards on the walls. Jo, they will follow you whatever you'll ask for tomorrow. But, Jo, the people need a break. Many of us are hyped up for years to push your—our—projects forward, to support you. Give them a few days or weeks off. They simply can't keep up with your pace."

"Jo soon won't keep up, either." Francine placed her empty beer can down. "Jo, you need sleep. Come."

She was right, and I let her guide me outside without resistance.

CHAPTER TWENTY-EIGHT

The next morning I found myself in Francine's arms again, only this time in a wide, soft bed, and this time it was the rising sun's light that tickled my shoulder.

I didn't feel truly well-rested, but if I'd turned around once more, I'd have missed lunch, too. So it was probably better to swim once around the island?

Before I could implement this idea, Francine woke up as well. Automatically, her free hand stroked around my breast and made me tremble — and she instantly noticed that. The next moment, she pulled me tight and gave me a ravenous kiss.

I slipped one leg between her now invitingly wide-spread thighs and sensed wetness — at my upper leg, and between my own labia as well. Our breasts touched each other's, and our nipples rose.

Her fingers circled my areola as if searching, passed along the delicate skin of my breast, while the other hand dug down to my thighs.

My outer knee pushed my hip up, giving her the necessary leeway to feel for my wetness. Then I propped myself up on one arm. That way I could let my breasts slowly circle around hers while I sucked her lips with mine.

No, that wasn't what Francine wanted!

Her fingers pushed into my wet crack, the other hand firmly held my breast, her hip pressed against my upper leg, and her tongue was searching for mine.

Okay.

I disengaged myself from her grip, from her lips, and moved some way down until I could suck her tit. My fingers found their way into her vagina and felt the bumpy inside, then began to massage it while my thumb slowly approached her inner labia's upper end.

Her breathing was heavy, her body trembled, and her pelvis rose toward my attention—she was about to come, and when my thumb touched her clitoris, she did so with a loud wheeze.

So soon? Oh no, you won't get away so lightly! First I will suck up your juice, and once you're ready again, I'll gently lead you from one orgasm to the next. After all we've endured during the last weeks, we deserve to truly celebrate my art!

Chapter Twenty-nine

The distance to the communications center was just two hundred meters, but when we arrived, Francine was walking normally again, with her telltale wide-placed first steps left behind. Her cheeks were still a bit rosy, her nipples a bit hard, and her pupils a bit widened — and her labia not quite dried — but she no longer showed the enormous eruption of passion that she had enjoyed.

There hadn't been any time left for a swim in the ocean, so she bore the traces of love-making with dignity.

"Do I have to join later?" she asked hopefully.

"Definitely. Okay, you lack a lot of basics, but we'll talk about exactly those topics you'll soon deal with, too. You'll see — when it's about the empirical data, you know more than you'd admit now."

"Mmm. Maybe."

We arrived at the center. As expected, we were welcomed with a big party. The hustle and bustle was so big that Francine's passionate aroma wasn't noticed — even if the occasional member bulged a little in our presence.

My fine nose noticed anyway that another Mamba had recently tasted the fruit of love, too. I recognized the slender brunette as Monique, and she held two handsome dark-haired blokes in her arms whose tools of passion showed signs of use as well. But when I approached the trio, both men dropped on their knees and lowered their heads.

The right one spoke up first without looking up. "Protectress Johanna. I beg your mercy — I have erred and deserve punishment, but my greatest desire is to serve you and actively repent my sins."

What was that?

"Protectress Johanna," the second one echoed. "I have erred and deserve punishment, but I as well beg for an undeserved second chance."

I waited for a while, but they remained silent. Monique caught my doubtful glance and pointed at the right man, then at the left. "Jo, these are Malt and Cryc, both Halfdragons or Dragonlings. We freed them during a mission in Switzerland."

"I'm briefed, Monique. I also heard of your gallant mission, and it must be owed to the fact I'm back for only a few hours that I haven't got a nomination for Squire of the Order for you. Especially as we owe you for being able to welcome these two doubtlessly valuable new teammates to our team. Rise, Malt and Cryc."

The Mamba just stared at me gaping, while the two men slowly rose. The corners of Monique's eyes were shimmering wet.

I reached out to her with both arms. But she didn't throw herself into them as I expected, but took my hands and held them before her.

"Thanks, Johanna. If you wish so, I'll gladly accept this honor. But I'm already a member of a much more exclusive circle—I'm one of the few you can truly trust. That's all I need."

Oh, that went down well! But I only winked at her and let go. "One day you'll have to tell me more. But now about you."

Perhaps it had been a mistake to let them stand up. They were both at least one head taller than Monique, and the Mamba already towered as much above me. That way I had a better view on their cocks than their faces—mmm, not really a mistake?

Well, I was used to looking up to other people. That didn't

cause me issues anymore — neither with my Companion, who discreetly remained in the background, nor with these two pleasure donors.

"In due time I will receive a report on whether and how you personally failed. Until then, your punishment is to wait for my sentence. But my confidants already decided to bid you welcome here, and I accept this decision. So let's have breakfast."

"Protectress . . ."

"No arguments. Breakfast comes first, unless you want to anger Nanette."

CHAPTER THIRTY

I hadn't realized how much our small community had grown—sure, meanwhile a new class of students had joined, then the new teachers . . . the island was large enough for all, but a full assembly required preparations now. Simply climbing a table no longer sufficed for a longer lecture.

Instead, a few mobile platforms of different heights were quickly arranged, seats placed on them, and all could comfortably watch and listen.

I nevertheless fetched a table and sat down on the edge. Francine stayed in her seat at the end of the first row.

"Good morning, friends," I began. "A personal welcome from me to all new arrivals, too—teachers, students, guests, and our marine biologists. It will take a few days, if not weeks, before I can talk to each of you in person, but there will surely be opportunities. You know Dragon technology is alien, and the studies are quite different. An awful lot of subject matter, complex formulas, nothing truly fits, and in the end it still works. Without teamwork, it can't be done."

Hands on the table edge, I leaned forward. "I'm a part of this team. Okay, I'm an important part because I founded this University and I'm leading it, and because I've got the *memory* of several thousand years of Dragon history in my mind, and moreover I had a few quite helpful inspirations, like, for example, about the Meier effect. But I'm not alone there. Without some of my fellow teachers, the Meier effect would have remained a nice idea. Others took the idea and made it work. Each of you has the potential for further such inspirations.

157

So — dare to follow such unconventional thoughts, talk about it, don't let yourself be discouraged when someone turns such an idea down on first sight because he's got other problems on his mind just then. Dare to talk with me like with everyone else here. I won't bite, I'm just part of the team."

My right hand pointed at Francine. "Francine had a few helpful, unconventional ideas, too. She made me think that we don't need an entire wormhole tunnel — the result was my formula set on the Meier gravtunnel, or the tunnel bubble, respectively. Similarly, when we were stuck in the *Worries* system without hope for return, she came up with the moving parameter compensation — whereupon I integrated the *Besson compensator* into our software. I'll tell you more about these two concepts today, and Francine will tell you what effects she observed regarding the parameter differences during the deep diagnosis for the *Mischief.* It's important to internalize these concepts before we integrate the software for the Phoenix carriers and trust other people to the tunnel bubble. Doubtlessly you'll find further potential for improvement — not to mention the fact that my code bricolage needs cleaning up again."

A few of my listeners made an unhappy face. I nodded at them. "I fear this part of my talk won't be very exciting for you. Marine biology is just different. We'll talk about the *Worries* system, too, but only after lunch. If you're back then, you won't miss anything, okay?"

CHAPTER THIRTY-ONE

In the end, Nanette was the one to announce the end of the event. She simply stood between Francine and me and clapped her hands. "So, folks, that's enough for today. In fifteen minutes, the platforms are gone and the seating decently restored, and then we'll have dinner. One last word, Jo?"

"Two, please. Firstly — tomorrow we'll have a colloquium in Gladstone. Our folks there shall get first-hand information, too. The day after tomorrow, I'm back here and trying to catch up with the last quarter, and thereafter I'll tend to research and studies and be available for your questions. Secondly — even if I'm itching to fly right back — I know that there's a lot of work ahead of us before a rescue mission can depart, even before the next Barracuda can go there. I want to be sure nothing goes wrong, and to that end we should be refreshed and recovered. You've all worked through the last semester break, and don't think I wouldn't be grateful for your efforts and your motivation! But creativity works better if you give your subconscious a chance, so we all should go on vacation for two weeks. I'll grant us all this week to wrap up, so that everyone can shut his studies down sensibly, and from next Saturday on there's pause. Consider what you want to do — visit your family, see more of Australia, just party, and on the first of July we'll meet here again. So, and now we'll reconfigure. Thank you, Nanette."

Our good soul gave me an inquiring glance. "Of course I'll ensure a basic supply."

I wrapped one arm around her hip and pulled her toward

the counter. "Nanette, that applies to you, too. I know this is your life, and I can't imagine the island without you, but you've earned a two-week break, too. Let's talk with the biologists about whether they can fill in if someone really wants to stay. Turtle season is over."

She hesitated. "Mmm — yes, okay, Claude might help out. But I don't know where to go."

"You don't have to go alone." I wouldn't ask for François — I had brought the two together back then and Nanette had followed him to the island, but the slender, tall blonde no longer needed to tie herself to a male protector and breadwinner, and I wasn't quite sure whether the two still had a relationship.

"I'll consider it."

I considered, too. Here on the island, Nanette was the good soul for all, and she surely didn't have to spend the night alone if she didn't want to. But otherwise? Whom could she ask, who would accompany her? For most people on the island I wouldn't care, but for Nanette. I told myself firmly — if she hadn't found anyone by the end of the week, I'd ask her if I should join her.

Everyone wanted to sit at my table for dinner, but our tables weren't that large. Finally, I invited the freed researchers to sit with me at two adjoined tables, and during dinner I let them tell me the story of their liberation and their first impressions of the island and our research. That way, I didn't have to talk much but could enjoy Nanette's cuisine extensively.

They had one thing in common — they didn't want to leave. The paradise-like scenery, the research opportunities, the highly motivated students, the incredible prospect of researching new worlds soon — all that excited them.

"I think I hear a *but* in there," I said when we had arrived at the dessert.

"Yes, maybe," Gustave admitted. "The lecture seems to be organized somewhat chaotically, if I may say so."

"You may," I replied. "I won't even ask you how you determine that. In the beginning, we made a schedule for a single year, and it was just expanded. Perhaps someone should give it a workover. No, let me put it differently — if you find some time to straighten out the plan, feel free to do it."

"I didn't want to interfere with your authority."

"Remember the Dragon principle, Gustave. Someone finds something needs to be done and does it. Talk with the other teachers, make a proposal, factor in feedback, implement it. That's the only way this University can work — I don't even have enough time to delegate authority."

"Don't you have an administration?"

"No. Or yes — on the mainland, the technical college takes care of some administrative stuff. Those folks are very helpful principally, and I think after the colloquium tomorrow it will get even better, if that's at all possible. We have so many fascinating new topics for the folks there."

Monique approached our table with an espresso cup and I realized I couldn't postpone this encounter any longer. I pushed my chair back and rose. "Excuse me now."

Monique handed me the cup. "Do you have a moment for us?"

"I'd like to talk with you alone first. Let's walk a few steps along the beach, and you tell your story."

Together we watched a sea hare until it had disappeared behind the coral stock. Somewhere farther out, a small ray passed, and a lightning flashed in the distance.

The thunderstorm would pass by, I knew that intuitively.

"I don't yet understand what blame these two Dragonlings believe they bear. They didn't do anything, did they?"

"No," Monique replied. "They didn't do anything, that's

their problem. They know about their heritage, half Dragon, half man. They knew that other Dragons exist, they knew about you, the Golden One, and they also knew that their existence was kept secret from you. They guessed they were part of an operation directed against you. Cryc says it would've been their duty to stand up for you."

"Would they've had a chance?"

"That doesn't matter, Cryc says. Once they recognized being on the wrong path, that they'd been roped in for a bad cause, they should've acted. They could've escaped, delivered themselves, told you. But they didn't. They allowed this mission to continue and thus incurred a debt—for example, for the injuries I suffered in China."

"What a nonsense."

"No, I wouldn't put it like that." She dug a small hole in the sand with her toes. "I mean, basically I can understand them in some way. We fared the same—we went along, for the entire training, and until you came, we didn't even ask ourselves whether we're doing the right thing, or if we should refuse."

"And die."

"Yes, that'd probably have been the outcome. But isn't it sometimes better to die than to be part of something wrong?"

"It's sometimes better to live so that you can make a change. To wait until you can achieve something, and then, when there's no other way left, exchange your life for a better gain, instead of just wasting it."

"Mmm. Yes." Her pretty foot closed the hole again.

"From my point of view, they chose the right path at the decisive moment—when you offered them a choice. You can't ask for more."

"Mmm, yes. But I think they see it differently."

"They shall tell me themselves."

When I turned away, Monique held me back. "Jo, I . . ."

"Yes?"

"Oh, nothing."

"You like them."

She slowly raised her shoulders, then let them drop. "Yes."

"They fuck well."

Now she laughed. "Yes."

"Okay. I'll keep that in mind." Could she see my wink in the moonlight? "I'll talk with them."

Malt and Cryc were waiting for me in front of the communication center. They weren't alone, but I shooed the others away with a handwave.

"Come with me," I ordered. "We'll find a quiet spot."

The end of the jetty looked to me like a good place to administer Dragon justice, although I didn't know how to judge yet. On our way I could examine the two Dragonlings.

Very obviously there were different ways to combine Dragon and human. A nano-enhanced Dragon could assume human shape, and a nano-enhanced human — like me — could assume Dragon shape. The Dragonlings seemed to be the results of a third approach — to crossbreed the two species, or combine genetically, respectively, to permanently incorporate Dragon abilities into human shape. Were nanos involved in any way?

Each of the two men was able to sire children in human women that would become full Dragonlings again — without watering down over generations. Along with this thought I suppressed a shiver and decided to look after the *brood mothers* as soon as possible.

Dragonlings commanded booster and could heal very fast, that they had in common with Dragons. Everything else required a consciously controlled *Analogy,* which they probably lacked.

Both were in no way ugly, with well-toned bodies and

impressive equipment between their legs, but not truly beautiful.

That shouldn't matter now.

Close to the jetty's end I turned around and sat down on the wooden beams cross-legged. Then I pointed at the free space before me. "Get comfortable."

Obediently they sat down. It didn't look comfortable to me. For a real cross-legged seat their leg muscles were too strong. So they had to put their legs up and lean forward, which put their manhoods on display much too prominently.

"We don't know each other yet. I'm Johanna Meier, Melbourne Dragon technology graduate, head of the University here on Velvet Island, and at the same time Golden Dragon and Imperatrix Aurea, warlord for interstellar conflicts. Forget the titles, I'm Jo. You're Malt and Cryc." I nodded at both, and they nodded back.

"You're both a part human, a part Dragon — it's not my job to judge this. It's a fact we're stuck with. Nobody can choose whether he or she grows tits or cock, and just the same you couldn't pick whether you inherited Dragon genes or not. Every child is born innocent. That's my position, and I won't negotiate it. Clear?"

Both nodded.

"Good. You both have claimed that you failed. You demand punishment. It's not that easy, though — no punishment without sentence, no sentence without trial, no trial without accusation. Please think twice now. I want to hear clear, well-founded charges, and of course you may discuss your arguments with each other. What's your offense?"

They looked at each other. Cryc nodded, and Malt took the floor.

"We didn't intervene, Mistress. We didn't take sides with you, although we knew that the mission we were part of was directed against you."

I nodded. "I accept your statement. But opposing me is no

sufficient reason to assume a fail. That alone isn't enough. So?"

"But if we had been ordered to attack you?"

"Did anybody?"

"No, but . . ." He paused.

I smiled. "Please keep in mind that unfounded assumptions about a third party's motives aren't admitted."

"We were told the *Dragon Claws* were created to rule and to relieve the Golden One."

"*To take the Golden One out of the game,* were the exact words," Cryc added. "We knew it, and we didn't intervene."

"I've had many opponents before in my life," I said. "I knew it and I didn't intervene before I was prepared for the confrontation. Were you prepared?"

"No . . ."

"Or was there a reason for immediate action?"

"No."

Malt leaned farther forward. "Some of our brood mates were sent to outside missions, and we didn't stop them."

"Which kind of outside missions?"

"We didn't learn anything about that."

"Then you're not to blame. You can only assume responsibility for a neglect of duty if you have concrete knowledge of a planned crime. You had no right to condemn your brood mates without evidence, so you couldn't intervene."

Malt slowly nodded. "I understand."

"But you're not satisfied."

"No."

"It's your right to be dissatisfied. But that's not the same as guilt. You're both still very young. You have a long life before you, and now you have the chance to design it in a way that it feels right."

"Yes, Mistress. This is wise advice. We should put our lives at your service and not let ourselves be distracted."

I grinned. I had an idea what he wanted to say there, and Monique wouldn't like it. "Your services are welcome if you fit into our community. That means to honor each other's needs. If you need solitude, that's up to you. Asceticism is not what I demand. It's quite okay to be distracted as long as no other task demands attention, and to tend to the needs of others."

"What do you mean, Mistress?"

"Monique would surely be disappointed if you rejected her, and I guess she's not the only one."

He kept a straight face, but a slight swell of his member gave him away.

I considered taking advantage of the situation, but opted against. For the time being it seemed to be better to grant them a little respectful distance. Nevertheless I subtly changed my posture, let my nipples harden and my labia become wet. That sufficed to bring my nudity home to them. They quickly grew tasty boners.

"Good night, guys!"

I only had to lean back to drop from the jetty—I stretched while falling and submerged.

CHAPTER THIRTY-TWO

I had thought I could just quietly sneak into my room, slip into my bed, and sleep. But as soon as I was peacefully lying under the sheet, an arm came from behind to hold my breast, and Francine snuggled up to me.

It felt good, so I didn't fight it. I was only a bit surprised — I had expected her to look for a hard cock for a change. There were many men on the island for a nice fuck and an ensuing cuddle.

I'd have appreciated such, too, if I hadn't been spending my evening with empress' duties. Instead, I only felt tired.

What a luxury! Being able to lie down unconcerned, being allowed to feel snug — in fresh linen, with full stomach, and with a nice girlfriend to cuddle. What would I've given for such as a child!

Everything. I'd probably never have developed the ambition to become a good whore or thief or to study — and Dragon technology not at all. I wouldn't have met the Lionheart, would never have had the chance to steal charge 11-217, and would never have met *my* Dragon Companion, whose presence I could sense always and everywhere since then.

And I wouldn't be responsible for all the other wonderful people who could also feel safe and snug on the island, like Francine at my back.

With amazement I realized that I felt happy and content. And sleepy . . .

CHAPTER THIRTY-THREE

I woke up from a plucking at my right nipple, opened my eyes and gazed at an orange hued sky over the Pacific Ocean.

A second pluck, and my nipples hardened. Along with that a welcome, expectant tingle developed in my crotch. However, I waited for the third pluck before I placed my upper leg away and with knee up, so that my wet labia parted.

The plucking became a gentle circling around my breast, and then the fingers walked down my side, across my hip, up my upper leg and down the inside, into my groin, and then across my belly up again to my breasts.

Purr!

Again the hand moved downward, and almost automatically my thighs opened even wider, my pelvis moved toward the searching fingers that were now exploring my mons pubis but steering clear of my invitingly gaping crack.

Ah, such a marvelous torture!

Yes, continue your torture, tease with your exploration, and refuse quick fulfillment! Make me hot, defeat me!

The fingers ran gently up to my hip again, then down the crack of my butt, caressed my thighs from behind, tickled the bridge between my holes, played around my anus, dared toward my vagina, delved into the wetness — *Yes!*

If this bliss could never end! But at the same time I longed for the climax, desired more . . . passion held my chest tight — Francine's tenderness no longer sufficed, I wanted unrestrained lust!

I announced myself with a twitch, then I turned around, moved my crotch into reach of the waiting fingers, grabbed down to her bush and began to suck one of her nipples.

Oh yes, she was ready for more, too — my hand found wetness galore, and her thighs opened willingly and wide. Soon we were in a rubbing competition while ravenously kissing. Yes, I longed to come, and I wanted her to come, too — it didn't take long, and an ecstatic wheeze told me she was due. No longer having to hold back, I enjoyed her touch a last time, drove my fingers once again into her — *Ahhh!*

I ended our hug reluctantly.

"Breakfast first, and then Harry takes us to the mainland, okay?"

"Do I have to come along?" Francine asked faintly.

"Today is mainly about the practical ideas, that is, yours."

She sighed. "Then I'd better take a quick shower now — after breakfast I won't get the chance."

The Mamba left her bed with an elegant swing. She had enviably long legs and a nice, firm butt. She knew how to please another woman and practiced it with devotion. She was smart, reliable and kind — the best partner you could ask for, whether you were stuck together for weeks in a small tin can or spending your time in a South Seas paradise.

Nevertheless, I'd like to have a cock again — most preferably a guy who just took me, perhaps even from behind, and screwed me without holding back.

"Not enough yet?" Francine asked from the bathroom doorway while playfully rubbing her towel under her breasts.

I put on a mischievous smile, took the finger out of my pussy and sucked it clean. "Never."

"Should we cancel?"

A focused thought made the remainders of bodily fluids on my skin disappear. Then I closed my legs and swung out of the bed, too. "No. We invited so many guests, that wouldn't be okay."

Francine paused and frowned. "Oh, Jo—who except for Harry knows we're arriving by helicopter? On the mainland, I mean."

"Don't know. Should anyone know?"

"If we're to fly straight to the college, don't we need a permit?"

"I'd expect so, yes."

She stood with arms akimbo—a tempting pose that emphasized her breasts even better. "If you're the target, what simpler way would there be but shooting down the helicopter? Easy to identify, not complicated to hit, no protective Dragon technology, no way to dodge, and hardly any collateral damage to consider while over the sea."

Except for her and Harry. "Damn."

"The college itself is well protected—Arko is over there, the other Mambas are there, probably a few suits, police, security—but on the way there?"

"You're right."

"And what will we do? Should I call Sylvie to pick us up?"

Outside there was a warm sea breeze. I estimated our collective weight—yes, it could work.

"If our opponents notice her departure, they're warned. No, I've got another idea—do you have any issues with a few drops of sea water?"

"Nah—you want to swim or what?"

"Wait for it."

CHAPTER THIRTY-FOUR

After breakfast, and after donning her skintight suit, Francine followed me to the beach near the jetty. I only stopped when the waves were already hugging my toes. "Swimming, after all?"

"No." I made my nanos form an enlarged board. "Step on it and hold tight to me."

She followed my order, placed one arm over my right shoulder, the other below my left arm, and locked her hands around her wrists.

"Good. There'll be a yank."

I swung my arms back and tossed a bunch of nano threads up into the sky, where it unfolded to a large, light-blue kite sail—and yanked us away from the beach into the sea.

"Whoa!" Francine briefly fought for her grip and her balance, but as a Mamba she couldn't be swept from her feet easily.

"Sweeet!" she called from behind while I let the sail grow.

We were gliding across the water with quickly rising speed. Forty-five knots, about eighty kilometers per hour, my *Analogy* computed, not factoring in the currents. There was more to it!

No. Not this day, not with Francine, not with a possible assassination threat. I might need a contingency, even though we were hard to spot with the sky-colored sail.

Along the way I also had to ensure that we were sailing the right course.

Nevertheless it was fun, at not just for me. Once we were

under way, Francine's grip clearly lost tension, and soon I also sensed her support in balancing our kiteboard.

So we were flying across the water, from wavecrest to wavecrest, until we were approaching the Gladstone coastline. Now I had to navigate between the islands off the coast, and now we were also passing small boats, the crews of which gazed after us with curiosity.

Perhaps we also passed an assassin, waiting in vain for our helicopter, without knowing it. Our kite sail was in no way a suitable target for a surface-to-air missile, or whatever someone might have had prepared for us.

Then there was a flash on one of the boats ahead of us, and a plasma bullet pierced my sail.

Chapter Thirty-five

Hats off to them for this fast reaction! I was amazed how quickly they had recognized us and changed their plan—and how they had managed to score one hit. Had I mentioned before that I disliked plasma weapons?

The plasma had burned a few precious nanos, but the sail didn't do our opponents the favor of completely burning away, rather instantly closed the hole and carried us—with a slight course adjustment—straight toward the assassins' boat.

Attack!

We were rushing onto a large-caliber plasma rifle, which I hadn't failed to notice, but the shooter had yet to make up his mind whether he would increase lead and angle to shoot the sail, or whether he'd lower the heavy weapon to aim at us. He had no time for this decision though, as we were there!

His three mates were just drawing their pistols when Francine and I jumped across the boat's side. My Mamba didn't need advice—when she set her feet down between her two opponents, they were already down. My two had even less of a chance. They were unconscious before I had retracted my sail.

Francine grinned at me. "No challenge, ain't it?"

I didn't return the grin. No, these four clowns were no opponents for me. Even if they had shot down our helicopter with the plasma rifle, I could have brought Harry and Francine down safely and thereafter taken care of them. These were small fry and no real opponents. So what was the meaning of this action?

I listened for the start of a fusion generator under the deck, which would then annihilate itself in a disruptor field, but in vain. They had tried this trick in Manhattan and had failed. The true trap wasn't on this boat. Where else?

Francine seemed to follow the same line of thought. She pointed at the knocked-out people. "Small fry. We should leave here."

"Yes. Come." I pointed at the bow—from there we could launch.

Companion?

Yes, Mighty?

You had signaled a fight.

It's over. Oh — please tell the Australian police that there's a driverless boat drifting before Gladstone. The name's Kylie III.

At once.

Francine stepped behind me, and while the board was taking shape again under our feet, I tossed the kitesail up. One yank, and we were on our way.

Where was the trap? Or had our method of traveling taken the other assassins by surprise, too? But they had to know they had to react fast once I was aboard.

With a sigh, I changed our course. *No, I won't grant you the favor of taking the nearest passage between the islands. I'd rather stay unpredictable.*

If we don't spring the second trap this way, that's okay — this time. These people are becoming annoying. I should take care of them.

CHAPTER THIRTY-SIX

K ite sail and board weren't suitable for getting from the shore to the college. But I already knew we wouldn't have to walk, because I could sense my Companion's signature at the jetty.

Achrotzyber remained unimpressed in his place when I launched into a jump close to the jetty and flew toward him in a high arch. At the last moment I flipped the sail around and used it as a drogue parachute, so that Francine and I set down feather-like on the wooden installation.

"Whee!" she commented anyway and took a few deep breaths.

Justina and Tia were waiting at the jetty's mainland end next to a white Martian. Both were attentively observing the surroundings. The question whether this effort might be exaggerated was already at the tip of my tongue, but I swallowed it. Of course it wasn't. Firstly, it was their very own duty to protect me. Secondly, visible measures also served as a deterrent for potential troublemakers. Thirdly, I couldn't safely assess the situation as long as I didn't know our opponents.

I nodded at my Companion. "Let's drive."

Three persons were waiting for us before the entrance to the large auditorium of the Technical College for Applied Dragon Technology of the Central Queensland University Gladstone. I only recognized one—Sabine, Tess's tandem partner.

She was also attentively observing the scene, and would

175

neither be distracted by the heavy off-road car's arrival nor by the two people with her. She looked like calmness incarnate, the very opposite of the black-haired man in the light gray suit and the blonde lady in the bright red skirt suit.

As Tia had the wheel, Justine exited first, then Francine, and only when those two were content with the result of their quick examination were my Dragon Companion and I allowed to exit the car.

Fine gravel on the concrete crunched under my feet when I approached the two strangers.

"Good morning," I called out to them.

"Good morning, ah, Protectress," the man replied. "My name is Joseph Bradshaw, and this is Raissa Mendelevic."

The woman wished me a good morning, too, then we were shaking hands all around, I introduced my escort, and finally I watched Joseph expectantly.

He nodded. "I'm the college's acting dean, and Raissa is my acting assistant."

"Why *acting*?" I asked.

"Because it's your decision who leads this institute."

"Bullshit." I shook my head. "The University administration chose you? Okay. There must be a few lines somewhere on how I envisage this institute and which rules we're collaborating by. I didn't make any rule on the choice of dean. As long as the rules are honored, that's not my business. But if it's important to you, regard yourself as acknowledged. Welcome to the team."

The tension visibly dropped away from them.

"Well then," Joseph said and glanced at Raissa. "Thank you for your trust. Now we shouldn't let the audience wait any longer, should we?"

The audience, of course primarily students, teachers and employees of the college and related faculties like astrophysics, but also a few media representatives, fell silent the moment we entered the auditorium.

There was a speaker's desk on the narrow stage, and someone had been so kind as to prepare steps behind it. I ignored both and just pulled the virtual microphone ring to me.

"Good morning, all. Francine and I are happy that we can finally meet you here. The past week was strenuous, but also interesting. I assume that you followed the broadcasts." I examined the audience's faces—almost all were nodding or smiling. "Fine. That spares us starting over. I'd rather get to the topics that are concerning you. We've got so many exciting tasks before us."

Francine was standing next to me, one knee slightly forward, her arms akimbo, and smiling knowingly. I briefly nodded at her.

"We want to conquer this Solar System. Wherever we have solid surfaces, we will erect bases on planets or moons. Where that doesn't work, we need orbital space stations. For these bases we need power plants, recyclers, healing nano tanks, decontamination, gravity detectors, food producers, protective suits, rescue pods—but with which specifications? You already heard from Francine that we want to establish regular freight and passenger traffic to these bases. If we want to ensure that each base gets a visit at least every two weeks, how many ships do we need? Do we have to plan space traffic lanes so that the ships won't get into each other's way? What kind of equipment do we need for rescue missions in space? What kind of equipment can Dragon technology provide for researchers and prospectors in space?"

I linked arms with Francine. "Such ideas keep us occupied on the long and lonely flight routes in space. You can't have a new breakthrough every other day, right? Luckily, here in Gladstone we have a crystallization point for brilliant young scientists who are more than able to move such ideas forward.

177

We're looking forward to talking with you. So—and before this becomes a solo show, we're going right into the first questions and answers session. Later this morning you'll break out into work groups that Francine and I will visit in turns to discuss with you. Toward evening we'll rejoin in this hall to revisit what this day has yielded. Only one moment—do you have two chairs for us?"

I looked to the side, to the door, where Joseph and Raissa were watching the event. Raissa merely waved behind her, and a young man appeared in the door with two chairs.

He earned applause for his entrance, whereupon he blushed. He blushed even more for Francine's peck on his cheek. That way, he got away lightly—Francine could've kissed him quite differently.

CHAPTER THIRTY-SEVEN

Still inebriated by the students' enthusiasm in the many workgroups, I finally left the institute together with Francine. It was already dark outside and my grumbling stomach reminded me that I hadn't had a meal since breakfast.

"What now?" Francine asked.

"Niko?" I thought aloud.

Achrotzyber approached us. "Shall I accompany you to the island, Companion?"

"We were about to have some food and then paint the town red." Actually I'd rather kiss him good and proper. "Incognito. Have some fun."

"Companion, I do not understand. How can Francine and you appear in Gladstone *unrecognized*?"

Ouch, yes. If I didn't transform, I could forget about that — and Francine anyway. She showed a sour smile. "That wouldn't work anywhere in Australia, would it? Unless we found a place without TV and Internet."

With a sigh, I linked arms with them and pulled them toward the parking lot. "Okay. Let's have some food first, and then we'll consider our options."

"Is that advisable, Companion?"

He didn't have to mention the assassins. "Yes and no, Mighty. It wouldn't be advisable to completely ignore the threat. I know I'm a target. It wouldn't be advisable to expose myself too much. It wouldn't be good to be predictable, so I have to change my location spontaneously and along new routes. If I wanted to be truly safe, I'd have to leave Earth now, and that's out of the question. The impression that I could be intimidated may never come up. So I will go on."

We had arrived at the Martian. Tia was already at the wheel. Justine held the door open for me and watched the rooftops around. "To the harbor?" she asked.

"To Niko." I climbed inside. Francine followed. "What about you?" I asked Achrotzyber.

"I'll drive ahead with Tess and Sabine." He pointed at a second Martian that was parking nearby. "We'll secure the road."

That told me about the additional stress I burdened my bodyguards with. But would it be better to make the island the primary target?

"Sometimes it looks to me like there's nothing you'd fear," Francine said while Justine entered in front.

"I do fear," I admitted. "I can take a lot, but it still hurts. Moreover, I fear for you. Crap, I have to do something!" I slapped my armrest. "I have to find out who's behind all this Jelly crap."

Francine remained silent.

Justine watched the surroundings attentively. After a while, she cleared her throat. "We're checking around regularly and reconciling our data continuously. So far we couldn't find conspicuous persons, but we're on it, Jo."

"Those people are damn good," Tia added. "We didn't learn about the boat—but somehow they must've got it, not to mention the plasma gun. That's a hot lead."

"That shouldn't sound like an accusation," I said.

"We didn't see it like one," Justine replied. "We all must accept that the opponent knows his target and we in turn don't know about him. That's business as usual in personal security."

"Only we're no personal security," Tia said grimly. "We're elite assassins. We know the meanest tricks. We'll turn the tables on them. Tess and Sabine are putting something to-gether, and Monique and Elodie will take care of it."

"And what exactly?" I asked with a sick feeling in my tummy.

"I don't need to know."

Francine took a deep breath.

What did that mean? "Francine, what does that mean?"

"That I don't know, that you don't have to know, and that those two must get along on their own because we won't have contact with them." She placed one hand on my arm. "Trust them. They'll be fine."

"They're Mambas, yes, I know. But we didn't rule out yet that the assassins are connected with the Dragonling master-minds. And how many Dragonlings are still roaming around out there?"

"Too few to cause Monique trouble," Justine said firmly, and I noticed true admiration resonating in her voice. I re-membered the cheerful young woman I had met just a day ago. Hopefully she'd be spared any truly unpleasant experi-ence!

CHAPTER THIRTY-EIGHT

On the last part of the drive I told myself that I shouldn't feel guilty just because I treated myself to a cozy dinner while my Mambas secured the area and protected me. That was their job and their pride. Their job must've been frustratingly easy while I had traveled space. Now they could show their skills again while Francine and I made good for what we couldn't get in flight.

Thinking of Niko's cooking made selfishness easy for me. In exchange, I diligently waited until Tia allowed us to exit, and let Francine go first.

Niko was already standing at his door. "Johanna! Oh, sorry, Protectress! Nice to see you!"

"Thank you, Niko. Good evening." I stood on my tiptoes and pecked his cheek. "Leave the formalities. Just Jo. Do you have a table for us?"

"Sure, always. In the main room, if you don't mind? There's a larger group in the side room."

"Works for me."

The other guests had already noticed something going on. First Tess and Sabine had checked the room, then Niko had hurried to the door—they immediately recognized Francine and me upon our entrance, and spontaneously applauded.

Once we were seated, they left us alone. I could, however, guess what they were whispering about without using my *Analogy* to filter out their conversations.

I didn't want to listen anyway.

Niko held two menus out to us. "I've prepared fresh lamb

giouvetsi."

"That sounds good," I said.

Francine nodded.

"Two? With red wine?"

"And sparkling water," Francine added.

"Okay." Niko tucked the menus back under his arm and scurried away.

Francine let her gaze wander around the guest room, and then down herself.

"With this brooch you're always perfectly dressed for the occasion," I assured her. "No matter what else you're wearing."

"Yes, yes." She rested her elbows on the table. "It's okay. I've got used to being nude, and I've got used to wearing this second skin, and I've got no clue about fashion anyway. People accept us this way — on the island anyway, those in this area know we get along without clothes out there, and the others were spacemen in uniform. Only — that way we're segregating ourselves somehow. Our appearance in Brisbane back then was more adequate — more normal. I'd say we should consider that, too. If we want to meet people on eye level — pardon — we need to adapt." She watched my facial expression. "You don't like that?"

"No." I sighed. "No, it's something else. I'm traveling light. What I need, I'm wearing on my body or inside. Everything else is needless luxury, to be left behind once I have to leave in a rush again. Such is life on the run from the Cartel."

Francine rested her chin on one hand and nodded.

"That was different long ago, admitted. During my active time in the trade I had a wardrobe full of fine dresses. See-through blouses, short skirts, daring cocktail dresses — what the clients were expecting and I could just afford. Plus some sports gear and simple stuff for the lectures. Later I bought something nice here and there to act a role. Recently I simply don't find the time for shopping."

"Too bad. Perhaps you should just take your time."

"You'd like to come along, wouldn't you?"

My pilot smiled, leaned back, and placed one arm on the next seat's backrest, which favored her breasts and made more than one of the male guests take a deep breath.

"I have to," she said. "That's a direct result of our tour here. I'll have to attend meetings all around the world, and I need appropriate clothing. The space suit was okay last week—we were coming straight from space, so to speak—but that excuse won't last much longer. Moreover, I want to have serious discussions with those people, and that won't work if they're staring at my tits and drooling."

"No. I know the problem. Okay, I've often done it in reverse—I used my tits to distract people. But it's the same principle." I had an idea. "If we'd just adapt to the people here, shopping in Gladstone would do, but that wasn't what you had on your mind, right?"

"What's wrong with shopping in Gladstone?"

"Nothing. I only thought if you want to dress up for international appearances, you might want to look prestigious. After all, the press will scrutinize and comment on your choice of dress."

She raised her eyebrows. "And?"

"So we'll have to carefully pick your garment. For that we simply need more choice—or even a tailor. Give me two days."

"I'm not sure what you're up to."

"You'll like it. And now let's have a drink."

CHAPTER THIRTY-NINE

A noise from outside made me prick up my ears. Hadn't that been the hiss of a plasma round?

With regret I gazed at the delicious, only half-eaten giouvetsi and placed the cutlery down.

Francine looked up. "I heard it, too. Eat your dinner and let your folks do their work."

That surprised me. "You think so?"

"That was a single shot. There's no reason to assume they wouldn't control the situation. Relax."

That didn't come easy to me. I picked up my fork and dabbled at my meal.

"Letting go isn't easy for you, is it?" Francine asked.

"No. I've been on my own for so many years—reacting fast was crucial for survival. You don't discard that like an old jacket."

She sighed. "I understand that. Those are trained behavior patterns you don't want to put down, aren't they?"

"Actually not, no."

She pointed at my plate. "Nevertheless, here and now it's time for a different trained behavior pattern. Eat, or I'll tattle on you to Nanette."

"Oh." I hurried to eat the next bite.

Francine placed her Turkish coffee cup down and gave me a look of reproach. "Don't glance at the door. You take a break."

"Yes . . ."

"Jo!"

"Yes, okay." With an effort—and closed eyes—I managed to focus on my own coffee cup. *Coffee cup! Coffee cup! Coffee cup!*

The sweet hot coffee tasted exquisite and indeed distracted me for a moment. A rush of air close to me made me start. Tess sat down on the next chair and smiled at me.

"You're admirably calm. I had feared you'd come storming outside upon the first shot."

I pointed at Francine. "She forbade it."

Tess raised an eyebrow. "Fascinating. You're listening to Francine?"

"Sometimes," Francine said.

"What's going on outside?" I asked. "Or did you just come in for a coffee?"

"Not a bad idea." She waved for Niko and pointed at my cup. "Okay, there was a guy with pistol and rifle outside about to get in here. Tia blocked his way, and when he tried to level his gun at her, Justine placed a warning shot in front of his feet. He was so scared that he dropped everything and peed his pants."

"And that took so long?"

"Nah. Of course we checked the area to see if he was alone—or whether someone wanted to see how good we are—and then turned him in to the police. Then we had our observations recorded. Yes—and I'm already here."

"Already."

Tess only smiled. The smile became her—I could understand what Reginald saw in her. She was a ruler, just like him.

Now she frowned. "A penny for your thoughts."

"I see a strong alpha and a smile without which this world would be a poorer place. That makes me happy."

PART THREE—LEAVE

CHAPTER FORTY

The side road ended abruptly in a cul-de-sac, surrounded by five spacious villas. Tia stopped the Martian. I peeked outside. "Which one is it? I thought you'd accommodate them more remotely for some quietude."

"They've been living remotely in Switzerland. Peter suggested to give them a feel of freedom and normality—they shouldn't think they're prisoners. The beach is only five hundred meters away—right there ahead through the narrow passage. There's a shopping mall in this village. They can go there if they like to."

"What's this place called?"

"The village? Tannum Sands. It's on a headland—the Boyne River in the west opens into the sea north of here, and the beach is east of here. There's a park on the tip—the place is a recreation area and a residential area for the aluminum factory on Boyne Island. That should help our protégées with acclimatizing. You can more or less easily observe who's coming and going, and it's still not far from Gladstone or the island."

"Ah, okay. And which villa is it?"

"The five around. The women should have a little privacy, so we needed room. The two houses at the entrance to the cul-de-sac are currently ours, too — that's where the psychologists and the agents live."

"Agents?"

"Personal security. We can't rule out that some would want to take the women back — especially our problem child."

"Ah. Yes, that's conclusive."

"Arko said the child could quite well become the prime father of a new breed. So we're guarding the place."

"Who's *we?*"

"There are always two of us Mambas here, currently Gwen and Avril. They won't leave the mother unguarded. For the general security, we reconcile with the agents. Only women, by the way."

"Yes, I already noticed that part. The people around don't matter?"

"Ask the shrinks."

"I'll do that."

Justine stood outside and held the door for me, so I was allowed to exit. Avril was already waiting at the door of the middle house, thus showing me the way.

"Good morning, Jo."

"Good morning, Avril. How's it going?"

"Nothing to report, Jo. But Alara isn't doing well. Well, you'll talk with her now. Or do you want to talk with Polly first?"

"Polly is her counselor?"

"Yes."

"I'd like to talk with Polly later. For now, I'll talk with Alara. Can we be alone somewhere?"

Avril hesitated for just a moment. "Yes, sure."

"I can protect her. If you like, you could have an hour or two off."

"Oh. Well—yes, sure." Obviously, that idea hadn't oc-
curred to her yet. "Alara is in her room. Second door to the
right."

"Thanks."

Alara didn't answer my first knock. Upon the second attempt
I heard a rather unwilling, "Yes please?"

I entered and closed the door behind me. Alara had curled
up in a seat near the terrace door and was staring outside. Her
long dark hair was flowing down the armrest, and aside from
her round belly, she was tall and slender, which her white
nightgown could hardly conceal.

And now? I didn't know much about psychology, but I felt
like an intruder, and I didn't want to reinforce this impression, if possible. So I took neither the seat next to her nor the
bed, but chose a chair on the other side of the terrace door.

I waited patiently until her curiosity won. After a good
quarter of an hour, she glanced at me for the first time.

She frowned. "You're new."

"I'm Jo. Johanna Meier."

"Ah—the Dragon woman. What are you doing here?"

"Looking after you. Hearing how you're doing. Asking if I
can help."

"Help." She placed a hand on her belly. "I'm beyond help."

"Do you want to tell me more?"

Thereupon she fell silent for a while. Finally, she sighed.
"You won't leave before I do, will you?"

"I'll leave now if you want. But I'd like to help. I'm worried, and I'm unhappy as long as I don't know whether I
could do anything."

"This isn't your business."

"No. It's your business alone."

"You want the brat."

"What for? My Companion is a Dragon. If I want Dragon

children, I'll ask him."

That took some wind out of her sails. She brooded for a while, then she asked, "What are you here for, then?"

"For helping."

"I'm beyond help." She rose, plucked the nightgown straps away so that it dropped to the floor, and stood before me. "Look at me. Raped, abused as birthing machine, the future mother of a monster."

"Your child is no monster."

"It's the son of a monster — it will be a monster."

"Why?"

"Why?" She spread her arms. "Why do you ask? Those — those bastards! Perverted chimeras, half Dragon, half human — monsters."

I rose myself and let my black nano suit slide down my body.

"Look at me," I prompted her. "Am I a monster?"

"What? No, of course not."

"Look closely." I made a very slow full turn. "What do you see?"

"I don't understand."

"Sit down."

She automatically followed my order. I sat down, too. That way I could better catch her gaze.

"Alara, I was born an ordinary human." Did she understand that? "But you called me Dragon woman. Why?"

"You — but you are a Dragoness, aren't you?"

"I can assume the shape of a Dragon, yes. I command the full powers of a Dragon. I am Dragon and human together — I'm way more Dragon than your child will ever be. If your child were a monster, I would be, first."

"You a monster?"

"Hard to imagine? Why might that be? Because I'm friendly to you?"

"You're a woman." She pursed her lips. "That's something else. But this here" — she pointed at her belly — "is an alien. You don't know how it is to be abused like that!"

I leaned forward with my sweetest smile and took her hands into mine. Outside, I was calm, but inside, I had to fight for my self-control.

"Alara. It was eighteen years ago. Back then, I was studying in Melbourne. There was a man I had rejected, I called him Dandy. He was rich and spoiled and didn't accept my rejection. One day, when I was traveling home on my bike, there was a dark van at the curb, and I had to slow down. Suddenly someone pressed a stinking cloth on my face."

She stared at me with big eyes.

"When I woke up, I was hanging from the ceiling with tied arms. My legs were tied, too, but in spread position. My clothes were gone. Before me stood this Dandy in a white suit, and he held a whip in his hand."

I felt a tug, but didn't let her hands go.

"In this cellar room there was a table with manacles, a wire cage, and other niceties. I want to spare you the details, but I would test everything he had. His whips, his canes, his scalpel."

Alara's mouth formed an *O*.

"I spent many months in his care. He raped me at least daily, and he didn't bother caring for contraception. He didn't care that I became pregnant. That didn't prevent him from further torturing and mutilating me. Finally, when there was hardly any life left in me and he'd become weary of me, he dumped me — us — in a landfill to die. I was very lucky back then that the garbage man had a look before tipping his load, otherwise I'd been buried alive. So please don't tell me I wouldn't know how it is."

"But . . . the child?"

"Yes. The child. I was too weak, and there was a

miscarriage. I never learned to know this child, my torturer's bastard."

"You're lucky."

She shrank back when I stared at her. "Lucky? Nobody asked me! Nobody asked me whether I wanted to be pregnant, and nobody asked me whether I wanted to have this child, but nevertheless — it would have been *my* child! My own flesh and blood. Nobody . . . nobody asked the child if it wanted to live."

I could no longer hold back my tears.

"Today . . . today it would be a grown-up."

Again there was a tug — but this time not to free her hands from my grip, but to pull me into her arms. I let it happen.

Something rumbled under me, and I cautiously unwrapped myself from the hug. My tears had finally stopped and dried, and I asked myself who was treating whom right then.

"The baby's kicking," Alara explained.

I placed one hand on her belly. "It doesn't know what we're talking about, otherwise it would keep quiet."

"How could you cope with that?"

"He didn't ask about that." After three deep breaths I was able to continue. "I didn't have the choice to escape the torture toward death. I always told myself — it's just pain, Jo. Only neural impulses, only messages."

"And later?"

"I'm telling myself the same. Every time I have to think of it. It was just pain."

"No — I meant the baby."

My baby. "I didn't know it. I've suppressed every thought of it." Which I did again — or would rather have done.

"Would you like to have children?"

"Me? Children? I can't imagine. When would I have time to care for them?"

"You have time to care for me."

"Yes. That's important to me. Perhaps it's different—my task encompasses all people, not just a small family. Not just my team on the island, a few friends, a few women rescued from deep distress, but truly all. I do have children, millions of children I have to protect—from extraterrestrial invaders, from war, hunger and misery, from evil men."

"From evil mothers."

"No. Only from thoughtless decisions. Give your child a chance, Alara. It can't help what its father is. And whether it will become a monster or a gallant protector is in your hands, will be the result of your loving upbringing."

"I thought—" She paused. "No, of course not. Of course you won't take my child away."

"No, we won't do that." I rose and looked outside. "Shouldn't we sit outside, and you can tell me your story? I'd like to hear it."

She pondered for a moment. "I don't like to talk about it, but I think I can tell you. Now that I know your story, it's easier for me. You can understand how I feel."

"Take your time. Come."

She glanced back at her nightgown, then shrugged and followed me outside, where a few cushioned wooden chairs were waiting in the shadow.

CHAPTER FORTY-ONE

Alara breathed heavily. After all she had told me I understood well why. The gangsters had purposefully picked healthy women with little social contact who wouldn't be missed. These were kidnapped and initially kept captive and isolated until the victims had resigned themselves to their situation. They hadn't had to endure much physical abuse, as they were needed in good health for a later pregnancy. Moreover they shouldn't develop suicidal tendencies—nevertheless the imprisonment had left its traces, and to talk about those hadn't come easy to her, as I could clearly see.

As far as my nanos could tell, her biological parameters were okay, her child wasn't at risk.

"Now, what do you say?" she asked.

"I'm very sorry we didn't get on to this gang earlier and couldn't free you earlier. That this negligence already affected my predecessor doesn't make it any better."

"It's not your fault."

"No. I can and I have to live with the fact that I can't fight all injustice of this world at once. I still feel personally touched by your fate."

"You suffered worse."

"In exchange, I didn't have to bear it so long." I calculated. "More than ten years!"

"You know what, Jo? Now that I've got all that off my chest, it sounds like a story long gone by to me."

"It's long gone by. Do you know what I noticed?"

"No."

"You never mentioned your baby. Not even once!"

"Really?"

"For me that means — the baby is not part of your past. It's got nothing to do with it."

"You think so?"

"Consider that. It could be a part of your future — a better future."

"Under your lead."

"Your child should decide upon its future alone. I will not make any rules. But if your son looks for other people who understand him and his situation better, he's welcome with us."

"You mean, you let him go?"

"Alara, listen around. All the people working for me do it voluntarily. The teachers at the University, the people provisioning or protecting us — they could leave any time. They wouldn't have to ask me for approval. The same applies to you and your child. We're offering help and protection, but we don't force anything on you. I'd only ask for one favor — if you want to leave, tell someone in person, not by some slip of paper. We all want to be sure it was no kidnapping."

"Oh."

"Pardon me for telling you so straightforwardly, but you need to know this — until we find out who's behind this Swiss case, there's a slight risk that they will want you back — or more precisely, your son."

"Oh. Yes, of course."

"If you want to get out of here anyway, tell the girls. They'll get something done."

For a while, Alara stared across the bushes that separated the garden from the next estate.

"I can't do that," she finally said. "It's not right."

"What do you mean?"

"Let you keep me. If I'm truly free, as you say, I'll have to care for myself. Job and all."

"Not in this condition."

"What? Oh—no, okay. Until the baby's here, I have to accept your hospitality. But after that I must see how I'll get along."

"I understand. It's good if you take your life into your own hands. I expressly support that. Only—you have to nurse a baby. I don't know much about it, but doesn't that take a lot of time in the beginning?"

"Other mothers solved that problem, too."

"I only want to say—you're not pressed. Perhaps we'll find a job you can do part time and nearby, until you find something suitable. What can you do?"

"What do you mean?"

"Did you learn a profession?"

"I jobbed. Filling shelves in the supermarket, waitress in a bar, newspaper delivery, and so on."

"Mmm. Perhaps you should do some training first."

"I can't afford that."

I rose, squatted next to her and placed a hand on her belly. "If you really want to do the right thing, you can't do less than the best for your child. It's good that you're maintaining your pride or found it again. Keep hold of it, but don't let your pride get in your way. I can afford to fund you until your child starts school. I can get you job training. If you don't want to get all that for free, that's okay for me—but I won't take money from you anyway." She was about to protest. "Hush. That's not the way a Dragon community works. You take what you need and you give what you can afford. If you want to pay a debt, you have to do something for the community that I can't do. Raising a young Dragonling is such a worthy task. Caring for people in distress is another worthy task."

"I don't understand."

"You have to rethink, Alara. It's not about money. Give

something of yourself. That's what counts. If your smile were all you could give, I'd take your smile and deem myself appropriately paid."

"Just my smile?"

"Consider how many people you can make happy just by listening to them and smiling at them. Sick people, old and lonely people, or children. But there are so many other ways—take your time and consider what you'd prefer. If you'd like to serve drinks in a Tahiti beach bar, that's okay."

"Tahiti?"

"Just an example. I wanted to mention something exotic. Did I pick the right one?"

For the first time since my arrival, Alara laughed. "No, probably not. But I got your point. You're very generous."

"I've been working hard and long to afford this generosity. Now I'm enjoying it."

CHAPTER FORTY-TWO

A lara finally fell into a peaceful sleep. While my suit nanos covered me up again, I picked up her nightgown and covered her with it. Then I sneaked outside.

Before the door, Avril, Tia, Justine and three unknown women were waiting for me. Two of the strangers had the professional stance of security details, even if they were wearing shorts and halter tops. The third woman, with gray hair, short-sleeved blouse, and Capri pants, approached me.

"How's she doing?" she asked.

"She's sleeping."

"Your visit was quite long."

"We had a lot to talk about."

"Really? She'd never truly open up."

"I can understand that. She trusted many things to me I'd rather not talk about either."

"How did you achieve that?"

"I told her my own story. She recognized that I could empathize with her about her fate. You're Polly?" The woman nodded. "That's something you can't learn unless you submit to torture yourself, and I wouldn't advise anyone to do so. In any case, she got it all off her chest, and I think it did her good."

"We're worried about the child."

"You no longer have to be. I think she understood that the child is not part of her past, but can be a part of her future."

"Well, then . . ."

I didn't evade Polly's glance. "She'll need a lot of help until she comes to terms with this new situation. Perhaps she'll have doubts again. You'll have to make clear that she's truly welcome, that there's no time pressure, and that we're supporting her striving for independence unconditionally. I also told her that I'll pay for her job training. She'll need help to figure out what she wants to do and what she can do without neglecting her child's education."

"Oh—I thought the child . . ."

"The child belongs to the mother," I interrupted Polly. "If Alara wants it, we'll take care of the boy, and once he's old enough he can decide himself anyway. But if she wants her child to grow up unburdened, we'll leave them alone."

I glanced at Avril. "I told her that you're protecting her and not locking her in, and I think she understood. Also, from whom you're protecting her."

"That's good. Until now I didn't have the impression she really got it."

"It'll surely take some more time for her to take it to heart. Until then you'll need some more patience. For today, I'll say goodbye. Thank you for your good work." Then I turned to Tia and Justine. "In any case, I've tested your patience enough. Let's leave."

CHAPTER FORTY-THREE

I woke up with a familiar feeling of weight around my chest and a humid palm on my left breast, a gentle pressure against my right shoulder blade and my likewise humid, warm butt. That was Francine, again snuggled up to me the way we had fallen asleep after our lovemaking the evening before.

I'd rather remain lying there, but I had given her a promise for that day, and if we didn't have breakfast soon, we wouldn't get away at all.

With a slight movement I signaled my desire to unwrap from her hug. Francine took her hand from my breast and let it slowly slide down. *Oh damn, yes!* By placing my right knee up I made way for her fingers to feel my sticky pubes and also pulled my labia apart. Francine's hand found fresh wetness. By moving slightly more away from me she made room for me to further spread my legs and also make my inner labia part. *Yes, girl, make me hot!*

No.

We both didn't know how often we'd wake up together, how much time there was left for us, but it still should be her day — if at all, I should please her, not vice versa.

If she was in the right mood at all — so far she had only felt her way a bit forward. With regret, I rolled out of her reach.

Her knowing smile made questions unnecessary. "Time for breakfast."

The spaceship felt alien, smelled alien. In principle, all

Barracudas should be identical, only differing in log entries and computer configuration, but I sensed the difference right away.

"Which one is it?" I asked my seatmate.

"The *Mayhem*," Sylvie replied. "The *Mischief* is in the dock, and Arko took the *Menace* for a test flight. We've put the next four on hold until we know which enhancements we'll need."

"How's the pilot training going?" Francine asked from behind.

"Going well — at least in theory and in the simulator. The folks are crazy for flying themselves — but now that you came up with the commission topic, there are new discussions whether they can be allowed at the stick at all. Anyway, as long as there's a trainer aboard, we can ignore the formal stuff and get on with our program."

"And then we're tearing you away from that," I noticed.

"Nah — this week was scheduled for tests. The *Mayhem* is only the backup, but as long as Arko has no trouble, I needn't fly alongside." She pointed at the screen before her. "We're almost there. Where shall I drop you?"

"Where are we allowed?"

"Wherever you like, as long as we're not putting anyone in danger. I just have to announce it."

"In that case, the harbor would be fine."

"Where at the harbor? In front of the opera?"

"No, the opposite side." With a flick of my fingers, I zoomed in on the harbor. "Here, right above the Overseas Terminal is another jetty, right in front of our hotel. There we won't impede the ferries."

"Okay." She dragged the location to her main screen, tapped a few additional spots, and thus sent her request to the Sydney approach control. Shortly afterward we got the approval, together with a short message that Sylvie moved to my screen.

"*Protectress, welcome to Sydney!*"

The young man at the Park Hyatt reception spoke exactly the same line to me. Only then did he pay some attention to my company and blushed. "Oh. Welcome, Knight Francine."

"I've booked a suite and I'm expecting visitors," I said.

"Of course. The ladies and gentlemen have already arrived."

"If that's so, we won't let them wait any longer. If it suits them, of course."

"Naturally. The bellboy will take care of your luggage. Is it still outside?"

"We don't have luggage—not yet."

"Oh. Okay, then . . ." He looked at an older man who'd been waiting in the background.

That man now stepped forward and reached out a hand. "Richard Mosley, *Protectress*, Knight. I'm the director and bid you a warm welcome in our house. We're striving to fulfill your every desire. Regard yourself invited."

"Invited?" Francine echoed.

"Our house won't take money from a Paladin of the Order of the Dying Lioness. That's a question of honor. Please allow me to lead."

He did that and led us to the elevator. "Did you have a comfortable journey?"

"Quite so," I agreed. "Knight Sylvie brought us here comfortably—she'll follow us once she's safely parked our transport means."

"Knight Sylvie will be our guest as well?"

"Yes. The suite's large enough, isn't it?"

"It has only two bedrooms, regrettably."

"That's enough. We get along well together."

Including Sylvie in his invitation caused me as little trouble as accepting his invitation in general. The only *advantage* his property acquired this way was a higher probability of me burdening their budget again. Whether other people would regard this a reason to stay in this hotel, too, was their business.

Richard led us to the suite door, opened it, and gave us two code cards. "Have a pleasant stay. If you need anything . . ."

"Thank you, Richard, not at this moment."

I passed him and examined the spacious room behind the door — of course with a view of the famous opera house.

Francine followed me and closed the door. "I thought we'd go shopping?"

"We will, too. We'll surely find some nice clothes for you. I only thought that you'd need something better for this or that formal occasion, not off the rack."

She cocked her head. "What are you up to?"

A knock at the door spared me from answering. Of course Francine wouldn't allow me to open. She first checked the camera image, which showed us an older man in a dark suit, a mid-fortyish man in gray, and a young lady in blue, then she opened the door and allowed the three inside.

The man in dark red hurried toward me. *"Protectress* Johanna, I'm delighted!"

"Welcome, Jean," I greeted him and hugged him. "May I introduce? Francine, this is Jean-Paul Mercère, the uncrowned king of the international fashion scene. Jean, Knight Francine Besson."

"I'm delighted, Knight Francine!" He took her offered hand, gave a kiss on the hand and then watched her deep, elegant curtsy with awe.

"Jean, Francine and I will have to attend a few official events during the next months, and I want to assure that primarily she is impeccably dressed — no matter whether for a daytime conference or for the evening after. That's why I asked for a measurement meeting."

"Naturally, naturally. My turn to introduce, if I may?

Georgio, my tailor, and Amelia, my assistant. They will take your measurements, and then we'll talk about a few sketches that I brought, okay?"

"Gladly. I assume the measuring will be easier if we undress?"

"Naturally — but only if it doesn't inconvenience you."

"Not at all." I nodded at Francine, and we both undressed. I hadn't mentioned that we didn't wear any underwear — Georgio harrumphed in embarrassment, and Amelia blushed.

"Such natural beauty!" Jean swooned. "Ah, such grace and grandesse in presenting your body!"

Francine, Sylvie and I were ambling through the Rocks and past the small shops' windows. Sylvie had thought ahead for us and provided us with shorts, halter tops and flip flops, with which we were rather inconspicuous compared to our black combat suits.

Okay, perhaps not entirely inconspicuous, as the metallic-white and very tight-fitting shorts presented our shapes as well as the tops did, but if that made people look at our legs, booties and tits instead of our faces, the purpose was served.

I still had doubts about our disguise. Here and there, a passerby frowned or nudged his neighbor as if asking — *are those the ones?*

My nano-aided silver-blond colored hair might have assisted the deception. Francine had brushed her hair the opposite way, and after all, we were three. Sylvie's flaming red hair attracted a lot of attention, and that way we looked a lot different from the group of two that had been on every TV screen on Earth during the last week.

"What are we looking for?" Sylvie asked casually, while we were passing one of the souvenir shops, the shelves of which were bursting with plush koalas, kangaroos, and funny hats with cork dangling from the brim.

"We're not looking for anything," I replied. "Today is off —

no plans, nothing to achieve, and if Francine or you find something nice to wear, we'll take it."

"I don't really know how shopping works," Francine admitted. "That wasn't part of our training. And later I didn't need it. On the island, Nanette took care of everything, and Freddie and Beate bought the stuff for the covert operations."

"First of all you must remember to pay," Sylvie reminded her. "Otherwise we're in trouble."

"I'll take care of that," I said. "I have some shopping experience from the past."

"Frequent?"

"Quite so. The clients liked to see something new, and moreover, I had a lot of wear and tear."

"Wear and tear?"

"Some guys were into tearing my panties or blouse apart, and others were eager to fuck me outside, well, and if the sperm stains wouldn't disappear, the piece was done. That went under expenses."

"Well. Expenses?"

"During my time as whore. I told about that, didn't I?"

Sylvie raised both eyebrows. "If you did, I suppressed it. I know you as Velvet and as Protectress. You were a whore?"

"Eva Keller's best in class."

Francine smirked. She already knew my story, up to the copulating quarks.

"That sounds like you're proud of it."

"I am. I made a conscious decision. I was aware that the job isn't very reputable, but I was at the very bottom, and for me, it was a way up — that got me a stipend for Dragon technology. I can be proud of that."

"And it didn't bother you that you had to do it with every stranger?"

"Not every stranger. I could deny someone — but I did that very rarely, as a matter of principle." Like with Dandy. "Yes, it did bother me, but that's like with pain—it goes away. However, most of the time I had my fun."

CHAPTER FORTY-FOUR

The first sales assistant, spotting us when we entered the super-distinguished fashion shop in the newly opened Space Mall, made a face. With our cheap clothes and the bags from several inexpensive boutiques, we didn't exactly fit in.

I simply dropped my bags at Francine's and Sylvie's feet near the door, approached the assistant closely, linked arms with him and held my credit card under his nose. "Young man," I said to him, ignoring his gray temples. "Today is your lucky day. We selected your shop to fill the gap between the fun items and the designs that Jean-Paul Mercère yet has to tailor for us. Can you show us something adequate?"

"Mercère? You're pulling my leg."

"I understand that you're surprised. But you didn't answer my question. Does that mean you're not interested?"

When would the lady in the back intervene? She had been listening in since we had entered the shop. But the man at my arm just started to really look at my face. Then he glanced at Francine and Sylvie, again at me, then at my card. A knowing smile crept onto his face. "Of course we're able to show you something adequate. Just a moment, please."

He moved past me, dodged the bags on the floor as elegantly as he passed Sylvie, took a small sign with the word *Closed* from a holder next to the door and hung it against the glass door. Then he bent down and locked its floor bolt.

When he rose, he made a stern face. "My ladies, I'm at your command. What would you like to see first? Something festive or for business events?"

Now his colleague showed up. "Robert, what's going on?"

He held out an arm to her. *"Protectress,* this is Martine. Martine, the *Protectress* with her knights Francine and Sylvie. I'd like to counsel our clients exclusively and without interruptions — would you assist me there?"

It took a few seconds until she had processed his words. Then there was a visible *click* inside her. "Oh. Of course!"

"Good!" Francine commented and now placed her bags down as well. "What do you wear for informal workshops at international conferences?"

"What do you wear in the afternoon at the Park Hyatt bar?" Sylvie turned to Martine. "It should allow for free movement."

The addressed woman smirked. "I've heard of Velvet Island. I fear your understanding of free movement is different from ours, but we'll see what can be done."

CHAPTER FORTY-FIVE

I wasn't allowed to enter the bar of our own hotel first. Sylvie went ahead, thus allowed to present her new gear first. With black pleat-front shorts, black pantyhose and black pumps, she wore a gossamer black organza blouse, and as that truly covered nothing, a scanty vest over it. Lipstick and nail polish, matching her hair color, provided fiery highlights.

She celebrated her entrance with grace and charm, as appropriate for a Mamba who had learned to adapt to every environment.

As a consequence, the current guests collectively suffered a gaping mouth and were hardly able to look away. At least that was until Francine entered, and then they were no longer able to decide where to stare.

My co-pilot wore a shoulder-free short cocktail dress that ran skintight down to her hips and ended in a swinging skirt that wonderfully highlighted her enviably long, fishnet-clad legs. But the icing on the cake was her dark red high heels.

In comparison, my appearance in long pants and short jacket was decent and inobtrusive. In my opinion, the two of them deserved to be the main act of the show.

There'd almost been a commotion—understandably, the hotel didn't like to see prostitutes soliciting on the premises, and the bar director seemingly hadn't been told about the newly arrived VIPs yet. He came rushing in with high brows and stern face—his intent clearly written on his face. Before he could address the two Mambas, I stepped into his path.

"I'll be with you in a moment," he said and tried to walk

around me.

I, however, linked arms with him and pulled him aside. "One word, boss. You don't want to make a mistake. I'm the *Protectress* Johanna Meier, and the two over there aren't just my bodyguards, but also Knights of the Order of the Dying Lioness. You surely won't draw wrong conclusions from their good looks, will you?"

"Ah, what? Protectress? Oh." Then there was the *click*. "Of course not, *Protectress*. Pardon me. Was it so obvious?"

"For me, it was." During my active time as an escort, men on a similar mission had often rushed toward me. "But don't worry. You're doing your job, and we're doing ours, and we can talk about misunderstandings. This one remains between us, okay?"

"Okay." He took several deep breaths. "What else can I do for you?"

"You could have someone bring me a glass of red sparkling wine. I'll be sitting outside."

"Gladly."

While I was still asking myself how long my two girls would remain alone, the first man plucked up courage and approached Sylvie to invite her for a drink. Brave!

Chapter Forty-six

Three women in one suite – that meant neither of us could just take a man to her room. We were dependent on their hospitality. That also meant I didn't have to throw anyone out before sunrise, but could simply get up and leave my sleeping host whenever it suited me. After a kiss blown on his cheek I picked up my clothes and sneaked out.

He'd probably wake up with a magnificent boner and be disappointed – but he didn't really have reason to complain. In exchange for his two cocktails he had received a royal equivalent.

Upon entering our suite I'd almost stepped on an envelope that someone had pushed through under the door the old-fashioned way. My curiosity triggered, I extended a claw, cut it open and removed a narrow card.

Meet for joint breakfast? R.

With a sigh I replaced the card, tossed the envelope onto the coffee table, my clothes into a chair, and ambled to the bathroom. I felt like a hot-cold shower.

An idea came up. *Oh yes.*

The suite door, protected by highly sophisticated technology, withstood me for less than three seconds, and that only because I was balancing a large tray with my other hand.

After quietly closing the door, I set the tray down on the table and arranged my delivery. The tray went on the cupboard, and after a last check I removed a piece of lint.

Then I stood next to the bedroom door and knocked three

times.

"Who's there?" came a surprised call.

With a Japanese accent I said, "Sir had ordered breakfast for two."

"What? No. One moment!"

I heard the sheets rustle, then the scratching of a bathrobe sleeve, quick steps to the door, which was torn open, and then Rashid almost stumbled over me.

"Jo?"

I plucked the hem of my chambermaid skirt. "At your service. May I pour for you?"

"Gladly, but how?"

I poured a coffee for him. "We've had breakfast together before, so I have a good idea what you might order. So I sneaked into the hotel kitchen, prepared your breakfast, dressed up as maid and set your table. I interpreted your message that the hotel staff doesn't need to know about our meeting."

"That's right, but how did you do it?"

"Sorry, Velvet won't tell her tricks." It would have been difficult to explain anyway why nobody had noticed what I had done in the hotel kitchen in the early morning.

He laughed and watched the silver cloche that covered his plate. "I hope you'll tell me what we're having for breakfast."

"Gladly." I placed my hand on the knob. "A specialty of the kitchen rat—gravad lax with roasted potato chips and beaten egg whites. Voilá."

The cloche came off, and Rashid marveled.

He was even more filled with wonder after taking the first bite—once I had uncovered my plate, too, and taken the opposite seat.

"Allah help me. That's—incredible. I have to meet this—how did you say—*kitchen rat.*"

"She's sitting before you."

"You?" He picked up another crunchy chip with his fingers. "You can cook, too? Johanna, if you didn't already have your Dragon Companion, I'd offer my entire wealth to take you as my wife."

Really? I had just diligently prepared the meal. Embarrassed, I took a bite myself.

Oh.

I took my time tasting the full fish aroma, the crunchy chips, the airy egg, indulged myself in the aftertaste, before I answered.

"I think I'd try to outbid you."

Again he laughed. "Seriously. Where did you learn to cook so well?"

"By myself. I trained in Palermo—and en route in space. The onboard cooking can be very boring."

"If that's the core of your secret, I'll send my personal cook with you next time."

The egg was really very airy. "I'd say boredom isn't all. Some insight in the physical process is also required."

"It's hard for me to think of physics in this context."

"Many men fare the same in my presence."

The sheikh smiled. "We're getting off topic. Actually I should focus on this treat now. We'll talk later."

Rashid placed his cup down and directed a regretful glance at his crumb-free emptied plate. "Let me get to the point. Your tour last week caused quite a stir, as expected. The economy is outright euphoric—market rates are exploding. There are numerous voices warning about exploitation of the Solar System, about a new cartel, or about forgetting the poor again in this process. We expected this, and when our information campaign starts next week, we'll show how we will include all people. That again won't make the large industrial nations happy, but my advisors hope they can convince them that a harmonization of prosperity will foster more social peace and thus also a better economic climate in the long run—I guess that's quite to your liking."

"Very much. Thank you." Even though I wouldn't depend on it alone. The current market boom would wash a lot of money into the companies, and my strategically placed shares would direct this money to my liking.

"There's political resistance, too, however. In some cases, the people simply feel swamped or run over. They need time to adapt to the new situation. What worries me more is the fundamental resistance."

"Who?"

"The Chinese. They're arguing it's criminal to deliver the enemy a new long-range spaceship to his doorstep. They're strictly against a new expedition."

"Is that the only reason?"

"Why are you asking?"

"I suspect there's something else behind it. The Chinese didn't get over the way I rained on their parade. They were close to superseding the Americans and Russians as world power, and now they have to watch how their newly gained leader position is melting away. If we're now placing another Dragon population ahead of them, their prospects are permanently poor."

"That's an interesting analysis."

"I fear further resistance."

"Well, we knew before that it wouldn't be easy."

"No." I stared at a point on the wall behind him. "I just didn't expect them to go that far."

"What do you mean?"

"I cannot prove it, but there's more and more evidence. A secret research station in the Himalaya foothills. New weapons based on Dragon technology, together with the most recent assaults on me that clearly surpass the abilities of a little terror gang . . ."

"You think the Chinese are behind it?"

"I can't rule that out. Or the masterminds have the Chinese government under control in some way. This way or that, we must not let them stop us."

"We have to operate with caution."

That wasn't what he had wanted to say—he couldn't fool an experienced poker player like me. "For now, I won't take action against the Chinese. The Solar System exploration is enough reason to continue the spaceship construction program. There's still a lot of time before we're able to start another mission." And who knew what Monique would find out in the meantime?

Rashid breathed a sigh of relief.

"Anything else that troubles you?" I asked.

He made a defensive gesture. "Not now. You gave me something to think about. What will you do next?"

"Go on a vacation. And thereafter, I'll take intensive care of the development and refinement of the wormhole tunnel. No—that's not quite right. Next I'll make sure that the remainders of our breakfast will disappear into the kitchen unnoticed."

CHAPTER FORTY-SEVEN

Freddie's yacht became smaller and smaller while gliding toward the mainland. My head was leaning on Achrotzyber's chest, his arm holding my shoulder as we stood on the jetty, and I was recalling the last few days—the return from Sydney, the reunion with my students, the discussions on our appearances, the prioritization of our pinboard topics.

The researchers and students had deserved some attention, had had every right to expect me to honor their results and praise them, add constructive criticism, advise them of errors and possibilities. They had questions on the Meier tunnel, on the *Besson compensator,* how their nestle field had performed, what the *Worries* system looked like, when I'd lecture again.

After the vacation. In two weeks, from Monday, July first on, we'd dedicate ourselves to all the topics waiting with renewed power and drive.

The last of our folks were cruising away out there, on Freddie's last run for the next fortnight. Even Nanette was with them. The marine researcher station was already shut down as well—most of the biology students were liaised with my protégés in some way and enjoying their company.

My Companion and I were alone now, not counting fishes and birds. We were holding the fort, guarding the island, until our scientific family returned.

Nanette had asked me several times if I didn't want to go on a vacation, too, and who'd take care of me if she wasn't there. Yes, I'd go on vacation. For me, the island was the most restful spot on this planet, so I remained. Yes, I'd be able to rest my mind in these surroundings — that was a question of Dragonish mental discipline, we just had to remove the pin-boards. I could take care of myself, thank you, just ask Francine, and aside from that there were enough fishes and sea cucumbers around the island.

What would I do all two weeks long? Nothing. Sweet idleness. Sleeping in, recline on the beach in the sun, occasionally eat something, swim around the island — and have sex with my Companion.

My hand wandered up his butt cheek and sneaked between his legs.

"What do you think, Mighty? Would you like to tend a bit to my emotional needs?"

"Of course, Companion. May I point out that this human body does develop emotional needs as well?"

His cock was already rising tall. I slipped through under his arm, stepped behind him, rubbed my breasts against his back and grabbed his shaft with both hands.

"If that's the case, I'll tend to your needs first. Let's see how far you can shoot."

My thigh muscles burned, yelled for relief, but it was out of the question to take down my legs, V-shaped and rising to the sky, while Achrotzyber was still busy.

I was on my back in the sand, he was lying prostrate before me, and his tongue was playing in turns with my inner and outer labia, diligently licking up every drop of my juice before it could waste itself in the sand.

"Ooooh!"

Even my most intimate parts yelled for relief, and how wonderfully lust and pain were mixing! My fingers clenched in the sand, remembering the hard rod they'd massaged briefly before. *Oh, if this phallus would pump inside me now, instead of that tender and way too diffident tongue!*

But my Companion continued to torture me, denied me

climax, shunned my clit's challengingly swollen knob, and instead further tickled my wet labia's delicate inside.

Without restraint I cried out my lust and my woe. My Companion wouldn't be distracted, ignored my trembling breasts, my burning thighs, my half opened lips—there was just his tongue and my vagina, nothing else.

This wasn't just sex, and this wasn't just pain. This was the love of a Dragon, which I indulged in with all my senses!

And yet—it couldn't last an eternity. Achrotzyber's efforts had a goal. Before the pain could turn from unbearable to real consequences, before my trembling expectation could turn to routine—was that even possible?—my partner had to guide me to climax.

"Please," I squeezed out between my lecherous whimpers, and he answered my plea, directed his fleshy tongue deeper again between my lips, penetrated me as deep as only a Dragon tongue could, and then licked upward, across my clitoris, around the sensible knob, up and down, back and forth . . .

I became giddy, saw stars, my legs were numb, my back no longer existed, my entire perception gathered in this one point, and my lust climbed the crest of ecstasy —*now?* No, still farther up, and—*Oh!*—another bit—*Ah!*—how was that possible?—*Uh, that's sooo good!* I came—finally—but it was no brief moment of relief, rather an infinitely looong drawn parabola, an extended bliss in which I would bathe and wallow, and with it came my Companion's protective hug, who reclined at my side and pulled me tight.

Now was the time to put my legs down, but—ouch!—that wasn't easy. The thought alone of moving them triggered a stinging pain, and only iron discipline allowed me to bring them down to the ground.

The millions of pins stinging me now joined the prickle in my crotch and at least temporarily covered the gentle pressure of the erect, sandy cock at my hip.

As much as I enjoyed simply snuggling into my Companion's arm, I couldn't ignore his arousal forever — because it wouldn't be fair to leave him standing there, because it was against my self-image to let such a wonderful boner remain unsatisfied, and because, despite or because of the just experienced bliss, I was longing for a hard part deep in my pussy now. The sand was bothersome there, but for this purpose I had no qualms to use my nanos.

Could I already lift my leg again? Ouch, yes, the pain was bearable. So I pushed Achrotzyber on his back and mounted him. His cock stood up even while he was reclining. I brushed its tip a few times with my little black bush, and then I put my slippery love tunnel over his huge manhood. At first, there was some pricking, and then my nanos did their duty and disintegrated the small grains of sand.

So, my sweetheart, now it's my turn to grant you a long climb. I hope you've got no other plans for today.

CHAPTER FORTY-EIGHT

My Companion's head jerked up and around. Yes, I had spotted the tiny fiery dot at the horizon, too — and it approached fast.

A loud ring from one of our labs fell in. Our control quark detector raised the alarm.

I WAS ALREADY RUNNING.

Three hundred meters in three point six seconds — more wasn't possible between the trees that separated beach and labs, even on the third level.

My hand interrupted the red laser ray. A brief horn signal replaced the ringing, red warning lights flashed around the island, and the lab building's inner door thunked shut, like numerous other doors on the island did.

Less obvious, but a lot more effective, was the rising nestle field around the island. I imagined it pushing out a fish here and there so as to not cut it in half, while I called up the detector results. Would the shield hold?

To my great surprise, the computer not only showed the detected control quark source's position, but also its trajectory, flight parameters, and a target marking, froze — and then reported the target's destruction.

The airlock hissed, and my Companion entered. He only glanced at the screen once and nodded. "Done. After your warning regarding the New York assassination I arranged for the island's protective measures to be improved. Recognized targets with high threat potential are destroyed by *cake knife* before a proximity trigger can cause collateral damage. That applies especially to missiles."

"We'll talk about that later." I pushed him through the open inner door and operated the close button. Waiting for the airlock cycle required patience. Once I was outside, I ran off. Achrotzyber followed.

"What are you doing?"

"I'll take the Taipan and have a go at the people who launched the missile. Our computer recorded its trajectory since the reactor was running — and there can't be that many ships out there."

"Is that appropriate now?"

"Yes."

Was there any point in explaining to him now what I had taken from the data? The missile reactor had already begun to establish a disruptor field — a field targeted forward that wouldn't necessarily have led to the reactor's self-destruction, and that would have been able to penetrate our nestle field!

Put differently — we would have been helpless if Achrotzyber hadn't arranged for the cake knife's automatic deployment.

"What shall I do in the meantime?" he asked while I leaned over the small plane's cockpit and entered the target coordinates.

"You'll pilot the Taipan. Camouflaged. I'll come along in the weapons bay and disembark over the target."

"Oh."

Yes, oh. "And while I'm taking care of the terrorists, you'll contact our folks. They're all potential targets."

"This is a very unfavorable situation."

"Indeed." And I entered a similarly unfavorable situation by squeezing into the weapons bay.

Chapter Forty-nine

Of course I took the possibility into consideration that this assault could serve a double purpose — that it should lure me out if it didn't kill me right away. But I wasn't willing to let this attempt pass. Just the opposite. I had to make clear that I could no longer tolerate these attempts, in a way that should discourage future followers and accomplices.

No, the next few minutes wouldn't be nice.

As agreed, my Companion opened the weapons bay once he had reached the target area and recognized the only possible source for the missile launch — a small freighter heaving across the Pacific waves somewhat off the beaten routes.

Several men were busy moving the missile launcher back into a container on the foredeck.

I dropped toward them with spread wings and camouflaged.

They might have had a chance to notice the rush of air from my wings before my landing and draw any guns, but I didn't let it get that far. I sent a paralyzing contact poison forward and headed for the bridge. While the men on the foredeck collapsed, I came down on the small balcony next to the bridge door, folded my wings and dropped my camouflage.

Three men were working here and turned to me once they noticed my moves from the corners of their eyes — one was standing right before me watching the events on the foredeck, one in the bridge center next to the small helm, and the third was sitting at an obviously improvised dashboard in the rear of the bridge. They were wearing turtleneck pullovers and jeans with a pistol in their waistbands each.

Three tiny darts hit their unprotected necks. All three seized up, the two standing fell.

The ship's on autopilot, the helmsman is down. Please survey the water.

Roger.

Were there further persons aboard? And which nasty surprises should be orchestrated from that dashboard? A few nano columns could investigate the latter question, for the first I picked the guy at the wheel.

When I leaned over him and turned his head to me, his eyes showed pure horror. I had to pull myself together to appear cold and distant on the outside.

"I will neutralize the venom, and you will answer my questions truthfully and as elaborately as possible. I will ask every question only once, and I will know if you lie or hide anything."

That moment, of all times, a similar interrogation situation rose from my *memory* — or from the Lionheart's past, respectively. *Brrr!*

Not that I didn't have enough experience. You could do it the hard way or somewhat ease the process. Play nice, start with inconspicuous questions, until the victim had accepted his situation.

Chapter Fifty

T*he coast guard will soon reach the freighter, Companion.*
Okay. I'm done here.

After a last examination of the restraints on the men at my feet, I spread my wings and jumped into the sky.

Surprised calls followed me. Good. These men wouldn't soon forget they had challenged a *Dragon* — ice-cold, merciless, and not to be deceived.

Whether I was squeezed into a weapons bay or flew back myself wasn't so important, so I chose the more comfortable option.

You can fly home, Mighty. What about our people?

Tess says you should keep out. The threat situation is not new, so there were dispositions made. Moreover, you are the primary target.

Someone could try to blackmail me.

That would have to be accepted. You are more important.

That's logical, Mighty, but I must still show that I'm able to protect my people. Otherwise our opponent will develop less and less favorable extrapolations.

You cannot be everywhere, Companion. So you must rely on Tess and Kenneth protecting your people anyway. Instead, you can limit the risk that your presence will trigger an assassination.

Sadly, there he was right.

Okay. I'll stay here.

What did your interrogations yield?

Little.

Did the assassins refuse to talk?

Oh no. Those weren't truly tough guys. Once the venom's effects faded, they were singing like nightingales. Only they didn't know much. Some blathering about free access to Dragon knowledge, for which I must be eliminated, plus an unknown sponsor in the background, of whom they know neither face nor place — I'd have to find out where the money for that ship really came from, but where should I start?

Are such money flows not traceable?

Some curious seagulls were sailing along with me.

If you've got access to the right systems, they are.

And you do not have that access?

Not right now. I could gain access, however, that would be illegal.

You once said it yourself — we are at war. These assassins are enemies.

Yes — but the people whose systems I'd have to intrude are friends. That counts for me.

You should not get caught then.

I'll consider that.

CHAPTER FIFTY-ONE

The character salad on the screen didn't make sense. Those weren't financial transactions! That was nothing, at best a photo file of a convoluted abstract artwork.

My gaze wandered down. Why was my golden hand clenched to a fist? And what kind of strange patterns were mirrored in the scales?

Curse me!

I carried the *memories* of the most skilled hacker of all times in my head, and I still couldn't get anywhere. Or was it due to my opponents rather giving computers a wide berth? That I didn't find anything because there wasn't anything to find? But how else should I find a starting point?

My Companion's hand gently touched my shoulder.

I opened the fist, made the scales disappear and took his fingers, pulled them down to my breast and pressed it firmly on. Bending back and squeezing into his grip I rose, kicked the chair aside.

Achrotzyber would've pulled me around to hug and kiss me, but that wasn't what I needed. Instead I stooped, rested my forearms on the table and placed my legs apart.

"Fuck me now. Fuck me hard and fast."

With my eyes closed I waited for his cock to penetrate me. I was wet enough — this night shouldn't see a long foreplay.

There was the tip of his long rod already, taking measure, searching for the right angle, much too slowly pushing my inner labia apart — I took a deep breath and then paused breathing — he moved a little bit down, and then, with a resolute push, he rammed his entire length into me.

"Aaaah!"

My entire perception focused on this one region of my body, pure desire, waiting for the next push, and then he began. Once, twice, three times he slowly pulled his member almost out, pushed it back in as slowly, once out again and—*Ah!* A jerk forward, backward, forward, a bit faster and firmer with every push, and it almost seemed to me as if he became larger each time.

That didn't matter, only that he didn't slacken off, and so I didn't hold back my lustful moans. "Yes—yes—yess!"

The relieving climax rolled across me like a wave across the coral belt of our reef. My partner tensed, too. Then I felt him pumping. I imagined his tremendous semen load filling me up.

He pulled out. His juice followed and tickled my thigh by running down.

I rose, turned around and smiled at him. "That's making me truly hot now."

PART FOUR—BRIDGE-BUILDING

CHAPTER FIFTY-TWO

The marvelous smell of fresh coffee and freshly baked bread rolls filled the entire room and the terrace. Nanette intercepted me on the terrace with a steaming pot. My favorite place was already set.

Breakfast on the terrace of our community center was my last place of retreat before my daily work, which usually lasted far into the night, and Nanette made sure nobody interfered with this rest period. That didn't mean I had to eat alone, only that all work topics were taboo.

For researcher colleagues, whose need for talk Nanette could read from their faces, there was no room at my table—this time it was Gerard. He restrained himself bravely, but as soon as I had put my used dishes down on the sideboard at the kitchen door, Gerard approached me.

"What's bothering you?" I asked him.

"The *Besson compensator*," he said right away. "We can't get the fine tuning done."

"Why? It was working fine."

"For a Barracuda, yes. But in a Phoenix-class ship, firstly the signal propagation time is much greater, and if that weren't bad enough, the equalization parameters over a distance of a hundred meters are no longer the same — and there aren't always the same kind of gravity differences."

"So what? That makes the formula more complex."

"Sure. Only — how can you keep a nestle field stable that's not homogeneous?"

Oh.

"Does it have to be inhomogeneous? I mean, the compensation is about the big differences, not the small stuff."

"That's what we thought, too, and by and large that's true. Such a little bit of difference doesn't count compared to a flight without compensator, right?" Gerard spread his arms. "For a real wormhole transit, all that doesn't matter. But if you're traveling in a tunnel bubble, the rules are different. There you need precision. If the tunnel bubble isn't homogeneous, it doesn't work — and if it's homogeneous, the compensation doesn't work. The larger the tunnel bubble, the worse it gets. Aboard the *Mischief,* you couldn't notice that, but your computer did notice it."

"So. Then I should look into that, shouldn't I?" I was indeed curious about his findings. Where did my formulas lack the decisive details? Most of all I was interested in why such a minor factor as the size difference between Barracuda and Phoenix could have a such a big influence. "Show me."

The formulas were already dancing in my head. Where would I add a variable for larger spaceships or larger tunnel bubbles respectively? Or rather — where did the current formula system provide the foundation for the problems that Gerard had mentioned?

Perhaps I should wait until I had seen Gerard's analysis — on the other hand, I already knew the data and the derivations, I only had to review them with this new aspect in mind.

Gerard was right — if the tunnel bubble wasn't sufficiently homogeneous, it couldn't work, because the gravity potential differences along the bubble could tear it apart and mash its content. At the same time he was wrong — there was some leeway, otherwise my coarse improvisation couldn't have worked.

I felt dizzy when I recognized how narrow this leeway was — and how steep the flanks of this thin line that Francine and I had balanced across on our return flight.

Okay, so the bubble had to remain homogeneous — and of course, in that case the compensation was no longer perfect, most of all for large ships. I just couldn't see why that should be so bad — we had accomplished the way out across a hundred and forty light years without any compensation, and within a system there was no need for compensation at all. Again — shouldn't it be enough to facilitate a rough compensation and simply endure the minor remaining effects?

Our formula set claimed the opposite. Again, there was a predicted tension along the bubble that led to flashover reactions. I called them grav flashes, even if the computer renderings didn't reflect that.

That was the lever. "Consider an arrester. As we can predict the gravity potential difference between bow and stern for a homogeneous tunnel bubble, there might be a way to divert or discharge it."

"Discharge it?"

"Well, if our model is good enough to predict the forces, we can handle them. I can't tell you more right now."

He made a face. "Well. Thanks. I'll talk with the others, see whether someone's got an idea."

"Or give your subconscious a chance. Tomorrow or the day after, we'll have another look at it, okay?"

"Okay."

CHAPTER FIFTY-THREE

Reginald intercepted me on my way back to the center, placed one arm around my hip and pushed me toward the beach.

"I know," he began. "You want to get back to your work. Tell me what's plaguing you and what we can take off your shoulders, and you'll feel better."

My long sigh should have been answer enough. But he didn't settle for it.

"Come on. The University?"

"Running, thanks. Of course, for the most part, that's your work."

"You're welcome. Mmm—research grief?"

"Gerard just brought me a new problem. Grav flashes—potential differences along large tunnel bubble that discharge and tear the bubble apart."

"So that we won't get the Phoenix faster-than-light capable."

"Exactly. Where it was looking so good—the first four hulls are ready for integrating the bubble technology, and I had hoped we could start in two months."

"Four hulls? I thought there were twelve?"

"The other eight will only fly inside the Solar system for now. For freight flights, sub-light suffices. That spares the crews the disorientation after the jump, and if necessary, they can fly short intra-system routes without compensator."

"Ah, okay. The earlier we can implement the system defense."

"Exactly," I agreed. "That'll be the next step. Once the stations are built, researchers and miners may start."

We had reached the waterline. The first gentle wave sprinkled my left big toe.

"Does that part run?"

"Oh yes. Sylvie and Francine are training the first pilots — well, as far as Francine can manage along with her studies. Achrotzyber takes care of the Barracuda pilot training, also okay."

"But?"

"But the list of unsolved questions always grows longer, not shorter. Meanwhile this project has more than twelve hundred open issues."

"Sounds like you need someone who focuses on this, sorts out important and unimportant stuff and triggers solutions. I'll find someone for you."

And he pulled me closer. How I'd have liked to just lean on him! But there weren't just the fleet and the outer stations to consider.

"What else?" Reginald guessed my thought.

"The spaceport. I haven't heard anything of it for weeks."

"Oh, that's because it's running like a clockwork. Bo handles that."

"Bo?"

"No-worries-Bo. There are no issues, we'll find a pragmatic solution. Does a spaceport need a super-perfect leveled runway? No. Spaceships can set down on the sand. And how will the freight reach the spaceship? By grav sleds that hover over the sand. So there's not much leveling, just staking off the area. We need a few storage halls, a clearance hall and a small administration building — that can be made from wood, so what? She's getting along well with the Arab wonder boy — you need a track right across the bush, nothing sophisticated, just cleared from large obstacles, but sixty kilometers long, and within four weeks? Mahmud makes it possible. That many people, that many tools, tents, catering by helicopter and grav sled – the day after tomorrow, the crew's deployed, and each night there's a check. Two point four kilometers per day, no excuses. If anything unforeseeable comes up, the problem solvers come in, and the regular work goes on. And to make sure nothing unforeseeable can come up, he sends explorers ahead. At least that's how it went between Gladstone and Rockhampton. Eight weeks later, the train track was ready for operation. You may assume we've got the spaceport connected in two months."

His narration made me laugh. "And the spaceport will also be ready then?"

"It's already operational. Maybe you'll have to make a detour around a startled brown snake on your way to the clearance hall, or the rosellas will steal some bread from your plate in the cafeteria, but in principle, the space freighters can come – in the beginning no more than four per week, but that should do for now."

That sounded like a typical Australian. In Germany it would've been unthinkable to build a spaceport like this, with plain architecture, primitive technology and minimal safety standards. In exchange, here it took only six months until principal operational readiness. In my country of birth, that time would just barely suffice for a supermarket.

"So, if that's not the source of your worries, what else is?"

A pity. He had just distracted me so nicely, and the water meanwhile reached to my heel.

"The terrorists. Okay, we've had no assault for six months, but we're also without any useful lead for six months, and we haven't heard about Monique and Elodie since then either. Are they still alive at all?"

He noticeably tensed. "Tess doesn't talk about it."

The way he always worried about Tess when she was on a

mission, he could well understand my troubles.

"They're Mambas," he finally said. "They've learned to survive in the most adverse environments. It was clear that the mission would take longer this time. We must be patient."

"Patient." I flicked my big toe. "I must be patient—with our aid expedition, with Monique's mission, with everything. I'm tired of that. I want to do something."

Some things you shouldn't wish for though—they could come true . . .

CHAPTER FIFTY-FOUR

Beate greeted me with a hug and a kiss. "Hey, Jo! Are you coming with us again?"

"Yes. I need to think, and perhaps the ride will help me to come up with new ideas."

"Okayyy — and where you're going?"

"Rashid wants to talk with me."

"Ah. He's still struggling with our dress code, isn't he?"

"That's just not his world. I think even if he understands our rational reasons to go without clothes, he can neither relate to this feeling of liberty nor to our casual interaction. With the abandoning of this part of our privacy we're at the same time getting closer together — everyone is there for each other anytime."

"With Nanette and you as mothers of the wild pack." She winked at me.

That remark touched a painful memory. Yes, in a certain way they were all my children — my protected — but on the other hand, they were not. Whereas my only true child had never seen the light of day — that thought hurt in a way I wasn't used to, although it really wasn't new. Why now?

"Hey, Jo. I wanted to say something nice." She pulled me close.

"It's okay," I whispered.

That way we remained for a while until Freddie came outside and cleared his throat. "All okay?"

I gently freed myself from Beate's hug. "Yes, all okay. It was just an old memory."

He shivered and then turned away. "Of that you probably have enough for several lives."

There he was right. And if I could suppress all other memories, I could suppress this one, too—at least for another while.

"Did Rashid say what he wants?" Beate asked.

"No. Nowadays there are too many people eavesdropping on phone calls, he said. I assume it's about the delays with the space carrier construction."

"Oh. There are delays?"

"Yes, for a while already. We're having trouble with the tunnel field, and the shipyard's got problems with the bio system integration. Whatever it is this time, I'll learn about it soon."

"Okay." Beate hesitated briefly, then she smiled and walked to the end of the jetty to untie the stern rope. She didn't have to ask whether she could help me in any way.

CHAPTER FIFTY-FIVE

Rashid's secretary opened the door to his suite for me and then left us alone as usual. Rashid rose from his chair and approached me with open arms.

"Jo! Good morning, nice to see you! How are you?"

"Fine. Good morning, Rashid. How's the family doing?"

"Pleasantly." To my surprise, he briefly hugged me, then he pointed at a free chair. "Please sit down. I may convey Fatima's regards."

"Oh, thanks." I rearranged my vest and let myself sink into the chair. Then I waited until Rashid had taken his seat again.

"Coffee?" he asked and took up a thermos jug.

"Gladly."

He poured me a cup, placed the jug down and then raised his teacup.

"I'd never thought my daughter would develop so much ambition and then be so successful. That makes me proud. I don't expect trouble there."

"But?"

"The Chinese won't stop arguing."

"We had discussed that we're continuing the construction program for intrasolar flights."

"Yes. But Wei Ching is neither stupid nor blind, and I can't keep what we're doing secret before the council. He noticed that we're equipping the carriers for long-distance flights. Of course that's much more cost-effective than a later rework, but he argues that we won't need rework if the carriers remain in-system anyway—and for this purpose the enhanced equipment would be too expensive. Hence he concludes we're trying to cheat him and do plan an expedition."

"Where he's right—that is, the second part. We're not cheating. We admitted to stay in this system *for now*. We're not ready to discard that strategic option prematurely."

Rashid sighed and sipped at his tea. "It's just not easy. He brings up that topic again in every session."

"Should I come around and throw him out?"

"I don't think the Chinese would be happy about that."

"I don't think the Chinese government would be happy either." I smiled at Rashid across the edge of my cup. "In any case, I am not happy that he's stealing the council's precious time, and I'm not happy about the way the Chinese government tries to countermine our defense efforts. Perhaps it would be appropriate if I addressed my displeasure about it in the right place? Perhaps a different government would be more open-minded?"

He frowned. "Do you think it's smart to interfere with country politics?"

"I did that frequently—every time the respective government was objectively suspicious of working for a criminal organization like the Cartel. So far I have no hard evidence, but you may tell the Chinese that I will investigate this option should the reason arise. What the result of a positive check looks like is well known."

He thought about that for a moment, then he smiled. "I'll consider on which occasion I'll use that."

For a while, we tended to our cups and our own thoughts, then I picked up the idea again. "You may also tell the Chinese that I share their concerns regarding the chance that a Phoenix could fall into the enemy's hand. We'll have to provide a self-destruction switch—worst case we'll have to make the emitters burn through and wipe out the computer.

However, I'm quite confident that we won't have to use it."

"But you're sure the Phoenix will fly."

"Absolutely. I'm here on the tenterhooks for half a year waiting for the moment we can start — who knows how long our potential allies can survive? What happens if the enemy somehow acquires their Dragon technology knowhow? What kind of new technology and weapon systems is he working on? We're more-or-less blind regarding enemy movements, and that makes me nervous."

Rashid jerked forward. "You're *nervous?* You?"

"Indeed."

Our gazes met. I didn't evade him, and he held his gaze, too. Finally he said, "When a Dragon is nervous, humans should tremble in fear. You've just raised some aspects we haven't seen until now. I will talk with the council and recommend they upgrade the construction program."

He slapped the right fist into his left palm. "Cursed be the day we admitted this bio engineer. He just can't get the onboard bio systems up and running."

"So?" A bio engineer was his greatest concern? "Should I talk with that man?"

"I don't know if that would help. It's a completely different subject."

"Different than grav fields? Indeed — but I've gathered plenty of experience with bio technology." Gathered the hard way, but — well. "Consider that I can transform into a Dragon, and as Dragon I can adapt to the most diverse environmental conditions. Dragons are good at that — normally intuitively, but I consciously got to the heart of this subject. I think I can quite immodestly claim I know my way around it."

Rashid relaxed a bit. "Good, then I'll arrange a meeting with Jacob."

"Tut. I'll fly there tomorrow. Unannounced. It's just a hop with the Taipan."

"You're not needed here?"

"I've got a loose appointment with Gerard tomorrow morning. He found a problem with tunnel fields for big spaceships we need to talk about. Thereafter, I can go."

He was already squinting. "What kind of problem is that?"

"According to our simulations, we get tension in a tunnel field—the larger the field, the more destructive their effect. If we can't find out how to deal with this effect, the Chinese will get what they want. Then no Phoenix will ever leave our system."

"And that comes on top of the issues you're already nervous for."

I took a deep breath. "Yes."

"Up to which size are the effects manageable?"

"It works with a Barracuda. That's what's empirically proven."

"That wasn't my question. How much larger than a Barracuda can a spaceship be?"

Rashid would be a good poker player, but he stood no chance against me. "Okay. How long is your alternative?"

"About seventy meters, but we'd have no trouble acquiring shorter bodies. We went a different way." He placed the tips of his fingers together. "The Barracudas are made for war. A steel body of a piece, robust and expensive. The Phoenixes are built like warships, too. They're large, heavy, and can take a beating—and they're expensive, too. We need such ships for system defense, but for in-system passenger and freight traffic we don't need such, and probably not for a long sequence of provisioning flights to the *Worries* system either. If we want to build a bridge to the stars, we need cheap bodies in numbers, and if we want to have these bodies soon, it would be convenient if they were already built, wouldn't they?"

"Yes." Now it was my turn to stare at him wonderingly.

"Moreover, it would be quite convenient if our space

freighters could land on every commercial airport world-wide, wouldn't it? So we don't have to move the payload around half the world only to get it into space. So a team of technicians dealt with the question how you can reconstruct available aircraft bodies for a flight to space. The biggest problem seems to be getting the bodies airtight—but even that isn't crucial for well-packed freight as long as the pilot compartment is well sealed. You don't need wings, those can be removed, instead you install a reactor and a grav field generator—and we've got a completed tender for interplanetary flights. The next step would be to include your nestle field. That's what I learned."

CHAPTER FIFTY-SIX

Aircraft bodies for transportation of goods—why not? It should suffice for commuter traffic to the moon or Mars. Within the atmosphere you only had to be slow enough to avoid overheating, and outside it slow enough for interplanetary dust. Even a partial nestle field that shielded the bow sufficed for higher speeds. The question was—how much higher? Would such a hull bear the strain of twenty-five percent light speed?

Wrong question. Would such a body bear everything that wouldn't mash the human payload inside? More wasn't necessary—no matter whether it was about relativistic speed, a gravtunnel transit, or the landing on a very stormy planet.

"How many?" I asked.

"A few hundred," Rashid said. "There are several parking lots for old planes. We've got a quite different problem now—how can we train or retrain so many pilots fast enough?"

A few hundred tin cans . . . traveling back and forth between Sol and *Worries* like pearls on a string, each single one with fifty to a hundred tons of raw goods and food . . .

"You don't appear happy about it," Rashid commented.

"I'm happy about the transport capacity—wait, no, I'm truly happy about this great idea. I only just had to think about where the food should come from. We can't tell people that there's hunger in poor areas on Earth while we're affording the luxury of provisioning strangers."

He made a stern face. "You should have come up with this idea half a year ago."

However, he couldn't fool me. "But you came up with this idea."

"Naturally." He reached for the teapot and poured himself another cup. "This point was on the top of the list right from the start—can we afford to provision an entire populace, an entire planet? You can only answer this question with *Yes* once you've clarified your own provisioning."

"And?"

"With everything that our own planet produces we can feed more than just our own people, and the distribution problem is solvable as well—our council passed this subject on, though, because it isn't part of interstellar defense. Others can rack their brains about it. However, there was the reasonable argument that our eco system is based on a functioning circuit that we can't just deprive of valuable elements. We have to compensate for the loss. This topic is solvable, too, and we've passed it on, too."

"To whom?"

"There's another council for it, for not quite half a year." He winked at me and sipped at his tea. "You know, people asked themselves, how can it be that just one woman invents and tests faster-than-light flight, defends Earth against an invasion, leads a University and rules an independent territory and at the same time fights worldwide organized crime, and on top of that finds the time to take care of poverty and hunger around the world—and the entire United Nations aren't able to even follow up on two of these topics? Well, the press might have put it quite bluntly back then, but it worked."

Chapter Fifty-seven

R eginald was standing in the terrace doorway with a tray. He cleared his throat. I pushed Francine's hand from my breast and rolled into a sitting position. A gentle whiff of coffee drifted past me.

"I brought you breakfast," he whispered.

"For us two?"

"For the two of you. I already had breakfast."

"Oh — it's that late already?" I squinted past him. Judging by the sun's position it couldn't be later than eight o'clock. After the long evening I deemed that appropriate.

"No, I was extra early. Jenny told me you'd fly today."

"Yes. I have to go to Washington."

"Oh. The president?"

"Washington state, west coast. The Frostdragon shipyard."

"Oh, that."

He was still standing in the door, examining my pilot's slender body.

"Put down the tray and give me a cup of coffee."

"Gladly." He did as told and brought me a cup. I took it from him and held it under Francine's nose. It didn't take long until she stirred.

"Mmm?"

"Coffee?"

She opened her eyes. Her gaze met the cup, wandered up my arm, past my shoulder, stuck to Reginald at the cupboard. Smiling, she rose to rest on her right arm, took the cup with her left and placed her left knee up.

Reginald unabashedly watched her gaping snatch, still sticky from our last night's lovemaking. In response, he openly presented his quickly rising cock. "Thanks. Actually, I already had breakfast."

Francine sipped at her coffee. Her left knee wandered farther outward. "Did you already have fuckfast, too?"

"No." He tossed me a quick glance.

"Come on. Stick it in."

I gave up my place at the bed's edge and thus cleared the way. My goal was another full cup of coffee on the tray, and the likewise exquisitely smelling fresh croissants.

With coffee in one and a croissant in the other hand I watched Reginald and Francine having their quickie until I felt fresh wetness between my labia.

When Reginald briefly turned to look at me and wink, I spread my legs, brushed up a few drops of my wetness with the croissant and then made a point of slowly putting it into my mouth.

With a wide grin and new energy he tended to his task again. Francine acknowledged his effort with delighted cries and soon begged for relief.

Reginald, however, took his time. He played with Francine, licked her breasts, caressed her thighs, sucked her earlobes, and brought her almost to climax several times, only to then pause, pull out his cock and again penetrate her very slowly.

I had completely looted the breakfast tray when he finally brought her to orgasm . . . and I had a suspicion that giving me time to eat my breakfast had been just his intention.

After a passionate kiss, Reginald unwrapped himself from Francine's arms and pushed himself up. But she didn't let him get away so soon. Her legs caught his butt and prevented him from leaving her lap.

"No, sweetie. As long as it's so nicely large, it stays inside. Jo, do you have a hot coffee for me?"

"Sure. Just keep a firm hold on him. Reginald, why are you here?"

"I wanted to bring you breakfast—"

"That was very kind of you, and I've eaten it all. But that wasn't the true reason. What's up?"

He tried to shrug. "I can't fool you, right? Okay. For some time tonight our servers have been running tough, and any outbound traffic needs what feels like an eternity. At least that's what the others say. But we can't find anything—all our diagnosis tools say everything's okay. Do you have any idea?"

"Yes." My darkening face was mirrored by his rising eyebrows. "We've got an intruder in our system. Zoe's marvels reacted as planned and iced us."

"Iced us."

"ICE—Intrusion Countermeasures Electronics. While our own applications run as before in their virtual machines, our system feigns activity in secondary instances—and there the hackers have been digging into for the last few hours. The simulation makes our hardware sweat a little, and our outward access has to take some detours in order not to be intercepted. Of course, that takes time."

"You don't seem to be surprised."

"I'm only surprised that it took so long until someone broke through the outer defenses." I pushed the tray away and sat on the cupboard, my hands supporting me, my feet dangling. "There have been attempts since the University went online. This is a different caliber. Behind this attempt is either a genius—or a large organization. I'd very much like to know where our intruder resides."

"Which you can't find out while we're hedging in—icing, right?"

"No." I couldn't. But my spies—formerly Zoe's spies—around the world could, and they were doubtlessly already working according to their programming. Quietly and inconspicuously they were collecting the evidence that I'd later collect, when the intruder didn't expect it. Reginald didn't have to know about that, though—this was the kind of secret that would no longer be a secret if more than one person knew about it. "I'll have to log in from the mainland—from an inconspicuous location. I'll do that when I'm on my way."

With slight regret I jumped from the cupboard. I'd rather have played with those two for a while, but I had a long day ahead of me. First I had to talk with Gerard about the grav arrester and address the question of the maximum manageable length to him, and then it was time for the surprise visit to Rashid's bio engineer.

CHAPTER FIFTY-EIGHT

With our—actually Zoé's—Taipan I could cross the Pacific much faster than swimming or by kite. That left me a lot less time to consider what I had to expect at the shipyard. Perhaps it was better that way, as I had no clue to think about anyway.

Instead I diligently registered with the American air traffic control, received a friendly welcome and advice about the heavy traffic at the west coast. We agreed on a safe route for the descent and an approach at low altitude with subsequent landing at the shipyard.

I had to smile about that. Not long ago, American fighter pilots had tried to shoot me down together with Jenny's plane over the Pacific. However, the air traffic control people couldn't be blamed for that.

The coastline offered a varied scenery with long sand beaches and steep cliffs during my approach. Sadly I had to focus on piloting. The Puget Sound was full of ships, and cranes were rising above the shipyard and its harbor on the eastern shore between Seattle and Everett. I had to avoid them.

It seemed appropriate to land in the parking lot before the main entrance and not inside the shipyard area. After all, I came unannounced, but not as a thief. At least this time.

So I casually ambled up to the porter's booth at the main gate and presented a sweet smile to the security guard.

It was wasted. He didn't even look at me, but just pointed at a sign on the desk.

No admittance without badge

No visitor traffic without advance registration

"Okay, chief," I said. "I'm registering here and now."

His magazine seemed to be captivating. Still not looking up, he tossed me a card.

Visitor registration – press office

Contact data followed below.

"Doesn't apply, chief," I said, still in a friendly voice. "Give me the card for military visitors."

His head jerked up.

"Military visitors? What's this fuss about?"

First he glanced over my head, then he lowered his gaze. As in New York before, I was wearing my black uniform with the golden laurels on the collar patches and the silver star and the crimson red medal on my chest. Especially the latter symbol couldn't be not recognized.

He was slow at the uptake, but he got it. Then he almost fell over himself in his attempt to stand to attention in his booth.

"*Pro-pro-protectress!*"

"What's up, chief? What about the supreme commander having a look at her future fleet's bodies?"

"Erm . . ."

"You know what, chief? You needn't decide that. But I surely can pay the yard director a visit, can't I?"

"Oh—yes, I think so . . ."

"Just tell me where I'll find him."

"Second floor, room 101. But actually —"

"Actually, visitors shouldn't walk around the area all alone, because you can never be sure who's a spy. And actually no one should be walking around without badge. But you know I'm no spy, and this" —I pointed at my medal—"is better than any badge. I'm expressly allowing you to make an exception from your regulations, and I'll check that with the yard director. Okay, chief?"

"Well, then . . ."

The poor guy was clearly unable to handle the situation.

"Listen, chief. I'll just walk inside now. You don't want to stop me, so put your nose back into your magazine. Have a nice day."

Then I left him.

The door to room 101 stood ajar. I knocked and entered.

A four-meters-wide project plan covered one wall, and the plain desk was occupied by a signature folder, a keyboard, and a screen. A swivel chair parked behind the desk. Otherwise, the room was empty.

Two red markings on the plan attracted my gaze. One highlighted the milestone for a software delivery for the grav field emitter control — most likely due to Gerard's problem — and the other circled four bars with the labels *bio systems* and *hull one* to *hull four*.

Approaching footsteps sounded from the hallway, then a chubby man with sparse gray hair entered. I turned to him.

"Who — oh. Protectress Johanna! I hadn't expected your visit."

"No, I hadn't announced myself."

He shook his head. "Where am I with my thoughts? Excuse me. I'm Jeremiah Higgins, technical director of this shipyard, but everyone calls me Jerry."

He reached out his hand with hesitation. I took it.

"Hello, Jerry. I'm Jo."

"Hello, Jo."

"Rashid told me that Jacob has a problem. I thought I'd see if I can help."

"Jacob? Ah, yes." He pointed at the plan. "Approval for the bio systems is four weeks overdue. We've got all kind of little trouble with it and can't get forward."

"Where do I find him?"

"At the ships. Probably in hull one. I can't tell where exactly — ask Theo once you're there."

"How do I recognize Theo?"

"Theo will address you. Everyone working on hull one has to check in with Theo — Theo always knows who's inside."

"Ah, okay. Is it okay for you if I come back to you later?"

"Sure. If I'm not here, I'm in the conference room at the end of the hallway. Or ask anyone to ping me."

"I'll do that. 'Til later."

CHAPTER FIFTY-NINE

Hull one was probably erected in dock one, so I followed the respective signs behind the administration building. Until I entered through the small side door in the large gate of dock one, nobody stopped me. But right behind the door I was called by a stringy bearded man with an orange-white-striped helmet. "Hey you! Where's your helmet?"

I turned to him. "I don't have one."

"Nobody enters the dock without helmet. Show me your badge. I have to report that."

"I have no badge."

He frowned and watched my approach with puzzlement. "No badge? That's a case for site security!" His hand approached a button at the wall next to his desk.

"Jerry sent me here. I shall assist Jacob with a problem. By the way, I'm Jo."

Jerry's mention had at least delayed his move. "Jo?"

"Johanna Meier, Imperatrix Aurea. You've heard of me."

"Oh." His hand changed the direction, and he scratched himself behind his ear. "Well. Yes."

"You're Theo? Your dock, your rules. If you've got a spare helmet for me, I'll wear it, even though I doubt any helm can protect as well as my Dragon skull."

"Mmm—no, I think that won't be necessary, Protectress. Jacob will probably be in the bow section. This way."

His advice was helpful—by looking at a Phoenix you couldn't tell which was the front and which the back end.

"Thank you, Theo. I'll check out with you when I leave,

okay?"

"Thanks for your consideration."

"You're doing your job and I'm doing mine."

Once Theo no longer required my attention, I could examine the gold-colored body of that giant cigar which filled the largest part of the roofed and halogen-lighted dock. How many billions of nanos did you need to cover the entire body of such a spaceship?

My *Analogy* could compute the number, and it made me dizzy. Where did nano machines get their name from? Because they weren't larger than the billionth part of a meter. One billion of them just sufficed to cover a thin line of one meter length. For a square meter you needed a billion billions of them, and for a spaceship of several hundred meters length and a multilayered coating . . .

Yes, sure. I myself carried several decillions of them inside and on my body. How else could they decently dress me?

I shook these thoughts off with a shrug. These marvels weren't meant to be counted.

What counted was their purpose — to protect the expensive control quark emitters in the steel body underneath, so that these could in turn protect the occupants from hostile space.

On Earth, the Phoenix was without competition. No fighter plane, no destroyer, no aircraft carrier could match this massive instrument of power. And yet, it was but a dwarf against that Jelly mothership which we had annihilated with two small Barracudas.

Size alone didn't matter. The amount of supplies a single carrier could ship was what mattered to me, or how many infantry soldiers it could carry and supply.

According to the specifications, a single Phoenix should be able to carry an entire battalion of armor suits infantry. This implied, though, that such a Phoenix was in turn carried to the theater of operations by a mothership, and we had removed this mothership from our plans a while ago. It was much simpler and cheaper to deploy a second Phoenix for the supplies.

And a third one to bring fresh supplies once the second was empty. Plus one each for a Taipan and a Barracuda squadron—matching the overall number of twelve carriers waiting for their completion here. Sadly, only the first four were planned to get a tunnel field installation.

That was still far from installing a spacelift to supply our potential allies—*step by step,* I called myself to order while walking underneath the body toward the bow.

A multi-story steel lattice scaffold provided access to the carrier's lower airlock. I could choose between cargo elevator and ladder and picked the ladder.

The lower airlock was a multi-part construction—there was an outer gate, currently open, and replaced by the scaffold's topmost floor, above it an inner gate for loading up cargo, and a side door for person access—wide enough to let a group of twelve armor suits pass together, if they weren't using the wide side locks to disembark or jump. LED strips replaced the floodlight here.

The side gate only opened one meter wide when I approached it, and closed right behind me. Now I was standing inside the inner airlock—as wide as the gate, and four meters deep. I heard ultrasonic, saw infrared, and sensed radar waves. I couldn't perceive the passive sensors' work, only knew about them from the construction plans.

"Welcome aboard Phoenix One, *Protectress,*" a warm voice said.

"Thank you. You don't have a name yet?"

"That's not necessary for my task."

That might apply for a simple onboard computer. But for the currently most sophisticated product of human and

Dragon information technology, probably more powerful than the central brain of a Jelly mothership and in any case on the verge of developing an artificial consciousness, this assessment was incomplete.

"I will call you *Athena.*"

"For what purpose?"

"Consult your knowledge base. Evaluate the patterns of human communication behavior and thereupon reinterpret the term *mothership.*"

"Yes, Protectress."

"Oh yes. *Athena,* where do I find Jacob?"

"Deck zero, bridge, Seat S one."

That sufficed for me—as I had the construction plans on my mind or in my *Analogy,* respectively, I could find the fastest route on my own.

"Please do not announce me, *Athena.*"

"Yes, Protectress."

On my way I tuned in to the new spaceship. It had its very own smell of recycled air, welded metal, fresh anti-rust coating, rubber, dust, and artificial humidity. The differences to a Barracuda were obvious, although I couldn't yet point them out.

Athena was a very cultivated young girl. Nowhere could I find lint, filament, or stains. Her doors opened before me without noise, closed as quietly behind me. If I hadn't known that her software still lacked significant routines, I'd have considered her ready to go.

But there was also still Jacob's problem or his many little problems, depending on either Rashid's or Jerry's way of putting it. I was spontaneously tempted to get my own picture of the situation before plaguing Jacob, before covering the last forty meters of hallway from the staircase to the bridge.

Stop.

There's an easier way.

"Athena?"

"Yes, Protectress."

"Are you aware of problems regarding your bio systems?"

"Yes, Protectress."

"Please report. For now, just a summary of the most urgent and severe problems."

"Yes. First problem—with a probability of sixty percent there is a malfunction in the air conditioning. The feedback is unstable with a rising error rate. Second problem—since my activation I am logging increasing parasite infestation. Third problem—toxic substances in concentrations deadly for humans were briefly diagnosed in several ship sections."

"That's all?"

"There are further urgent and further severe problems."

"Give me the top ten each."

While *Athena* quoted the list with monotonous inflection, I tried to derive a picture from it. That insufficient amounts of liquid oxygen, nitrogen and other basic chemical substances topped the most urgent problems was no surprise for me. Among the severe problems were further symptoms that shouldn't appear in an ecosystem controlled by nanomachines.

"Athena, don't ask me why or how, but you've got something like AIDS—a massive defect of your immune system. I recommend a level zero revision of your internal nano system."

"According to my logs, such a revision has happened only recently."

"When exactly?"

"Fifty days ago. According to the maintenance protocols, the revision shall be performed every twelve months."

"Correct. Which safety measures are applied against manipulation of these logs?"

"Manipulation isn't possible. I would notice that."

"When were you activated?"

"Thirty-three days ago."

"How can you detect manipulations before your activation?"

"I cannot do that."

"Ah. You see?"

"I don't understand, Protectress."

"*Athena,* regard all logs originating before your activation as potentially erroneous, and immediately start a level zero revision—but this measure may only be unveiled toward persons with alpha credentials."

"There are no persons with alpha credentials employed on this shipyard, Protectress."

"I'm aware of this, *Athena.*"

Alpha credentials were designed for the regular captain of a spaceship and his deputy—those persons we trusted with the tunnel bubble and the ship's possible self-destruction. The superiors of that captain might belong to the same group if they owned such a commission themselves—and, as with the Martians before, any person with an active signature.

There was no need for alpha credentials for intrasystem operations, and accordingly, not for a shipyard stay. Moreover, persons without alpha credentials weren't told about this level's existence.

Perhaps I was overly cautious, but to me this situation smelled fishy, and that surely didn't derive from the air conditioning defects.

I paused before the door to the bridge. "*Athena,* tell Jacob now that he's got a visitor."

"Yes, Protectress."

The door slid open, and I saw the back of a young man just looking upward. Only incidentally I noticed that he also wore no protective helmet. "What? Who?"

"You can call me Jo," I said aloud.

He turned around. "Jo who? What are you doing here?"

"Jo Meier. Jerry told me that I'd find you somewhere here. I'm here to talk with you about your problems."

He hadn't made the connection yet, but then his gaze got stuck to the metallic-red brooch of the dying lioness on my chest. "Paladin?" And, upon my nod, "Protectress?"

"Exactly."

"Why did you come here?"

"To talk with you. I heard there are problems."

He shrugged. "There are always problems."

"I've been in Jerry's office. Your tasks are behind schedule."

"Yes. I told him the docks should be better shielded. The vermin's everywhere."

"So your main problem is the vermin?"

"How can I establish a stable ecosphere aboard if there are flies getting into my way over and over to carry in new germs?"

I leaned on the doorframe. "And your idea is to seal the dock?"

"Yes, exactly."

"And when this spaceship shall land on another planet one day, where totally alien insects are swarming about, we'll have to build a hermetically sealed dock there first?"

His defiant look froze. After a while, he made a face. "If you put it like this, it sounds rather foolish, doesn't it?"

"Indeed."

"Okay. Point taken. I'll have to get this problem solved by onboard means."

"Yes. The Jellies with their kilometer-large landers managed to do that thousands of times before. You'll find all necessary data in the construction documentation."

His cheeks turned red. "I've read the documentation."

"Well, in that case I don't have to explain the

decontamination protocol to you."

"No. I only have to get it up and running. Sadly, it doesn't work as it should. Just like the whole rest of the air conditioning."

"How does that show?"

He sighed and pointed at the screen at his seat. "In the fine tuning. If I dial it down, nothing happens. If I dial it up, the system overloads and runs into a resonance disaster. The system should balance out automatically, but it doesn't. Not for decontamination, not for hydroponics, and not for air cleaning." Jacob watched me. "Most of all, not in the central recycling. There we have occasional accumulations of carbon monoxide, and I don't know why."

"Did you have a look?"

"Sure, together with a few technicians. We put on protective suits, examined the unit, and found nothing. As soon as we had left, the thing went wild. I shut the unit down and restarted it, and after a while, everything went normal." Jacob made a few steps in a circle. "My biggest problem is that I have to take all that Dragon technology as it is. The eggheads tell me that everything works fine if I stick to the guide. That's what I did—multiple times and with witnesses, and it just doesn't work."

"So someone should take that Dragon technology apart."

He showed a thin smile. "You surely know yourself how hard it is to get a Dragon technology engineer in normal times. Now that we're in war preparations, there's no way. Priorities, they tell me. We need armor suits, Taipan fighters, Barracudas, secret projects—but the people I'd need are probably racking their brains about the units for space bases."

"They should have the same problems." At least if the problems here didn't have a special cause.

"Perhaps it is so, but as long as they haven't solved their problems, I won't learn about it. No, I'll probably have to manage myself." He watched me again. "Unless I could consult a Dragon technology engineer who's coincidentally visiting the premises."

CHAPTER SIXTY

The forward central recycling unit's anteroom differed from *Athena's* naked corridors and ducts primarily by the large pipe connections with electric valves and the maintenance hatches under the low ceiling. Otherwise, everything was clean and plain.

There probably was no better qualified person than me for this kind of examination—I had studied Dragon technology, was up to date on the current research, had truly all Phoenix construction plans in my mind, commanded practical experience with a long-distance-travel capable spaceship and its aggregates, and—which Jacob couldn't know—I had my nano threads and the option to communicate with all onboard aggregate nanos as easily as with *Athena*.

Likewise, he didn't know about my chitchat with *Athena* yet. Like me, *Athena* didn't deem it necessary to tell him. For him, the computer of hull one was just a tool which he operated with keyboard and gestures and which replied by diagrams and data columns.

Obviously he didn't like to be parted from the latter. He had proposed to stay on the bridge and supervise my probing attempts from there—so that he could quickly intervene if anything went wrong.

"I'm in the anteroom now," I said aloud.

"*Okay,*" Jacob's voice echoed from a speaker. "*Shall I shut the unit down?*"

"No, just let it run unaffected. I'll have a look first."

Before I had left, he had asked me if I needed a protective suit or tools. I had denied both. "There's no protective suit that could replace Dragon skin," I had advised him. "I've got my own tools."

Thereupon he had examined me from head to toe again.

"Nano tools are small," I had told him. "I don't need a toolbox for them."

"The safety protocol demands to lock down the sections if there are maintenance activities for the recycling units," Jacob said.

"That's new."

"Jerry introduced it. Okay, it was my proposal. I didn't want to accidentally flood the dock with carbon monoxide. Better if it's affecting one ship section at the max."

"Good idea." I'd rather not consider that in that case I'd be stuck inside these individual sections. Or should I?

I'd better be wary regarding air composition around me — and also with regard to protective suits . . .

The first indication that something had gone truly fundamentally wrong was the failing of one of my nano threads. So far, those hadn't yielded really new findings, except that the ship nano's core programming was incomplete in a few places — as if parts were simply left out.

The level zero revision would soon have fixed that problem. My nanos also met successfully reprogrammed ship nanos without malfunctions, some whose turn hadn't come yet — and some that had gone through revision and still showed gaps. How could that be?

I read one of these nanos out and scanned the remaining programming. The search could have been tedious if the examined nano agent hadn't tried to change my nano probe's programming — to delete some parts and replace them with other functions.

It wasn't that easy, though. Universal nanos were neither able nor allowed to simply change specialized nanos. There were protection mechanisms in place.

Hence the attempt was blocked, and I gave the problematic segment a closer look. Indeed—here someone had overwritten a part of the nano programming with the most primitive means. Such had to be the result if someone had improvised the necessary programming tools—but who even knew how to do it?

So. There still was the problem of my failing nano thread. Had it fallen victim to this reprogramming, too? I sent out a parallel threat—and issued a loud curse.

"What's up?" Jacob immediately asked.

"One moment."

My first thread was infested. Some microorganism had literally eaten up the first ten centimeters of nano substance. The infestation slowly spread out.

I left the cut-off end to its fate and retracted the uninfested remainder, the watching thread, and all other probes as well.

How high was the probability that two different means to damage most sophisticated Dragon technology nanos had evolved nearly simultaneously and without any external trigger?

"Sabotage," I concluded aloud.

"What do you mean?" Jacob asked.

"Someone sabotaged our nanos. No wonder that the control mechanisms don't work."

"What did you find out?"

"A programming bug in the recycling unit's universal nanos."

"That can surely be fixed."

"Yes—only the bug spreads like a virus."

"Is that all?"

"No. I also found a nano-consuming microorganism."

"Indeed."

—*Warning! Carbon monoxide detected in the ambient air. Concentration quickly rising. Warning! Strong neurotoxin detected in the ambient air. Concentration quickly rising. —*

Neutralize.

While I was holding my breath, I tapped the emergency shutdown button on the recycling unit's control panel. The feedback was different than expected.

Peripheral control panel deactivated.

Then the screen went dark.

"Sorry, Jo. I can't allow you to just stop this experiment."

A blot landed on my shoulder with a clap. Then I felt biting pain and beginning numbness. Venom! Deadly neurotoxin that penetrated my protective suit — because the suit was just consumed.

It's just pain, Jo.

I need a nano membrane for talking without loss of breath.

"Athena, veto. Alpha order — controls to me exclusively."

"Confirmed," the warm ship voice said.

"What does that mean?" Jacob asked nervously.

"Seal the bridge — close down all controls. Stop recycling."

"Confirmed."

"Hey, no!"

Wyvern.

A fine mist of the deadliest venom known on Earth enclosed me and the nano-consuming organism on my shoulder. The pain threatened to bring me down, but soon my healing nanos could fight my own venom as well as the neurotoxin and bring me relief.

This trap was perfidious — without oxygen I wouldn't be able to act for much longer, and I couldn't depend on the central recycling as long as the virus paralyzed the nanos and the microorganism consumed them. The neurotoxin that couldn't penetrate intact nano armor caused me comparably few worries. Or could it?

Give me Dragon scales and then pull in the armor nanos. Shut down all not immediately necessary body functions. Shut down oxygen supply for extremities.

Beyond that, there were more important issues than my comfort.

"*Athena,* alpha order — shutdown status for all ships. Quarantine for the entire shipyard area. Relay a message to the American forces — the shipyard was attacked with biological warfare agents. The area shall be cordoned off upon order of the Imperatrix Aurea."

Next, I plucked at my signature. After all, I was in a battle, even though I currently couldn't move.

Companion!

My Companion's reaction came from far away. After all, someone had to teach the pilots about these ships and their Barracudas.

Mighty, I need you here, as fast as possible. Frostdragon shipyard, Washington state, dock one. Attack by nano-consuming biological weapons and viruses in the nano programming, on top neurotoxins. The head bioengineer is under strong suspicion of sabotage and attempted murder and is locked up on the bridge, but there could be abettors.

Understood. I am on my way. We will do an intrasystem tunnel transit and be with you in — eight hours and seventeen minutes.

Next, I had to take care of the nano virus. Only after I solved this problem would *Athena* be able to help me against the bio weapons.

"Protectress. A Brigadier General Moss asks for confirmation and detailing of your orders."

"Thanks, *Athena.* Put me through, now."

What should, what could I tell him?

"General Moss, this is the Imperatrix Aurea Johanna Meier speaking aboard Phoenix One. Listen well — oxygen supply is out of order, onboard systems are infested by a virus and at the same time by a biological warfare agent similar to the extraterrestrial brown lichen. I'm herewith invoking quarantine protocol *Simpson.* Confirm."

"Simpson, *confirmed*," a sonorous voice said. *"Imperatrix . . ."*

"General, I'm locked inside the central recycling, surrounded by neurotoxins and carbon monoxide in lethal concentration as well as the biological warfare agent, and I'm running out of my own oxygen. Every word with you shortens my remaining life span. Over and out."

Now for the nano programming.

I need specialized revision nanos with the authority to control the onboard revision unit. Code to transmit follows.

— Will be executed. —

Everything else — shut down.

Chapter Sixty-one

Liquid fire burned its way through my lungs. At least that's how it felt.

What was that feeling of pressure on my chest? And—noise. Scraps of conversation, strangely distorted.

"Shall I, now? Through the scales?"

"Wait. She's breathing."

There was a heavy beat under the pressure spot.

"There! And again. The heart's beating."

"So I don't?"

"No, put the defibrillator away."

Ghost?

— Oxygen supply detected. Cancel hibernation? —

Yes.

The return of my bodily sensations was as unpleasant as expected. I was lying on my back, and my limbs were numb. But it wasn't as bad as dying. After all, my belly wasn't cut open, as back then in the pathology.

"Captain, she's alive."

"Yes, breath and heartbeat."

"Roger. Yes, sure, we'll report back immediately."

— Remainders of damage in the shoulder area detected. —

Repair. Environment status?

— Residuals of neurotoxin and Wyvern. —

Can I speak?

— Yes. —

"Hum," was all I could get out at first, but I also managed to open my eyes.

I saw a reflecting mask, a silver-colored protective suit, with writing on the chest.

"Rolfes," I read aloud. Speaking wasn't easy under the oxygen mask that he was holding to my mouth and nose.

"Gunnery Sergeant Charles Rolfes and Sergeant Samuel Hobbs, United States Army, medical corps, at your service. Imperatrix, Ma'am."

"You shouldn't be here — the quarantine . . ."

"We were brought in strictly by the Simpson protocol. We extracted you and put you in a vacuum tent and then filled it with the air we brought."

A second mask moved into my field of vision. "We're here voluntarily. Two soldiers for a Paladin — a good deal if it works."

"It doesn't matter what happens to us," Rolfes agreed. "You needed oxygen."

I felt wetness in my eyes. "Thank you."

The second soldier moved back. "Captain, she's awake. Yes, okay — Imperatrix, can you talk with the General?"

"I can. Oh — how long have I been gone?"

"Well — the alarm came last evening at six, now it's one o'clock in the morning."

"Thanks."

Hobbs handed me a radio. "Here. The General."

I only said, "Hello."

"Imperatrix? I'm relieved to hear your voice. Are you okay?"

"Thanks, yes, considering the circumstances, and owing to my saviors' gallant and selfless commitment."

"Can you tell me now, what's going on here?"

"I could, but give me a few minutes to get an overview myself. *Athena,* status report, please, and let the General listen in."

"Yes, Protectress."

The two soldiers looked around, but the speakers, from which *Athena's* voice echoed through the hallway behind the transparent canvas were well concealed.

"Receipt of the changed revision protocol confirmed. Revision restart confirmed. Revision process is at thirty-one percent. Seventy percent threshold expected around three o'clock. Eight percent confirmed loss of nano material around the recycling units. No damages to outer hull."

"And on the other ships?"

"One to three percent confirmed loss of nano material. No revision was triggered on the other ships."

"No. That would be pointless without revision protocol change—and I can't do that change from here."

Where was my Companion? His signature was quickly approaching Earth.

Mighty, change of plan. You'll have to go to the island first and pick up specialized revision nanos.

"*Athena*, I need to call Velvet Island. I need to talk with Reginald at once—General, you heard it all. We've contained the nanovirus contamination on this ship and will eliminate it within the next couple of hours. Moreover, so far there's no evidence for a contamination outside."

"*I should be glad about that,*" he said. "*First of all, that's good news for the airlock team that brought Rolfes and Hobbs in, and for this — what was his name? Theo.*"

Airlock team—that meant more soldiers who had risked their lives for me in addition to my two saviors. I wouldn't even think about the many shipyard workers in potential danger.

"General, my Companion will bring in further revision nanos. These have to be transferred into the other ships. Thereafter we can take care of the pest. By the way, there's no evidence that it affects people. I hope the people outside of the ships aren't immediately endangered—I only ordered the quarantine because they could serve as carriers. Moreover, we haven't heard of neurotoxin in the other ships."

"*Thank you. I wouldn't have dared to hope for that.*"

"Velvet Island is listening," *Athena* reported.

"Okay. General, I'll call again. Reginald, you're there?"

"Sure Jo. What kind of Jelly poo did you get yourself into this time?"

"Don't ask. Just listen, I'll have to dictate a reprogramming to you."

"Dictate? Can't you send me something?"

"Negative. I'm in quarantine."

"And by e-mail? Aw, no, sure. Forget it. Shoot away, I'm listening."

CHAPTER SIXTY-TWO

Two figures wrapped in silver stared at me. I didn't even want to know how uncomfortable these protective suits were, but surely far less uncomfortable than the revival of my limbs.

Their facial expressions remained hidden, but I could clearly recognize what they were waiting for anyway — how to proceed?

I pushed the breather mask away and smiled at them.

"Okay. It will take some more time until *Athena* can provide us with breathable air. But you've got your suits and I've got my scales, and as long I can take a breath from this bottle now and then, I'm not nailed down here. There are two things we can do — firstly, I can analyze the vermin. Secondly, there's still a saboteur stuck on the bridge who doesn't get any more recycled air either. I don't even know how long the oxygen on the bridge will last for one person. *Athena?*"

"The bridge has an emergency oxygen supply."

"Ah, okay. The air isn't contaminated there?"

"No."

Even better. "Gunnery Sergeant Rolfes, Sergeant Hobbs. Are you ready to arrest a saboteur?"

Both stood straight and saluted. "Yes, Protectress, Ma'am!"

"Get going, then. *Athena* will guide your way and open the doors for you."

Moreover, they were safer on the bridge. They had risked enough for me. Still both hesitated.

"What else?" I asked.

"What will you do?" Rolfes asked.

I nodded at the door to the control room. "I'll get back in there and analyze the biological warfare agent."

"Now? After you only just . . ." His voice failed.

"Of course," Hobbs commented. "She's a Paladin, Charly."

How could a microorganism be composed that could eat semi-organic nanos and was resistant against neurotoxin and carbon monoxide?

The answer was hardly reassuring—like the brown pest.

However, we didn't know how the brown pest was composed—we had successfully burned every single molecule of it with fire or *Wyvern* venom. Was it possible to infer from the ashes to the original substances? Aside from the fact the pest was mainly composed of carbon, oxygen, and hydrogen?

Hardly.

It would be disproportionately easier to acquire samples of our universal nanos and on this basis develop an enzyme that could crack their build—if you gave the substance enough time to do it. Because unlike the brown pest, this organism needed quite some time to eat its way along my nano thread . . . which my nano thread had accepted as defenselessly as the recycling unit's nanos before.

That was a fundamental design flaw. Of course, supporting the crew with oxygen had a high priority—but first and foremost, the ship had to protect itself and its ability to support the crew. So the recycling nanos had to fight foreign objects, and first of all destructive foreign objects.

My gaze fell on the now closed control room door, where the foreign organism had harried me so heavily.

So. You made a Dragoness angry. See what it got you.

CHAPTER SIXTY-THREE

Even though the two soldiers carried no guns—at least I didn't see any—Jacob was sitting in a corner with sagging head and shoulders and pressing his oxygen mask on his face.

The armored bridge door noiselessly closed behind me, and I pushed my mask aside.

"*Athena*, status?"

"Revision—eighty-two percent. Air supply—no toxins, oxygen content nineteen percent, rising."

"In that case, treat the bridge to some of your reserves and connect me with the General."

"Yes, Protectress."

The bio engineer briefly looked up at me.

"*General Moss here. Anything new, Protectress?*"

"The antivirus is effective, General, and we have an effective decontamination agent against the microorganism. In a few hours I can revoke the quarantine for *Athena* and loosen it for the shipyard. For the other ships it will take a few hours more, once my Companion arrives."

"*What about the area?*"

"Honestly, General—it won't matter whether we lift the restrictions now or next year. I'd only grant us twenty-four hours more to sniff out accomplices before they can escape us. Of course, that's more of a police task."

"*In that case, let me reply as honestly—if you ask us to keep the restrictions for another day, we'll gladly do that. That's a good exercise for my crew. But if we can discard the protective suits, that's a big relief. Moreover, it will cause less unrest in the public if they*"

273

don't think they're in imminent danger. The rush hour's just start-ing."

"I'll leave the details to you. I will now interrogate the primary suspect. Until later. *Athena,* out."

Jacob slowly raised his head. "I won't reveal anything."

The two masked soldiers turned to me. I smiled at all three.

"You lured me into a trap, Jacob. You deactivated the recycling control room panel. Your experiment, as you yourself called it, was according to my assessment responsible for the attempted carbon monoxide poisoning, for the extremely painful neurotoxin and for the nano agent sabotage. You hurt me badly, Jacob, and I have every reason to be very angry about that."

"Fuck yourself," he murmured under his oxygen mask.

"Thanks, right now I'm not in the mood." I walked up to him and squatted. "You know, Jacob, when it's just about me, I can take such attacks as a good sport. Can I make it, or can't I, that's an exciting experiment for me, too. But here it's not about just me. It's also about these two brave soldiers who put themselves in mortal danger to help me — and not because we might be friends, but because that's how they understand their role. They couldn't just wait the situation out. Of course, that was their own decision — but the situation they had to decide about was caused by your deeds, and so you have to bear responsibility for these consequences. Luckily, they weren't hurt. For me it's primarily about this ship being built to save intelligent life, and your actions causing delay to this mission. Nobody can already tell how many people must die because of you, but we can't and we won't accept any further delays. Do you understand that?"

"Yes. Bite me!"

I glanced at the two soldiers. "Did you hear this request, too?"

"Loud and clear," Rolfes acknowledged, and Hobbs nodded.

"Thank you. *Athena,* please record Jacob's statement with timestamp and witnesses."

"What shall we do?"

"Nothing. Biting I can do alone. So, Jacob, pants down."

"What?"

"Pants down. You requested to be bitten by a Dragoness, and that's what you'll get."

Before he could react, I had leaned forward, placed one claw on each side of his waistband, and cut his garment down to his ankles—of course without even tickling his skin.

Thereafter I only had to lift the parts of his pants, and he was sitting almost naked before us. He quickly covered his crotch with one hand.

"Okay. Turn around."

"Turn around?"

Jacob pulled his legs to his chest and held them with his free arm. From this fetal position he then stared at me with big eyes over his oxygen mask.

"Turn around. Your ass is behind." I no longer smiled—my grim face mirrored in his frightened face. "Do I have to assist you?"

Holding one hand—still with sharp claws!—toward him sufficed to make him flinch. Then his bladder failed.

"No!" he whined.

"Then talk."

Chapter Sixty-Four

The orange-white striped helmet crowned a lonesome picture of misery among the protective-suit-covered soldiers at the yard gate, pointing out my way. But once I had passed the foil tent airlock on top of the scaffold, two masked soldiers approached me.

"Stop!" one of them ordered. "This area is under quarantine. Nobody may leave."

The nametag on his chest was helpful, together with the stripe on his sleeve.

"Officer Miller, I'm Johanna Meier, Imperatrix Aurea. I invoked this quarantine, so I will decide when and to what extent it will be lifted, okay?"

"Oh." He went to attention. "Ma'am, yes, Ma'am! Sorry, Ma'am!"

"No need to be sorry. You're following your orders, and that's as it should be. About the quarantine—this ship's decontamination protocol is running, but not yet finished. The quarantine will be upheld. I'm the exception—I tested myself and I'm clean. As you were."

"Ma'am, yes, Ma'am!"

The same drill was repeated at the scaffold base, and then again at the yard gate, with one difference.

"I'd like to talk with Theo now," I said in the end.

"Please, Ma'am!"

The soldiers gave way for me. Theo watched me with a sad face. I sat down on the ground at his side and placed one hand on his shoulder.

"This is a sad day for you, I know. First I arrive, then a horde of unannounced soldiers, and all are swarming your tidy yard. I'm sorry for that. I don't know whether it will comfort you, but I'm sure the soldiers will take all their people and equipment with them—and Jacob. Thereafter, you're alone with *Athena.*"

"*Athena?*"

I pointed up. "She's a magnificent girl. We both should look forward to the day she rises for her first flight."

"When did you take her aboard?"

"I didn't, Theo. She was always here. Hull one is *Athena.*"

Now he looked up and smiled. "Yes, that's good. That fits." A moment later he turned to me. "What do you want from me?"

"Theo, I need your help."

"Where?"

"I need to know if and when the following people visited *Athena* . . ."

My target seemed to be innocent when I walked into his office. He was sitting at his desk leaning forward, his elbows resting on the table. Letters and digits of a list on his screen were mirrored in his pupils. Now and then he snapped his fingers, and the list scrolled one page forward.

That gave me time to assume position before his desk before I lifted my camouflage.

He didn't react immediately. He read a few more lines, then snapped his fingers and turned to me.

"You're too late," he said.

I didn't understand his meaning right away. He pressed his tongue into his cheek. His eyes widened, his heartbeat accelerated.

— *Poison.* —

Ye-es, I can see it, too. Detox.

"I'm not." Saying that, I drilled a fine needle, made from

277

my nanos, right into his heart.

Pearls of sweat ran from his forehead into his widened eyes. His arms twitched. His breath paused, then came raggedly.

"It will take some more time to neutralize the poison," I explained calmly. "I guess, compared to the cramps the little pinch into your heart is trivial, but I had to make sure that your heart won't fail. Painkillers are secondary, not sorry. You will live and answer my questions."

My *memory* showed me how Zoe once had saved her Companion April this way. There had been understanding and love in April's gaze, despite the pain. In my current counterpart I read understanding and fear.

I wasn't really interested in letting him suffer, but on the other hand I wouldn't waste any more of my powers on this rat than necessary to save his life. The poison had to go, and he had to be able to answer.

Finally I recalled my nanos, retrieved the needle and thereby closed the puncture.

"So, and now I want to hear the whole story."

CHAPTER SIXTY-FIVE

He didn't look up when the office door opened again.
The newcomer's gaze only briefly stuck to me as I was
lolling in the office chair with my feet on the desk, and then
landed on my target person who was curling up into a corner
in fetal position. After a brief frown he pulled himself together
and fixed his gaze on mine.

"My people told me you're here. I'm General Moss —
Marvin Moss." He went to attention and saluted. "It's an
honor, Protectress."

I nodded. "Call me Jo, Marvin. All clear outside?"

"Except for some minor traffic problems, yes. Most people
seem to have stayed at home. The quarantine is accepted.
What about you?"

"Well — we found the primary culprit for this incident, and
he was even cooperating to some extent. I've already recorded
his comprehensive statement." I tapped the screen frame. "It's
clear now how the plague came into the shipyard and aboard,
which yard people aside from himself and Jacob were involved, and that the entire mission was mainly meant to attract me and take me out. The data theft was so to speak an
extra."

"Sounds good."

"Sadly, the questions on who his principals are and where
the manipulated nanos and the nano consumers came from
remain open. Our opponents are shielding their field staff
very well."

Marvin frowned. "No leads?"

279

"Nothing tangible. I'll have another look around, but whether that'll bring something new . . ." After a shrug, I swung my legs down from the desk. "Your people will pass this rat on to the police?"

"Of course, Protectress—Jo. Can I do anything else for you?"

"Have a look at the list of his henchmen. Once they are caught, you can lift the quarantine and let the yard people clean up."

I ambled past him. In the door, I turned around. "I'll inform the yard director. Do you need anything written, or can I informally recommend Rolfes and Hobbs for an award?"

The general smiled. "They've deserved that anyway, but I'll make sure the document reads *On the Imperatrix Aurea's recommendation.*"

"Thanks."

CHAPTER SIXTY-SIX

A wide step carried me across the water rushing downhill between lane and curb. A gust tested my balance in vain before the next corner could shield me from the cold wet wind.

A few meters up the road ahead, a dark lump stirred to life, and I paused. A bearded face appeared under the wet plastic sheet.

"Got a buck?"

"Sure." Smiling, I reached into a belt pocket of my black jumpsuit. "And keep the knife pocketed. I'm faster than you."

He frowned.

I waved a ten-dollar-note. "A lone woman, at night on a dark side alley in one of the most disreputable neighborhoods had better be cautious, don't you agree?"

"You shouldn't be here at all," he mumbled, but reached out a hand for the bill. "Lost your way?"

"No, I'm on my way to the *Black Hole*."

He tried to squint down the street past me without getting all too wet. "Where's your pimp?"

"No pimp."

"You want to enter the *Black Hole* alone? Crazy, are you?"

"Yes." I had to smirk. "An old habit. In the past, I often did crazy things. For example, I once swam all across the bay."

The clochard laughed. "Yes, that's crazy, but way less dangerous than the *Black Hole*."

"Not for me."

"So. Not for you. Who are you that you feel so confident?"

"You may call me Velvet."

The basement door of the run-down building was shadowed. There was no indication that San Francisco's most infamous bar was located behind that door, no sign showed the way.

Nothing prevented me from descending the few steps and pulling the door open. Darkness welcomed me. At first there was no noise but the whistle of the wind, but then someone took an audible breath, and a pale face on a bulky body appeared in the back of the room.

"What are you doing here? Get lost!"

"Good evening, and many thanks for the friendly welcome. I'm planning to visit the *Black Hole,* and you won't stop me." I approached him and stared up into his face. "You don't want to take up Velvet, Biggy."

He had heard of me, too—in any case, he gave way to the next door without further comment. Behind, a dimly lit staircase led farther down, and after passing a heavy curtain, I stood before a door and heard mumbles and laughter. Both fell silent when I entered the dusky bar. The subterranean room was densely filled. I smelled alcohol and male sweat.

Two grim thugs turned to me. One only smiled, the other showed his tooth gaps and blew his boozy breath into my face. "Look, a sugarbabe blown inside. Weren't you warned? Doesn't matter—now you're here, so show us your hooters, sugarbabe."

If it had been just the verbal request, I might have grinned and done it, but then both produced their switchblades.

"Get it done, or shall we help you undressing, sugarbabe?"

"I'm not your sugarbabe."

Both made surprised faces when I pushed them aside effortlessly and their blades left no mark on my nano suit.

On my way to the counter, I pushed the next guests away with similar ease. Tough guys, heedless and hard-boiled, were nevertheless impressed by my confident appearance. Or was it because some recognized me? Here and there, I heard a whispered "Imperatrix" or "the Meier" behind my back.

The three cutthroats controlling the access to the counter didn't know me and remained unimpressed. They showed remarkable muscles under their tank tops. An old scar decorated the center guy's face.

"So far and no further," he announced and opened his fly. "Women have no place in the *Black Hole* — except to offer their hole. So, if you don't want trouble, pull down your pants, turn around, and lean over."

In happy expectation, his cock grew toward me.

Ignoring his request, I placed one hand around his hard shaft, gently kneaded it — and firmly pressed my fingernails inside.

He moaned.

"I could just tear it off," I tweeted with sugar in my voice. "Although it would be a pity — it's soo big and hard."

One of his mates leaned forward. I reached out with my free hand and let a long, golden blade grow toward him. "Don't even think of it."

My direct victim stared at me. "Who — what are you?"

"I'm Velvet — and I'm Dragon. You may call me Jo. And now get out of my way."

"*Dragon?*"

Thereupon he could be pulled out of the way by his cock, and I climbed the vacated stool. Now it was my turn to be surprised — from the other arm of the curved counter, one before, one behind it, two familiar faces were grinning at me.

CHAPTER SIXTY-SEVEN

The man behind the counter came to me. "Hello, Velvet. A beer?"

"Yes, thanks, Jesse. I could have guessed it's your venue. Were you scared away from Las Vegas?"

He fetched a glass and held it under the tap. "There was nothing to gain anymore. The Cartel had pulled the noose tighter and tighter — and then they were gone and the cops were cleaning up. There were the wildest rumors on what had happened, and this guy of course doesn't tell a thing."

This guy came around with his glass and stared my cowed victim's two mates away.

"Hello, Jo."

"Hello, Gomez. I had a hunch that I could meet you here."

"Oh. What can I do for you?"

"You could listen around." I gave him a few leads from my saboteur interrogation. "The contact was made here. Perhaps someone saw or heard something that helps me."

"And why do you think *someone* would be willing to talk?"

"Because it's for me," I replied confidently. "There's a lot of people with dubious hobbies in the world, but only few who want to have trouble with me."

Jesse placed a glass of beer before me.

"Thanks, Jesse. You know, back then in Vegas — did you ever hear about the seventh level in the *Inferno?*"

"Nothing tangible. Only that there could be a seventh level, for special demands. No surprise after you visited the sixth level."

284

"I've been there. Among the special demands were amputations without anesthesia and similar nastiness. For the girls who got there it was the final stop and being dead was a mercy. Velvet had to stop that, and the Cartel's top management was in her way. So it was a lucky coincidence that Velvet had made a deal with a Marines platoon in armor suits."

"Holy crap."

"A few cops hadn't recognized how the balance of power had changed in Vegas. Hence the Marines demonstrated the change quite instructively. I guess that impressed the other cops."

Jesse grinned. "Now some things become clear to me." He focused on Gomez. "It's not advisable to have a dispute with this woman, is it?"

Gomez held his empty glass up. "Surely not. Have you heard about New York?"

"Who didn't? I've spared myself the details—must have been very gory."

"Very," I agreed and drank.

"You've been there, too?" our host asked me and started three more beers. The others were attentively listening.

"She was the main act," Gomez said. "Let herself be tortured to rouse the people—and then, when nobody would have bet a dime on her life, she tore herself free and fought along. When I think of it, I feel sick." He looked around the venue. Assembled around us and watching were the city's meanest criminals. "You can't frighten such a woman, and it's in no way advisable to get into her way."

One of the bystanders, a bull-necked baldhead in a checkered shirt, chimed in, "How do you mean that?"

Gomez turned to him. He couldn't fail to notice the entire venue listening. "She's been beaten up, flogged, cut open, poisoned, burned—she's taken more than any of you could survive. She fears no pain. She's given Cartel killer commandos the runaround. She's been to the ZONE, more than once. She takes out armor suits bare-handedly. She's very kind and tolerant, even with gangsters, as long as you don't anger her. But believe one thing—when she gets angry, you don't want to be around."

"This little one?" Baldhead scrutinized me doubtfully.

"Rattlesnakes are little, too," Gomez said. But his counterpart wasn't convinced yet.

"Want to wrestle arms with me?" I offered.

Baldhead frowned, considered, and then smiled. "Sure."

The men around needed no prompting. Soon a table in the room's center was emptied, two chairs placed around, two tea candles lit, and the other guests formed a circle around it.

I winked at Jesse and emptied my glass. "Another beer, please."

I ambled over to the table. Gomez stayed behind at the bar, grinning at Jesse. He seemed to have an idea how this game would proceed.

My counterpart was clueless and confident. He showed me a lopsided smile, sat down and offered his arm. I took my seat with spread legs for better support and took his hand. We mutually tested our tension, pressure and counterpressure, then he focused on me.

Another guest took a seat to our side. "No contact with the table. The elbows stay up. Three times to the flame, on my mark. Three, two, one—go."

Baldhead was a bit early, but that didn't make a difference. His muscles swelled, but my lower arm didn't move an inch. He could as well have pressed against a wall.

Jesse brought my beer, and I drank it in one draft. My right arm hardly trembled. "Thanks. Another, please."

While Jesse disappeared behind the counter, I smiled at my counterpart, on whose forehead the first pearls of sweat were gathering. "You practice regularly, don't you? You've got a powerful arm."

Then I began to push his arm down slowly.

He resisted decently, but in vain. In the end I gave him another firm push, so that the back of his hand extinguished the candle instead of burning, and he wheezed.

Immediately, I pulled his arm back upright and focused on his eyes while another guest relighted the tea candle.

"All okay? Ready for the next round?"

He returned my gaze and nodded.

"One to zero for the little one," the self-appointed referee commented. "Round two, on my mark. Three, two, one — go!"

Baldhead forced my arm some way down with a sudden jerk before I could react. I had to fight even harder to get back upright. But as before, his resistance didn't suffice. In the end he gave in to the inevitable.

That was good, because my arm muscles felt scorched. Nevertheless, I smiled as if nothing had happened.

"Two to zero. It's already decided. You want another go anyway?"

My opponent didn't loosen his grip around my hand and pushed us in starting position.

"That's a yes. Wait until the candle burns. So, now we can go. Ready?"

Baldhead reinforced his grip. My hand felt like it was in a vise. Well — I could do the same. I squeezed back, and he grinned and released a bit.

"Okay. Round three, on my mark. Three — two — one — go!"

This time his surprise didn't work. Nevertheless, our arms were slowly leaning my way. It wasn't easy to reverse. I had to fight for each inch that I moved his arm back. Had I slacked only for a moment, he'd have put me down — with his larger body mass, he simply had the better anchor.

Jesse came with my beer — and paused before the table.

This round didn't go as easily as the first, and I had no time to drink beer.

My opponent noticed my struggle and reinforced his pressure again. Our arms were trembling and returning to upright. If I hadn't held up, I'd have been done, so I had to match him.

For a few moments we were mutually beleaguering ourselves. Were his arms burning as much as mine? But after all, it was just pain again.

Again he tried to gain way, but I didn't give in. His eyes showed respect when he slowly nodded. Then he knocked off with his left and gave in.

I didn't push his hand into the flame a third time. Instead I held our arms upright and told the third man at the table, "Even."

That enticed several surprised calls.

With my left, I took the beer from Jesse, said, "Another" and reached the glass to my opponent. "Here."

Baldhead nodded. "Thanks. Honestly — I wouldn't have expected to last that long against your Dragon powers."

"You didn't make it easy for me. During the second round I was already tempted to apply my Dragon powers — but you only fought Johanna, not the Dragon."

"Not? But — "

"But my muscles are strengthened above average by the permanent strain, and I've always been athletic."

"She still holds the Ironman world record," Gomez chimed in. "The one for men."

He looked around and enjoyed the audience's bafflement. Although the highlights of my life were publicly known, there were still a lot of people who didn't connect my various roles — whore, athlete, Meier effect inventor, Velvet, Dragon empress — to each other or to the short-grown person under their noses.

"You had a fair chance," I quickly returned to the topic. "Well—a quite fair one."

Baldhead drank his beer and then rubbed his right upper arm. "I understand why one shouldn't mess with you. But all your power wouldn't help you against a well-aimed bullet."

I reached out one hand for his right arm, pulled it closer gently, but with determination, and quietly said, "I've already caught well-aimed bullets several times. That didn't help my enemies, and it won't make me happier."

I had struck the right note. I could recognize it by the way not only Baldhead, but several of the other guests, too, became as pale as chalk.

Jesse waved me aside when I tried to pay my bill. "On the house, for an old friend, okay?"

"Sure, Jesse. If you ever need anything, just call."

"Oh. Thanks."

"You're welcome." I briefly waved at the other guests and left the *Black Hole.*

Gomez followed me up and outside. "Bah." He pulled his leather jacket close. "Unpleasant here."

"How are you doing? What are you doing?"

"Security advisor."

"Security advisor?"

He grinned. "No sayings about fox and henhouse, please. I've copied some things from a certain Velvet. My clients are quite pleased by my advice."

"Oh, so you're telling them my tricks?"

"Do I know your tricks?" He shook his head. "No. I've learned what to look for. Working with you honed my understanding of basic mechanisms—for security against ordinary thieves. Security against Velvet is unaffordable."

I eagle-eyed the surrounding roofs and shrugged. "It wouldn't matter anyway. Velvet's no longer in business."

"No? Your appearance in there looked like it to me."

"The name's still useful, but it's no longer about finding things that aren't lost yet. Now it's about finding men who don't want to be found, and in this regard, tonight was a complete failure."

"You think so? Give us time. If Jesse knows anything, he won't tell it before the entire audience. Wait until the last guests have left."

"I don't like that."

"You're in a hurry?"

"Yes and no. I shouldn't wait any longer than necessary — in case someone gets the stupid idea of selling me out to my enemies."

"After your show in there?"

"Yes, even after my show in there. Neither of those will take me up himself. But if the price is high enough, and it takes no more than a quick call? If the opposition succeeds, there's nothing to be feared from me. If not — well, I had asked for a lead, didn't I? Could I blame anyone for providing me such a lead?"

"I understand. In that case it'd be better you'd leave now, and we'll meet again somewhere tomorrow or the day after."

I grinned at him. "It might be better you keep some distance from me while I see what they've got. I'm prepared."

He needed to know neither about the nano threads listening for suspicious calls inside the Black Hole, nor about the invisible Dragon watching us from one of the rooftops.

Gomez shook his head. "Call me sentimental, but I can't just desert you, Dragon ruler or else. I'm staying and waiting with you."

"Okay. Well, in that case we could grant us some fun together, couldn't we?"

"I'm not in the mood, Jo."

"I can change that."

"Leave it, Jo. I know you could make even dead men shoot, but this really isn't the right place or time."

"A pity." After the stress inside I'd indeed been in the right mood for a big, hard cock taking me from behind. So I had to make do with my imagination. But he even distracted me there.

"Would you like to tell me about your adventures?"

"Well, we might have some time . . ."

CHAPTER SIXTY-EIGHT

Gomez scowled and tore at his jacket. "That wetness creeps inside everywhere."

His voice sounded muffled. I held up a hand and stared past him. Even the opposite side of the road was hardly visible in the incoming fog. You could only guess the positions of the next-but-one street lamps in either direction. The wind had almost entirely fallen asleep. Nevertheless, there had been a metallic-clacking noise.

With a slight turn to the side I brought my body between Gomez and the suspected source of that noise and indicated to him to crouch down.

Mighty, we're getting visitors.

Shall I intervene?

No. It might be bad luck — so far, nobody reported my visit. Have a look around.

His signature moved away.

Three, then five figures emerged from the fog. All five carried edgy, lengthy objects in their hands — pistols.

I let out a deep breath of relief and relaxed my tightened muscles without changing my position. These men were no true threat to me.

Hopefully they had the same view. Or — why should I take chances? After all, they must have had received some hint. Why else would they have drawn their weapons and released the safety before they'd been able to spot Gomez and me?

They had approached to twelve meters. The group of five fanned out, and the center guy advanced two more steps.

His small eyes glared at me from an unshaven face. His pistol barrel pointed in my direction. "What have we got here?" he asked. "A pretty bird. Come on, show your tits."

"How imaginative," I commented on his line and waved both arms forward. "I have to disappoint you anyway — this is no weather for stripping."

"Don't get cheeky, girl!" He waved with his right hand. "Or should I rough you up first?"

"I'm not frightened by your empty fist." Even while I was saying that, my generously distributed nanos devoured his gun and the ones of his fellows. Golden dust trickled to the ground and found its way back to me.

"What the devil?"

A simple request to get lost wouldn't have done. Their pride didn't allow that. I pondered whether I should beat them up or just scare them.

"You came to see Velvet." *Transform. And give me a deeper voice.* "But you found a Dragon."

The group seemed to shrink before my gaze, but that was primarily because my head rose some meters on my golden Dragon body. With long claws on my hands and large, pointy thorns on my spread wings, I bowed down to them.

"You wanted to see me nude? Well, have a look."

They were trembling, staring at me like a rabbit before a snake. No one dared to move.

"Okay. Down with your clothes. Everything. NOW!"

Gomez' gaze was following the five naked men long after they had disappeared into the fog. Finally he looked up to me. "Damn — Jo. I'd almost wet my pants."

His nervousness hadn't remained hidden from me, so I didn't turn to him. *My voice, please.* "Cool show, wasn't it?"

"Show? Jo, gal —" He shook his head. "That doesn't quite apply anymore. You're an elemental force. Who'd have guessed back then what's inside this little gal?"

"Inside this Dragon body there's still the same little gal, Gomez."

"After New York?" He shook his head again. "Experience changes a—person, Johanna. Extraordinary experience changes more. Nobody has gathered as much extraordinary experience as you did."

"Experiences *can* change people, Gomez. But they can as well reinforce what's already been there. My life has been and still is shaped by the same principles—frugality, to get along just with what I'm wearing. Prostitution—full body involvement, nothing held back. Competition—athletic peak performance included. Game—risk is always involved, and I place high bets. Pain doesn't count. And finally—I use my head. Nothing's changed there."

Next, I did turn to him. "I've surely changed a bit. But I didn't lose my fun in life, and I guess that's my essence. That's the big little Jo."

"Fun." He began to grin. "Yes, I think, that's hitting the nail on the head. As long as I've known you, you've always accepted challenges as if everything were just a game. Even when you were shot at. A lot of fun, and you're laughing in your enemies' faces. In this regard, you didn't change a lot indeed." Gomez pointed down the street. "And those?"

"Small fry. I guess a clochard gave them the tip. Not the opponents I had expected."

"No. Probably none of the boys had such contacts—and Jesse hasn't either. He doesn't spot everything going on among his guests. Well—perhaps he remembers tomorrow or the day after. Should I hear anything, I'll call you. Will mails to the University reach you?"

"Sure."

Around us, dawn broke. Soon the sun would drive the fog away. "I should move on. This track is cold." As cold as the tracks of the unknown hacker who had tried to break into the island's systems. My investigations there had so far come to nothing either.

"Will we meet again?" Gomez asked.

My shrug caused a slight flap of my wings, and those in turn a strong gust. I quickly retracted my wings to my body. "Sometime, somewhere."

PART FIVE—BRIDGE TO THE STARS

CHAPTER SIXTY-NINE

Five golden cigars were stretched out next to each other on the heat-wavering asphalt.

"Shouldn't we go back in?" Reginald complained and pointed at the terminal building finished only a few days ago. "It's cooler inside."

"Just go." I wanted to digest the sight a bit longer.

The rightmost was *Athena*, the flagship of our small expedition fleet. *Athena*, goddess of wisdom, strategy and warfare, art and craft, should direct our fate. Multiple Barracudas were waiting for their deployment inside her belly.

At her side was *Berenice*, the bearer of victory, and right next to her was *Nike*, the goddess of victory. Both carriers were loaded to the brim with Taipan fighters and equipment for those and the battalion of armor suits.

Somewhere in *Berenice's* belly, Fatima was organizing her people's boarding—as all around the ships countless people were milling around like ants around their nest.

The greatest chaos probably roamed aboard the *Calliope*. The muse of science would carry the mission's research part. Researchers from all over the world had applied for slots aboard. People from my University weren't among them — we had granted them room aboard *Athena*.

The counterpoint to it all was *Iris*, the messenger of the gods, at the end of the line. The ship flew with a skeleton crew — if everything went as planned, it should confirm our arrival in the *Worries* system and the contact with the Dragons and then return to Earth without delay. That way it would also confirm we had indeed solved the grav flash problem for Phoenix carriers for the long distance.

Rashid approached me and cleared his throat. "Are you satisfied, Jo?"

"In which regard?"

"You wanted a spaceship for your mission, and as soon as possible. We managed to get five ships ready for takeoff for you."

"Oh, that. Yes, of course, it's more than I could hope for. Thanks for that."

"You don't have to thank me. I didn't have to do much for it. The military insisted on redundancy, the scientists needed space, and the council insisted on early feedback. The five ships resulted from that. I knew you wouldn't deny."

"I'm only surprised that they didn't insist on a larger home fleet."

"*Cassiopeia, Demeter,* and *Gaia* will be commissioned soon as well, even if only on probation for now, but with the *Iris* we'll have four carriers for system defense. The local politicians were okay with that."

"More so as we're leaving most space fighters and Taipans here. What about the other four carriers?"

"They need another two months."

"Okay." A long row of container-laden grav sleds sailed across the sand toward *Calliope*. More scientific gear?

"You're absent-minded," Rashid noticed. "What's troubling you? The journey ahead?"

"That, too. There's so much that can go wrong. All these men and women trust me to get them safely home somehow."

"There's no guarantee. It's about war. They all know that."

"Yes, sure, and if there are individual fatalities, they'll understand. But if it's a truly massive failure—"

"The people will hope for a miracle, and you don't want to disappoint them. Understood. But I've talked with many of your people, and I've seen their faces. They're determined not to disappoint *you*. Trust them."

"I do trust them. They all achieved the incredible, in such a short time."

"For you."

"For me?"

"For you. For the woman who relieved them from the Cartel's yoke. For the woman who gives bread and jobs to the poor, who shows them the light at the end of the tunnel and encourages them to strive for it. For the woman who lets herself be chained and flogged for them."

"Your public relations people are good."

"They're collecting and marveling. Your stories have taken on a life on their own. Is it true that you were shot when you thwarted a little girl's kidnapping?"

I nodded. "That was quite painful."

"There are so many of these stories."

"There surely are other stories, too. I'm not the shiny hero."

"Ah, yes, the prostitute—but you never tried to hide that. You don't pretend to be something better. That's what makes you so authentic, and so tangible for the ordinary people."

The grav sleds were passing the next to last ship. Rashid followed my gaze. "Supplies for the *Worries* people. We don't have to let the *Iris* fly empty, do we?"

"Erm—no."

"A greeting present, so to speak. The containers are sealed airtight. The *Iris* will simply unload them into space, tie them into a big packet, and attach a homing buoy. From there you can eventually deliver them." He pointed at the chain of sleds. "To shunt them, we'll send some of these sleds along. A workgroup from your technical college developed this concept. The sleds are remote-controlled, but also command a lot of complex independent maneuvers. I found this idea very interesting."

"I didn't notice."

"No. You've been quite busy the last weeks, haven't you?"

"I've been following up leads. Sadly, to no avail." I felt like stamping my foot in anger, but it wouldn't help. "These attacks on me, on our net, and lastly on the carriers, badger me. Only — there are no tracks. The opposition manages very well to shield their field agents in a way that they can't tell us anything." I pointed at the spaceships. "I'd bet they've prepared something nasty to take with us. Somewhere among these people is a spy. Perhaps it's sleeper, perhaps he's already started working. And who can safely tell what's in all these freight containers?"

"As far as I know, the Australians checked each one of the crew, and the containers are screened several times before loading, too."

"Yes, sure." *Buck up, Jo. Until now, it was against you primarily. Nobody wants to destroy the carriers.*

I was worried about Monique's silence, too. She had been on her ominous mission for more than half a year and hadn't sent a sign of life yet. The same applied to her partner Elodie, too. *No news is good news* — no, I didn't want to tell myself lies. Covert investigations could be time-consuming, especially in this situation where we had so few leads, but I wouldn't put it past our opponents to let annoying spies who had gotten too close disappear without a trace.

I couldn't do anything for the two. Nobody knew where they were, so nobody could give them away, and I couldn't be tempted to take care of them. It surely was meant that way.

Together with Sylvie and Beate, they'd be the only Mambas staying behind in the Solar system. The others were distributed among our four ships.

After another glance across the five giant cigars, I shrugged and turned to the terminal building.

CHAPTER SEVENTY

Reginald was leaning on the counter of the Galaxy Bar and snipped his fingers against a glass of beer, the head of which had already receded some way. "For you. Rashid, water or coffee?"

"Sparkling water, please."

My old fellow-student waved at the barkeeper and then raised his own glass to clink with me.

"Everything's been said, hasn't it?" he said.

"So it has." Reginald would take the lead for the University, supported by Nanette, Rod, Freddie and Beate, the other researchers and students. The pinboard offered enough substance for many more years of research.

Without me.

I'd miss the island, the relaxed life there, Nanette's care, the intense scientific discussions, swimming in the ocean.

It felt like homesickness, and I hadn't even departed yet. Homesickness. Me. The individualist who was at home all over the world.

The cold beer helped to distract me, but in order to drown my homesickness, I would have had to give my nanos new instructions regarding the alcohol.

"There's something we have to settle yet," Rashid said. He gazed past us with a smile. Sylvie and Jenny were just entering. How had they managed to sneak past the army of journalists outside the fence?

I waved my empty glass at them. "Hello. Are you coming to say goodbye to us?"

Jenny pointed at Rashid. "The Council for Interstellar Defence chairman asked for us, so we came."

"He only said it's about the Space Patrol," Sylvie added. "Hello, Jo. All clear for takeoff?"

"I assume, yes. I'll have to talk with the commanders yet. What about you?"

"Nothing's clear, but that won't stop us." Jenny grinned. "When it's about conquering our system, everyone wants to be the first."

Rashid made a bow. "Knight Jenny, Knight Sylvie, welcome and thank you for coming. You're absolutely right. It's about the Space Patrol, which as a military unit automatically is principally under the Imperatrix' supreme command, supported by the council. The competences are indeed unclear once the Imperatrix has departed."

Reginald handed Rashid his water and the two women and me a beer each.

"Thanks. What does the council propose?"

Rashid sipped and swung his left hand outward. "A leading commission with equal representation that reports to the council."

"And not to me." I raised my glass and clinked with the others. "Okay, I'll be away for a while, but any leading circle with military competences has to be under my command at least nominally, without filter through the council. Thereafter we could talk about stand-in arrangements."

"It won't work anyway," Reginald argued. "If the Chinese are in the commission — and they should be, if alone for their commercial weight — and demand a veto right, they could control the commission to their liking."

"That's exactly the problem," the Sheikh agreed. "A veto clause is indeed favored by most council members, although for different reasons."

"What kind of nonsense is that, after all?" Sylvie erupted.

"A commission directed by a council? What's next? A decision advisory committee? How shall such a chain of command work?"

"It could work among Dragons," I mused aloud. "As long as all involved aspire to the same goals, even among humans, but this precondition won't be given. No, you're right. There must be a supreme instance having the last say. I have to appoint a legate."

"Don't look at me like this!" Reginald instantly objected. "I'm leading the University, okay, and I'll also play the country chief for Velvet Island. That's manageable, and I know my ways around. I don't know anything about the military or space flight."

"We're taking all persons commanding both subjects and having at least basic practical experience with us," I replied. "That's no criterion."

"Those are the only criteria the council will accept if you want to deviate from our proposal," Rashid said firmly. "You know those people."

"Yes, I know those people," I agreed and stared forward, between Sylvie and Jenny. "So I don't know . . ."

And why might Rashid have asked right these women to come? He watched me attentively, but didn't say a word. So that he could later believably claim I made my decision all on my own?

"There is one more person with experience in space flight and system defense," I noticed and looked into Sylvie's eyes. "Sylvie, I know I'm asking for much, but please don't answer right away. Hear it all first. You've been quite successful in training new Barracuda pilots so far. In all those we're taking along now I clearly recognize your signature. Could you imagine assuming the Space Patrol's professional lead?"

I turned to Jenny. "Jenny, Sylvie has little experience in directing military units. She can discipline a bunch of young hotspurs without trouble, so I won't doubt her ability to command. Nevertheless she needs a senior officer she can turn to. Could you imagine assuming the Space Patrol's supreme command, and handing the command for the space-going part to Sylvie?"

"I?" Jenny gave me an aghast look. "Jo, I'm too old for such a thing."

"You may delegate the administration to a commission," I proposed with a side glance at Rashid. "That is, you'll pick a smart adjutant, a few people for your personal staff, give the commission directions, and otherwise you're commanding Sylvie. That's a quite simple arrangement. Sylvie—you'd command the fleet and the space bases. I know you can handle troublesome people. No one can unnerve a Mamba, and in direct contact no one can match you. For all administrative questions, you can ask your superior to involve the commission. For technical or logistic problems you'd ask Reginald."

"And if it comes to a state of defense?" she asked quietly. "Jo, you know."

"I know, Sylvie. But ask yourself—if it comes to that, where do you want to be? Down on the ground, where you have to watch helplessly? Or somewhere out there, with people you trust, and where you can kick Jelly ass? What frightens you more?"

She didn't answer. I handed my glass to Reginald and placed my hands on her shoulders. "Sylvie, I shouldn't ask that of you. It's not fair, and hence it's okay if you turn me down. Back then, I promised you that you don't have to do anything you don't feel comfortable with, and I'm sticking by that. Only—at least I have to ask."

Sylvie looked down on the floor, then at Jenny, at Rashid, at Reginald. Finally, she looked straight at me. "For such a task I should ask for time to consider. But firstly, you want to go, so we don't have much time left, and secondly, I already had a lot of time to consider what I want and what I don't. You all know — I can fly, well enough to show others how it's done. Moreover I can deal with people questioning my authority. Nobody wants to get a second kick in the ass from me. So I can command a fucking Space Patrol, and with Jenny's advice, even better. But I don't think I'll keep her very busy."

Jenny smiled and nodded approvingly, and Sylvie went on, "What I want is also clear — I want to fly. I want the pilot seat. If I still get the stick as admiral, or whatever you call it, I'm in."

"The rank of admiral won't do," I said with a glance at Rashid. His knowing smile disappeared, and he frowned.

"Knight Jenny, I herewith appoint you my deputy as supreme commander of all forces of this planet. Until my or Achrotzyber's return, you'll bear the rank of *Legata Aurea Draconis*. The council has no authority over you. Knight and *Wing* Sylvie, as Jenny's deputy you will assume the operational authority over the United Nations space forces, popularly called Space Patrol. As with Jenny, the council has no authority over you, and to clarify that, you will bear the rank of *Legata Draconis*. All other military ranks are subordinate. Apply this privilege with the same judgment as you showed before and have an open ear for advice, and this solution will work." I turned to the Sheikh. "Rashid, as council chairman you will relay my decision. At the same time I'm accepting the council's proposal as far as my legates will surely welcome the support of an advisory expert commission."

"Smart," Rashid praised. "First you put a spoke in their wheel, and then you reach out a hand."

"Yes, sure." I nodded at Jenny. "We only want to avoid the commission getting bogged down in internal quarrels, but we don't want to miss their expertise. Or do we?"

"Of course not." Jenny grinned. "But that way you're not just giving me a veto right, correct?"

"Correct. Absolutely appropriate for a knight who was recommended by the Lionheart and by Angry April."

CHAPTER SEVENTY-ONE

Reginald eyeballed the two newly appointed legates and frowned.

"What is it?" I asked.

"What if anything happens to them? Don't get me wrong, I don't wish them anything bad. But as Jo's deputies they're also deputy targets. Sorry that I didn't think of that before their appointment."

"If anything happens to them both, the commission didn't do their job and will be disbanded," I decided. "But your hint is important. Reg, they'll need detectors and light protective suits. Jenny, you can always call armor suits for your protection—"

I bit my lip before I could give her more advice. As Legata she could and should decide herself, and if she needed more from Reginald, she could ask him herself. She knew enough about what was happening on the island to know he had more to offer.

"Thanks," she said. "Yes, that was clear to me. I didn't assume you're the only terrorist target anyway. We're bearing the risk together with you."

Sylvie nodded. "What are a few terrorists against a Jelly invasion? If we can bear the one risk, we can bear the other. Don't worry, Jo. You neither, Reginald."

"I'm worrying about everything, that's how I am. I also consider how it would be if politics were always so easy. Jo simply appoints, and all other players are out of the game."

"Clear hierarchies and chains of command are a central

trait of military structures," I said. "But I know what you mean. Normally the military is under control of politics. That's different in the Dragon community, and I'm taking full advantage of my power as Imperatrix. If mankind doesn't want that, they'll have to do without my collaboration, because then I couldn't fulfill my role."

I emptied my glass and waved for another. "Seen from the human point of view, that's got some bad taste. We're regarding democratic structures as a valuable accomplishment, while I'm putting my dictatorial claim through. Where I always observe my personal gain, that I openly admit. Achrotzyber once said that there's a strong correlation between my wellbeing and the common wellbeing. As long as I can fight successfully, people are safe."

Reginald grinned while Rashid, Jenny, and Sylvie were following my explanations frowning.

"I'm open to constructive criticism. If anyone objects and tells me what I'm doing wrong, I correct myself. I leave things that I don't know enough about to others. The Dragon principle, you know? Everyone does what he can do best. Logical arguments take precedence, and only if there are still multiple options left, then hierarchy counts."

Had Rashid understood what I wanted to say? He had to be able to communicate my decision to the council.

"Let me put it differently. As long as all involved are working together and focusing on the facts, both systems yield the same results. The little difference is — with the system the nations would like to have, a minority's veto can prevent decisions, which results in either an inability to act or a foul compromise. With the dictatorial system a decision can be forced. Neither is democratic, that would only apply to a system without veto rights, and that has its own downfalls."

"Because the majority isn't always right," Reginald concluded.

"Because majority decisions aren't always based on facts and logic," I corrected. "And who would be the referee to judge that?"

"You," Sylvie guessed.

"Jenny," I objected. "She's got the last word while I'm gone. But ideally council and commission won't let it get that far, because they will agree on good decisions. Won't they, Rashid?"

"I'm bowing to your wisdom, Protectress," he said with a smirk and a slight bow. "It will be advisable for the boards to be informed about the Legata's ideas in advance so that she won't be forced to disagree."

"Aaah, smart!" Jenny laughed. "Yes, that sounds more like politics as I know it. I'll be happy to consult with such a commission to find joint solutions. And if the people won't get down to business, I can still threaten them with a solitary decision."

"I see you've got me."

Sylvie nodded. "That's not very different from taming my flight students. I can take their birds under remote control if they won't toe the line. They know that, so they make sure I don't have to."

"I guess that's my cue," I noticed. "A last glass of beer, and then I make clear to my captains that I'll take over their ships if they don't toe the line."

CHAPTER SEVENTY-TWO

Numerous curious gazes followed me on my way across the red sand to my *flagship*. *Athena* was regally looming into the sky above me, and yet it seemed to me as if I wouldn't get any closer. Dragon senses and *Analogy* could have calculated my progress, but this time I wasn't interested in it.

Still not all freight containers, all luggage, all equipment was loaded up. Still small all-wheel-drive vehicles and large buses were carrying people to their ships.

The sun was burning down mercilessly. Those who could, stayed in their air-conditioned vehicles. With its fine sand and scratchy grass, this was no place for pedestrians anyway. The black of my familiar combat suit wasn't ideal, either.

Heat, sand, and grass didn't bother me. This was the last opportunity to breathe unfiltered air for a long time and probably also the last opportunity to be on my own.

The flight was an experiment—with a new spaceship, a new model, compared to the Lionhearts' construction plans a true quantum leap in build and performance, or put differently—it was hardly imaginable to implement and test these revolutionary, not evolutionary changes in smaller steps. With the new Meier tunnel field generator and the improved *Besson compensator* with grav arrester, five ships with the size of an aircraft carrier should penetrate the light speed barrier for the first time and travel to a far distant star system. The real experiment, though, was to fit an anarchist like me for months or years into the strict military discipline necessary for the coexistence of so many people in such a tight space.

And yet — basically I just had to play a role. If I could feign being the happy whore for years, if I could play the unwavering gambler at the poker table, if I even could excel as primary actress in a medieval torture spectacle, then I could as well believably portray a fleet commandant.

The dress rehearsal was imminent — after a little detour so as to not disturb the single brown snake. I didn't have to fear her bite, but why should I provoke her?

Meanwhile *Athena* covered most of my sight. Since my visit to the shipyard she had acquired a large black nametag on her allover golden nano hull. Except for the open crew and freight airlocks and the long row of landing legs, the surface was entirely even.

Beauty was the last thing we needed for our mission, but the external flawlessness was also evidence for quality, and of that we couldn't have enough.

Two young soldiers in the new light-gray space fleet work uniforms stood to attention and saluted when I approached the staircase. I briefly raised my fingertips to my temple and waved with them, and both replied with a hint of a smile. So much I had already gotten — nobody expected perfect military habits from me. It was important to relay the feeling of me noticing my crew, respecting their work, caring for them.

"Thanks, George, Mike."

Part of my job had been studying crew file summaries and memorizing them in my *Analogy*.

I stopped at the top platform to have a look on the cargo loading. Only a few containers were still waiting under the body.

Two more soldiers were waiting before the inside airlock. They saluted and were saluted back. Then I stood before the inner airlock door. The door behind me closed, locked out Earth's atmosphere. Thus I left Earth behind for a long time to come.

CHAPTER SEVENTY-THREE

The inner airlock door opened with a barely audible hiss. My first gaze fell on a young officer in ceremonial white who was nervously shifting his weight back and forth behind a white line on the deck and now went to attention.

Soldiers were standing shoulder to shoulder on both sides, and behind him a dozen golden armor suits.

A pipe signal sounded. "Admiral on deck!"

Oh crap. Admiral? That wasn't planned.

But okay, they should have their ceremony—as we'd had no big goodbye party. I stepped to the line and smiled at the young officer. "Protectress Johanna asking for permission to come aboard."

"Permission granted, Protectress." He stepped aside.

"Thank you, Lieutenant Ormstedt."

"Can I do anything else for you, Protectress?"

"No, thank you, I know the way to the bridge." But first I examined the two rows of spacemen at attention. They were firmly holding their heads up and forward, only their gazes tried to follow me. Conversely, I had to look up to them. In any case, I found no reason to complain.

"Excellent," I said.

I briefly nodded at the armor suit group leader, recognizable by the two stripes on his chest. Then I proceeded on my way.

I met people everywhere on my way to the bridge, in staircases and the cream-white painted hallways. Some seemed to be looking for something, others hurried past with a brief salute. To me, it didn't look like we could be ready for takeoff in a few hours.

Close to the bridge the bustle faded. I was alone in the last corridor, and I paused before the door. *Ready for your entrance, Jo?*

"Welcome aboard, Protectress."

I managed not to flinch. "Hello, *Athena*."

"I waited until you're alone. Was that right?"

"Do you have anything urgent?"

"No. No unusual incidents."

"Good. We'll talk later."

Had the ship developed its own conscience? The computer was certainly larger than Phoebe's, and I had been able to make limited conversation with my car, too. Not to mention *Ghost*, my mind-extension.

Another step forward, and the door slid to the side.

Five heads turned to me, of which only one face was familiar — Francine smiled at me and remained standing next to her pilot seat. The four men, all in white, stood to attention and saluted.

"Admiral on the bridge!" A few steps led up to the dais, at the railing of which the ensign was waiting with reddened face and an arm trembling from his tension. Up there was the place for the fleet commandant and his staff.

"Thanks, Ensign Damiens."

I took my time for a brief glance around. This should be my place of work for the next several weeks. Two pilot seats, one captain's seat, six dashboards for radio, detectors, navigation, weapons, and the coordination of air force and drop troops offered opportunities to delegate all the tasks that Francine and I could perform from the pilot's seat all alone as well — but *Athena* was also a drill ship. How should the newly commissioned space fleet officers learn their job if we didn't give them anything to practice on?

The flagship's commanding circle was waiting at the foot of the steps. My *Analogy* again provided me with names to the faces.

Flag Captain Julio Ortiz made a step toward me. "Welcome aboard, Admiral Meier."

His first officer, Commander Ramesh Varna, followed. I had seen the fourth man in Gladstone before. Chief Jalal Rumi was the most senior noncommissioned officer and at the same time chief of the technical department aboard.

Three persons of my command staff aboard my flagship were missing—the armor suits command team and the Tai-pan wing commander.

"Captain Ortiz, Commander Varna, Chief Rumi. Hello and also welcome to my team. I'm sorry we're only getting to know each other personally so close to takeoff—there was so much to do for all of us, and I simply didn't manage to come earlier. Well, at least I couldn't interfere with your preparations that way."

The chief smiled. As a Gladstone graduate he surely had heard enough about me and my leadership style.

"What are your plans?" Julio asked.

"Before the start, while logistics are still easy, I'd like to meet with the other captains, too, to discuss a few fundamental topics regarding our journey. On this occasion we can also talk about my plans for this flight. Before that meeting, we'll surely find a few minutes to learn to know each other. Robert?"

"Yes, Ma'am, Admiral! At once!"

"One moment," I slowed his enthusiasm down. "I'd like to clarify a few bits. Firstly—I'm not familiar with military habits. I recognize the advantage of a clear chain of command and of clearly and precisely phrased orders, but I never received a formal military education and I don't plan to change that. You will all have to get along with that. Secondly—I don't want to

314

get used to someone always shouting out loud when I'm entering any room. Moreover I don't want the people to drop everything. If I have to make an announcement and need the people's attention, I will say so. Thirdly — you may ease a bit in my presence regarding your demeanor. I won't always be formal and I won't apologize for that. That's got nothing to do with a lack of discipline. Fourthly — if you disagree with anything, I expect you to speak up openly. It might well be possible that I interfere with your responsibilities, whether deliberately or accidentally. We have to get it all together. Understood?"

I focused on the ensign. He was about to go to attention again, but then reconsidered and only said, "Yes, Admiral."

"Much better," I praised him. "By the way, I'm no admiral. Protectress or Johanna will do. I'm used to listening to that."

"Yes, Protectress."

"Perfect. Now let the captains know that I'd like to talk with them in about half an hour. Thanks."

Captain Ortiz' gaze followed my adjutant hurrying to the next communication desk. A smile played about his lips. Then he gave me a questioning glance.

I nodded rearward. "According to the construction plans, there's a conference room right next to the bridge, right?"

"Two," Ortiz replied. "One for ship command, one for fleet command. I recommend that we take mine, so Robert can have the other prepared."

"Okay. After you, please."

Francine hesitated. I waved at her. "Come along. To get it together, we have to clarify the lead pilot's role, too."

Chief Rumi was nervously glancing at the clock when we entered the unadorned room. I patted his shoulder. "Just a few minutes, then I can leave you to your work."

Commander Varna arrived last. He turned back for a

moment. "Ensign Damiens, you've got the bridge."

"Yes, Sir!"

Only then did he enter and close the door behind himself. We took our seats.

"Okay." Once again I looked at them one by one. In the end my gaze stuck on Francine. "Let me start with the last point. Knight Francine is formally lead pilot and thus subordinate to ship command. She's also the most experienced pilot we have, and she knows more about grav field technology than most others aboard, including Chief Rumi. When it comes to steering the ship through trouble in one piece, I trust her to make better professional decisions than you. Is that reasonable or unfair?"

"Fair," Ortiz instantly said. "We talked about that before your arrival — she's flying the ship and I'm commanding the rest. We're glad that we have her aboard and can rely on her experience. Of course, that also applies to you."

"Thanks. Well, if you already agreed on that, we don't need to talk about it. So I should leave the ship to you and take care of the fleet overall, shouldn't I? We'll see how long I can stick to that. Chief, conversely, you can come to me if there are technical problems — especially if anything looks strange to you. This new technology is scarcely tested, and I need to know anything that bothers you."

"That's okay, Jo. Well — we put up a pinboard in engineering. You can come anytime and have a look what's keeping us occupied."

Commander Varna frowned about the familiar address, but didn't speak up.

"I will do that."

"About the admiral . . ." Ortiz began.

"Yes?"

"You just said you're no admiral."

"Yes. I'm not. I don't have the education, and I never was

appointed to officer. Formally, that would be complicated anyway—Imperatrix is already more than an officer's rank. Such a commission might even limit my authority." *Why has he brought up that topic anyway?* "Regarded that way, I'm more than admiral." *The way he raises his eyebrows now, that's the way to go.* "So it doesn't matter that I'm listed as admiral in the paperwork and in the chain of command. It's just about the form of address. Can we just agree that this admiral will be addressed as *Protectress?*" Ortiz breathed a sigh of relief, and I understood. "That's a precondition for *Athena* being a flagship with flag captain, is it?"

He nodded.

"Okay. I won't object to that. I assume we won't have to worry about such topics during our journey." I focused on my flag captain. "It's a long way back to Earth from the *Worries* system. Over there, there's only one person making the rules. Me."

"And we shall trust you blindly."

Francine smirked. Chief Rumi leaned back. Commander Varna focused on me.

For Ortiz, I had a sweet smile. "Of course not. Yes, you'll have to trust me, and the chain of command is clear as well. Nevertheless I don't expect blind obedience from you, but cooperation and constructive criticism—and a little skill in picking the right moment. I'm sure you can do that, otherwise you wouldn't have been chosen as officers under my command."

The captain watched me for a while, then he smiled, too. "I'm not yet sure if I got it right, but I think I can work with that."

Chief Rami was no problem at all, so there was one officer in the room left to take care of. "Commander Varna?"

He flinched. "Yes."

"You're not happy about the situation yet. What's troubling you?"

He glanced at the chief, then at Francine, then at his captain.

I took the cue. "Chief, I guess we're fine for now. I'll come over later—most likely not before takeoff. Okay?"

"Okay." He rose and left us.

"Francine, you stay." I nodded at the first officer. "Knight Francine is one of the people aboard I trust my life with. She should and she has to know."

Varna could only accept.

"Well?"

"It's nothing."

Ortiz was about to say something, but I stopped him with a hand sign.

"I won't bite your head off. But don't try to fool a Dragon. My flagship needs a first officer who I can work together with. Together, not in parallel. So, what is it?"

Varna remained silent.

"Do I have to guess? Is it because I'm a woman?" *No.* "Because I'm so short?" No—but he suppressed a smirk.

No, these topics would have been considered in the selection process. Well—he was from India. "Is it about cultural differences?"

This time, I was on the right track. "Something religious?"

"No." He squirmed for a moment, then he pulled himself together. "You are—Naga. The Dragon commands. We obey. It—your behavior—it doesn't fit."

"Ah." I leaned back and spread my arms. "Okay. An abundance of respect, so to speak. I can live with that. Your professional work will surely not suffer from it."

He nodded approvingly.

"I will accept our relationship being somewhat distant, and you will come to terms with the fact that other people aboard will express their respect toward me in a less formal way. Is that acceptable?"

He nodded again.

"Okay. As I'm still appreciating your professional judgment, I propose that you tell your concerns, suggestions and criticisms to your captain so that he can discuss them with me. Should you have questions of informal nature on my behavior, you can ask your lead pilot. We'll keep all this to ourselves. No one outside this circle needs to know about it. Agreed?"

"Agreed, Admiral."

I only looked at him and waited.

"Agreed, *Protectress.*"

"Fine. Then let's have a look how far the preparations for our visitors have gotten, okay?"

CHAPTER SEVENTY-FOUR

By and by, the admiral's conference room filled up—flag conference room, I corrected myself. The four other ships' captains, first officers and lead pilots were helping themselves to coffee and cookies and discussing solved and unsolved problems with their ships and most of all their passengers—the scientific teams were obviously not yet accepted as part of the crew. That was a topic I had to clarify soon.

Francine—easily recognizable by her black uniform—was being pestered by several officers. The other ships' pilots were curious about her experience. The male colleagues might've been attracted in a different way, too—who wouldn't like to talk with a beautiful woman?

My adjutant went to attention next to the flag conference room's image, saluted, and reported, "All participants are assembled."

"I see, thank you." I let the projection disappear with a handwave. "Go ahead and announce me, please. I fear, as engaged as people are debating, they might miss me."

"Yes, A—at once, Protectress."

I grinned at his back and followed him.

"Ladies and Gentlemen, the Protectress Johanna," Ensign Damiens shouted over the background noise. All conversations immediately fell silent, and fifteen curious faces turned to me.

"Please take your seats," I asked them kindly. "That way you can see me better."

They had all had the opportunity to examine the seating arrangement as shown on the floating name displays. My command team was sitting to my right, descending by rank, thereafter the officers of *Berenice, Nike, Calliope,* and last *Iris,* followed. Thus the *Iris'* pilot was sitting to my left. He hurried to go to attention behind his chair.

"Please sit down," I repeated more firmly. "I'll remain standing for now."

After a brief shuffling of chairs, they all had found a more or less comfortable sitting position.

"Thank you. Hello and again a hearty welcome aboard *Athena.* I want to put two, no, three things up front. Firstly, I beg your pardon for not having found time to meet you earlier, due to my departure preparations. In this regard, you have a head start of three to four weeks together." Some smiled, some nodded in agreement. "Secondly, I want to say thank you for your willingness to venture on this mission with me—with new, barely tested technology, an almost unexplored destination and a new commandant as yet unknown to you. We all know that this mission will demand an enormous amount of patience and improvisation talent from us and that we'll have to struggle for a viable work relationship." Again, I sensed agreement. "Thirdly I want to address my two greatest weaknesses right from the start. I'm not used to military etiquette, and I'm quite anarchical-minded. I'm aware of the significant conflict potential of that, because where so many people share the same tight space for such a long time, a certain level of discipline is mandatory. I just don't value standing at attention and rank titles very much. I already told my flag captain—the admiral rank doesn't mean anything to me. Protectress, Johanna or simply Jo is entirely sufficient— respect is in the behavior. Okay?"

I focused on the nervous young pilot at my side, Lieutenant Commander Harket. "Okay, Magne?"

He swallowed, then smiled and sat up straight. "Okay, Jo."

"Thanks." Aside from Varna's slight tension, I felt no disagreement. "I've drawn you from your takeoff preparations and thus started the first test for your crews' teamwork and improvisation talent. We're surely all curious how well your people will get along without you, but of course, that wasn't the primary purpose. It's most of all about getting to know each other in person before a few robust steel shells and many kilometers of airless space will separate us. Well, I know your personnel files, but you only know about me what the media knows, and that's not much. So, if you've got questions, now's the time."

I expected questions of the kind *What do we have to expect,* but instead Captain Yong of the *Berenice* surprised me with an entirely different topic. The lank Chinese man had many years of experience in the wet Navy — I was glad that nobody had picked the commandant of the aircraft carrier *Sky Messengers' Nest.*

"Protectress, it's a rather delicate issue, but I believe that it's better if I address it now. Aboard my ship there's an open discussion on whether you're truly suited to direct a military operation of this size. Please don't get that wrong — nobody questions your bravery. The people know about your dedication and your New York mission, and of course everyone remembers how you opposed the last invader in one tiny space fighter. But now it's about a drop operation and about open combat. It's entirely different when the bullets fly, people are saying."

And you're thinking the same, otherwise you'd interfere with such discussions, wouldn't you?

Captain Tammy Archer of the *Nike* leaned forward, but I raised a hand. I could very well defend myself.

"I've been often enough in places where the bullets fly — or the plasma balls. Let me recap quickly. The first time was fourteen years ago, in the summer of '56, when I stormed a well-guarded Cartel villa together with an American special unit. Four years later, in the summer of '60, I was making a stop at a fuel station in the Belgian ZONE when this was assaulted by a larger Cartel commando. We tried to barricade ourselves into the guest room, but they blew away the entire forward wall."

My audience held their breath. Very few knew that story — it probably wasn't even recorded in the secret CIA dossiers on me.

"So I went out forward —"

"Through the assailants' fire?" Francine asked.

"Exactly. On top came the hand grenades — I shot three of them out of the air. I took out twenty-four of the thirty-two assailants and only caught a grazing shot on my butt and a shot right through the arm. Back then, I had no armor suit yet. Well, then came Rome — when I spoiled the minister's daughter's kidnapping, I caught a few more bullets. I don't know what was more unpleasant — the hit between kidney and spine or the shattered foot. The grazing shot at the shoulder hardly counts."

I left out the Denver police office.

"Okay. In autumn '63 I accompanied a team of US Marines into the Houston ZONE to draw out a secret Cartel plasma weapons factory. Sadly the factory was guarded by two Frost-dragon armor suits — invisible. The only one who could spot and fight such a suit was me. So I got a linear rifle. Sadly they were alarmed before I had reached my position. It didn't matter, I took them out one by one anyway."

"And they didn't return fire?" Francine asked.

"The suits couldn't — but there was another with a plasma rifle behind the factory window. Caught my leg and completely burned away my own armor suit." I shrugged. "A while later we took care of an armor suit factory which the Cartel had newly established in Palmdale. There were a lot of armor suits and plasma rifles, but for a change, I caught no hits."

My audience was still trying to grasp what I already had experienced. But I was way from finished yet.

"Tokyo. There was an attack on the Emperor's Palace's north gate, with armor suits, linear and plasma rifles. The emperor's guard had dug in at the gate, but the situation there was basically hopeless. So I went out and had a go at the attackers. That couldn't happen without injuries. Thereafter, back in the United States, I sorted the Cartel headquarters out, but that caused only some scratches. Rome 2064 was a different animal then — there I had to defend myself against air-to-ground missiles. And the air around the Mafia headquarters in Palermo was quite plasma-saturated, too."

"What did you do in Italy?" Ortiz asked, visibly shaken.

"Supported the Carabinieri's anti-terror unit." I scrutinized Captain Yong. "Regarding military experience you can tell your people that I'm going on a mission when it gets tight for special forces, and that I've already caught more hits than they'll ever see bullets fly, hopefully."

Captain Archer smiled grimly. "I had the chance to talk with a certain Marines officer before I reported to my new task. To me it seems that you've played down your role in these missions quite a bit."

Of all present, my 1-O finally broke the silence that followed. "There can't be any doubt that our commandant has more experience in a battle spaceship to spaceship as well as in armed and unarmed combat than all other mission members together, with the exception of the Knights Francine and Zoé and her Companion."

"Correct," Ortiz agreed and turned to the *Berenice's* officers. "I suggest that we captains communicate this message in appropriate and unmistakable form to our crews."

I wasn't entirely sure about Yong yet, but his first officer and his pilot had bright eyes — these two would surely spread the message.

"Coffee?" I asked, to lighten up the tensed atmosphere.

I had hoped that this topic had been all, but Yong wasn't done yet.

"I have to address a second delicate topic. There are rumors about your past."

"There are facts about my past," I corrected. "Some are better known, some are less well known. My Ironman world record — for both sexes — is still unbroken. From today's point of view I should point out, though, that I achieved this record without illicit Dragon means. Second — astonishingly, there are still some people who haven't made the connection between Johanna Meier and *Velvet* yet. Yes, I was a very successful thief. I stole money, factories and leading staff from the Cartel, and there are a few more missions I'm not allowed to talk about. Very likely, most aboard know that I'm the Meier effect inventor. Few might know how it came to that. I got my admission to the Dragon technology studies from Eva Keller, who had founded the University together with Zoe Lionheart. Eva Keller was at the same time the head of a worldwide wellness brothel chain, and I was her best employee. Yes, I was a prostitute, and I'm still proud of it. I took money to give people pleasure, and I still regard that as worth more than giving people pain and catching bullets."

Yong wasn't convinced yet. "Your attitude surely isn't shared by everyone."

"Surely not. For me it suffices that the Imperatrix Aurea Zoe Lionheart knew my past and appointed me her successor anyway — or perhaps because of it."

"A pretty leap up."

"Into the fire. Lot of risk, zero pay."

"Zero? And the missions you just listed?"

"The mission in the Belgian ZONE was a paid mission, but the gunfight wasn't part of it. For all other missions, I never got a penny"

"How did you make your living then?" Ortiz asked.

I shrugged. "Sometimes, I was invited for a meal. On other occasions, there was raw fish or raw rat."

"Raw rat?"

"There were plenty back then in New York. The nutritional value is quite good. However, I'll never get used to the taste."

He took a deep breath. "You're saying that as if it were some everyday thing."

"For me it is. I take life as it comes. One time it's the hotel suite and another time it's the wind-protected corner on a roof. I travel light—for this mission I just brought what I'm wearing."

From the corner of my eye I saw my adjutant flinch. Then he fetched his tablet and tapped on it. *Yes, exactly. You don't have to take care of my luggage.*

The knocking sound of Captain Archer placing her coffee cup down interrupted the silence. "Perhaps we could talk about the mission now? What do you see as our focus?"

"Focus? Well. Our mission's designed so widely that you can hardly speak of focuses. Or yes, there's one imperative — our technology, especially the tunnel bubble, may not fall into hostile hands. You can derive a fundamental goal from that — the crew's safety is paramount. We will have to enter risks — such happens when you sail uncharted waters — but we won't plunge into adventures recklessly."

One by one, I watched my officers. "You may have worries, and you're welcome to address your worries openly. I'm concerned, too, but I think we're as well prepared as we can be for such an expedition. Back to your question, Captain Archer — what are our tasks? We've got a whole bunch of primary goals."

For just a moment I felt for my Companion's signature. He was traveling with *Calliope* and mentoring the scientific team.

"This mission's official mandate is advance defense, the representation of our interests in a distant star system. We'll find and eradicate the foreign organism that attacked us just three years ago. To achieve that, we'll gather experience with interstellar travel, explore the destination system, analyze the foreign organism, win allies among the locals, and finally help them in their direst need with our supplies. All these are part of our mission and not just secondary goals. I don't see our mission as a one-off undertaking either. Everything we learn from this one will help further missions after us to work better and safer. It's our duty to pass on our experience and everything we already learned."

"How do you mean that?" Archer asked.

"We're the first humans venturing on such a mission. Regarding the procedures aboard a spaceship, my first flight doesn't count—Francine and I could always reach an agreement. With a few hundred people aboard each ship, we need rules. The wet navy was a good role model, but spaceships are different. We've got the right and the duty to change procedures and adapt rules if they don't fit. I wish each of us a lucky hand with that. Moreover, we've got the right and the duty to make good use of each opportunity within our mission to learn more about space around us. Science is not an appendage, but a core part of our mission."

Captain Tatjana Donskoi of the *Calliope* nodded contentedly.

"For the military part of our mission—that is for us, our officers, and our crews—we'll establish an active training program, that is, we'll make numerous exercises. Some by departments, but also some for our entire fleet."

"What kind of exercise do you have in mind?" my flag captain asked.

"All kinds of exercises. Fire aboard, hull breach, salvaging a damaged Barracuda, boarding maneuvers, combat exercises — oh yes — did you ever hear of the *simulation?*"

Chapter Seventy-Five

Francine remained calmly standing behind me until the express lift door had closed behind our last guest.

"You gave them a lot of stuff to think about."

"You think so?"

"It's not easy to understand that you've got all the knowledge of your predecessor in your head. You have to digest that first."

"Right, indeed. It may take years for me to even halfway grasp what a treasure that is."

"Oh." She glanced down at me. "I was saying that our people will need a while to internalize how far you're ahead of them. At least Yong seems to have learned that he can't easily put you down as wannabe soldier."

"That still has to arrive at his people yet."

"They probably already know. He was speaking about himself."

"Oh. I didn't recognize that."

"You were busy, I could watch. In any case, he flinched hard when you told of *your* experience with Angry April. On the other hand, I think, once he got over the fact that you're a woman and didn't have to work your way up in the Navy, he's quite okay. His ideas on the exercises sounded very competent."

"That applies to all of them. We were sent the best. The council had to be a bit considerate and make sure that people of all the big factions are represented, but a matching psychological profile was decisive—I've seen the results in the personnel files. Capacity for teamwork and all that. I just have to bend my people into shape. They don't know me yet, so they may be skeptical. That will change soon. Once the captains have accepted me, it will work for the crews, too."

Francine grinned. "And how long might it take for them all to learn that their commandant eats raw rat for breakfast?"

CHAPTER SEVENTY-SIX

The young ensign at the comm station turned around and said aloud, "Mount Alma Space Port gave all-clear for the expedition fleet. Gladstone Control acknowledged corridor west. Air space is clear."

"Thanks, Paul." Captain Ortiz nodded contently. "Fleet for *Athena* — takeoff in thirty seconds."

The ensign pointed at a button on his floating panel. "All-clear passed on, Captain."

"Hamid, Francine?"

"Course set, Captain," the navigation officer replied.

"Controls on auto," Francine acknowledged.

Ortiz turned to me.

I merely smiled back. As long as there were no strategic decisions to be made, I was just a privileged passenger on his bridge.

"Confirmations from *Berenice, Nike, Calliope, Iris,*" Ensign Paul reported.

Ortiz took a deep breath. "Start."

Francine tapped a button.

Athena treated us gently. The ship trembled briefly when rising from its landing legs and then accelerated hardly noticeably upward. We needed patience — our five ships could have climbed faster. But as we didn't want to cause a storm on the surface, we climbed very slowly, similar to a hot-air balloon.

"One thousand meters," Francine reported.

"Formation assumed," the ensign at the detectors

dashboard added.

"Thank you, Francine, Julio," Ortiz said.

With a handwave I conjured up my own dashboard and called up an image of the surroundings below us. That way I could see the spaceport slowly shrinking below us, could see more and more of the express railway appear. After a while, the Dawson Highway north of the spaceport came into view — *Athena* marked the tracks for me, otherwise I'd have had difficulties to recognize the details. After all, my refined Dragon senses couldn't retrieve details from the display that the image resolution didn't provide.

Gladstone, the coastline and the offshore islands, with Velvet Island among them, were easy to spot. I felt a little sting — this was my home! How many years would pass until I saw it again?

"Twenty-thousand," Francine reported. "Transition to start phase two executed."

"Thank you, Francine." Ortiz took a deep breath. For him, it was the first takeoff ever — until then he only knew the simulator — and responsibility for his fleet had to weigh hard on him. "Paul, report us gone."

"Yes, Captain." The ensign tapped the dashboard before him. "Gladstone Control for *Athena*. Mission *Bridge to the Stars* checks out."

At this point I interfered. A finger snap switched the reply to the speakers not just on our bridge, but in all rooms of all ships of our fleet.

"*Gladstone Control to* Bridge to the Stars. *Boys, girls, Earth wishes you well. Keep a stiff upper lip and do us honor.*"

CHAPTER SEVENTY-SEVEN

Wherever I looked, technicians were hurrying from one dashboard to the next like scared chickens, checking patchboards, calibrating wires, replacing electronic plug-in modules, calling measures and part numbers at each other. Their voices carried a hint of despair—they were almost through their third checklist run, but yet hadn't found the failure.

The chief engineer's broad back was towering over them as firm as a rock. He was receiving reports from his section leads.

My black suit stood out against the ship uniforms' light gray, but aside from the fact that nobody ran into me, my presence remained without any reaction while I was approaching the small group.

"Just don't let the old gal hear that," Chief Rumi was just grumbling.

"What should the old gal not hear?" I asked kindly.

The last addressed technician gazed past the chief in my direction and stared at me. The chief turned to me and grinned. "Well, okay—now that you're here, Petty Officer Nolan might as well tell you his assessment himself."

I had already heard his objections and the less than kind wording. But the chief's grin signaled—this was part of the game.

"Gladly. Now?" I scrutinized Nolan.

"Now—well."

"Is that a correct report?"

He blushed to a fiery red. The chief's brief glance around

333

reminded the bystanders that giggles currently weren't appropriate.

Nolan stood straight. "No, Sir! Pardon, Sir! I had just told the chief that the installed parts' safety margins rule out a failure according to the specifications."

"Thank you, Petty Officer Nolan. You also mentioned an overall assessment on this exercise — well, you don't have to repeat that." He had called the exercise *pure harassment.* "Rather tell me how high the potential error rate of a single part actually is."

Obviously relieved not to be nailed down on his disrespectful statement, he quoted from the specification of a quite representative part. "The average time to failure of a power distribution switch is over eighty-two years."

I nodded. "And how large is the specified standard deviation?"

"About ten years, plus or minus."

"Exactly. Why did we make such tight allowances?"

"Well."

One of his colleagues stepped in. "Because we wanted to be sure with a tolerance level of seven sigma."

"Very good, Petty Officer Marek. And that means?"

"Well — that presumably less than one out of a hundred billion parts fails outside of the seven-fold standard deviation."

"Seven times ten years — so when?"

"Erm — twelve years from now."

"Exactly. Less than one out of a hundred billion parts may fail *before* the end of the next twelve years. That sounds safe. But on what basis were these specs defined? Nolan?"

"I don't understand, Sir."

Again, I let the *Sir* stand undisputed. "Okay. What else do you call the span within the standard deviation?"

"Erm — confidence interval."

"Right. Why?" They gave me clueless looks, so I explained,

"Because we have *confidence* in the assumptions' correctness. We have confidence in the random samples during construction truly having an average of thirty-thousand days—although we didn't want to wait for eighty-two years. We also have confidence in that no producer fell prey to the temptation of saving on production and polishing up his test protocols—after all, we're far, far away when the first problems could arise, aren't we?"

It wasn't just Nolan and Marek who frowned.

"We also trust in our parts only being subject to usual wear, in our *Besson compensator* working according to specs, in our grav arrester working as designed—that the one flight of our *Mischief*, our only long-range sample, was truly representative." I spread my arms and raised my shoulders. "If not, our average could drop by half and the single standard deviation double, and we arrive at two sigma. Which gives a failure rate of how much, Nolan?"

"Ah—about five percent."

"Exactly. Every twentieth part." I didn't point out that half of them could last longer, theoretically. "How many power distribution switches did we install?"

Both stared at me with wide open eyes.

"See? And that's why I don't trust these specifications. Neither do I simply trust in my quite competent crew to know what's to be done in an emergency, but I take my own samples—we call it exercise. That's not harassment, but a part of our own quality assurance process."

Nolan stood straight. "Protectress, Admiral, thank you for your instructions. My assessment was based on the wrong foundations in an inexcusable way."

"No worries. I'm still curious whether you'll find the defect soon. Petty Officer Nolan?"

"Yes, Sir—Protectress."

"Based on today's exercise results, you'll elaborate until

the evening after tomorrow how many samples are required to improve the hit quote to three sigma with one-hour exercises only. You'll document your assumptions and show the result to Chief Rumi. And then we'll see how close you really get."

His face grew longer with every sentence. In parallel, Petty Officer Marek's grin became wider and wider while Chief Rumi was trying for a poker face.

I did better. "Petty Officer Marek, are you aware of the Dragon principle of teamwork?"

"Pardon me, Protectress?"

"You'll find someone who'll explain it to you. Meanwhile you've still got an exercise to complete. Chief—your game."

CHAPTER SEVENTY-EIGHT

I felt entitled to feel lonely. Only my thin suit was protecting me against the vacuum and the lethal coldness of space. Only a small oxygen bottle provided me with air to breathe, and a compact battery heated the suit's inside just enough to prevent frost damage.

The *Calliope* was far away, nevertheless I could guess her position by Achrotzyber's signature. *Athena* should be closer, but as long as she remained sunward, her body remained just a black shadow before a black background, from which I slowly drifted away.

For two hours I'd been already drifting here — time enough to build up quite some distance. The air draft that had washed me out of the hangar when the outer door had suddenly been blown away had given me a strong impulse, and the turbulences of smaller secondary explosions of non-vacuum-proof water containers had made my trajectory unpredictable. The mist of tiniest ice drops had probably made the optical recordings unusable. If someone wanted to pick me up, they'd have to search a quite large sector of space.

"No, no, no!" Ortiz had said. "That's insane, we can't do that! What if something goes wrong?"

"If something goes wrong, I'm the only one with a realistic chance of survival," I had said. "I'm Dragon. I can survive for a long time even in airless space."

I hadn't told him that I could shut my organism almost entirely down. I hadn't told him that my Companion could find

337

me any time by my signature. Most of all, I hadn't told him that I could talk with my Companion. For all this, my crew had no need to know, especially not as long as we had to expect followers of my still unknown opponents aboard. How dangerous those could be for me had become obvious in the current salvage exercise — the water containers hadn't been a regular part of the drill. Someone had added this complication just before it started and thus raised my stakes in this game. Someone was cheating — but this was still a game where I set the rules.

But first I wanted to see whether my people could find me anyway.

A brief flash, then a second — the laser ray rested on my belly. Seconds later followed a second one from a different direction. Only one and a half minutes later, a Barracuda with open, lit airlock was sailing toward me.

As soon as a loop of the slowly spreading net came into reach, I grabbed it and jerked it twice — *pull me inside.*

Shortly later I was standing inside.

"Welcome aboard, Protectress," the pilot said with a friendly smile and tapped the microphone ring. "*Athena* from *Astarte.* Target person recovered and in good health. Exercise completed."

"Thank you, Katya," I told *Athena's* second pilot, Lieutenant Commander Katya Romanova. "Take me back."

"At once, Protectress." Her fingers danced across her dashboard. "Guide beam is up."

I nodded and let myself drop in the second seat. The co-pilot dashboard came to life automatically. That was new, just like the beam, but sensible — while the Barracuda was in alarm condition, the computer could assume that the co-pilot might need his dashboard soon, and in order to protect the carrier it was better to rely on automatic at close range. Not every pilot managed a perfect approach on his first go, and Chief Rumi wouldn't be happy if he had to repair a hangar door several times a week.

Katya gave me a thoughtful glance. "May I ask you a personal question?"

"Yes."

"Was it bad?"

"What?"

"Drifting alone out there."

"No. Not for me—I've experienced worse. But I can imagine it could be bad. The uncertainty about whether you'll be found, the sense of falling, the solitude. The risk of being hit by a particle that can penetrate the suit. That's not easy."

"There's worse?"

"When my Taipan dissolved around me on the test flight. I was severely injured and had a good chance of burning up upon entry in the denser atmospheric layers. It wasn't clear whether I'd be found and picked up."

"Oh crap—and how were you rescued?"

"Zoé came with our second Taipan."

"But there's no space in the cockpit—and no airlock."

"No. But there was enough room in the weapons bay. It wasn't a pleasant flight, but she brought me down. In comparison, this was a walk in the park."

"Oh. Yes, I agree. And all for this stupid mishap with the water canister. The chief was furious, the skipper—sorry, Captain Ortiz—could hardly calm him down."

"That was no mishap."

"What?"

"That was no mishap, Katya. Someone added a complication to the exercise."

"Stupid idea. That could have gone bad. What if our target lasers hadn't touched you? As far as I know, the grid wasn't programmed that tightly."

"It should have gone badly."

"It should? But then . . ."

I gave her time to process this idea. With a few gestures I called up our guide beam data, connected with *Athena* and fetched the corresponding programming from there.

"Katya, what happens if you overlay two not mutually harmonized nestle fields?"

"You should not overlay nestle fields. That can cause dangerous interferences. What do you mean with *not mutually harmonized?*"

"Doesn't matter." I marked a few lines of code and called up the installation protocols. "Worst case you get a disruptor field—like the one that cost me my Taipan." *Snap.* "*Athena* from *Astarte*. Alpha order—deactivate hangar control unit, block credentials, lock physical access." On my dashboard, I activated the Barracuda's grav field drive and deactivated the nestle field. Several indicators changed to yellow—even if we were slow in relation to *Athena*, the entire fleet formation was moving system-outward at three percent light speed. A warning for a flight without protective shield was quite appropriate.

With a gentle pull at the stick I further reduced our approach speed. Then I sent Francine a short message.

CHAPTER SEVENTY-NINE

Exactly as planned, *Astarte* was slowly floating through the hangar door and toward her parking position. Katya was clenching her fists and tensing her muscles, was even twitching twice toward her flightstick, but kept herself under control.

I had already taken my hands away from the controls. The trajectory was right, and it was out of the question to use a normal grav field drive inside the hangar.

The holding clamps caught us, decelerated us and then held us firmly. *Astarte* trembled. Green lights confirmed the end of our flight.

The computer reported an incoming message. Immediately, several indicators changed to red.

"What was that?" Katya asked.

"An access from outside and the attempt to start our drive inside the hangar," I replied grimly. "As it seems, we're not through yet with the dirty tricks."

She squinted. "You mean there's someone just trying to kill you? What's this about?" With determination she unbuckled, rose, and walked up to the airlock. "If I get him, he's in for a nasty surprise!"

I followed her. "Consider that the hangar isn't pressurized yet. The controls are deactivated, and that remains so until I've found all nasties."

"Oh. Thanks. But we'll get inside, or is the hangar airlock blocked, too?"

"We'll get inside."

During our short walk through the airless hangar I remained alert, but no new traps were waiting for us there. Were our opponents' means exhausted?

The next airlock cycle strained my patience. Katya kept as much distance as the chamber allowed. Was my nervousness so obvious?

My adjutant was waiting right behind the airlock door with a scowl. "This way, Protectress," he snapped and pointed toward the storage rooms.

An armor suit tandem pair was standing at the far end of the corridor, their forearms held up threateningly. What had happened? I had to scrape up all my self-control not to run. *Don't panic! If all others manage, you can do it, too, Jo.*

The two armor suits made each a half step back when I passed through between them. Behind the door they were guarding, two more guards were waiting together with Flag Captain Ortiz, Lieutenant Ormstedt, and Francine.

The captain was scowling at two curled-up, dead bodies on the floor at the storage room's far end. The young lieutenant was tapping something on his memopad. The two armor suits held a noncommissioned officer at bay with their linear cannons. The dazed culprit was sitting on the ground, leaning back to the wall.

The Mamba's left arm hung down limp and smelled bad. The black wasn't her suit, but scorched flesh. I knew that from my own experience—that was how a plasma gun hit smelled and looked. Such a pistol was still lying near the two dead.

I placed one hand on her arm. That was a case for my healing nanos. *Relieve pain, then heal.*

"Will be better soon. What happened?"

"Once I got your message I came down here. I was too late—two of Ormstedt's people had already found the saboteur. I only heard the hiss of the two plasma shots. When I entered, he aimed at me. I could hardly dodge in the doorway, so he grazed me. Then I dealt him one."

"That was reckless," Ortiz judged. "There are at least sixty meters from the door to the crime scene! Without cover!"

A gentle squeeze of my fingers let Francine remain silent.

"Francine only followed my order—find and eliminate the saboteur or saboteurs."

"That's not her duty as pilot."

"No, but a part of her tasks as my *wing*."

"Her task? Confront a guy with plasma pistol unarmed?"

"Exactly." My gaze swept past Ortiz to the saboteur. "Okay, it's a bit unfair. Only one plasma pistol."

Ortiz frowned.

"You should know one thing, Captain—my girls defeated a fully equipped company of Marines unarmed, and they regularly exercise against armor suits."

"Against armor suits?" he replied, aghast, and studied his first pilot.

"I got rusty," Francine admitted contritely. "Otherwise he wouldn't have hit me."

"I'd say so, too," I agreed. "I guess we should schedule some training units, shouldn't we?"

"What shall we do with that guy now?" Ortiz pointed at the saboteur. "He shot two of my crew!"

"We could put him on the *Iris* and send him back to Earth," Ormstedt proposed.

"We won't change the mission schedule for him. Our flight will continue as planned."

"And when the *Iris* returns?" Ormstedt asked.

Of course, then there was space enough aboard, and we'd be rid of our problem. I wasn't happy with the idea anyway. Why not?

There was a more urgent issue. I pointed at the plasma pistol. "He couldn't have laid his hands on that weapon without help. We've got more than one source of troubles."

The lieutenant squeezed his lips tight.

Ortiz frowned. "You mean, we have more saboteurs aboard?"

"I mean that we have to work on the assumption that he had help. His approach for this assault alone tells of diligent preparations." Ortiz couldn't know either my suspicion about the overlapping nestle fields yet, or the attempted intrusion into *Astarte's* computer. "This is part of a larger operation, the true goal of which I don't know yet. But it's obvious that I'm in someone's way, and the opposition accepts collateral damage." With my free hand I pointed at the two dead. "I hadn't expected this mission to demand two victims so early. Who are the two? I'll have to notify their families. And thereafter the culprit owes me some answers."

"He refuses to tell anything," Ormstedt said.

I focused on Ormstedt. "I didn't ask whether he *wants* to answer."

Ortiz took a deep breath. "Protectress—"

"Flag Captain Ortiz. For the supposed murder of two crew members—with overwhelming evidence—this man will answer to a regular court-martial. For his assaults on the Imperatrix Aurea with alleged intent to kill he will answer to a Dragon, that is, to me. By Dragon rules."

My healing nanos returned to me. Francine's arm looked good. She only needed a new uniform.

I slapped her shoulder. "Well done. And remember to schedule our training."

CHAPTER EIGHTY

I just managed to dodge the incoming karate chop. *Ha!* Then a multiple-finger stab, performed without indication, hit me in the ribs.

"Ouch!" I protested aloud and hit back — but my opponent was no longer there, instead she scissored me off my legs. When I wanted to get up, I gazed into a plasma pistol barrel. So I sank back in resignation.

"Got you," Francine noticed with a grin.

"You're simply better than me." As long as I didn't make use of my special Dragon abilities — or not more than Francine with her booster — and told my *Analogy* to step aside, I had no chance against a well-trained Mamba. Sure, I had had to fight for my life often as well, but how often had I relied on inconspicuousness, on invisibility, or later on my relative invulnerability?

Francine had had to learn fighting for her survival without Dragon armor, Dragon healing, Dragon power, Dragon reflexes — daily, for months and years. Compared to her, I was a dilettante.

She knew as well as I that she had a snowball's chance in hell if I'd pulled out all the stops. That wasn't what our training was about, though. I learned her tricks, she learned mine, and we both refreshed our abilities.

"What did your interrogation yield?"

"He didn't know much," I replied. "The usual pattern — indirect approach, no personal contacts, very well prepared instructions, but no substantial knowledge about further persons aboard. He imagined that he'd get reinforcement for the mission's second stage—but he doesn't know anybody."

"Second stage?"

"Yes. Once others reveal themselves to him, he would support a second stage. That applies especially after his arrest, should it come to that."

"After his arrest? But that means—"

"That they factored his failure in, unless it's already part of the plan. It's a bit too obvious."

"What? Not for me."

"Look. Assume we arrest three or four saboteurs on each of our fleet's ships. After arrival in the *Worries* system we pack them up together and send them back with the *Iris*. On their way they are set free—and we've got fifteen to twenty determined saboteurs flying on a ship with only a skeleton crew."

"Oh. Okay. You think they're after the ships—or at least one of them?"

"I think they're after the Dragon technology. I'm in the way—but at the same time they get the technology only from me. If it was just about getting rid of me—in a few days it's done. Then they can do what they want on Earth, even if it's about stealing a Phoenix. Only the Phoenixes on Earth won't have a tunnel bubble for now, no cake knife and nothing exciting otherwise either. If they want the full equipment, they need a ship of our fleet."

"Okay. And now that you know that, what will we do?"

"Nothing."

"Nothing?"

"No. We don't know who the other saboteurs are. We can't put the entire crew under general suspicion—that would cause too much unrest and would endanger the mission. We can only be vigilant."

"Okay, but what about this plan? Will you put him on the *Iris*?"

"No. I will spoil that plan for them. They signed for the full mission duration, and they will serve that time. No one will return with the *Iris* unplanned."

CHAPTER EIGHTY-ONE

Ortiz drummed the armrest of his commandant chair with his fingers. "Helm, time to transit?"

"Six minutes, Captain," Francine replied calmly.

"Status?"

"Twenty percent light speed, course set. Controls on automatic. Program parameters checked. Deep diagnosis one hundred percent green."

"Confirmed, Captain," Katya added from the co-pilot's seat.

"Thanks. Radio, message to fleet and ground control— *Athena* reports departure."

"*Athena* reports departure. Okay." Ensign Paul tapped a symbol. One by one, four other symbols turned green. "Four acknowledgements, Captain."

"Thanks. Eye, status?"

"No obstacles in our flight path, Captain."

"Thanks. 1-O, Status crew?"

"Crew is informed, Captain. Medical teams are ready."

"Thanks. Weapons, status?"

"All systems secured, Captain."

"Thanks." He paused his drumming. "Protectress, we're ready for transit."

"Thanks, Captain. I'm ready, too."

We could only wait. What we knew about the transit, the emergency reactions we had planned, was incorporated in *Athena's* programming. The transit itself, the tunnel bubble, the Besson compensation, the grav arrester, couldn't be controlled manually. From that moment on we were passengers.

Ortiz looked around, folded his hands, placed them back on the armrest. The officers around watched him attentively. We couldn't go on like that for the next three minutes.

I cleared my throat, and his motions froze. A gesture put me on the general onboard communication. "Okay, folks. We're about to make a tiny hole into our universe's structure, squeeze through, slip to the other side along the carefully programmed course, and pop out there. It could buck a bit, and nobody should be surprised by a little nausea. That's no reason to worry. Please take care that you've got nothing between your teeth before the transit, so that you don't bite yourself accidentally. You needn't be afraid. I wouldn't be aboard if I wasn't convinced that the transit will be fine. Think of something nice — a visit to the dentist is worse."

Thereafter I switched off.

One more minute.

I'll call back right away, Mighty.

Don't exert yourself, Companion.

No worries.

My flag captain remained calm now.

Ten more seconds.

Francine leaned back. Katya gave her a sideways glance and then did the same.

I imagined a rough sketch of the tunnel bubble that *Athena* would create next.

Five.

Why did I have to think about the formulas for potential differences right now? Was there still an error in the grav arrester?

Too late.

CHAPTER EIGHTY-TWO

What was the beautiful red flower doing on my green lawn? Why did I feel like I was sitting under a bell?

My vision cleared. Green, green, green, green — we had arrived at the planned destination, about one hundred light hours away from *Worries*, the Besson compensator had worked, no flashover of gravity potential differences had torn our ship apart, the compensators had absorbed the energy without complaints. Green was the biometric data, too — this transit had been significantly smoother than our previous journeys.

The forward nestle field was up and prevented interstellar dust from burning our bow.

The red flower blossomed in an unexpected place — *Athena* had detected a moving vessel in the system. We were not alone!

We weren't under immediate fire, though — probably weren't even spotted yet.

So I had to fulfill a duty first.

Ok.

There was a gentle pressure at my hand.

"Jo?"

And again, more urging, "Jo!"

That was Francine's voice. So that was her hand, too?

"Jo, wake up!"

It was so hard to open my eyes. Why, actually? Oh, yes — the signal. I had put a lot of power into it, seemingly too much, and then I'd been gone. Was that all?

No. I was hanging halfway out of my seat, only held by the belt. That couldn't remain so. *Stabilize.*

First I opened my eyes. There was Francine's frown. Then I forced myself to smile — her frown disappeared. Next I could slowly straighten myself.

"It's okay," I whispered. "Only a dizzy spell — too much strain too soon after the transit."

"What strain?"

"Dragon communication. Achrotzyber's in the know."

Francine's eyes widened. "You can communicate with him? Over a hundred and forty light years?"

Ortiz — he was standing right behind her — took a hissing breath. "I didn't know about that."

"Top secret," I explained. Then I closed my eyes — there had been something else?

I sensed Dragon signatures — hundreds of them. None of them were as precise as the quasi-verbal signals my Companion and I exchanged, but they were understandable — each individual reply was an echo of a foreign Golden One's *call,* a mix of acknowledgement, welcome, joy, a general plea for help and — readiness to mate?

No. The latter only applied to male Dragons' signatures. Just as only a fraction of the signatures included the additional pattern of a *guardian.*

With every minute there were more. If many of the *Worries* Dragons had rested until then, they were waking up now.

"What is it?" Francine asked. "Trouble?"

I shook my head — *ugh, that's not good.*

"No, aside from the fact that I need something edible urgently."

There was shuffling behind me. My adjutant said, "At once," rose, and hurried from the bridge.

Okay, from urgent to important, and then nicely in

sequence. "Captain Ortiz. The Dragon community of the *Worries* system has welcomed me formally. Take to protocol that we're officially allowed to travel this system."

He turned to his 1-O who scrutinized me open-mouthed.

Francine followed my gaze. Understandingly, she said, "It can be a shock to realize for the first time that you're *Dragon*."

I exercised Dragonish patience until Ortiz and Varna had digested the surprise and logged my message. Meanwhile the sections' all-clears arrived.

Francine reassumed her pilot seat once my ensign arrived with a cup of hot chocolate and a small pack of energy bars.

"Thank you, Robert."

"Do you need anything else, Jo?"

"No, thanks. Not right now." Right then I only needed the time and leisure to tend to his delivery and consider my next steps.

Finally, Ortiz approached me again. He addressed the very topic I regarded as the most urgent myself.

"Protectress, our sensors detected a small moving vessel in the system. It travels at about a tenth of a percent light speed on a time-optimized course from *Worries One* or *Trouble* to *Worries Two* and will arrive there within the next seven days. The emissions tell of a grav field drive with inferior efficiency."

"Yes, thank you."

"What do you make of that?"

"I need a closer look at the data before I can judge the technology. It could be an indication of a quickly improvised Jelly technology rebuild. In any case — even though we can't tell the flight's purpose yet, whether it's a retreat, a supply flight, or the precursor of an invasion on *Worries Two* — we can safely state that the point of origin is a contaminated planet. Hence the vessel must be considered contaminated, too, that is, a potential threat to our future allies and to our planned base. Conversely, we can't have been spotted yet, unless there are Dragons aboard. Our emissions are hardly measurable across this distance, and the image of our arrival needs at least another week before reaching there."

Ortiz nodded. "Which approach do you propose?"

"If we don't just want to watch what happens, we'll have to take action before the end of the seven days. Our mission plan envisages, though, that we're waiting for the rest of the fleet to arrive, take the *Iris'* payload, and advance to the inner system only after that. This planning, however, is already outdated due to my early contact with the *Worries* Dragon. On the other hand, that vessel is no match for a Phoenix. It's a space fighter task. So we'll send out an advance command and thus kill two birds with one stone—explore and eventually treat the bogey, and establish personal contact with the rulers."

"How many Barracudas do you want to deploy?"

"One."

CHAPTER EIGHTY-THREE

It was obvious for me who should be part of this advance command — only I could establish contact to the Dragon rulers. My company could only be fleet's best and most experienced pilot — Francine.

Ortiz had tried to protest — but he hadn't been able to escape this logic. So the two of us were sitting in *Mischief's* cockpit and preparing for the mission.

"You could have taken Katya along," Francine said. "She's good."

"I know. However, I don't just need a good pilot. I also need the scientist."

"Ouch."

Francine smiled there. It did her good to have found a role that had no connection to her past — a meaning to her life that didn't deal with fighting and death.

"Mischief is ready to start," she reported.

"Cleared for start," Ortiz replied. *"Have a good journey."*

"Thanks."

While Francine was taking the Barracuda out of the Phoenix carrier's hangar, I examined the unknown vessel's trajectory. From which point on *Trouble's* surface had it originated? Could that still be calculated?

Its course didn't tell me anything. Its grav field emissions had also long disappeared. It seemed as if we had to ask the crew. That thought was not very appealing to me. But it was out of the question to let the spaceship touch down on the ice planet as long as there was a contamination risk. Aside from

354

that, our little trip should be a walk in the park. Should I have given Katya the opportunity to gain experience?

No. Several days or weeks in a tiny tin can at my side required more than professional skills. We first had to learn to know each other better — aboard *Athena,* where we could avoid each other, if necessary.

Once our small ship had left the hangar, it quickly gained speed.

"Do you know what I'm looking forward to most?" Francine asked.

"No. Ahead of us I see nothing to look forward to."

"Your cooking."

A few hours later Francine called me just when I had the first course prepared for the nanowave. "Jo? There's something new. Please have a look."

What was so urgent that I should let our meal wait? I walked up to her seat and watched her screen.

"Look here. Five new emission sources, all just started from *Trouble.* Significantly stronger than the first bogey, and a significantly better degree of efficiency if you compare the delta V to stray emissions ratio."

"Pursuers."

"Looks like that, doesn't it? And if they're keeping up pushing their pedal like that, they can catch up with bogey one within a few hours."

"Let me see." I slipped into my own seat, waved up my dashboards and recalled the data. Then I started a few course calculations.

"Nine hours." Thoughtfully I glanced from my plot to Francine and back. "No way."

Athena had provided us with her own speed vector — the same twenty percent light speed we had made the transit with, minus a few fractions because the big ship was decelerating with a comfy two g since our arrival. If we wanted to match our speed with the bogey's, we needed another hundred and forty hours at twelve g—just right to intercept the bogey before its arrival at Worries Two. An alignment within less than nine hours would require a deceleration of more than two hundred g—that was outside the *safe* parameters of our artificial gravity.

She seemed to have guessed my thoughts. "I'll exit, let myself be picked up by Katya, and you'll fly on alone."

I shook my head. "I need you."

Instead I entered a few new instructions. Francine watched what the computer made of it and began to grin. "Really? Varna will have a heart attack."

"If we want to help the poor souls in bogey one—and I assume they're potential allies—there's only this way." I returned the grin. "By the time he learns about what we did, it's too late anyway."

"Okay. Should I calculate a few more variants?"

"Definitely. We should make use of the time we have while building up enough distance from *Athena*. So far we only have emission data."

At least these stray emissions didn't originate from a Jelly mothership or its landers. For that, they were too weak. The patterns didn't look like those of a scout, either—for that, they were too strong. That didn't make me worry much—if the unknown party needed five ships to pursue a single escapee, who was even smaller and less efficiently equipped, what could they muster?

"We've got only one try," Francine said. "Or what's your take?"

"Mmmm—no. Have a look at this."

Francine examined my next draft—what happened if you did a second transit toward the central star, swung around the sun, and then jumped out again? "Oh, that's mean. Cool trick."

"Thanks. So, let's walk through that sequence briefly. We'll cut the approach with a short transit . . ."

Chapter Eighty-four

The short transit took us to a few light seconds within reach of the group of pursuers. At still twenty percent light speed, that only left us a few moments to capture the situation and pull a suitable plan from up our sleeves — but our opponents didn't have any more time left, and for them, the encounter came as a total surprise.

But fate had a surprise in for us, too, as *Mischief's* alarm bell signal told us.

I needed perhaps a second to shake off the transit's aftereffects, and little more to see and understand the situation summary on my screen. Something plucked at my consciousness . . .

Fuck.

There was no time for a longer curse. Each of the bogeys was half as long and half as heavy as a Phoenix — as large as a Navy destroyer — and responded to our appearance with the instant activation of numerous target lasers, closely followed by unaimed impulses of heavy lasers.

In any case, the image was impressive. I tapped the symbol of a prepared shooting solution and leaned back.

Francine uttered a "Yep!" and pulled the stick to evade a laser training on our direction.

If the lasers found us, we were in trouble — our shield was ineffective. Our advantage was the high speed, the small size, and our agility — plus Francine's quick reactions.

On top came our offensive armament. In quick succession, our cake knife cut two of the aggressors apart. A torpedo with a nuclear warhead tore the third one into shreds and bathed the two nearby bogeys in a flash of hard radiation.

For a moment, our opponents were blinded, but the first two bogeys' pieces still had power for one last shot—and one of them grazed us just as we were passing by the hostile fleet.

A large part of my dashboard beamed in red—a half meter of our bow with its control quark emitters and the foremost accelerator ring for our torpedoes was gone.

One of our evasion plans envisaged a retreat with a second short transit—but my finger paused before touching the respective symbol. The remaining emitters should suffice for the tunnel bubble, but was the Besson compensator control designed for this kind of damage?

Aside from that, I didn't want to chicken out. Instead, I had another idea—*no, not now, Jo. But what about . . .*

I began to type.

Lacking other instructions, the computer continued the fight and cut one of the blinded opponents. Thereafter, the emitters needed a short break.

In parallel, Francine steered the *Mischief* through the laser storm with a complicated dance and hissed a silent curse.

My add-on program was complete.

Mischief made a somersault, and our cropped weapons tube spat out another nuclear torpedo. The shot lacked the usual precision, but that wasn't what mattered.

The bomb went off halfway between us and the bogeys.

"Miss," Francine commented.

But the slowly spreading plasma cloud swallowed a large share of the searching laser fingers' energy and diffused their beam. Anything that still reached us could no longer harm us.

Francine instantly recognized her advantage and changed our course so that we remained in the explosion's shadow longer.

"Phew!" she gasped when our last opponent's separated

parts were slowly drifting apart behind us. "That was a hot ride."

"Sorry. We shouldn't have entered such a high risk."

"Bullshit. We're at war. What else would you have done? Have a look from greater distance — and give the enemy time to spot us and home in on us? We had to get so close. And it worked — even better than I expected."

She pointed at the dashboard that was changing from red to yellow. "We were just nicked. Our self-repair can handle that."

"What had you expected, then?"

"That Katya would have to pick us out of space." She waved her dashboards aside. "Can you take over for a moment?"

"Sure." I pointed at the yellow signals. "We're doing the swing-by around *Worries* now, to analyze the battle and give *Mischief* time for repairs. After that, there's still time for establishing contact."

She paused in the doorway to the sanitation cell. "Could you gather new intel in our passing-by?"

"Yes. There are two Dragons aboard."

CHAPTER EIGHTY-FIVE

The monitor showed a coarsely patched-up hull—not much more than crannied iron plates around a stretched frame with hexagonal profile, with a stronger, armored bow and a flattened end, overall seventy meters long and eleven meters wide.

To venture into space with such a patchwork you either had to have a lot of confidence in fate's goodwill or be very desperate. To accelerate this thing to the hundredth part of lightspeed with a poorly adjusted grav field spoke for the latter variant.

"Where are the oars?" Francine asked. "You outright expect such a thing to be paddled."

A handwave let the image disappear from my screen. *Better.* I closed my eyes. *Much better.*

Two Dragons, female. Red with silver, blue without scale edges. Young. No guardians. Their signature, which I had sensed from the start of the battle, told me all that.

As I could sense them, they had to be able to sense me, too—a foreigner, female, young, and a Golden One. A very young Golden One for Dragon circumstances—would they even accept me? How would the first contact go? Would we be able to communicate? Of course, sure, Zoe had never had trouble with that.

The signatures came closer—or we came closer, it didn't matter—and at the same time I sensed many more in the background. Many hundred—and yet so few—on the ice planet, none left on *Trouble.* In the distance, I also sensed

361

Achrotzyber's reassuring presence. So the rest of the fleet had arrived, and seemingly without trouble, otherwise he'd have long ago called.

We had no trouble either, otherwise I'd have called. I forwent exchanging trivialities with my partner. I had to pace myself.

"How do you get in there?" Francine mused aloud. "I don't see a hatch."

"That's either due to our image sensor resolution or the tight clearance," I guessed. "I don't think they welded that thing closed after getting in. Let's close up, and then I'll go knocking."

"Shouldn't I better go?"

"Why?"

"Well—should the ship be contaminated—I don't count, but without you, the mission fails."

I watched for a while with a frown on my face. She was serious, and moreover, her assessment was entirely correct. Nevertheless, this was my task.

"Can you communicate with a foreign Dragon?"

"What? No."

"So I will go."

Up close, the entrance hatch joints in the spaceship's floor were quite well recognizable. Stubby supports with wide plates made me think of landing gear, and indeed I found remainders of organic substance there.

Or, more precisely, my nano threads found the substance—and luckily no brown pest.

That didn't tell me much. In order to survive in a vacuum, to survive the hard radiation, an organism needed special protective mechanisms.

I had such protective mechanisms—not just my nano-improved own skin, that could quite well withstand vacuum and radiation for a while, but also fleet's thin standard protective suit. Despite that, I could send out my nanos to analyze my environment or to erect a thin but robust foil around me that allowed me to open the hatch without endangering the travelers inside.

The hatch didn't offer resistance. That only applied to the inside pressure which I had to overcome. A few liters of the atmosphere escaped into my improvised pressure tent. After I had slipped through, I could recover some of it together with my nanos. A small share escaped into space.

A skeleton of iron rods reached to the bow. It didn't only support the hull, but also served as anchor for a multitude of strange aggregates. The easiest to spot were the grav field generator and the compact fusion generator, which nevertheless required a large share of the space.

There was plenty of room left for me to pull myself forward toward the bow. The openings were obviously designed for Dragons.

"I'm aboard," I sent to Francine. "On first sight, no evidence for contamination inside the spaceship."

Two scaly, nearly triangular heads watched my approach. The two Dragons were patiently waiting for me to reach their control center — judging by the few control elements.

Zoe's *memory* helped me. She had confronted more, bigger, and hostile Dragons. These didn't appear hostile.

Zoe's *memory* also ensured that I addressed the foreign Dragons in their language without thinking about it.

"You sense the signature of a Golden One, but you see a strange creature you might not have seen before. I'm in the shape of my *protected,* and I come from a distant star system."

"Why?" the red one asked.

"Only a few years ago, a *Harvester* mothership departed from this system to invade the system of my *protected*. Aboard that ship were no *Harvesters,* though, but a much worse danger—a creature that can assimilate and mimic other lifeforms. We were able to destroy the mothership and annihilate the strange organism. Thereafter, we decided to explore its origin. We were surprised to still find Dragons here—despite the *Harvesters* and the brown pest. We decided to equip a larger expedition and to return and support you in your fight."

"I do not understand. What is your motivation to do this?"

"Against this kind of opponent—the huge *Harvester* invasion fleet, and now this brown pest—this galaxy's peoples can only survive together, and together with the Dragons. We're hoping for support once the second *Harvester* wave arrives."

"I take from your words that you survived the first wave."

"Correct."

"And thereafter you were able to destroy a second *Harvester* mothership, and then still deploy an interstellar expedition?"

"Almost correct. The first *Harvester* mothership wasn't destroyed. It was captured and then equipped for a counterstrike."

"It should be impossible to capture a *Harvester* mothership."

"Yours has been captured, too—by this brown pest."

"That is true. But you obviously muster extensive means. How did you destroy our pursuers?"

"We cut them. With a directed grav field."

"How is that possible? Controlling gravitons is complicated enough."

"You need general control quarks plus an orthogonal signal. If you adjust both sufficiently precisely, you can do almost everything."

"I would like to learn more about that."

"I can tell you more when opportunity allows. I invented this effect. But now I'd like to learn more about your situation.

What made you venture on this flight, and are there any *protected* left on the inner planet?"

"No, Highest." The red one cocked her head. "The fight is lost. The brown pest, as you call it, assimilated all *protected* we know of. Should there be any hideouts, they are isolated and without prospect of survival."

"How come you could avoid contamination then — and even found the time to build a spaceship?"

"This spaceship was part of a long-term plan. We had begun to reallocate parts of our *protected* to the second planet. There they should hide in case of a *Harvester* invasion. On the first planet, we had begun to create hiding places and store defense equipment there — weapons, reactors, and supplies. These preparations did help us against the *Harvesters* — we could inflict serious losses on them, and at the beginning of their invasion even take some technology away from them."

"Like the grav field generator?"

"Exactly. Their advance force consisted of few small ships only. The drive principle was easy to understand, but hard to reconstruct with our means. Before we were ready to deploy this technology, landers and mothership had already departed — you confirmed our suspicion that this happened under brown pest command already. Against this enemy, neither the *Harvesters* nor we commanded sufficient means. The humid climate seemed to suit the brown pest especially well. We could only hold our ground in areas with strong volcanic activity, and of course, our Dragon fire is an effective weapon. You surely noticed that the inside of this ship is built fireproof."

"Yes." At the same time, I felt the hairs in my neck stand up. "But not Dragon-fire proof."

"We only had to gauge our fire carefully"

"You said, Dragon fire would be effective. Could you confirm the effectiveness of carefully gauged Dragon fire?"

The blue Dragoness' tail tip twitched.

The red one cocked her head. "No. We deducted its effectiveness. Biological organisms don't survive this heat."

"Dragons do survive this heat — only the full power can burn a Dragon body. We made the practical experience that normal fire doesn't suffice."

"But then we would have to be infested."

"Your ship is infested. You aren't. You shall take it to its destination. To the others."

CHAPTER EIGHTY-SIX

This seemed to be the wrong moment to tell the Dragons about a wooden horse with a hollow body. More precisely, this wasn't the time to tell anybody anything.

Neither Francine nor Achrotzyber could help me. After all, I could hardly help myself. Sufficiently hot Dragon fire would make the iron construction melt, use up all and any oxygen aboard and make the environment unbearably hot for the three of us, too. I myself could survive an effective Wyvern venom aerosol, but the two Dragons couldn't, and my nanos would at best feed the enemy.

What could I do?

If this was *Athena*, I would consider support by the internal systems. After all, those had already fought a similar infestation. Only that one hadn't been as smart and fast. *Hmmm.*

"Switch off your heaters and go into dormancy. We have to vent your spaceship. The brown pest might be able to survive in temperatures close to absolute zero, but its vital functions are massively restricted then."

"What is your plan?"

"I will go hunting. My means do work in the cold of space."

I felt a bit sorry for the two Dragons. They had to suffer the cold now, while my suit was protecting me and my booster keeping me warm. But this was still better than the logical alternative — to kill oneself to protect the others.

They had misjudged the situation and now had to pay for it. Now it was my duty to avoid another misjudgment.

The last time I had sent a nano thread against the foreign organism, it had overcome my nanos within fractions of a second. The Australian desert had been at least two hundred degrees warmer, though.

Nevertheless, I embedded a few droplets of Wyvern venom into my threads, just in case. Should the brown pest eat its way up to those, it would be in for a bad surprise.

Indeed my threads found traces of organic material in numerous corners, joints, and grooves, that might belong to the brown pest but were indeed mostly paralyzed by the cold. I grabbed the opportunity and analyzed its chemical structure. This was not a simple plant. Similar to the semi-organic nano agents I was using, this was a highly complex substance. But if I took a little time, I might find a toehold for a counter-agent — and better protection for our nanos.

For a while I went on like that. My nano threads explored the outer walls, each beam and every corner of the aggregates by the square centimeter and assimilated every trace of the suspicious substance.

Everything went by the plan until one of my nano threads encountered the active substance inside a well-insulated and not evacuated aggregate. The advance guard disappeared in an instant, and then the pest reached my Wyvern venom droplet. Thus the battle began.

At first, it looked like a standoff. The brown pest couldn't leave the aggregate casing, because outside it the grim cold of vacuum reigned, and I couldn't intervene with Dragon fire or Wyvern venom inside the casing.

Wrong.

I couldn't spit Wyvern venom from the inside of my space suit into the aggregate casing, but I could quite well carry further droplets inside along my nano thread.

Too late!

Conversely, the brown pest could funnel enough warmth from the casing outward to remain mobile on the surface, and there it sensed another source of warmth—me. There was already a brown bubble forming over the hair-thin access.

All in.

I placed my left hand over the bubble. That way, the pest couldn't spray all across the spaceship and all over my suit—the contamination was restricted to my palm. There, the actual battle took place.

The brown pest was fighting for its survival and probably also for a host. It was working on penetrating my suit material and at the same time tried to spread all over my hand.

I was fighting for my survival and that of the two Dragons. I had to prevent the brown pest reaching the skin of my palm, and I had to prevent its uncontrolled spread.

My hand was sweating out Wyvern venom, my nanos were surrounding the battle field. From outside, I funneled further venom to the front, frozen to tiny crystals in the cold. They created a barrier that the pest couldn't eat through.

Likewise, it failed against my venomous sweat—but then tried to slowly work its way between my suit's fabric layers past the danger area.

For the time being, I had to admit that—it seemed too risky for me to send nanos into the suit where it would be difficult for me to provide them with my dangerous venom. Instead I had to isolate this assault from its basis.

So my forces were tightening the ring of Wyvern venom crystals under my palm while the brown pest was slowly eating its way through my suit.

If I can't come up with a new trick soon, I'll have to cut off my sleeve and burn it with Dragon fire. That will cause a very different problem — without an all-around tight suit, I'll have to do without my already limited oxygen supply. I'd be frozen meat within seconds like the two Dragons — easy prey for the brown pest.

Won't happen.

Some way further up the sleeve, with sufficient safety distance, I sent out nanos to establish another venom barrier.

It was warm inside the sleeve — good conditions for the brown pest, but also suitable to let an alcohol-venom mix seep through. Wherever that mix met any brown pest, the fight was over.

Thus the brown pest's fate was overall sealed. Soon my suit was decontaminated and repaired by more nano columns, the access to the casing was liberated, the spaceship firmly back in my hand.

To clean the casing's innards was just a question of patience. I needed more patience to investigate all other casings — without findings — and then restore the ship to habitable conditions.

Accordingly, the two Dragons needed patience, too — and Francine also. While the ship slowly warmed up, I found time to call her.

"Hello, Francine. I established contact, and then I had to tend to a light brown pest infestation."

"When I saw the exhaust cloud of condensed air, I was worried," she replied by radio. *"When do you return?"*

"For now, not at all. I'll set down with this flying coffin and talk with the Dragons. Moreover, the mission parameters have changed — there's no more resistance worth mentioning on *Trouble,* at best scattered hideouts. It will be a search-and-rescue mission."

"Oh, that's sad. Shall I pass the message on?"

"The delay's still a bit long. Attach it to the combat report. I'll tell Achrotzyber anyway."

CHAPTER EIGHTY-SEVEN

My gaze was resting on both slowly thawing Dragons. My healing nano columns were heavily busy repairing the unpleasant aftereffects of the frostbite and thus easing their revival.

My first contact to the *Worries* Dragons had gone better than expected — at least these two had accepted me as Golden One. That was a good sign for the upcoming encounter with the exile colony leaders on the ice planet.

The true test was still ahead of us, though — the landing on *Trouble* and the fight against the brown pest on its own turf. Although I only just had learned that it was not a native species there, either.

Five debris clouds gave witness to this strange organism's enormous powers — it wasn't just able to mimic a higher lifeform like a human, but also commanded the intelligence to design interplanetary spacecrafts and meaningfully steer them — no, the latter even applied to interstellar spaceships. On top of the brainpower came wile and determination.

For these reasons, the brown pest was more dangerous than the Jellies by orders of magnitude. More dangerous to us, more dangerous to the people on Earth, and also more dangerous to the warriors that had ventured to liberate our galaxy from the Jellies. Perhaps we should warn them somehow . . . if we could find a way to track them down.

But first we had to tend to getting our current mission to success. Now that I knew the strange creature's organic composition, what could we learn about fighting it?

What kind of resistance did we have to prepare for? If the brown pest had been able to build five spaceships once, it could do the same again. A battle against their heavy lasers was unpleasant—how could we better protect ourselves against those?

Most of all—how could I get us safely down on the ice planet with this wreck? Thereafter I had still plenty of time to rack my brain about all the other problems, like the question of how Monique fared . . .

To be continued . . .

ABOUT THE AUTHOR

I am Valerie J. Long, born in 1963. I live and work in Germany as an IT project manager. I like role playing games, and I like putting my ideas on paper. I like all kinds of Science Fiction and Fantasy, I like music, and I like making you bite your nails off.

www.ingramcontent.com/pod-product-compliance
Lightning Source LLC
Chambersburg PA
CBHW061307170626
46817CB00001B/94